[if there are three hundred Ramayanas]...there might be three thousand or thirty thousand Mahabharatas.

A.K. Ramanujan

THE LAST KAURAVA

A Novel

KAMESH RAMAKRISHNA

FROG BOOKS

ISBN 978-93-52015-49-8
MRP INR: 525/-

First published in India 2015 by Frog Books
An imprint of Leadstart Publishing Pvt Ltd
1 Level, Trade Centre
Bandra Kurla Complex
Bandra (East) Mumbai 400 051 India
Telephone: +91-22-40700804
Fax: +91-22-40700800
Email: info@leadstartcorp.com
www.leadstartcorp.com / www.frogbooks.net

Sales Office:
Unit No.25/26, Building No.A/1,
Near Wadala RTO,
Wadala (East), Mumbai – 400037 India
Phone: +91 22 24046887

US Office:
Axis Corp, 7845 E Oakbrook Circle
Madison, WI 53717 USA

Editor: Padmini Smetacek
Cover: Mishta Roy
Layouts: Logiciels Info Solutions Pvt. Ltd.
Illustrations: Junuka Deshpande
Map: Harshad Marathe

Typeset in Palatino Linotype
Printed at Nikeda Arts Printers

For my parents

ACKNOWLEDGEMENTS

My grandmother introduced me to these stories. In a traditional dinner-time routine, she would seat my siblings and me around her on the floor and efficiently get us to eat, doling out a tablespoon of *thayir-sadam* with a spoonful of *sambar* in our hands. With each spoonful came a bit more of an episode from the great epics.

My father introduced me to reading. He did not control the quality or quantity of the books I read, both bought and borrowed. As a boy, I often settled down for hours in the India Book House in downtown Mumbai, and the British Council and the USIS libraries in Delhi, while he completed errands.

My mother scolded me when I told her that I was "writing the Mahabharata" as this epic tale of intra-family war is believed to bring bad luck to the extended family of the writer. So I was surprised when she asked for a copy of my work-in-progress and read the whole manuscript in one long sitting. She then told me that we need not worry – what I had written was not the Mahabharata after all – the curse would not apply. She was the first reader of this curse-free version. She even said she enjoyed the story, an accolade not ever bestowed easily. After that ringing affirmation, I had no choice but to get on with it and publish the book.

My wife and daughters have been tolerating my obsession with the Mahabharata for a long time and they are overjoyed that I am finally done with this book. I appreciate their patience; through their love and support, they created a world in which I could write and not worry.

Finally, my thanks go to my editors Jayashree Anand and Padmini Smetacek for their careful reading and their encouraging comments. Their critiques have been crucial for finishing this work.

INTRODUCTION

As a child, the Mahabharata fascinated me – not only did it have heroes, heroines, villains, and fast-paced action, but it also raised profound human questions about fairness, the need for revenge, the horror of war. When I became interested in history and pre-history, I struggled to fit the stories into what the archaeological record showed on the ground. The histories of other vanished cultures of the ancient world, Greece, Egypt, and Sumer seemed to be grounded in verifiable fact while this epic history of a still-alive-and-beating culture seemed to lack any foundation in the reality we could unearth.

One fact we do know from satellite images and excavations – around 2000 BCE in South Asia, a great river with almost a thousand urban settlements on its banks dried up and disappeared. This river, the Sarasvati, is mentioned in the *Puranas* and the *Vedas*. The vanished settlements, called the Sarasvati-Sindhu Culture (SSC, initially called the Indus Valley Civilisation after settlements first discovered on the banks of the Indus) were spread out over modern-day Pakistan and western India. When the river dried up, the SSC towns collapsed, sending refugees in all directions. Refugees moving east into the Gangetic plain would have encountered a native, forest-dwelling, non-urban population, leading to conflict. These were unresolvable conflicts with no compromise – one side had to lose and the other side had to win. War would be the solution, both awful and unavoidable; with peace would come a new way of life.

The Last Kaurava is a novel set against the background of a crisis circa 2000 BCE caused by the drying up of the Sarasvati. Hastinapur on the Ganga is a frontier town that is overwhelmed by immigrants. Social policies set to manage the crisis fail and set the stage for the Great War that destroyed one civilisation and established the first empire in the region.

A frame story, set in 850 BCE (over a thousand years after the Great War) reimagines the meta-episode in the epic of how the god Ganesha agreed to be Vyaasa's scribe, subject to unusual conditions. I connect what might be a metaphor to known events from a time when the city of Hastinapur (literally, *The Elephant City,* or perhaps, *Ganesha's city*), was destroyed in a flood. Its oral archives including an epic poem about the Great War, held in human memory by the guild of bards was threatened with extinction as almost all the bards of Hastinapur had died. The solution was to write it down. But how?

I *imagined* a highly evolved, non-literate and orally based culture in 850 BCE, utterly unlike its "literate" Western (i.e., Persian, Assyrian, Greek, etc.) contemporaries. The decision to write down the memorised archives was not just a break with tradition. The bards did not know any script, they could neither read nor write and needed help – just like Vyaasa needed Ganesha's help in the original. Vyaasa called upon Ganesha to be the scribe – the bards asked the Elephant City to provide the scribes who would write down as they recited. This was an expensive proposition that the city was unhappy with and every delay or slowdown would provoke demands to end the project – just like Ganesha's demand for non-stop recitation of the poem by Vyaasa. The guild of bards cooperated with the guild of traders and merchants to solve problems that arose. The solution? It's in this novel.

I followed some ground rules. Nothing fantastic – no gods, goddesses, or demons; no magic; no magical weapons; no miraculous conceptions; no karmic explanations. Situating the Great War in 2000 BCE limited the technologies available – for instance, no nuclear weapons, but more to the point, no horses or iron or million-man armies. Iron was scarce or unknown; armies were small; horse-drawn war chariots would not exist for another two hundred years; transportation was by carts drawn by oxen or onagers (the "Asian wild ass"). The people were not all that different from us – they loved, they hated, they were kind, they got angry, they acted without thinking, they plotted, they lied, they demanded the truth, etc. Not better than us, and not worse either. They were just like us.

The result is this novel.

Many other writers and texts have influenced me. The great scholar and poet A. K. Ramanujan's collection of folk-tales acted as inspiration; likewise, Iravathi Karve's *Yuganta's* analysis of the main characters of the epic; J. A. B. van Buitenen's translation of the critical edition produced by the Bhandarkar Oriental Research Institute was a key reference; information about ancient India came from the *Brihatkatha*, the *Jataka* tales, and the *Panchatantra*; the controversial anthropologist Marvin Harris (*Cultural Materialism)* provided a theoretical foundation; insights into ancient cultures came from Robert Graves (*The Greek Myths* and other works); and the amazing novelist Gore Vidal (*Creation* and *Julian)* provided a model for the writing.

I take full responsibility for this work of fiction. Its contents and the opinions in it are a product of my imagination. All my life I have read widely in the fields of history, archaeology, mythology, philosophy, science, and technology, and I drew on this to create this story. I do not claim historical authenticity or scriptural validity. The novel does not represent my beliefs about what may have "really" happened. This novel does not represent the views of the Publisher or anybody else. It is not endorsed as authentic or historical by the Publisher or by anybody else.

Table of Contents

PART 1

The Prisoner

Amba's Visit

The Pandava Camp
Circa 2000 B.C.E.

"I am Amba."

The voice rang in Devavrat's ear like a forgotten melody. Initially, the voice evoked in him a sense of lightness; it enveloped him in a warm glow like the break of dawn cradling the river Ganga. Ancient memories from lost time veered in and out of focus. The memories came with flooding questions. *How could it be Amba? What was she doing, here and now?* The questions stuck in his throat, refusing expression. Then the voice fell to the ground and a grey miasma, a grey that he associated with pain and anger, seemed to crawl out of the fallen voice – the glow faded and the grey fog grew until it shadowed every coloured point. *Amba. She is here. I must see her.* He tried to turn. The stub of an arrow, sticking under his left shoulder, made him pause with every move, however slight.

"You killed Shikhandin. You killed my son."

The greyness increased. *Yes, he had killed Shikhandin.* His mind raced ahead of his turning head. Shikhandin had lured him into an ambush. He had dealt Shikhandin a fatal blow. Then the ambushers attacked and a well-aimed arrow had penetrated under his arm to his lungs. His arms rendered useless, he had fought and fallen by Shikhandin's side. He was now a prisoner. Shikhandin and he had been transported to the Pandava camp in the same cart and he had listened to Shikhandin moan as he died. *Shikhandin was Amba's son*? He should have known. It explained so much. It had been so easy and comfortable for Devavrat to trust him. An image of Amba's profile as she looked out at the sunrise over the garden town of Varanavata, his model town for resettling the Panchnad refugees, melded into a profile of Shikhandin looking out over the Ganga at the remains of a settlement burnt in the war. That was why he had dropped his guard as he followed Shikhandin into the ambush. He recalled the surge of anger when he discovered Shikhandin's betrayal; that was why he had slashed Shikhandin down. *Shikhandin,*[1] *well-named and well-aimed, truly an arrow aimed at him,* was the only person he had killed in this war, for at his age he was useless in battle but an asset in conducting the war. *But... there were so many buts.*

"You killed your son. Die."

The greyness became darker. Devavrat wanted to face Amba and deny the astounding charge, but then he felt her hand push on his left shoulder, the one with the arrowhead. The bed pushed back against the broken shaft of the arrow.

The pain... the pain exploded all over his body, a burn that would not stop. He was a warrior. He said to himself, *I will not scream,* and he threw himself into this struggle against the scream with the roar he had used in battle. He was *Devavrat Bhishma,* Devavrat the Terrible, four times Regent of Hastinapur, the bulwark of an empire built to last an eternity, an empire that must save the refugees fleeing from their ancient home of Panchnad in the west into the embrace of the Ganga and the

---

[1] One of the meanings of *Shikhandin* is "arrowhead".

Yamuna. He was the saviour of that civilisation, and he would not scream.

His challenge did not stop the arrowhead – *Shikhandin!* – from pushing deeper past his lungs to his heart already fractured by the presence of Amba. His last memory was of a glimmering haze into which guards rushed in and pulled Amba away, and regrets that he had not been able to look at her face.

Writing an Epic

OVER A THOUSAND YEARS LATER

KAUSHAMBI/HASTINAPUR
CIRCA 850 B.C.E.

"You were too fast for me, my friend. I couldn't write it all down." Bhargava the trader, doubling as scribe, had given up trying to write down the words and listened to his friend Vaishampaayana tell the story. He held down a pristine palm-leaf with his left hand on the small wooden platform, gripped a sharp scribing stylus in his right, and frowned at the few marks he had managed to make on the palm leaf. He shook a cramp out of his fingers. *I am getting old. This sharpened and charred bamboo twig is no good. I should bring the iron stylus that the trader from Assyria gave me last year.*

Vaishampaayana, the one-hundred-and-eighth Vyaasa[2] to head the Kavi Sangha,[3] rubbed his temples with his fingers as he watched Bhargava. *It was hard to recite the story in this manner. Bhargava's fingers are already complaining. Would Bhargava be able*

---

[2] *Vyaasa* is the traditional author/compiler of the Mahabharata. In this novel, the Vyaasa is the title of the head of the Kavi Sangha (see below).

[3] *Kavi Sangha* means "Society of Poets".

to continue writing? Bhargava had not understood the scope of the task when he signed up for it; Vaishampaayana himself had doubts that the project could be completed, but he had kept those doubts well hidden. Even if he could finish it, would he be able to do so with the meagre support promised by the leaders of Hastinapur?

Vaishampaayana and Bhargava were seated on reed mats under the ficus[4] tree outside the house that had been allotted to the Vyaasa. A small alcove had been cut into the tree and a little knob of stone was placed in it, daubed with red lead and grey ashes. It reminded the Vyaasa that they were on Kashi-controlled land. *Pashupati's land.* There were no clouds in the sky. Despite the sun, the air was cool. *Not as cold as it would have been in Hastinapur,* the Vyaasa thought. He had only come out at the urging of Bhargava. The sun felt alien, was alien. *I haven't seen the sun in many days.* It wasn't strictly true, but he had stayed in his bedroom far longer than was reasonable. *I will spend the rest of my life in this room.* Again, not true, but it felt like that. The only hindrance to seeing the sun had been the quilted curtain on the doorway of his personal room. The light of the winter sun just reaching its southernmost extent elbowed its way through windows and doors, but not through that last barrier. He had been in a diffused light, not the direct brightness of the sun's beams. Thinking about the task ahead reminded him of his friend Jayakumar, who had been the co-bearer of the city's historical archives. Now Jayakumar was dead, a victim of the flood, and he, Vaishampaayana, was alive. The Great Goddess's gifts came with a bitter aftertaste.

He shook his head as if to dissipate the worries clustering around him. Nothing could come of replaying these thoughts. The flood had come and gone, leaving a destroyed city in its wake.

---

[4] This tree is the *ficus religiosa,* called the *peepul* by Indians. It has been considered sacred in South Asia for over four thousand years (it even appears in seals found in Mohenjodaro and other sites).

If not for the people of Kashi, who had rallied to the cause and transported the residents of Hastinapur to this new, temporary location, Hastinapur would have vanished into the fog of time, much like the empire of which it had been the capital. Kashi was the capital of an empire now – it had extended its charity to the old capital and resettled the traumatised survivors on the banks of the Ganga at a place they called Kaushambi.

His mind refused discipline and continued to wander. There were so many similarities between the crisis Kashi faced now to the crisis faced by Hastinapur in the story that Bhargava was writing down. The story he was reciting was part of the oral archives of Hastinapur, maintained by the living stores of the much-reduced Kavi Sangha; he, Vaishampaayana, was the only complete living store left, along with junior members who maintained parts. All the other senior members, along with many younger members, had died in the flood. The people of Hastinapur were unhappy and discontented refugees, not unlike the Panchnad refugees in this remembered history. Hastinapur was dependent on the charity of Kashi, a city of benevolent strangers. The unhappy and discontented Panchnad refugees had been dependent on the charity of ancient Hastinapur. Kashi was the prosperous capital city of an empire that could provide for the refugees from Hastinapur. For the Hastinapur of that past age, years before it became a great city, the refugees were an overwhelming crisis.

Hastinapur had been a small, if prosperous, trading outpost just beyond the frontier of the Panchnad civilisation. The outpost had existed in uneasy equilibrium with surrounding forest dwellers and had only very recently established its hegemony over a small tract of land surrounding it. Then the refugees had flooded in and overrun everything – in time, the refugees became immigrants and then became the rulers of Hastinapur. Between the old and the new, they created a new culture shaped by the exigencies of the situation on the ground. Hastinapur became an empire, the first empire in that land. This was nothing like the

Panchnad the refugees had left behind. Peace had reigned in Panchnad, conflict being the exception; the empire that Hastinapur became was a militarised state that responded violently to trouble. Traders and their concerns had been primary in Panchnad; the Hastinapur Empire, concerned about maintaining and extending its hegemony, focused on its growing army. In Panchnad, the cities governed themselves under the benign oversight of their own matriarchs and their councils; Hastinapur, the trading outpost that had become a fortified capital, was ruled by its King, a trader-turned-warlord, and his council of war.

Yes, a listener could acquire a lot of merit by listening closely to that ancient history.

His meandering mind was brought up short by a sound. Bhargava's voice broke through Vaishampaayana's reverie.

"Vais! Wake up!"

"Yes, yes! I'm awake. I heard you, I heard you."

"And..."

Bhargava's protest had to be addressed.

"You want me to go slower?" said Vaishampaayana.

"Yes, Vais," said Bhargava.

Vaishampaayana sighed. Bhargava should not call me that in public. People will interpret it as lack of respect. Memories came crowding in and his eyes lost their focus again.

"What's the matter, Vais?" said Bhargava. "I know you can go slower, I've heard you perform."

Vaishampaayana moved his head from side to side to stretch his neck and shoulders. *These depressing thoughts are making me slump.*

"I'm fine. I was just thinking. I'll begin now."

Vaishampaayana began again: "I am Amba."

850 B.C.E

"Hold on," Bhargava said. "Are we at the beginning of the recital?"

"Yes, of course."

"Didn't the city council say that they wanted the written version to be like the recital in every way?"

"Yes?"

"I've been to quite a few recitals and they never began with an episode."

"Huh? How did they begin?"

"There is usually some kind of introduction praising the listener, or a god, or the sponsor, or a blurb about the benefits of listening carefully."

"Ah-ha! The benediction."

"Yes."

"We leave that to the bard responsible for the recitation. He has to customise it to the context of the recital."

"Hmm. He makes it up for the occasion?"

"Yes."

"What would be the occasion for the recital of this written text?"

"I don't know," Vaishampaayana said. "The Kavi Sangha's archives do not constrain the context and so we do not memorise a prepared benediction. There is nothing to write down."

"You know the city council will not accept that."

"What do they care? We had asked for ten apprentices to be trained to replace the bards who died in the flood; we had asked for support for them and the rest of the Archivists who should be busy making duplicates of the archives, not working at earning their livelihood."

"Vais! That's what you wanted. What did the city council want other than writing this down?"

"Other than cutting expenses?"

"Yes."

"Cut more expenses."

Bhargava pretended to knock Vaishampaayana's head with his knuckles. "My friend! Stop that. There's no point being cynical."

Vaishampaayana sniffed. Then he said, "Exactly what I told the council. They think that cheap readers can be trained to replace expensive bards reciting this epic. Yes, that would cut costs, if it became possible. I gave in on this because the Kavi Sangha, the guild of bards, will disappear if we do not recover now after the flood. I've agreed because we need to survive. I think the council will learn how foolish their ideas are after the first few recitals."

"You think you will be proved right when they are forced to employ a bard for the benediction. Before even one word is read? Is that it? You think it shows how committed you are to this project."

Vaishampaayana pursed his lips and closed his eyes. His friend was right – the council would doubt his sincerity if a bard had to be hired just to start a reading recital. He had not planned it, but it would certainly look like he had plotted it that way.

Bhargava said, "Tell me this, my friend. Floods come and go. Hastinapur is not the first city in the world to be destroyed in a flood. After a few years, people rebuild and go on. That is what Hastinapur will do too. Both you and the council seem to think that this writing down of Hastinapur's history is important. I don't understand. If I remember correctly, these events occurred over a thousand years ago. Why is this so critical?"

Vaishampaayana said, "History must be remembered. Without history, we are like the animals in the forest."

"Please do not mouth platitudes. Yes, history is important. It is more important to stay alive, to restore everyday life, and to restore agriculture, brick making, home building – commerce, in short. You made demands on the council that they could not possibly meet, given those everyday demands. You, of all people, understand that it is critical to start living a normal life."

"There are times, Bhargava, when that thought crosses my mind. Why does it matter that a thousand years ago we were a great city? That will not feed the refugee stranded in one of our camps over there. Yes, yes, I understand the impulse to ever go forward. However, my friend, history forgotten is history repeated. Here we are, on the verge of repeating history."

"What do you mean 'repeating history'? Hastinapur has almost nothing. It isn't going to repeat anything, especially if it comes at an exorbitant price."

"I meant exactly that. We could easily 'repeat history'. Even the council understands that. That is why they were willing to fund this project. When I told them what it would take, they balked. Then somebody came up with the idea that if it were written down, it would cut future costs. That was it – after that they would not listen to my asking for more – I had to accept."

"Vais, you keep repeating it like a mantra. Perhaps, like history, huh?"

"Yes, exactly. We repeat history if we do not learn from it. The forge that built Hastinapur and made it the great capital of a growing empire was caused by water. Even so, the path to greatness was strewn with one disaster after another that threatened that future – each disaster caused by the foibles of an individual ignorant of the past.

850 B.C.E

"Our city has been destroyed by a flood. A thousand years ago, at a time when Hastinapur was a small and failing settlement, it was threatened with destruction, not once but many times over four generations. That is the story told when we recite the *Jaya*.[5] Knowing it makes us wiser."

"I see," said Bhargava. "We will then be wiser about... what exactly?"

"Riverine changes destroyed the civilisation that our ancestors had built in Panchnad, the land of the Sindhu and the Sarasvati. The resulting flood of refugees threatened to destroy Hastinapur. Natives, some of whom resisted, occupied the land that these refugees wanted to settle as immigrants. The leaders of Hastinapur could not agree on what was to be done. Personal issues and personalities exacerbated these disagreements into outright conflict and, for the first time for that culture, large-scale war. Nobody came out unscathed – the natives were expelled from the areas occupied by the refugees, a militarised empire came into existence and the immigrants were subject to a new and rigorous yoke, that they called Dharma. During the era of peace that followed, the empire's hold faded away and the world we live in came into existence. With this recitation we celebrate the victory of that empire centred on Hastinapur.

"The recent floods have destroyed our city and by the grace of Kashi we have been saved. Already, already, we put a burden on Kashi. Kashi cannot support us forever. We are the refugees; we are a burden; and we are a threat. This will not resolve itself in my lifetime, or the lifetimes of the remaining senior members of the Kavi Sangha. We must find a way to save the history of the past, for we may need to learn from it. The Kavi Sangha can no longer do this by memorising – we do not have enough bards to hold these memories.

---

5 *Jaya,* means Victory. The word also refers to a poem composed in an epic style (a "lay") to memorialise a famous victory.

"That is why I agreed to write down the archives of the Kavi Sangha. If we are to learn from history, we must not forget it."

Bhargava shook his head. He said, "People listen to your recitation as it entertains. You are an optimist if you believe that they will learn anything from this history."

"Now, it is you who is being cynical, my friend."

"No, Vais, I am being a realist. I have visited the lands to the west of Moolasthan;[6] you have not. You have not seen how they live, despite their never-ending wars. Their rulers profit from the war for it is the source of their power over their own people. Each city accuses the enemy of disrespect to the gods, the first of whom is the god of the city itself. A male military class rules roughshod over all the other residents; the military recruits men rather than women with the result that the man is valued and the woman not; instead, beautiful women become choice prizes that the men fight over while the rest of the women are treated like cattle and only considered fit to give birth to children."

Vaishampaayana said, "You are one to criticise them, with a woman in every town from here to Su-meru.[7] I understand that – you are a realist, after all."

Bhargava said, "They are not my property – I am a man to each of them when I visit them – the women stay behind to rule their family, and I follow their rules when I visit. Each of my wives runs her own establishment over which she has complete control, without me to tell her what to do. As a Master Trader, only the caravan is my property; in the towns whose rulers I trust, I own property that my wife or other agent manages. That is why I have no wife or family in Sumer – the women there are expected to manage only the 'women's affairs', know little about the family's

---

6 *Moolasthan* is near the modern city of Multan.

7 The name "Sumer" could easily morph into the Sanskritic "*Su-Meru*". Future references to the Mesopotamian city will use the name "Sumer".

affairs, and are subject to a man's rule – under those conditions, I would not have the liberty to be absent for long periods.

"My wives are from trading families and they are matriarchs in their own house – they have power independently of their men and therefore do not seek to bind him to a single wife like your bards. We've been friends for a long time; surely you know this about me."

Bhargava had stood up during the discussion. He was frowning, and his eyes refused to meet Vaishampaayana's eyes.

"I'm sorry," said Vaishampaayana. "Yes, I do know something of it and someday you should tell me more about how it works. I apologise for my thoughtless remark."

Bhargava grunted, but he stayed standing.

Vaishampaayana said, "Come, my friend. We've known each other for too long to fight over this matter. Let's drop this digression and return to our tasks."

Bhargava slowly sat down on his mat. He said, "You still haven't convinced me. What's so important about saving your ancient archives?"

"The events in the *Jaya* portray a breakdown fuelled by anger between refugees and their hosts. We are refugees here – we must find a way to be grateful to Kashi and not resent them. We must find a way to return to the old relationship. Among other aspects, the *Jaya* is a story of a failure to accommodate and adjust.

"Reflect on it, Bhargava. When you have heard the whole story, I will ask you your own question. For now, let's return to the benediction."

Bhargava nodded. "Alright, I'll accept that challenge. I still have a problem, though. A benediction is just that – a small thing that says little. Why can't you just say a prayer to your gods? Compose something like that and I'll write it down."

Vaishampaayana shook his head. "That does not work. What's the context? Who is the sponsor? What good does the sponsor expect to receive? What god or force is being invoked? Those are the elements of the benediction."

"What do you think the city council would want?"

"Bhargava, I see where this is going. Keep in mind that a written benediction must cover future sponsors and future listeners, maybe unknown future contexts. The sponsors this time are the city councillors, but membership of the council changes with time as well – so the sponsor is the city, not its council. The Kavi Sangha is also the sponsor for without our cooperation this will be lost. Yes, yes! I'll weave it all in."

He continued, "The listeners are the people, all the people, not just the *jana,*[8] the electors, but all the listeners gathered there, the *gana,*[9] if you will. The gana are both the sponsor and the listener and it is for their entertainment and understanding that the recital is being held. The context? That's a little trickier."

"Why don't you make it appropriate for all events conducted by the city?"

"We don't recite this *Jaya* at every event held by the city, only the most important – the four *melas*[10] for instance. The gana wait eagerly for entertainment at these festivals. The god can be *Ganapathi,*[11] the god of our city, for he is also the god of the people."

"That leaves us with the good that the city and its people might expect from the recital."

---

[8] *Jana* probably means "the people", but could also be "the citizens/electors".

[9] *Gana* means "the people", but with a lower class connotation (so can be everybody not covered by *Jana*). A pejorative interpretation would be "the rabble".

[10] Annually, the city holds four *Mélās*, (meaning a fair) – on the two equinoxes and the two solstices. See Endnotes on redistributive festivals.

[11] *Ganapathi* means the "lord of the Gana(s)". Pejoratively, "leader of the rabble".

"A smaller budget?"

"Tut-tut. Something else."

"Don't worry, I have something," Vaishampaayana said. He closed his eyes.

Bhargava waited. A few vighatis went by. Meanwhile Bhargava discarded the palm leaf he had been using and prepared a fresh one.

Then Vaishampaayana said, "I have made up a benediction. Are you ready?"

"Vais, my friend, I am ready."

Vaishampaayana began. "Write this. The *Jaya*, composed to memorialise this war, begins and ends with Devavrat. That is the tradition. That is how we tell this history. In accordance with the tradition, we begin with Devavrat's death and narrate his story. Though we begin with the story of Devavrat, we are narrating the history of our city, Hastinapur, the city of the Elephant, Ganesha's[12] city."

"Hold it. You'll have to go slower."

"I am going slower. That was about one *vighati*.[13]"

"Well..."

"I can go even slower. The slower I must go, the more I despair of completing this project. My mind wanders and I repeat the arguments I made to the city council. *Give me apprentices who will become bards, and I can teach them to memorise and sing the history.* The old way is the only way to save our history. Writing is useless. The city council will not listen to me; this is their solution... You want me to go slower, I'll go slower."

---

12 *Ganesha* is another name for Ganapathi.

13 A *vighati* is a unit of time equal to twenty-four seconds. A *ghati* is sixty vighatis, i.e. twenty-four minutes. See Endnotes.

"Vais, I am not part of your debate. I'm only doing it because… I volunteered. You think that a trader's business goes on without his presence? I am losing opportunities to trade even as we speak. Go slower or I quit."

"Bhargava, you leave me no choice. I agreed to this only because they said you would write for me."

Bhargava squinted at his friend. "Is that true, Vais?"

Vaishampaayana smiled but with frown-lines showing on his brow, "Well… in a manner of speaking. I'll go slower. From the beginning, then."

He spoke slowly. "The *Jaya,* composed to record this war, begins and ends with Devavrat. That is the tradition. That is how we tell this history. In accordance with the tradition, we begin with Devavrat's death and narrate his story. Though we begin with the story of Devavrat, we are narrating the history of our city, Hastinapur, the city of the Elephant, Ganesha's city. It is the story of a city on which was built an empire, an empire of the people. It is a story without end for the story of this city, this empire of the people, is the story of humanity – how can it end? Devavrat was named so by his mother at the beginning of his life; he was called *Devavrat Bhishma*[14] by the people at the end of a long life. Just as we sing of the life of Devavrat Bhishma, so shall we write of the life of Devavrat Bhishma. As the bard enters the soul of Devavrat to speak for him, so will the reader enter the soul of Devavrat to read his words. When Devavrat speaks through the bard, he must speak the truth; likewise, when a reader utters Devavrat's written words, he must read the truth.

"The truth, whether uttered or listened to, makes both the speaker and the listener free. We offer this truth to Ganesha, the protector of the ganas. Lord Ganesha, extend your grace to us, the denizens of your city, the city of the Elephant, our city,

---

[14] *Devavrat Bhishma* means "Devavrat the Terrible". How he came by this name is part of this story of his life.

850 B.C.E

Hastinapur, the city of the Snakes, our city Nagapura.[15] We offer this truth to our ancestors, protectors of our family. Respected Ancestors, shield us from evil fates, and as we prosper, so shall you rest in the after-life. This truth, the story of Devavrat Bhishma, heard with respect, will free seven generations of ancestors from purgatory. Read with respect, the reader should expect to gain merit of the same magnitude." He paused.

"You got all that, Bhargava. Written it down?"

"Yes."

"Jaya."

"Jaya-he. Are we done?"

"Write that down."

"What? Write what down?"

"Jaya."

"Jaya?"

"Yes. Every telling of a *Jaya* begins with a benediction and the pronouncement of *jaya*. The bard proclaims 'Jaya' to which the audience responds with 'Jaya-he'."

Bhargava wrote down the last utterance.

"I got that," Bhargava said. "I have a question – since the benediction is made to suit the occasion, should we include some guidance on how the reader is to use this benediction?"

"The city elders wanted a reader to tell the story in public exactly the way a bard might. That is not possible. The writer cannot cover all the contingencies of a future reading. I fought against this order. You know why they did it? Hah! Of course you do. They don't want bards anymore. Readers and announcers will replace bards – that's their hope. I am glad you brought up the benediction, for if we do not include at least one

[15] *Nagapura* is another name for Hastinapur.

such benediction, the idea itself – the idea of the introductory benediction – will be lost.

"That is what happens when you have readers, not bards. A written down item, when lost, is lost forever. Bards may forget to recite a verse, but it is not forgotten. Other bards will have memorised it too. Our descendants, in a time when writing dominates, will remember nothing. That will be our future. To let go of memory passed from the cold and unresponsive past to the warm present and welcoming future. To let go of the Songs that link and bind all our bards from the first Vyaasa, Guru Vasishtha,[16] down through the chain of teachers and disciples to our future bards.

"An even greater loss is the loss of participation in the creation of memory. Every recital recreates and reimagines the story for the benefit of the audience. That is why a recital is not like a memorised mantra, but partakes all facets of *Naatya*.[17] A recital is a reimagining – what, indeed, is a *reading?* I do not know what is to come when readers replace bards, but the reader's eye is on the palm-leaf and where the eye goes, there goes vision, with vision goes thought, thought carries the mind, and the mind, that hound-dog of habit, is mired in its expectations of rewards from smooth reading and anticipation of the content of the next leaf to be read. Reading is not Naatya. The connection to the audience, so essential to recital, to Naatya, is lost. Both reader and audience will become observers and not participants."

Bhargava said, "Yes, yes, Vais, I see. I'm sorry to have interrupted the grand chain of poetic transcreation. Let us continue."

"My apologies, Bhargava, I am lecturing. I'm not offended that you would rather not be subjected to my digressions and

---

[16] *Vasishtha* is a famous sage of antiquity. In this novel, he is the founder of the Kavi Sangha.

[17] *Naatya* is the traditional Sanskrit term for all kinds of performance art, ranging from acting to dancing to story-telling.

exegeses. What you did when you asked a question about the benediction is exactly what I want you to do when I recite the history. Question me. A bard responds to an audience. I cannot recite the poem without an audience. You are it. It is your duty – to stop me and ask questions. Consider it your dharma."

"Hmm… I see. You could go a little slower, perhaps? Even if I can keep up, my apprentices won't when it is their turn."

"Slower than this?"

"Yes. I know that it is hard and you are not used to being told how to perform, but you must go slower if we are to finish this."

"We shall see. Did you get the whole benediction?"

"Yes. This time. Slow down, please. Let's continue."

"Jaya."

Bhargava of Kamboja, a trader by profession, involuntary scribe, an old friend of the Vyaasa, wrote down these words recited by the Vyaasa.

Vaishampaayana, the last Vyaasa, the last head of the Kavi Sangha, last living Archive of Hastinapur's History, of the city destroyed by a flood, continued his recital.

"'I am Amba.' The voice rang in Devavrat's ear like a forgotten melody. Initially, the voice evoked in him a sense of lightness… His last memory was of a glimmering haze into which guards rushed in and pulled Amba away, and regrets that he had not been able to look at her face.

"Thus ends the confrontation of Devavrat Bhishma and Amba Nagini as the Regent lay on his death-bed in the forest camp of the Pandavas, enemies of the Empire he had built."

850 B.C.E

The End of an Era

A Father's Boon

The Pandava Camp
circa 2000 B.C.E.

"I give you this boon, my son – you can choose the time of your death."

On his deathbed, Devavrat's father Shantanu had laboured to whisper these words to him.

If it sounded like nonsense to him then, it was definitely nonsense now. He must be dead, for he was floating. All about him was a white nothingness, undifferentiated by shadow or colour. *This must be death.* That was not possible; he had not chosen to die. Then he heard something, off to his left and behind him.

"Will he die?"

Devavrat couldn't see anything, but his hearing was good enough that he could identify the speaker – it was his grandnephew Yudhishthira. His thoughts formed questions. *Was this a dream? Why am I floating? Who was Yudhishthira talking about?*

An unfamiliar voice came from his left side.

"Not right away, sir. When he wakes up, he may be in pain. I will do my best to help."

The whiteness started fading, becoming a little greyer. *Where am I? How can I hear a discussion between my grandnephew and a stranger?* The greyness became darker. *Somebody was going to wake up soon. Who? Who were they talking about?*

Devavrat felt a sensation. It was a touch on his chest. He looked down. There was nothing to see. He could feel four touches, close by each other, on his invisible chest. The greyness had definitely become darker. *If it gets any darker I won't be able to see anything.* It wasn't a whiteness anymore, it was a blackness. Meanwhile, the touch continued and moved. *Are they really touching my chest?* If so, there was a spot just below his left nipple that was sensitive. If they touched it, he should feel ticklish. A short time later, he felt the touches on the sensitive spot. To his relief, he twitched. The voice continued.

"His heart is in good shape. I do not hear any worrying sounds. The tip of the arrow is almost touching his heart. Do not move the arrow. At the first large movement of the arrow, his heart may be punctured, blood will pour out into his lungs, and he will die."

Now Devavrat could place that voice. It was the doctor who had worked on Shikhandin when they were first brought in. The conversation he was listening to was in the medical tent. He was floating again, in another blackness somewhere near the medical tent. He still couldn't see but he could hear. Yudhishthira and the doctor were discussing some injured person. *Who could it be?* Whoever it was, he had a lung injury from an arrow. *Just like me.*

"Will it heal at all?" Yudhishthira said.

That was Yudhishthira. *His voice reminds me of his father. Caring for everyone, even a wounded prisoner.*

2000 B.C.E

"No," said the doctor. "The Regent will die of this sooner or later."

The Regent was going to die. The Regent? I am the Regent. They are talking about me. He must be in the medical tent and not floating around. He was not dead. He was dying. *What happened to my father's boon?* It had been a strange utterance, possibly the strangest, from his father, delirious on his deathbed. Even in delirium, his father had been completely serious and convincing. Occasionally, in idle moments, Devavrat would wonder what his father had meant. Apparently nothing, for here he was, fatally wounded and soon to die.

Why can't I see? He was prepared to die, but he had always imagined himself entering death with eyes wide open, seeing everything. Moments passed; it felt like eternity, and fed a growing sense of panic. He found himself back in his body, and now he could feel the pain in his shoulder pulsing and alternating with his heartbeat. It refused to be ignored. He opened his eyes. The doctor was there sitting by his side, along with Yudhishthira. The doctor had bent low and leaned in to place his right ear on Devavrat's chest. Devavrat closed his eyes.

After the doctor raised his head, Devavrat heard Yudhishthira say, "How long?" The doctor said, "Two days, a week, perhaps. Not more than that. I'll be back tomorrow to check." Then there was quiet.

The first thing that struck Devavrat when he opened his eyes again was the sunlight streaming in through the open door-flap. His bed had been turned around. Now he faced the entrance of the tent and could no longer see the mat on which Shikhandin's body had lain. His left leg was tied, as before, to one of the tent-poles. He could turn a little more freely to the right, but a roll of cotton placed behind him prevented him from rolling onto his left side. The cotton was matted and felt rough on the skin of his back. His shoulder was sore and he found he could not move his arm.

"He has opened his eyes," Yudhishthira said.

Devavrat knew now that they had been talking about him all along. *I am going to die, and fairly soon at that.*

Amba was nowhere to be seen. Yudhishthira, his grandnephew, smiled at him, but his grave eyes gave the lie to the smile. Yudhishthira's calmness radiated and seemed to calm the people around him. That by itself made him different from his cousin Suyodhana. A sensuous pout of the upper lip characterised the descendants of the old Queen Mother. *My stepmother*, he thought. She had it, and so did her father and her brother Shukla, the current Vyaasa. It marked her descendants, made them attractive, and encouraged people to defer to their wishes. Her grandson Dhritarashtra had the pout, and despite his almost-complete blindness women came to him, and he did not dissuade them. Dhritarashtra's son Suyodhana had the pout. He looked dissatisfied. He was dissatisfied, all the time. Yudhishthira, the son of her grandson by Ambalika, had not inherited the pouted lips. That had settled the matter for the Queen Mother – she demanded proof that Yudhishthira was truly her great-grandson and, therefore, the heir, *her* heir, but there was no proof and no known way of establishing the truth. "Yudhishthira is not my descendant," she said. "You must support Suyodhana, he is my only true heir."

That curve of the lip, with its hint of subtle pleasures, also drew people to Suyodhana and his brothers. Devavrat knew the look, for despite all that had happened, it had the power to make him want to please his stepmother. After his father's death, he and his stepmother had clashed frequently, and he would compromise with her even when a compromise was not warranted. Even when his anger at his stepmother was so great that a compromise seemed unlikely, her brother Shukla, with the same feature, could persuade him to cooperate. Because of that look.

The unanswered questions about Yudhishthira's legitimacy was one of the reasons Devavrat supported Suyodhana. *That's not the only reason for this war,* Devavrat thought. *The Pandavas will destroy what I have built.* His life's work, accomplished during four long terms as Regent for one descendant or the other, was the empire he had constructed around Hastinapur. The refugees fleeing the famine in the west caused by the loss of their great river, the Sarasvati, could have been sent back to certain starvation and probable death; they could have been forced to go further east into land inhabited by the forest-dwelling Nagas[18] and Rakshasas[19] and left to fend for themselves, to die or to survive on whatever terms they got. His father had tried and failed at that, for the forests were not easy to clear, the land was hard to till, and, bar some, the refugees were urbanites, not farmers. They all wanted to immigrate to Hastinapur. Despite their poverty, they did not consider themselves refugees – they were immigrants. Before the crisis, immigrants were welcome in Hastinapur. The Kauravas[20] were immigrants. All the non-Naga residents of Hastinapur were immigrants. In normal circumstances, immigrants would have been welcomed in Hastinapur.

However, the circumstances were far from normal. The river Sarasvati,[21] which hosted most of the Panchnad cities, used to receive snow-melt from the Yamuna, which flowed about ten yojanas[22] to the west of Hastinapur, and from the Sutudri,[23] which

[18] The Hastinapuris gave the name *Naga* to the forest-dwelling, matriarchal bands living along the Ganga.

[19] The Nagas gave the name *Defender* (in their own language) to the hunter-gathering tribes who dwelt in the forest to the east of modern-day Patna; the Hastinapuris translated that into the Panchnadi language as *Rakshasa*.

[20] *Kaurava* means "descendent of Kuru", but is usually applied specifically to Suyodhana and his brothers.

[21] *Sarasvati* is the hidden river of Hindu legend, flowing invisibly to merge with the Ganga and the Yamuna near Allahabad..

[22] *Yojana* is a measure of distance. See Endnotes.

[23] *Sutudri* is the river Sutlej.

flowed even farther west. The earthquakes in the Himalayas had changed this. The Yamuna had shifted east, and the Sutudri had turned to the west, depriving the Sarasvati of water. That had initiated the migration.

The Yamuna's eastward shift was not an immediate gain for the eastern lands – the waters had no riverbed to flow on and flooded the land. The Khandava forest to the west of Hastinapur and areas further south were flooded and could not be used to provide for the immigrants. Instead, any settlements they built would have to be in the lands to the east and south of Hastinapur – lands already occupied by the Nagas, hitherto friendly.

These immigrants did not want to be pioneers creating new settlements that would take a generation or more to become as liveable as the towns they had left. They wanted to live urban lives rather than frontier lives. Devavrat's accomplishment had been to marshal the unhappy refugees into work crews that built dams, created lakes, constructed waterworks – they created the infrastructure that supported new settlements.

All this had come at a cost – the Nagas, who had been friendly to Hastinapur, were being squeezed out of their traditional range. The lands that they left fallow, to recover from the stress of slash-and-burn agriculture, were being taken over by immigrants. As each new settlement grew, all the arable land near water would be taken and the Nagas would not be able to live the way they used to. Either they would give up their way of life or they would leave. If necessary, they would be pressured to leave.

The Pandavas might, no, they *would*, undo all that he had accomplished. They would justify their rebellion, just like their father had justified his, in the name of fairness and justice for the Nagas. Suyodhana would not do that. Suyodhana, like his father Dhritarashtra, did not care about the Nagas. Like his father, he had many ties to the immigrants. Some friends, many lovers, many allies. *He will soon outdo his father in the number of wives and concubines from among the immigrants.* Hastin's descendants had come a long way, transitioning from the trading family that founded Hastinapur to the family of warriors they now were as rulers. Suyodhana would not interfere with the administration of the empire that Devavrat had established.

The doctor spoke to him. "Do you feel any pain?"

Devavrat's heart was no longer racing the way it had when Amba had pressed on his shoulder. *Where was she?* His breathing was still ragged. He could feel the stubby edge of the broken arrow against his upper arm. *It had not gone away; it was still there.* He shrugged and essayed a smile.

"A little," he said.

The doctor's face did not change.

Yudhishthira said, "I have bad news for you."

"Uh-huh."

"Your injuries continue to worsen. Not because of what Amba did," Yudhishthira said. "She was upset over her son's death. I approved her request to collect her son's body. I did not anticipate her actions."

Did they know what Amba had told him? Did anyone? Had Amba told the truth? *I must talk to her. I must reassure Yudhishthira that I am not afraid of her.* Devavrat tried to smile, but the pain kept his lips closed. He said, "She should be angry. He was her son. I still want to talk to her when she is less angry – perhaps in a month."

Yudhishthira's eyes looked down away from Devavrat. His shoulders slumped a bit. Then he slowly raised his head and looked straight at Devavrat. "That is not likely."

What did he mean?

Yudhishthira said, "You will die soon, Grandsire." For a brief moment, Devavrat saw a ripple of worry spread across Yudhishthira's face and the calm set of his eyes vanished.

Devavrat frowned and his eyes narrowed. Yudhishthira continued, "The doctor here refuses to remove the arrow. Amba pushed the arrowhead past your lung, and it is now near your heart. He says it missed all the vital spots along the way. You should have bled to death –you are alive because the arrowhead is plugging its own hole. The doctor does not expect you to last a week."

Was that all? He had heard that while his eyes were closed.

"You would probably die immediately if the arrow were removed. At best, you will last a few ghatis."

Was this how my father's boon manifested itself?

"You mean to say, I can choose when I will die."

"Yes. That is one way to put it."

Yudhishthira's Request

The Pandava Camp
Circa 2000 B.C.E.

Devavrat had not expected it to hurt so much. He was a warrior, and an old one at that. He had survived much. He had been cut by the edge of a sword and had lived through that. He had felt the sting of a sharp arrow before. He had felt the bone-numbing pain of slipping down a hillside after missing a step and then recovering his balance to keep fighting. That was physical pain, and only physical pain – he knew he could overcome physical pain.

This time, it was different. The thoughts that echoed in his mind could not be subdued like bodily pain. They grew with each rehearsal and tore open an old wound that he believed had been cauterised by the passage of time – over five hundred moons – yet Amba's visit had re-opened that one. She was angry because he had killed her son. He could understand that. *Why did she leave in the first place? That was a puzzle.* If he had known that she was pregnant, he might have... he was surprised that he did not recall anymore why he had been absent when she disappeared, but if he had known of her pregnancy, he would not have been absent. *Shikhandin was my son!* He thought he had become inured to surprises – the onset of war at Suyodhana's impulse, the Pandavas' escape, their alliance with Panchala, the alliance of the Yadavas, led by Krishna Gopala,[24] with Panchala – the list of surprises was long, but this one beat them all. The dead Shikhandin was his son. *I killed my own son.* Shikhandin was the son he had vowed would not exist and now he had made good on that promise. He had no son. *Truly, I deserve to be called Devavrat Bhishma!*

It appeared as though Shikhandin's paternity was a secret from everybody else too. His great-nephew Yudhishthira had apologised for the attack – he had approved Amba's visit to take her son's body and had not imagined that she might find an opportunity to kill his killer. The apology revealed nothing more – nothing in what Yudhishthira said indicated that he knew that Shikhandin was his granduncle's son, an uncle of a king in his own right, or even that he knew of a prior connection between Amba and Devavrat.

Yudhishthira had taken care to see that Devavrat was safe and comfortable. The other Pandavas, Bhima, Arjuna, and the twins, had come by, their voices subdued, and a slump to their shoulders in his presence. The nurse assigned to him was brusque and abrupt in his actions – there was no love lost for the enemy commander. *Only my great-nephews, the leaders of this camp, care if I live or die. To the rest, I am the enemy, better off dead.* The feeling was different in Suyodhana's camp – Suyodhana, his brothers, and their hangers-on did not seem to care if he lived or died, but the rest of their army had deferred to him with respect. Who, indeed, was his ally?

---

24 *Gopala* means "cowherd".

The entrance to the tent punctured its eastern wall. A flap of leather kept the direct rays of the morning sun out. His bed was laid out along the southern wall so that his head was towards the entrance. Alongside the western wall, there had been another bed with Shikhandin's body, laid out on his back. Devavrat had puzzled over the profile, how it seemed to tug at a corner of his mind. With Amba's revelation, that mystery was explained. Amba must have taken the body away the previous night and come back when she realised that Devavrat was in the same tent. She had returned to kill him. Once upon a time, those wide eyes and high cheekbones had made their way into his heart to give it life; now they had returned to reclaim that life. *No matter, I am a fortunate man.* Before death claimed him, memories, from so far back that he almost doubted their reality, had materialised to lighten his heart. Those memories would assuage the sorrow that now welled up within him, as he recalled watching his son die. The son he had not known he had. *Just once, before Yama takes me,* he thought, *I was permitted a glimpse of a small pleasure from lost time. I do not blame Amba; she has been the only light in my life. That is enough.*

His grandnephew posed a different problem. Yudhishthira looked subdued, as though depressed by the thought of Devavrat's demise. If there were one thing he could change, it would be this – relieve him of this misery. He had liked Yudhishthira as a boy and he liked him now as an adult – he had changed from a slight youth with faraway eyes to a dignified man who held himself like a warrior and behaved like a commander of men. However, the legitimacy of his claim was in doubt. The compromise Devavrat had forged once, many years ago, that made Yudhishthira the Chief Magistrate of Indraprastha,[25] the breakaway republic that was their father's legacy, had collapsed under the weight of Suyodhana's ambitions. Devavrat had not expected the

[25] *Indraprastha* means the "City of Indra".

compromise to survive forever, but it did not even survive the first generation, let alone reach the next generation. It had not been intended to last forever – his plans for the continued growth of the empire ensured that eventually Hastinapur would rule all the surrounding lands, including Indraprastha – but the compromise had barely lasted a few years.

Yudhishthira's manner indicated genuine concern for his granduncle. He said, "Grandsire! I wish the doctor had said something different."

"Yudhishthira, my boy! I am an old man and have seen much. That my wound is fatal, I know myself. Your doctor is right. I do not have much time left. I accept it."

"I am sorry we had to capture and disable you, but that was necessary," Yudhishthira said. "This war was… is, unnecessary. No matter, now we must win it."

"You did what you had to, my son. I am sworn to protect the dynasty and ensure legitimate inheritance. As long as I live I would have to oppose you."

Yudhishthira did not respond. Devavrat's public oaths were known to all – his acceptance of his own disinheritance – but they made for hidden whispers hinting at treason. There were secret oaths as well – celibacy and unquestioned support for the Queen Mother's children – made to his father and stepmother – these were only known to a few: Sanjaya, the family bard who would sing publicly of Devavrat's vows if he were not terrified of Bhishma; the Vyaasa Shukla, the golden-voiced head of the Kavi Sangha who knew all that Devavrat knew and probably more; and, lastly, his nephew Dharmateja, called Vidura by the world for his wisdom, intelligent, of closed mouth and open mind, born alongside his royal brothers Mahendra and Dhritarashtra, the child of the royal wet-nurse, perfect in every way that the other two were not, but ineligible to be king because his mother was not royal, not a wife, merely a maid-servant of the queen and wet-nurse to the princes born to the dead Vichitravirya. *Did Yudhishthira know of these vows? Was he about to question my decision to oppose him?*

Devavrat did not expect Yudhishthira to say anything. *Why should he touch the subject?* The question of succession would be resolved through battle. Yudhishthira had refused to be drawn into the ancient debate over legitimacy. His father had acknowledged him as his son, eligible to be Master Trader of Hastinapur, and that was the final word.

"Our dynasty will live on," Yudhishthira said, "Its survival is not my concern. What am I concerned about? The crisis that began in your time continues to confront us. My father rejected your path, and now I reject it as well. We may not undo all you have done – but we will stop the continual grab of Naga land and the eviction of the Nagas. The Yadavas have promised not to come further north. We have more than our share of refugees, immigrants or not. The next batch can go further west, beyond the mountains to Bahlika.[26] I want you to explain why you chose to create this empire. It will perhaps help us follow a wiser path, one that the Matsyas, the Yadavas, and Panchala can support. My cousins felt threatened by our proposals. You did too. War was inevitable. You may be too old to fight but your hand marks all their strategy. That is why we plotted to capture you. We only intended to capture you – we did not intend to injure you thus, let alone kill you. We thought that with you as our prisoner, Suyodhana would be left with Kutaja,[27] the master of weapons and the martial arts teacher, as the only competent advisor regarding the conduct of the war."

---

[26] *Bahlika* is believed to be either Bactria or Baluchistan. It is said to have been founded by Shantanu's brother Bahlika who abdicated and left Hastinapur. See Endnotes.

[27] *Kutaja* means "mountain peak" or "jar". Later, the martial arts teacher would be called *Drona,* (also meaning "jar", but one that holds an hallucinogenic drug). Drona is possibly a pejorative name. See Endnotes.

"What grieves me," he continued, "is that your injuries are fatal and you will die as my prisoner. I have no options in that matter. I cannot send you back. I must keep you a prisoner. My men are afraid of you and your cunning – even now I am being asked when we will execute you."

Cunning? Devavrat mused at that description. *Of course, they were right. Only the cunning survive to an old age.* He had survived. He must be cunning.

"What do you want from me? As you say, the crisis continues. Clearly we have not been wise enough, for we have added war to the furnace."

"I want to know the history of the crisis. How it came about, what was tried, and what did not work. You are the only person whose knowledge goes that far back."

"Not the only person..."

"The only person I can talk to. The Queen Mother refuses to have anything to do with us. Uncle Dharmateja tells us that he supports our claims but then, being Vidura, chooses to stay in Hastinapur, at Suyodhana's side, and refuses to explain his actions. He has always helped us when we lived in Hastinapur. My mother says she will not move out of Hastinapur but that I should fight for my rights. The Vyaasa Shukla can move freely within the city – he comes and goes as he pleases – he takes care to speak in parables that nobody understands.

A sour taste rose in Devavrat's throat. Remembering on command. Remembering was what he had been doing ever since he had been captured, but those were not the memories anybody wanted.

"I need time to think. I am tired and it is late. Can you ask me tomorrow?" *With luck I shall be dead.*

"Yes, I will," said Yudhishthira. "I will come ten ghatis after sunrise. I will bring along Indraprastha's Archivist."

2000 B.C.E

An Archivist. So they were getting some help from the Kavi Sangha. Devavrat mused as he carefully let his shoulders lie back on the cotton roll.

***

THE PANDAVA CAMP
CIRCA 2000 B.C.E.

Lomaharshana,[28] the Archivist, woke up that morning to find one of his younger colleagues sitting by his bed.

"We have a message from the Vyaasa," the junior said. "He will visit us soon, a quiet visit, without any ceremony. The Pandavas are rumoured to have a senior prisoner in their camp. It is imperative that you archive his memoirs. Ask the eldest Pandava, Chief Yudhishthira, for permission and for any questions he might want answered. There cannot be any delay."

As Lomaharshana prepared himself for the day, a messenger came from Yudhishthira. "We have a prisoner whose memoirs you must archive soon for he is on his death-bed. I've told him what I want to know and he understands my requirements. You must start as soon as you can."

Lomaharshana rushed through his morning rituals and meal and went to the hospital tent. He recognised the prisoner. He was the Regent. *The Regent. The Terrible.* It was a shock to see the man, whose name had been used to scare him as a child, tied to a hospital tent. Then it hit him that this capture could well mark the end of the war. The morning meal weighing down his belly suddenly lightened. *Capturing Devavrat the Terrible was a great achievement. If this will not make peace, what will?* The Regent was still asleep. A nurse was replacing a bloodied cotton roll placed behind the Regent with a fresh one.

"There is an arrow still stuck in his shoulder," the nurse said. "He will act as though it doesn't matter, but from time to time he will acknowledge discomfort. The doctor says he will

---

28 *Lomaharshana* means "one who makes hair bristle or stand on end".

die if we extract the arrow, but then, he will die in a few days anyway. Why they don't let him die, I don't know. They aren't even questioning him – I would put him down on the ground and jiggle the arrow until he told us everything. Instead, we've been taking care of him, making him comfortable, doing what we can to comfort him. I clean the wound with fresh turmeric water and keep it covered. While you are with him, just keep doing whatever makes him comfortable. Not too much though." The nurse gave a lop-sided grin and left.

Lomaharshana sat down at the foot of the mat and waited for the Regent to wake up.

"Amba!" the sleeping Devavrat mumbled. Lomaharshana leaned forward to hear the whisper. *Who or what was Amba? Maybe he said Amma? Was he calling for his mother?* Despite the coolness of the autumn morning, Devavrat's throat showed beads of sweat. His cheeks glowed with a thin sheen of moisture. Lomaharshana cleared his throat loudly but the Regent did not respond. The nurse came back and said, "He's up. Here," and before Lomaharshana could protest, he pushed the sleeping Regent's arm with a finger. Devavrat flinched and he tried to turn his head. The pain woke him up completely, his eyes wide as he tried to control his response. He saw the Archivist sitting near his feet; his eyes narrowed again and he said, "Who are you?"

The Archivist said, "Lomaharshana, sir. I am the Archivist. I have been asked to work with you. Please do not worry; there is no reason to hurry. The Commander will explain it all to you. I am waiting for him."

"Commander?"

"Chief Yudhishthira, Consort and Head of the Queen's Council. He will be here soon, sir. I would like to wait for him. I am ready, otherwise."

The Regent said, "Yes, you would be ready! You are the Archivist. Does Shukla know you are here?"

"Shukla, sir?"

"The Vyaasa, Shukla."

"Yes, sir, he does."

"Where is he?"

"I don't know, sir. These days his movements are a secret."

Devavrat looked around the hospital tent – it was large and empty, as if erected just for him. The sun was bright outside Devavrat's tent. It was still early. Outside the shelter, the long shadows cast by the early morning sun grew shorter and the fuzzy edges became sharper. It had been a month since the monsoons ended and the autumnal equinox had been celebrated. In a normal year, the harvest should be in progress. In a few days, the farmers would be busy again, preparing for the winter crop.

I am a warrior, not a farmer! That was what Suyodhana, encouraged by his friend Karna had proclaimed when Devavrat had counselled patience. *They are wrong. A warrior needs to know all that a farmer does about the cycle of the seasons.* Yudhishthira's request had to be dealt with. What did he want to know? It was not as though Devavrat had had many policy choices. First Yudhishthira's father, and now, Yudhishthira, acted as though there were choices. The easy-to-till land was limited. The Nagas with their slash-and-burn practices used the forested land inefficiently. They did not create permanent settlements, just ramshackle villages that were abandoned after ten to twenty years,[29] the spent field left fallow for at least two generations, until no one in the band recalled living in that spot. Any itinerant settler could exploit the situation – all he had to do was occupy the fallow land and scream if a Naga threatened them. He, Devavrat, had tried his best, but there was no "fair" solution.

[29] For agricultural purposes, the solar year is defined from one winter solstice to the next winter solstice.

Yudhishthira came on time, by himself. Again, Devavrat was struck by the difference between the cousins. A king had an entourage. Suyodhana was a king. He called himself King. He moved in Hastinapur with a coterie of courtiers who waited on him. Yudhishthira did not call himself King, or for that matter, Emperor, as some of his troops called him. He walked around the camp without an entourage. He had chosen to make his city a *janapada,* a state governed by a council chosen by the people. That harked back to an old and almost forgotten tradition of the Pauravas of the cities of Panchnad, the land between the Sarasvati and the Sindhu. A hereditary matriarch, advised by a council, headed the janapada. A matriarch had never ruled Hastinapur, with its unusual evolution from caravanserai to city. Indraprastha, Mahendra's town, a new settlement born of Hastinapur, had chosen to return to the past, with some changes.

Yudhishthira sat down by his head. His voice was soft. "Did you sleep well? Are you comfortable?"

Devavrat found himself smiling at the minor courtesy – he had become used to the forceful language that ruled in Suyodhana's court.

"Your people carried out your instructions perfectly, my son. You have competent hospital staff. They propped me up so that the arrow would not be dislodged. A boy attended to me every time I woke up. Why care so much for a dying man, an enemy at that?"

Yudhishthira smiled. "Should I torture you to get information about Suyodhana's war plans? I have been asked to do that. Fortunately, I do not need that from you. I have other questions, as I said yesterday. Do you remember our conversation?"

"Yes. I've thought about it all evening and I was concerned that I would not be able to sleep. Then night fell and, fortunately, sleep took me. You want me to regurgitate ancient memories?"

2000 B.C.E

"Yes," Yudhishthira said. "There is much I do not know. I was young, perhaps too young when my father told me some of the history. He died just as I came of age. When we returned to Hastinapur, my mother was concerned that all the children were only being taught martial arts. She asked Uncle Dharmateja to take charge of our education, but he had to deal with all five of us. He taught me about the administration of your Hastinapur Empire. There was no time for anything else."

"True, we did not have any time for you. Or, for that matter, for your innumerable cousins."

"Grandsire, that isn't the past history I want to hear about. Tell me about your childhood. Tell me about your father, great-grandfather Shantanu, and what he did."

It's so easy to like this man, Devavrat thought. *He is very direct, just like all of Satyavati's descendants. Maybe we are wrong to doubt his parentage, lip or no lip. There are differences – he is polite, whereas Suyodhana and his brothers are arrogant. He wants history, not an artful story with the twists and turns that please storytellers. I cannot give him either version.*

"My childhood? You cannot understand my childhood without knowing everything else that was going on."

"I can listen. Begin as early as you have to. Begin with the founding of Hastinapur, if you will."

"I'll need some time to collect my thoughts."

"You can work with Lomaharshana, here," Yudhishthira said.

"Yes, I have met him," Devavrat said and nodded to the Archivist who was standing silently at the foot of the bed.

Where is Devavrat?

The Kaurava Council
Circa 2000 B.C.E

"Damn it! Damn, damn, damn, Karna! I do not want to make peace with those Naga-loving Pandavas. Don't they get it? I want war!"

"Suyodhana, my friend. Cheer up!" Karna said. He had come as soon as he was called, for Suyodhana had stormed out of the council meeting.

"That meeting was a waste of time. Why did I call it?"

"It was a waste. We got what we needed, though. Permission!" said Karna.

The morning had begun with bad news – Devavrat Bhishma was missing. He had left on a secret mission with Shikhandin. It had been a week and he had not returned. It was frustrating to work with the old man – he had ruled as Regent for so long he could not stop ordering people around and doing things without permission. Now he had gone off on a mission that Suyodhana and Karna had tried to ignore – a fool's errand to make peace.

I do not want to make peace with those Naga-loving Pandavas. Only Karna understood how Suyodhana felt – only Karna had tasted the bitter fruit of rejection by his inferiors that Suyodhana swallowed every day. His spies relayed to him the word on the street – they watered down what they heard, for Suyodhana's anger would burn the messenger – Yudhishthira was wise, Suyodhana was not; Yudhishthira was a mature adult, Suyodhana was a spoilt baby; Yudhishthira tried to be fair to all, Suyodhana favoured his immigrant friends.

The siege of Indraprastha last year had been an extraordinary success, bar one inexcusable failure. The Pandavas had been trapped and their allies, the Panchalas and the Yadavas, had been unable to come to their aid. Blocking the upstream dam had cut off the water supply to the city. Then they had diverted the excessive snowmelts of the spring into channels that went a long way away from the city. The Pandavas' *City of Indra,* Indraprastha, had become a cemetery with thirsty and starving people and dying children. In another day or two, the people, the citizens of the republic, janas as well as the ganas, the *janapada,* the people whom the Pandavas had so proudly sponsored, would have handed the Pandavas' heads to him on a platter. *Five platters,* he corrected himself. *It could even have been seven if his guards had not been tricked by the wily Krishna the Yadava and Krishnaa Agnijyotsna the arrogant Matriarch of Panchala.*

The inexcusable failure had been to permit the Pandavas' successful escape from the city into the surrounding forests. *The fools had let them go!* After they left, Suyodhana's troops had looted the city and he had ordered its destruction – the citizens were ordered to settle elsewhere. Granduncle Devavrat, *Regent* Devavrat, had objected. *For somebody called Bhishma, he was soft.* The victory would have been a celebrated one as the Pandavas had left everything behind – wealth, clothing, slaves, and much else – all the things that made life worth living. The victory should have made his life, Suyodhana's life, a glorious one, definitely worth living for, if it were not for the virus that had infected his own people – the spread of praises of Yudhishthira sung by the exiles from that destroyed city – and had made victory taste like mud in his mouth.

Recalling the botched victory reminded him of the debacle earlier that morning that had left him feeling angry and despairing. *I need Karna here and now.* Karna was the only one who could pull Suyodhana out of the depression that chained him whenever he thought of the Pandavas.

"Send for King Karna," he had said to the attendant at the door. The man had gone to find Karna. That was when the news of Devavrat's disappearance was brought to him.

As Suyodhana had waited for the arrival of his friend, he heard a commotion outside. He went to inspect and found a man lying sprawled on the ground near the door to the chamber. He was panting.

One of the gatekeepers said, "He asked for King Suyodhana!"

"Bring him here," said Suyodhana. They picked the man up and brought him into the almost-empty chamber where Suyodhana recognised him as one of Devavrat's attendants.

"What exactly did he say?"

"The Regent Devavrat has disappeared. He says he was last seen with the stranger Shikhandin, who has also disappeared," said one of the spectators.

Suyodhana shook his head in disgust – the old man could not do anything right!

"Karna!" he said as his friend appeared at the door. "What are we to do? Our field marshal has disappeared. The slippery Shikhandin, too. I knew we should not have trusted him. Devavrat may be dead. He may have been captured by the enemy."

"Does it matter?" asked Karna.

"You are right – we don't need the old man. We captured Indraprastha without his help. If it had not been for the interference of my treacherous uncle Dharmateja, we would have the Queen of Panchala serving us. We do not need him, but we cannot lose him – Granduncle knows all our defences. If he is not dead but is a prisoner, they will torture him and extract that knowledge from him."

A meeting of the war council was in order, to deal with the crisis. The council consisted of Devavrat, who was absent, Kutaja, Suyodhana, Suyodhana's brother Duhshasana, and Karna. Sanjaya, the court poet, attended in support of his father, the blind King Dhritarashtra, *"King" by the grace and sufferance of Devavrat, the generous, abstemious, self-sacrificing, ever-critical Regent.* All his life Suyodhana had endured the taunt "the son of a blind king". His uncle Dharmateja was on the council but Suyodhana arranged Dharmateja's absence by not informing him of the meeting. *What was the point of having an avowed critic of war on a war council?* He had been one of Devavrat's appointments to the council, and Devavrat was not there.

Suyodhana called the meeting and asked their martial arts teacher, Kutaja, to chair it. He had all but begged him to focus on the immediate crisis caused by Devavrat's death or capture. Kutaja was an obstinate, unyielding disaster – nothing that Suyodhana or Karna proposed was to his liking. *What did he think – that he was the king?* His attitude itself was wrong – it was as though negativity was the order of the day. There was no point organising an expedition to find Devavrat and rescue him if he was still alive, for they did not even know where the Pandava camp was. Nothing was possible if it was in Panchala territory. It might be in Yadava territory – they should collect the appropriate intelligence from spies before trying to find them. They could even be hiding out with the Matsyas (though Suyodhana could not imagine a more dreary part of the country). Only Karna and he wanted to send out a full-fledged war party.

The council wanted more information before they decided. Devavrat's guard who had returned was suspect – he said the second guard had run away, but how could he prove that? He had revealed very little useful information – Suyodhana thought it might be necessary to threaten him with torture. Kutaja recommended that a small troop investigate the site of the kidnapping. The council had agreed. *They'll support anybody but me.* Suyodhana had left the session in a rage.

It had been a waste of time. It rankled. *Investigate first, indeed.*

"What am I going to do, Karna?"

Karna said, "My friend, calm yourself. What you got is good. The council has not appointed an investigator or specified the size of the troop. Until the council meets again, you are in charge."

Suyodhana smiled. "Of course. I may not be King yet, but the Regent is absent too. My father will do whatever I say. You can be the lead investigator."

"I will need a team with three hundred men."

"Good. You be the investigator. I will mobilise the rest of our army so that we are prepared to act on whatever you discover."

PART 2.

The Son

CHILDHOOD

THE PANDAVA CAMP
CIRCA 2000 B.C.E.

At Yudhishthira's request, Devavrat narrated the story of his early days. Much came to mind – they were the memories of a child, and like the memories of some children, there was no trace of crisis or turmoil: either then, or to come. He knew that his mother was sometimes pregnant, and as he grew older, he realised that his brothers or sisters disappeared soon after their birth, but these events hardly had an effect on him. He was not shown his siblings, and then they were gone.

He skipped past his earliest memories with brief descriptions – the occasional regal visits from his father, King Shantanu, and his mother, Queen Ganga, interrupting a repetitive routine that seemed like it would never end – of playing with the attendants who took care of him, of crying when his parents or his attendants demanded obedience to some rule, of ordering the servants around the house, of running along the river-bank and building sand-castles. As he learned to talk, visits from his mother became more regular and patterned. She hugged him and called him "laḍla".[30] He, in turn, called her "avva".[31] He would wait for her hugs even as he moved from one caretaker to the next and from one teacher to the next.

In the beginning, the King did not seem to know what to do with a toddler. Devavrat was his one and only son, and Shantanu envied the boy's easily expressed affection for the Queen. As Devavrat learned to speak and became articulate, his father came by more often. He asked to be called "bābō"[32] by his son, rather than *Raajan* or *Mahaan,*[33] or other names used by the people around Devavrat, who were always deferential to the King. It was awkward at first, but once the King's wishes were known, everybody encouraged Devavrat to be informal. Devavrat took his cue from them in the beginning and was formal, but he also wanted to please his father, so he tried to be informal when at home with his father.

Shantanu also took Devavrat along to public events and Devavrat took pleasure in his father's pride. He took Devavrat to council sessions where the boy sat quietly to the right and behind his father's high seat. It seemed reasonable to be proud of this indulgence and to see how his father conducted himself as the leader of the council, a role Devavrat was being prepared for. He observed the chain of decisions involved in being the Chief – judging, rewarding or punishing, and finally, facing up to the consequences of those decisions. His family seemed happy and secure. Until the day his mother died.

---

30 *Lāḍlā,* pronounced "lard-la". This is a Gondi word (the Gonds are a forest-dwelling people in India, believed to be the first people of India) meaning "dearest/sweet/darling" boy.

31 Avva (*Avvā,* pronounced "uv-va"), is one of many Gondi words for "mother". The rest of this book will use "mother", even though avva's connotations lie between "Mama" and "mom" in English.

32 *Bābō,* pronounced "ba-bow", is one of many Gondi words for father. The rest of this book will use "father", even though bābō's connotations lie between "Papa" and "dad" in English.

33 *Raajan* is usually translated as "King" with the connotation of "Glorious One" or "Resplendent One"; *Mahaan* means "Great One".

At this point Devavrat voice trailed away and he stopped. Yudhishthira watched him slow down. "If it pertains to this war, you must tell me," he said, his voice still soft and quiet, but with the authority of a Ruler. *Why am I telling this story?* Devavrat thought. *Was what happened to my mother relevant?* It might bother him like the incessant flapping of a hummingbird sipping from a jasmine flower, but that did not make it relevant. What had happened to his mother that day was not inconsequential – it had shadowed him for the rest of his life. The events of that day made him the Regent he had been. They influenced key decisions that led to other actions and forced more decisions. It could be said that the events in his mother's life led to this war. Yudhishthira could not know of the chains of action and reaction that led from his mother's death. His mother's dying had everything to do with policy, and its effect on him was relevant to Yudhishthira's questions about policy.

Devavrat said, "When my father and mother had a disagreement, the house would darken and the air would become hot and humid like the herald of a monsoon storm. I am sure this was in my mind for the mansion was never heavy and oppressive. All the staff walked on tiptoe then, trying to avoid attention. Even though I was only eight years old, both Mother and Father would be short with me; my Mother tried to balance the irritability with an impulsive excess of unexpected hugs. I made occasional attempts to ask my mother what the matter was, but she did not answer – I later concluded that she was preoccupied and did not listen to my questions. I was not used to being taken seriously by my parents, so that was no surprise. This is a report of my observations – I came to understand the situation many years later and my memory is undoubtedly coloured by that knowledge.

"I was eleven years old when my mother died. I understood everything that led to that death. You may be surprised at that. This was a consequence of my education, which even for that generation, had deviated from the traditional. It made it possible for me to memorise perfectly conversations that I heard – even if I did not understand them then, I could rehearse and understand them later."

"What was different about your education?" Yudhishthira said.

Devavrat said, "As was customary for the first son and heir of a great trading family, I had started my schooling at the age of six. Yes, the Kauravas were becoming warriors, but they continued to be a trading family. My schooling would follow an established pattern appropriate for the future master of a caravan. That pattern has changed, for the Kauravas have become warriors, as our ancestor Samvarana wanted. Suyodhana's cohort, warriors all, looks down on traders. My father's descendants today would not recognise the kind of education I received.

"What is in a trader's education? We were peddlers, though not the kind of peddlers you might see in the marketplace. A peddler sets out from home with a cartful of goods – we put together a caravan of goods owned by many manufacturers and merchant families. A peddler keeps in mind the lands he intends to visit in a cycle that lasts six to nine months – we plan a cycle that might last two or more years. A peddler brings back goods that have great value in his home country – we take orders from buyers for items and quantities. We also take orders from sellers about the kinds of products they want in exchange. A peddler must be constantly on the alert about the safety of his person and his goods. The wise peddler listens well, speaks little, remembers everything – well, not as much as bards, but still almost everything. The careful peddler befriends travel companions who will accompany him on bandit-plagued sections of roads. That is how a peddler becomes a merchant – he makes friends or finds a family in the places he visits along the way, who will receive him and help him on the next step. A merchant who has such a home in every destination along a well-worn path can become the leader of a caravan. The families that support him are often trading families themselves. Over many years, trading families build up links with each other – they sometimes consider themselves a single family even though they speak a different language, follow different customs, eat different foods, bow to different gods, and perform different rituals.

"Not every member of a trading family becomes a trader – many choose to stay in one place and never go on a trade expedition. They stay home and distribute the products obtained from afar as peddlers in local markets. Some go overboard, becoming explorers who travel to strange lands looking for new products. In the course of time, some of the traders become leaders of caravans – their extended families will help them put together syndicates of manufacturers and sellers and buyers at every stop.

"Considering all this, the training for a trader, at least in the first year, is not that different from the training for bards. For instance, there might be a list of objects for trade such as a lapis lazuli necklace, a choker of pearls, ear-rings of copper and tin, gold ornaments for the nose, a pendant for the forehead, a jar of unguent for the lips, a whitening cream for teeth, rings for the fingers and toes. A second list might be the directions for a trip of two months with choices to be made every day and distances to be travelled. A third list would be a list of people's names that is then expanded to include how they relate to each other. The difference is that bards are trained with a much wider variety of memorisation tasks while traders focus on the marketplace – for instance, a good trader will learn many languages and customs, while bards develop their skills in just one.

"This training started as soon as I could speak meaningful sentences describing actions by others. Speech proved that I was not mentally disabled. The test showed that I could interpret simple actions and sequences of actions performed by others and describe them in simple sentences. Once schooling started, I did very well and advanced rapidly in comparison to the other traders' children of my own age. I had nothing to do and being bored, I joined the bards in their training sessions – by the age of twelve they were expected to accurately memorise complete conversations that lasted for at least half a ghati, recall shorter conversations with intonation, and the core content of longer conversations of up to three ghatis. I enjoyed these classes.

"Trading families believed in training their children in multiple skills – the only guild that used to do that systematically. Memorising the manifest of a caravan was one skill; being prepared to fight off bandits to protect the caravan was another – both were necessary. Thus, we also trained to fight – this consisted of exercise routines to develop the strength of various muscles in the body – the hands and feet as fighting instruments, the centre of the body as the source of power, the eyes as windows that not only let in light but also expose one's innermost thoughts.

"After memorisation and martial arts, the third aspect of my education was unique to me as the son of the Kaurava ruler of Hastinapur. We Kauravas had to do more than defend ourselves – we had to inspire the warriors we led into battle. The guild of mercenaries selected promising apprentices to undergo training in command – they called it officer training. Guru Vasishtha, the first Vyaasa, had persuaded the master of the guild of mercenaries in his time to train the officers in Samvarana's army. Guru Vasishtha had also persuaded the senior-most Matriarch of the Pauravas that a form of the training that prospective matriarchs received should be provided to Samvarana, the Master Trader of Nagapura, as well as his chosen descendants, as long as they were the guardians of the Panchnad frontier. There is much superstition about this training – no, we do not have a command voice that compels obedience; we do not enter a mystic trance in which we consult with past matriarchs before we come to a decision; we do learn what it feels like to be at the reins of a runaway cart. We learn to steel one's gut and take decisive action in the face of uncertainty.

Panchnad – The World in a Bygone Age

The Pandava Camp
circa 2000 B.C.E.

"This brings us to the greatest change between our world and that of Panchnad – the Master of a caravan is a *man* who wields supreme power, while in a Panchnad city the Matriarch wields power with the advice of her council. This is as it should be, since a caravan may have to go through hostile territory controlled by bandits, or may meet criminals who pretend to be friends and act as spies for enemies. The Master must have a free hand to make crucial and deadly decisions under pressure. Guru Vasishtha and King Samvarana made this the model of governance for Hastinapur. The ruler of Hastinapur, like a caravan Master, is ever ready for battle. Panchnad was a land in which cities settled conflicts without war – Hastinapur and its neighbours settle conflicts by war and nothing else."

"Granduncle!" Yudhishthira said, "You've mentioned this before – I recall, quite distinctly, you telling me many years ago that in Panchnad conflict was not settled by wars. I was unable to understand you, for all my life the prospect of war has never been far away. How did Panchnad settle conflicts without war? All the foreign cultures that I have heard about, from travellers and traders, engage in war. How did Panchnad become a war-free culture?"

"As you found," Devavrat said, "Traders who went on caravans to the West will attest to the unique features of Panchnad, the most unusual being how society was organised. This organisation was the key behind the absence of war. Most of the ordinary citizens, not being traders, barely knew that these were unique features of their culture. The people of Panchnad did not understand how unique they were.

"My son, you want to know how this one-of-a-kind society came about. I will tell you, but remember this – it will be impossible to recreate. That was your father's confused goal.

"The scholars in Takshashila[34] have an explanation. They call the period in which Panchnad developed, the Third Age. We live in the troubled times of transition to the Fourth Age. What the Fourth Age will be like, nobody knows. You, or more likely, Suyodhana, will experience it."

***

Kaushambi/Hastinapur
circa 850 B.C.E.

"I've come across this idea that we are in the Fourth Age, many times. Many times," Bhargava said. "But only in Bhaaratavarsha – no other culture says anything like this. What are these Ages? You also said that this ancient history we are writing down is from the Third Age. Tell me, what does that mean?"

Vaishampaayana said, "The Kavi Sangha records show that the belief in the four Ages of civilisation was widespread in Panchnad. They believed that they were not in the last Age, that there was one more Age to come, they just did not know when. Now we know that we live in the Fourth Age, the *Kali Yuga*. It has been called the Dark Age; the Iron Age, for iron is black; the Age of Strife, for war is its way of life; and, sometimes, the fourth and last

---

[34] *Takshashila* was called Taxila by the Greeks in Alexander's time.

Age, for at the end of the Kali Yuga, the world will be consumed by fire and water and all human beings shall die, except for the seven immortals whose duty it is to repopulate the world. The world is a game of dice – in a dice game, a throw of one is called 'kali' for it is always a losing throw, and the Kali Yuga is the era of complete loss.

"This story of the Great War is the story of how the Third Age, the *Dvapara Yuga* ended. Devavrat lived during that Age. It has been called the Red Age and the Yellow Age, for those are its colours; or the Copper Age, for copper is red; also, the Age of Bronze, the hard yellow metal that emerges from the mixing of soft ores; the Age of Settlement, for in this Age the mothers ended the wanderings of their clans and put down roots; and, sometimes, the Third Age, the last but one of the cycle of four ages that make up a *kalpa*. At the end of the Dvapara Yuga, mountains move, rivers overflow their banks, and perforce, people abandon their homes and go seek new lands to settle in, for settlement tires the land and drains its soil of life – the land must rest lest it become desert. In a dice game, a throw of two is called 'dvapara' – it will lose to all other throws except 'kali', and as such the Dvapara Yuga is the age of little victories and big losses."

"I see," Bhargava said. "We live in the last Age, after which the world is consumed." He paused, then continued, "Who comes up with these ideas?"

Vaishampaayana said, "I don't know. Even the archives of the Kavi Sangha have little to say on the origins of these beliefs. Your question mirrors Yudhishthira's puzzlement."

"I am listening."

***

THE PANDAVA CAMP
CIRCA 2000 B.C.E.

Yudhishthira said, "I want to know more about Panchnad and the world in the Third Age. Tell me what you know of the Third Age: the world at large, and Panchnad in particular."

2000 B.C.E

Devavrat said, "This is what the world looked like in the Third Age. At the very centre of the world, that unmatched mountain, Meru,[35] rose into the heavens where the gods keep their secrets. That sacred mountain peak is home to Amaravati,[36] the city of the gods. To the extreme north of Meru lies Uttara-Kuru,[37] the original northern home of the legendary Pururavas, ancestor of Puru, who left that home in a time lost to memory. Just south of that is the frozen northern wasteland where the Danavas,[38] asuras by nature, hide from the wrath of Indra in the summer. Through this ice-bound land flow the unnamed mighty rivers that empty into the northern sea – when the sun goes south these asuras emerge to freeze the rivers and inflict pain on the unfortunate denizens of that land. Still further south, closer to Mount Meru, we find the homes of the brutal horsemeat-eating Shakas[39] who range from the eastern desert to the western lakes, from the foothills of Mount Meru to the northern wasteland. To the east of the great peak, lies the plateau of the Bo[40] and the Ronga on the way to the plains of Su-wa-Xia.[41] Through this plateau flow great rivers: the mighty river Lauhitya,[42] also called the Bo Ganga; the Xia Ganga that flows to the land of the Xia; and other great rivers called the Ganga because they purified

---

35 *Mount Meru* is a legendary mountain believed to exist north of South Asia, approximately in the centre of the Pamirs in Tajikistan.

36 *Amaravati* was the city of the gods, located at the top of Mt Meru.

37 *Uttarakuru* is the mythical "Arctic home of the Pauravas" covered by ice all through the year. The Pauravas claimed to have come from a land far to the north of Mt Meru. Some optimists have located this in the North Pole. See Endnotes.

38 *Daanava* are demons, children of *Danu*, one of the wives of the mythical sage Kashyapa who fathered all beings (except the highest gods).

39 In historic times, the *Shakas* are identified with the tribes that the Greeks called Scythians.

40 The Tibetan plateau inhabited by the Botias and the Ronga.

41 *Xia* – the plains of China, through which flow the Yang-tze (Xia Ganga) and the Huang Ho (the Ho Ganga).

42 *Lauhitya*, meaning the child of *Lōhita* (iron), is one of the names of the river Brahmaputra; other names include Bo Ganga and Tsang-bo.

whatever they touched. Immediately to the west of the mighty peak lie the lands of the Mlecchas and the Parsakas; further west are the lands of the brown, the red, and lastly the black people of Egypt. The rivers that flow here are deep and fast, hence called Sindhu (swift) – the Arvand,[43] beloved of Indra; the River of Egypt, sometimes called the Krishna[44] for the colour it imparts to the land, sacred to the blue-necked Eashwara; and the Supurna[45] that fulfils all desires. Finally, to the south of Mount Meru lies Jambudvipa,[46] the most fortunate of continents, watered by the rivers Sarasvati, the giver of wisdom, the Sindhu, the swift river, and the Ganga, the purifier of the soul. Many more rivers, of various merits, water this land and all of them empty into the southern ocean, the *Brihatsagar*,[47] either through the Western or the Eastern Seas.[48] To the east of Jambudvipa beyond the Lauhitya are the rivers Iravathi,[49] mother of the Mahanaga Airavath, and the Hme-Ganga,[50] the great river that vanishes into the unknown world of the east. To the north, the Himalayas, the snow-covered White Mountains, are an endless source of water and a barrier impassable by enemies. The centre of Jambudvipa in the Third Age is Panchnad, settled by the most honest, the

---

43 The *Arvand* is the Tigris (the Swift River, also *Sindhu*).

44 The *Krishna* (the Blue/Black River) is the River Nile (also called "the Black River") flows through lands sacred to Osiris (translates to *Eashwara,* the Lord in Sanskrit) – these were the Black Lands, also called the Land of the Temples of Ancestral Spirits (Egyptian word translates to *Pitr-vihara-naad*).

45 The *Supurna* ("fulfilling" or "completed well" in Sanskrit) is the Euphrates (meaning "well-fertilised" in Greek).

46 *Jambudvipa* (*The Island of the Jambul*) is the ancient name for South Asia (from the Hindukush to Assam and from Ladakh to Kanya Kumari). See Endnotes.

47 *Brihatsagar* is the Great Ocean surrounding Jambudvipa (referring to the Indian Ocean).

48 The Western Sea is the Arabian Sea; the Eastern Sea is the Bay of Bengal.

49 The Irrawady, that originates in the Himalayas and flows through Burma to the Bay of Bengal.

50 The Mekong, named for the Hme/Hmu/Hmong people, that flows through Thailand, Cambodia, Laos, and Vietnam and empties into the Indonesian sea, a region not known to the Panchnadis.

most honourable, the most peaceful, and therefore the richest and most prosperous people in the known world. Panchnad can be divided into regions, each settled by an ancestral clan – the Bhaarata-Pauravas to the west and north of the juncture where the Drishadvati and the Sutudri join the Yamuna to form the Sarasvati, a wide, swiftly flowing river; further south, the Vanara,[51] the Raishyava,[52] and the Mayura[53] clans have settlements along the banks of the numerous lakes that slow the Sarasvati down; having slowed down, it widens to suit the flat plain it flows through; finally, the southernmost settlements are those of the Yadavas, all the way to the place where the river enters the sea. Over two thousand such settlements live in peace; the citizens consider themselves fortunate to have been born to such prosperity.

"Each settlement was independent of others; each settlement governed itself in the traditional manner, with a matriarch advised by a council of the wisest and most experienced dwellers; the citizens were consulted through assemblies called when requested; the council advised the citizens who, in turn, were informed and engaged; the seven independent guilds were disciplined and guild members obeyed the rules and regulations established by their guild and the government in performing their tasks. The guild of bards witnessed the acts of the current assembly and could report truthfully on the important events during the time of the last seven matriarchs. Six other guilds – weavers, potters, smiths, builders, farmers, and doctors – reported on their activities, successes and failures, and knowledge of distant events that might affect the settlement. The guild of mercenaries, traditionally not considered a part of any settlement and whose

---

51 *Vanara* means "ape", probably the langur.

52 *Raishyava* means "unicorn". The myth of the unicorn is believed to have originated from this source.

53 *Mayura* means "peacock".

members disavowed allegiance to any settlement, sent observers who would participate if guild-relevant matters were discussed. All the major families participated in trade under the leadership of the founding family – trade was the usual source of wealth and power and entry into the guild of traders was controlled by the leading family – the guild of traders did not need a separate representation in the councils of the state.

"A settlement might contain more than one family headed by a matriarch – the matriarch of the first family, the family that had established the settlement, considered herself the chief and headed a council of matriarchs. The families were usually related to each other and conflicts among the families of a settlement were rare.

"There was one aspect of settlement life that was not dictated by matriarchs. The eldest son of a matriarch could expect to be the next male head of the family supporting his oldest sister as matriarch. Consequently, the eldest son was trained to be a chief. Sometimes one of his brothers might also be similarly trained in case the candidate for chief died prematurely. The other sons of the matriarch did not have that option.

"As a result, it became the duty of the father of a boy to manage his son's education. The simplest way to do this was to enrol the son in the father's guild as an apprentice. Similarly, the younger daughters of a matriarch, the ones not destined to be matriarch, would be guided by one of their aunts into an appropriate guild – that aunt would often be performing the same guiding role for her own daughters as well. As a result, entrance into a guild was largely passed on from father to son or from mother to daughter.

"The survival of the settlements depended on all these guilds, but prosperity depended on trade. The settlements traded with each other, of course, and with the far-off lands to the west and northwest – they shipped their fine clay pots, the rice, wheat, and barley that they grew, rice wine, pepper, sesame seed oil, and other goods west to Dilmun[54] and sometimes directly north of Dilmun, to Susa,[55] the capital of Elam,[56] and all the way into Ur;[57] the smiths imported faience beads from lands north of Takshashila and fashioned jewellery which was greatly in demand in Dilmun. They exported textiles of cotton that were in great demand. In turn, they imported gold from everywhere, for the people were fond of brilliant decoration; they imported tin from secret mines in the far north and exported it to the western world through Dilmun, paying a fortune and making a fortune; they imported decorative objects made of alabaster from Egypt, the land of the Black River; and imported dates from Elam and woollen textiles from the cities of Sumer on the Arvand. The land was at peace and had been at peace for many generations.

"The practice of war, so common in the west, was considered odd in Panchnad. It is tempting to call these present times that we live in, the fourth Age of the world, the baleful Age of Kali, the Age of Strife. I say this with conviction, for most of my life the world has been at war. The coming of the Age of Kali was presaged by its shadow on the lands to the west – Parsaka, Sumer, Elam, and even powerful Lauhityapada[58] abandoned trade as the path to prosperity and succumbed to war, with external enemies as well as internal ones. The effluent of war

---

[54] *Dilmun* was either Bahrain or Oman – the Sumerians considered it an incredibly prosperous trading centre that allowed them to trade with the mythical land of Meluhha to the east.

[55] Susa still exists as a city in modern Iran.

[56] Elam was an ancient non-Semitic culture in southern Iran that frequently conflicted with the Semitic Sumer and Mesopotamia. In 2000 BCE, Elam was the hegemon and once-powerful Sumer was reduced to poverty. By 850 BCE Elam and Sumer were no more and the Assyrians ruled Babylon.

[57] The first city of ancient Sumer.

[58] *Lauhityapada* means the "Land of the Children of Red (soil)", or, maybe "People of the Red Way". One of the names used by Egyptians for their country was *The Red People's Land.*

clogged and then blocked the river of international trade and then stopped it completely.

"Yudhishthira, you asked and I have told you what I know, of Panchnad and the greater world."

The Pauravas Venture into a New World

The Pandava Camp circa 2000 B.C.E.

Yudhishthira said, "Tell me – what made the Pauravas of Panchnad establish an outpost like Hastinapura."

Devavrat said, "During the Third Age, in a period long before the events of this war, the Sindhu and the Sarasvati held pride of place among the people of Panchnad. Ilina, a descendant of Pururavas through the prideful Nahusha,[59] the self-indulgent Yayati,[60] and the self-restrained Puru,[61] wished to expand the trading for which his clan was famous. The land available in Panchnad on the Sarasvati was limited, hemmed in by other settlements, and not usable as a trading hub. If he left the banks of the Sarasvati and headed east he would reach a great river, the Ganga. If he settled there, he would be leaving Panchnad – the Ganga went east into uncharted territory and did not connect with any Panchnad settlement at all. Ilina vacillated between staying in Panchnad and increasing trade with the West, or going to the Ganga and developing new markets in the east. Ultimately, Ilina hedged his bets and established Kaalindini,[62] named after his mother, on the upper Sutudri, almost at the

---

[59] *Nahusha* was a legendary ancestor of the Pauravas. Nahusha's pride led to his fall. See Endnotes.

[60] *Yayati* was a legendary ancestor of the Pauravas. At the end of his life of over a thousand years, he is not satisfied and asks his sons to give him their youth. See Endnotes.

[61] *Puru* was Yayati's youngest son – he fulfils his lustful father's desire for one more youthful year and becomes the heir.

[62] *Kaalindini* was probably close to the current town of Ropar, just before the point at which the Sutudri changed direction and flowed west to the Indus. It was positioned to be an important trading centre for Panchnad.

foothills of the Himalayas. Kaalindini was close to the other Panchnad settlements. Though the Sutudri was not navigable, the residents of Kaalindini would still share its waters with Panchnad. Kaalindini was also closer to the Ganga and within the reach of the forest-dwelling Nagas. It was positioned to monitor and manage any trade with the east – Ilina was certain that this would come about and he wanted his family to be prepared to benefit. Kaalindini was not as hospitable as other Panchnad towns and the decision to stay was a strategic bet about the future of trade. Ilina's ambivalence about this decision could be considered a family trait – every generation after him considered the question of moving east (and abandoning Kaalindini), or declaring failure and returning to some Panchnad town, or staying put, doing nothing. The residents felt that migrating to the banks of the Ganga would break their links to Panchnad. They also feared that this separation from Panchnad would make it difficult to attract immigrants who would grow the frontier town.

"Ilina's grandson Bharata was greatly successful in his dealings and trade with the West and he ignored Kaalindini. Interest in the east declined and was not revived until Bharata's great-grandson Hastin determined to try his fortunes in the east."

Devavrat paused. He did not want to stop – the narration kept him from thinking about the arrow. *I do not want to die now. Not so soon. I may not change Yudhishthira's mind now, but he will think about what I am saying. He will come to realise that what I did was the only path for all of Panchnad and Hastinapur.* This was the right path for all, even for the Nagas, even for Panchala. Devavrat's dilemma was that fear of Hastinapur kept the Nagas from listening to him. His mouth was dry and his voice had voice had become gruffer and gruffer.

Yudhishthira said, "Are you tired? Should we stop for a while?"

"No, I am fine… A little water would help."

Yudhishthira signalled to the Archivist. Lomaharshana fetched a small cup of water. The nurse who had been hovering outside the door came in and said, "Be careful – the old man cannot drink too much water at a time – he throws it up."

Lomaharshana nodded. He used his fingers to moisten Devavrat's mouth and then held the cup to his mouth.

"I am most obliged to you, my son," Devavrat said. "That's enough."

Lomaharshana sat back.

Yudhishthira said, "I've been to Kaalindini – it is a pleasant small town that has been largely abandoned. I was told that the Sutudri turned away from them. Was that the furthest east you could go and still be part of Panchnad?"

"Yes, that is true."

"Does that mean that there were Nagas immediately to their east? How close were they? How did the Nagas react – were they friendly?"

"I'll answer some of those questions as I continue," Devavrat said.

"By staying on the Panchnad side of the watershed," he went on, "the Pauravas intended to reassure the Nagas that they did not want to displace them, and that they wanted to trade with them peacefully. Previous attempts to settle on the Ganga had threatened the Nagas – the Nagas avoided conflict and did not try to evict the settlers, but they had refused to trade or cooperate with them. With the establishment of Kaalindini, the threat was removed and relationships with Naga bands immediately to the east improved. The bulk of the Nagas still lived a long distance (and past dense forests) from Kaalindini, and trade was not as central to the Naga way of life as it was for Panchnad – despite that, more Naga-produced goods came to market to barter for Panchnad's products. Nagas would bring unusual produce – fruits, vegetables, or animal meats and pelts; and minerals – rock salt or other minerals used by smiths, but occasionally copper and very rarely, small quantities of tin. They wanted tools, ceramics, and utensils of bronze. Bronze was scarce in Panchnad, and not easily found in the market, but an exchange for a larger weight of copper could be profitable. By persistence and some sacrifice, the Pauravas of Kaalindini maintained a monopoly on the Naga trade as it became profitable.

"The Panchnadis were familiar with monopolies. They approved monopolies as a valuable strategic tool for a trader when dealing with foreign cultures. Any Panchnad trader could ask to share in the monopoly. The Paurava monopoly was different – the Naga trade was too small to share and the profits came from importing into Panchnad, not exporting. The Nagas consumed little and almost the only product they asked for was bronze. They gave too much stuff in exchange for bronze. This roused both jealousy and anger. By comparison, the Yadavas, who settled around the delta of the Sarasvati, established the great port city of Tripura and controlled the trade with destinations reachable by sea, such as Dilmun, Elam, and Egypt. The Yadava monopoly was a vastly more lucrative one than the Paurava monopoly at Kaalindini, but it was seen as a service benefitting all of Panchnad. Small things can have magnified effect in society. The Pauravas of Kaalindini were considered miserly and grasping, while the Yadavas were considered generous benefactors, even though they behaved identically.

"The Pauravas of Kaalindini were concerned that the other cities of Panchnad were jealous of their success. Hastin, a Bhaarata,[63] proposed to address this by deflecting that resentment away from Kaalindini. He set up a caravanserai on

[63] *Bhaarata* means a descendant of the legendary emperor Bharat, who was said to be the first ruler of a unified Jambudvipa/Bhaaratavarsha.

the banks of the Ganga due southeast from Kaalindini. Usually a caravanserai was a place where caravans stopped on the way to a market or city – this caravanserai was a destination, for there were no known markets or cities to be reached from there. This caravanserai was not a settlement but a service centre for trade – it provided a marketplace for Nagas to come and barter with peddlers and traders from Panchnad. Little changed as far as Kaalindini was concerned, for the profits still flowed to the Pauravas. However, the caravanserai provided a service in a potentially hostile environment, and its fees were not resented.

"Hastin collaborated with the local Naga clans in establishing the settlement and called it Nagapura – this further insulated the Kaalindini Pauravas from the disapproval of the other Panchnad towns, at the expense of Nagapura. Nagapura was intended as a trade centre and nothing else. It was organised like a caravan rather than like a settlement, the leader of the caravan being a male trader who exercised absolute powers. Nagapura did not even try to become self-sufficient as an urban settlement would – instead, it bartered for food from the surrounding Naga bands. The Nagas became partners in the success of Nagapura and it succeeded where previous, more conventional, attempts to settle on the Ganga had failed."

HASTINAPUR, CAPITAL OF KURURASHTRA

THE PANDAVA CAMP
CIRCA 2000 B.C.E.

"So, it was all going well," said Yudhishthira. "What changed? How did an otherwise unremarkable trading post become a city so different from the rest of Panchnad? The changes are extraordinary – it was governed by a Master, not a matriarch; the Kauravas were warriors not traders; the settlement first collaborated with the Nagas, then became the ruler of some of the Nagas, and, finally became their oppressor, all the while asserting the sincere desire to cooperate with them."

"Your father speaks through you, my son," Devavrat said. "Hastin, the great-grandson of your ancestor Bharata, founded the frontier outpost of Nagapura on the right bank of the Ganga. Naga bands were sparse but the location was near a convenient ford for crossing the river that Nagas used. It was an ideal trading location and Nagas came to Nagapura often. By the time of our forebear Samvarana, Naga settlements had appeared around Nagapura, for the population had increased, but there were few conflicts as the settlers of Nagapura avoided agriculture and relied on the Nagas for food. The Nagas were used to growing just what they needed and had to be encouraged to grow some more, so that there was a surplus to support Nagapura – the exotic cotton textiles, the bright jewellery, and the superior metal tools of Panchnad were bartered for food and other products. The Naga population had expanded towards the north on the right bank of the Ganga, despite the thick forest near the river. Over ten yojanas to the west was the Yamuna, but as it went south, it turned west at the northern ridge of the Aravalli[64] range to join the hundred little streams of the river we call the Sutudri. The unfortunate land to the south and west of Nagapura was protected from the rain by the Aravalli range – deprived of the water of the Yamuna and of the rain, the land was bone-dry, receiving little or no rain. This arid wild land, unsuitable for cultivation in the Naga manner, we called Khandavaprastha. This arid cursed land stretched south until it encountered the Charmanavati[65] River, also monsoon-fed, but draining a vast plateau in the Vindhya mountains.

"Nagapura was prosperous because of trade and only because of trade. The Bhaarata Hastin had recognised an opportunity – occasionally Nagas would come into Panchnad with small quantities of almost pure copper and some tin. Tin was a precious metal – it was scarce in Panchnad and in the rest

---

64 *Aravalli* is a mountain range in Western India stretching from Ahmedabad to Central Delhi.

65 *Charmanavati* is the river Chambal.

of the world. The Panchnadis had discovered a source far to the north past Bahlika, and had kept it secret, but eventually that secret would be revealed and Panchnad would lose that monopoly. Hastin thought he might be able to establish a more permanent trade in tin and other ores. That was how Nagapura succeeded – it became the destination for tin and copper ore brought by Nagas from the east in small boats. Nagapura prospered with increasing trade.

"In the beginning, Nagapura was managed like a caravan, not like a Panchnad settlement. The head trader was a man who managed all aspects of caravan life, and negotiated barter deals with his Naga counterpart. Over many generations, the head trader's role became the permanent entitlement of the descendants of Hastin. Nagapura never became a Panchnad-style *janapada* ruled by a matriarch and her council. The head trader's family wanted to retain control and the role of head trader passed from father to son, a practice imported from the Parsakas across the snow-covered Himalayas west of Panchnad.

"The situation was not completely peaceful. On the left bank of the Ganga was Panchala, a confederation of Naga bands. Panchala had slowly but surely extended its rule over other Naga bands of the left bank. Panchala wanted to rule over the Nagas on the right bank as well. The Ganga was too wide to construct a permanent bridge, so such a bond would never have been easy to maintain. When Nagapura entered the picture, it became practically impossible to dream of unification. Nagapura's success led to prosperity for the Nagas who allied with them and traded with them. Panchala refused all interaction with Nagapura. The Naga bands on the right bank did not want to join Panchala. Shortly after our ancestor Samvarana, Hastin's great-grandson, became the head trader of Nagapura, he faced an ultimatum from Panchala – *You are on Naga land. Pay tax on all your deals.* When Samvarana laughed off this demand, the Panchalas did the impossible – an army went north and found a place to cross over the Ganga and invaded Nagapura. They drove a surprised Samvarana and the Pauravas out, and took over Nagapura. Samvarana sought refuge in Kaalindini. He did not find support from the other Panchnad cities, for external war was not their forte. Nor did he get support from the guild of mercenaries, for the war to recover Nagapura was unlike anything they had executed in a long time.

"The cities of Panchnad dotted the banks of the Sarasvati from its beginnings at the merge of the Sutudri, the Drishadvati, and the Yamuna, all the way south to the western sea. Cities like Moolasthan and Takshashila similarly covered the banks of the Sindhu and its tributaries, many yojanas to the west. The population was still growing. The great teacher and strategist, Vasishtha, had established the Kavi Sangha as an organisation that would help address the expected problems of growth. Vasishtha believed that expansion to new regions to the south and to the east was essential but neither he nor the Kavi Sangha persuaded anybody.

"Samvarana's exile proved to be an opportunity for Vasishtha – sensing an opportunity to establish the credibility of the Kavi Sangha, Vasishtha offered his advice to Samvarana. He and the Kavi Sangha helped Samvarana train an army of warriors – the first such army in Panchnad. It did not consist of mercenaries. Mercenaries fought for an employer; this army was a managed and maintained organisation pledged to fight for Nagapura and owing allegiance to Samvarana. One innovation that the Kavi Sangha borrowed from the other cultures that Panchnadis knew about – the army was an all-male army that did not include any mercenaries or other guild members. This allowed them to create the army without requiring approval from the matriarchs of Panchnad.

"In the meantime, the Panchalas had troubles of their own. They did not understand how to run a market or a trade entrepôt. Nagapura's prosperity faded and the surrounding

Naga bands also suffered. The takeover of Nagapura was a disaster for Panchala and as the years passed, they maintained a smaller and smaller force to keep control of Nagapura. When Samvarana returned with his army, he found a disaffected population that welcomed him. The small Panchalan force was routed and Nagapura returned to Samvarana's rule. Vasishtha and the Kavi Sangha gained in stature and this victory marked the acceptance of the Kavi Sangha as a formidable strategic, political, and intellectual force in Panchnad. Under Vasishtha, the guild of bards merged with the Kavi Sangha. *Vyaasa,* the title of the head of the guild of bards, became the title of the Panchnad-wide head of the Kavi Sangha as well.

"The Panchalas, by evicting Samvarana and then, in turn, being evicted by him, established the seed of an empire – Nagapura with its new permanent standing army, became the hegemon in its immediate surroundings. Samvarana's army did not consist of mercenaries, but career warriors who stayed together. The troops stayed when the fighting was over and were supported by taxing the surrounding Naga communities in exchange for 'protection' from Panchala.

"Samvarana's son Kuru used the army to send expeditions to the east to find the source of the tin and copper. Many yojanas to the east, the Ganga encountered a great plateau to the south and turned north.[66] A monsoon river, which we call the *Hiranyaganga,*[67] emerged from the plateau to join the Ganga. At that juncture, Kuru established a small trading post called *Laghu*[68] Nagapura. The plateau was peopled by a different

---

[66] Modern Varanasi/Kashi is located a little east of this turn to the north. Kaushambi is also close by (about 75 kilometres from Allahabad). After flowing past Varanasi, the Ganga turns east again and joins the Sone (see next footnote) at Patna (old Pataliputra, the capital of Magadha).

[67] *Hiranyaganga* means the "Golden Ganga", possibly because gold was brought down this river from the plateau. Later the name would change to "Son-ganga", further shortened to Sone.

[68] *Laghu* means "Little".

forest-dwelling culture – the Nagas called them *Defenders,* which Kuru's men translated as *Rakshasa*. The Rakshasas of the plateau lived a double life – they had settlements that were permanent and depended on the surrounding forest for game and food, but they also had a mining establishment, permanently tied to the location of a lode of ore – copper, silver, gold, or other tradable mineral. They had developed techniques for extracting almost pure copper from the rich lodes they treated as owned by the settlement. The plateau Rakshasas had access to tin, though they would not, or could not, explain where it came from. Laghu Nagapura became the market in which the plateau Rakshasas exchanged almost pure copper and tin ore for products from Panchnad, such as cotton, textiles, bronze tools and utensils, and fine clay pots.

"Laghu Nagapura was not considered suitable for smelting arsenical bronze – the Rakshasas did not know how the shiny golden metal was made, there were no local sources of arsenic, and Kuru did not want to create an incentive for raiding. Instead, bronze foundries were established around Nagapura, to smelt arsenical bronze and further work it into tools and jewellery. Nagapura produced copper and bronze items – cooking utensils, carpenter's tools, expensive armour, and hunting weapons. Smiths and artisans from the rest of Panchnad came to Nagapura. Nagapura prospered as a Third Age manufacturing site, and its surroundings were dotted with foundries in the middle of growing swathes of clear-cut forest. Nagapura began to look more urban, like a traditional Panchnad settlement, and less of a nomadic caravan stop. To recognise this evolution, Kuru renamed Nagapura – the new name was Hastinapur in honour of the founder Hastin.

"Later, Kuru's son Viduratha and grandson Arugvata, also called Anashwa, found a source of arsenic ore in the plateau of Laghu Nagapura and moved the manufacture of bronze ingots there, while the artisans remained in Hastinapur. Arugvat gave the Rakshasas a stake in the production and protection of the bronze by handing over the furnaces to them. A Rakshasa band that raided the site for stealing stockpiled bronze only hurt another Rakshasa band and the response would be immediate and devastating.

"The Rakshasas responded to the new technology and new production by increasing native copper production in order to produce more value-added bronze. They also increased cooperation with the Hastinapuris and exchanged information of mutual interest. Arugvat discovered that the tin came through traders who hiked from the headwaters of the Hiranyaganga to the head of a river the Rakshasas called the Great River, which the Hastinapuris translated as Mahanadi.[69] The Great River flowed east out of the plateau and emptied itself via a delta into the Eastern Sea.[70] The traders were met at the delta by ships that claimed to come from the other side of the Eastern Sea. The ships carried tin ore as well as linen, salt-water fish, unusual fruits, and coconut oil and other palm byproducts. They took back copper ore and gems – lapis lazuli, beryl, and shell – as well as animal pelts. Live animals – tamed elephants and domesticated dogs – were a favourite item.

"The demand for arsenical bronze, tin, and tin-based bronzes in Panchnad led to the establishment of a great trading route from the unnamed land[71] across the Eastern Sea to the mouth of the Great River, across the plateau, to Laghu Nagapura, then up the Ganga to Hastinapur and thence to the plains of the Sarasvati and the Sindhu. Hastinapur, as the entrepôt, controlled the trade and prospered – more than prospered, for Kaalindini and Hastinapur came to be respected in the councils of the Panchnad cities.

69 *Mahanadi* means "Great River".

70 The upper reaches of the Mahanadi are a few days trek from the upper reaches of the Sone.

71 Probably Malaysia or Siam. See Endnotes.

"Kuru's explorations increased Hastinapur power and profile in Panchnad. Hastinapur had been a caravan – it was going to be a city, while retaining its unique features. One difference would prove to be important – Hastinapur was not a matriarchy. The legacy of its long existence as a caravan outpost, headed by a male trader, continued. To conform to Panchnad customs, the chief's sister, or sometimes the chief's wife, was called the Matriarch, but the lineage and control passed through the male chief to his sons and not through the Matriarch to her daughter and son. Kuru, in turn, was recognised as the patriarchal dynast – Hastinapur was no longer the trading outpost of a glorified caravan, but a successful city, controlled entirely by his descendants called *Kauravas.*

"This change in inheritance seemed like a small change – it was expected that when the crisis was over, the traditional Panchnad model would be followed. The Kavi Sangha did not expect the change to last more than a generation or two. However, not only did the new model of patriarchy continue past the next few generations, it has been the standard. Your own claim rests on your father inheriting from Vichitravirya.

"Many Hastinapuris resented the lack of support from the Bhaaratas of Panchnad during Samvarana's exile. Kuru's success in establishing Laghu Nagapura gave him the wherewithal to declare independence from Panchnad and make Hastinapur a state, called Kururashtra. With its standing army of trained warriors, this state could assert its rights in hostile surroundings."

Yudhishthira's brow was creased. "So the Hastinapur practice of the sceptre passing from the king to his son was new. Before that, was Panchnad more like the Panchalas?"

Devavrat said, "Panchnad was like no other society in the world. Let me explain."

"There was no war in Panchnad," continued Devavrat.

2000 B.C.E

"Yes, the trading families taught some fighting skills to their members. That is not to say that they were trained as warriors. A trader would never become as expert as the traditional mercenary of Panchnad. Why did Panchnad need mercenaries if the land was at peace? There were bandits who preyed on travellers, so the roads needed to be patrolled. Caravans needed protection, especially when visiting the lands beyond the Himalayas – once you cross the pass to the plateau of Gandhara,[72] you leave the land of peace and enter a world in which war is endemic. There, gangs of thieves might attack an unprotected caravan. The caravan might blunder into the middle of an armed conflict between cities in foreign lands. In Panchnad, there were no conflicts between the cities, for land was plentiful. The final critical difference was that no city aspired to dominate the others.

"This did not mean there were never any conflicts. Conflicts occurred. You could say it is human nature to find a cause for which to fight. The conflicts did not end in the kind of war we have now, the kind of war that is ubiquitous in the rest of the world. Two cities in conflict would be encouraged by their neighbours to negotiate. Panchnad had been settled by the steady splitting up of bands with a daughter band settling the frontier with help from its new neighbours as well as its parent band. Neighbouring cities were tied to each other by familial as well as economic and cultural bonds. Conflicts affected everybody and the result was that negotiations rarely failed.

"Negotiations rarely failed. That is to say, sometimes, negotiations failed. Attempts at reconciliation by neighbouring cities failed. When reasonable means fail, one must try unreasonable means – for instance, the not-reconcilable parties

[72] Now called Kandahar in Afghanistan, the province of Gandhara along with the province of Arachosia (southern Afghanistan) would be the two richest provinces of the Persian empire under the ruler Cyrus the Great (*Maha-kur-esh*, The Great Lord of the Kurus) of the Achaemenid dynasty (*Agamana*, the Returners).

would be encouraged to decide by a competition – the winner of a race or a competitive game or the winner in a game of dice – these sometimes worked when everybody agreed that there was no fair way to choose sides.

"The last unreasonable means resorted to was war. When the opposing parties were adamant in their positions, and would not accept the result of blind chance that games or a throw of dice represented, the parties would be allowed to go to a *managed* war.

"Nobody wanted war, even a managed war. More than anything else, the matriarchs who governed each band and clan understood that dependence on uncontrolled war to settle conflicts would change the culture by creating the need for an army. On average, a man was stronger than a woman, and a very strong man was stronger than a strong woman. The difference was slight, but it would be enough to create a preference for an army of men, led by men. Such a force soon became an army for men – a danger to the power of a matriarch. Neighbours collaborated to prevent or eliminate such developments.

"A managed war was a war that felt like another game, like a game of dice. The difference was that warriors could still die. A few deaths were preferable to uncontrolled war that would kill the culture. This is how the practice of ritual war came into being.

"The Panchnad civilisation was a trading civilisation. Ships sailed from the ports on the Western Sea to Dilmun and other lands inhabited by Mlecchas. Caravans crossed the mountain passes into the lands of the Asuras, the Medes, and the Parsakas. The caravans and the ships needed to be protected and a guild of guards existed that raised competent fighters and warriors.

"Fighting a war is a skill, like any other skill. The guild of guards expanded to become a guild of mercenaries who could be used to conduct war games. The guild of mercenaries provided the warriors, the advisors to the opposing cities, and the arbitrators who decided who lost and who won.

"If negotiation failed to settle a conflict between cities, the cities would go to war with mercenaries hired from the guild of mercenaries. This was ritual battle – the cities stated their demands before the battle and the side that won the battle would dictate terms restricted to those demands. Since a wealthier city could always hire better and more mercenaries, a poorer city would rarely choose this path, preferring to negotiate instead, or to create a coalition that might oppose the wealthier city. As a result, even managed war, when it happened, was between approximately equal coalitions of cities.

"You would not recognise a Panchnad war. One side would challenge by announcing a goal of capturing something of value from the other side – for example, its commander-in-chief. The judges would assign a value to this challenge, specify the time within which the task was to be accomplished (ghatis, days, or other time period) and judge the winner. The defenders would announce their strategy – perhaps an armed formation to protect its commander for the time specified by the judges. If capture was successful, the challenger won and the challenger's client might declare victory. If enough judges did not accept the claim of victory (the required number of judges would be agreed upon before the war), the challenge would be reversed. The defending side would issue a challenge in its turn. It did not have to do so – possessing the disputed resource and keeping it during the original challenge might be enough to claim victory. The judges might uphold the claim. There was no limit to the number of challenges a losing side could bring. The cost of such challenges could become unsupportable even for the wealthiest city.

"The members of the guild of mercenaries, even those on opposing sides of a battle, were often related to each other. They preferred to capture an opposing warrior rather than kill or even maim them. At every engagement, the goal would be to capture, not kill, one or more senior commanders of the other side. The mercenaries did not overtly change their own behaviour – their clients would get nervous by the loss of the trusted commanders. The arbitrators might make a snap judgement if one side lost enough senior commanders (by capture or, occasionally, death). The result of a Panchnad war was peace.

"A Panchnad war was also the training ground for the guards of a caravan – when raiders attacked a caravan, its guards would create a defensible encampment and ward off challenges and try to wound the attackers until they left. Only rarely would a Panchnad troop chase and destroy raiders. They preferred to wait out the raiders or negotiate safe passage, paying tax if it seemed feasible.

"This has all changed. As a trader, I learned some bardic skills, some warrior skills, some linguistic skills, and some skills in observing cultures. Now the Kauravas are warriors and this war, your war, is like no other war in Panchnad's history. The Kuru family are not traders any more, but warriors and empire builders.

"To repeat, this change has its origins in the exile of Samvarana by the Panchalas, your ally. Hastinapur was a border town that was treated as a glorified caravanserai. The Nagas of Panchala drove out the Kuru leader Samvarana. He returned and re-took Hastinapur with the first Panchnad army that was trained to kill its opponents, not capture them. Samvarana's Guru, Vasishtha, helped create and train this army. The army became a permanent institution to protect Hastinapur from the Panchalas. Hastinapur was no longer a Panchnad town, but a militarised state, perpetually ready for war. Meanwhile, Vasishtha's organisation, the Kavi Sangha, became the foremost advisor of the Kuru family."

"I understand now what my father talked about," Yudhishthira said, "when he denounced the patriarchal city. It came about through war and was sustained by an army. In turn that army presented a fierce face to the world and ensured the continuance of hostility."

"Yes," Devavrat said, "the Kauravas were traders and warriors, but we also created the first patriarchal state in our world. My policies were built on this framework. As you point out, your father disagreed: strongly enough that he exiled himself rather than work in a state that he could not change. He took you away and raised your brothers according to his values. In hindsight, that was a mistake – he should have stayed. You would have been educated, not ignorant of necessary knowledge and skills.

"As it was, when you and your brothers turned up in Hastinapur, we could still train your bodies. Bhima and Arjuna have become formidable warriors. Your mental skills were just what your father taught you. You could not have become traders, even if you wanted to. There is much more to being a warrior than brute strength, and we left you to learn those other skills on your own."

"To the extent I learned anything, I have much to thank Uncle Dharmateja," Yudhishthira said, "I know, though, that you are right – my brothers were enamoured of the warrior's path that you opened for them and did not choose to learn from their wise uncle."

"Yes, Dharmateja tried, but I do not believe he could have succeeded," Devavrat said. "I was surprised when he took such an interest in your education – for most of his life up to that point he had been like a restrained version of Dhritarashtra. I knew that his brother's defiance and self-exile had impressed Dharmateja – he paid many visits to Indraprastha and brought back useful information. He is a wise advisor now, if only Dhritarashtra and Suyodhana would listen to him."

"Yes, his visits were welcome ones," Yudhishthira said. "When I was young I had no idea who he was. He played with us, brought news to my father and my mothers, Kunti and Madri, of events in Hastinapur. He was a kind uncle. He taught me a lot."

"Dharmateja was the child of a servant, not a Kshatriya, so even though he was the son of the King, he was not educated as a warrior," Devavrat said. "He was raised alongside Mahendra and Dhritarashtra, so he learned things he would never have learned otherwise. Even so, he could not have made you a greater warrior than Suyodhana. Do you understand why I think you will lose to Suyodhana? Excuse me for saying that, but I have no use for tact now. Suyodhana received the education you and your brothers did not – as a warrior."

For the first time, Yudhishthira raised his voice and interrupted Devavrat's remarks.

"Grandsire! I do not take offence at your critical statements about my education or that of my brothers. Surely it is irrelevant to the story you were telling? How does this relate to the immigrants? How does it relate to this war?"

"The deficiencies in your education and that of your brothers are relevant," said Devavrat. "Suyodhana is a skilled warrior. He has skilled strategists working for him. His education, just like mine, trained him in war. Unlike me, he has trained to be nothing but a warrior. He is capable of recognising a thousand distinct sounds in their context and reacting accordingly. His hands and fingers were trained to be flexible and strong – sensitive enough that blindfolded they can identify unseen objects by touch, strong enough that his grip is unshakeable – that is the origin of his battle-name *Duryodhana*.[73] I know that the name has been used to mock him and he is easily irritated by the insults. He had the best teachers on strategy we

[73] *Duryodhana*, means "Bad Warrior". However, the connotations of the adjective "Bad" are controversial. It could be interpreted as "difficult" or "malevolent" rather than "unskilled" – the latter being pejorative while the first two imply great skill.

could get from Parsaka, where war is a persistent way of life for the cities. This, too, I don't expect you and your brothers to appreciate. You may have tactical successes like my capture, but you will fail to win the war."

"That may be. If we fail, we fail. Our consolation will be that we will have tried to move the world down the kinder, gentler path that my father wished for."

Devavrat sighed. Had Yudhishthira not understood him? Had his bluntness fogged the message?

"I will return to the story of my father's policies," he said.

***

Kaushambi/Hastinapur
circa 850 B.C.E.

Vaishampaayana stopped – it was later than usual and the sun had just disappeared behind the curve of the horizon and the soft grey of dusk covered them.

"I'll stop here – Devavrat has gone over the aspects that made Panchnad unique, and resulted in a uniquely peaceful society. Tomorrow, he will get to his own life."

An Archive in Crisis

Friends: A Debate in the Marketplace

Kaushambi/Hastinapur
Circa 850 B.C.E.

"How old-fashioned can you be? Stop memorising oral contracts."

Vaishampaayana brooded over these words. These were the first words Bhargava had said to him when they first met fifty years ago. The resulting debate had formed the basis and motif for their friendship. They were both getting old – their words continued to express a vigour that their bodies couldn't sustain. He couldn't sleep. He lay back on the padded cotton mat, his head on a roll of cotton, and mulled over his friendship with Bhargava.

As a trained memoriser, it was very easy to remember superfluous and useless stuff. It took work to forget. Every bard in the Kavi Sangha learned the techniques for forgetting. Every evening, after a small meal and before the faint outlines of dusk yielded to the dark of night, he would sit facing the west and apply those techniques to the detritus of the day's hearings. He had forgotten much but he had never been able to forget these first words. He had forgotten many other words and sentences that meant the same, but these exact words had proved to be unforgettable.

Bhargava had left a few ghatis before sunset. It was hard to discern his mood – he was clearly in some pain from scribing, but he refused to acknowledge it. That was typical of Bhargava – he was incapable of acknowledging defeat. Vaishampaayana smiled as he recalled the day he had met Bhargava, fifty years ago. They were young.

***

HASTINAPUR
CIRCA 900 B.C.E.

"How old-fashioned can you be? Stop memorising oral contracts."

Bhargava would say this to the Archivist on duty whenever he had to come to the market to sign or to release an oral contract. The bard who had just memorised his contract would ignore him. The supervisor, if present, would stare at him and then ignore him – but after that, the guards would watch him until he left. Bhargava enjoyed creating this minor storm of worry for the Kavi Sangha's bards who profited from the system.

Bhargava was a member of a trading family whose range covered all of Bhaaratavarsha– an area that sprawled from the delta of the Ganga in the east to Moolasthan far southeast from Hastinapur and to Takshashila in the north. Kashi was the largest city, and as the Emperor's home, claimed to be the capital of Bhaaratavarsha, but it was more the idea of an empire than one in reality. The Emperor ruled by persuasion and consensus rather than force. Bhargava's family, the Kambojas, ran one of the largest trading networks and had representatives in all the major janapadas – traditionally sixteen – and the larger chiefdoms and kingdoms. Moolasthan, in its turn, was the eastern hub of the great trade route that unified the known world towards the west. Takshashila was the gateway to the vast grasslands of the Shakas. Bhargava's family, the Kambojas, even conducted trade missions across the Eastern Sea.

Bhargava had come to the market to register a contract. Vaishampaayana was on duty in the bard's tent. The rain started as a drizzle while they were memorising the contract and by the time they were done, it was a downpour. Bhargava sat down – he would have to wait out the rain. No other trader came by.

Traditionally, members of the Kavi Sangha provided the memorising service for the marketplaces in Bhaaratavarsha. With their skills at memorising and retrieving old memories, one or more bards would memorise contracts and, when required, would retrieve the contract from memory and recite it. In ancient days, this function had been provided by the guild of bards, but when the Kavi Sangha (the organisation that Vaishampaayana now headed as the Vyaasa) absorbed the guild, it took over the responsibility of archiving contracts.

The Kavi Sangha had begun as a small group, consisting mostly of bard guild-members, but also included some traders and some leaders of mercenaries – the leaders of the Kavi Sangha tried to generalise from cultural experience to rules that addressed strategic issues and arbitrated between cities. Under Guru Vasishtha, it aided Samvarana and became an organisation with a lot of power. People did not know the full extent of the Kavi Sangha's power – it seemed to be merely another service guild, the guild of bards and memorisers, necessary to perform at festivals, register contracts, and archive family histories. As the guild of bards, the Kavi Sangha had access to the history of the city; being spread all across Panchnad, it had access to a repository of experience that far exceeded anything that any other groups could bring to bear. As a multi-city network of advisors, it had far greater influence than any other institution from Panchnad. One of its greatest accomplishments was to sustain a unified culture over the extent of Bhaaratavarsha.

900 B.C.E

Archiving contracts was tedious. Fresh, newly qualified bards were assigned to the job. After a few years at the job, tedium would set in and errors of omission and commission would increase to an unacceptable level, and the bard would be relieved of duty. Other tasks, more popular, included reciting mythological stories at festivals (perhaps the most fulfilling but also the most exhausting task); performing an inventory of a caravan's manifest for traders (tedious but routine beyond boredom); and, registering the taxes paid to the market managers and memorising the tariffs charged by the market administrator.

In principle, archiving an oral contract was simple. Two traders would agree to barter say, fifty ceramic bowls decorated to order, for five bronze arrowheads and a bronze chest plate. Since this was to be consummated in the future, perhaps in the following year, it had to be registered. They would approach the memoriser provided by the Kavi Sangha in each marketplace to witness the agreement. The memoriser would meditate briefly on the Goddess in her form as Sarasvati to achieve a neutral frame of mind. When ready, the terms of the contract – what was being exchanged and when this was to be accomplished – would be described by one of the traders while the other assented. Then both traders would recite their full names, a set of about ten to fifteen phrases that named the trader's key ancestors, the place and time of birth, the names of the trader's father and mother, and their clans, and lastly the trader's own given name. The memoriser would rehearse to create a permanent long-term memory – it would take a few vighatis. When the memoriser was done, the trader would receive a token that could be used to identify the memoriser and the contract. Later, disagreements over the terms of the contract were resolved by asking the memoriser to recall the oral agreement – the token would allow the master of the market to determine the memoriser who had acted as the proof of the contract. Usually a backup memoriser would also be present.

900 B.C.E

Things got interesting when one of the traders was from Sumer or from Parsaka – they would go through the oral memorisation routine, but would also insist on a written version of the contract as per their practice. Two tablets of clay would be prepared. Each would specify the objects to be bartered, using a mutually understood pictorial code that was impressed on the wet tablet. Then the seal of each trader would be impressed on both tablets. In Bhaaratavarsha, the seal of the memoriser was also impressed, as well as a pattern that specified the date. The two clay tablets were placed side-by-side in an open kiln and fired until dry. This written contract could not be enforced in Bhaaratavarsha; the oral contract was not recognised outside Bhaaratavarsha.

Bhargava sat in the Kavi Sangha tent waiting for the rain to stop. It was tiresome. He felt impelled to make observations. He said, addressing Vaishampaayana, "Why do you follow this archaic custom? A bard must remember each oral contract! Only oral contracts are firm contracts? Is the rest of the world crazy? Your 'True Witnesses' are so… so… unnecessary. In the West, contracts are written! A trader does not need to go to someone to archive a contract. Traders exchange *written* contracts. On fired tablets, in duplicate, hardened mud. Once fired, the tablets are immutable, readable by anybody. Each tablet would specify the terms of the barter. Conflicts can be settled by openly confirming that the two copies are identical and then *read* to establish the terms of the original contract.

"This system of written tablet agreements had been invented in Sumer and was in common use all over the West. Even Bahlika now uses written tablet agreements," Bhargava was emphatic. "Only the people of Jambudvipa, in the lands that make up Bhaaratavarsha, refuse to write – they live an oral life. They prefer to waste brainpower and time. What is the point of wasting all this time?"

Vaishampaayana glanced at this young stranger. He had just completed his training and had been assigned to the market.

How can this man make such claims, he thought. The rain had made it a slow day and this man had been one of the few who had come to do business. He faced him and said, "You can't change your written contract, modify it, or extend it. Yes, yes, I know that you can always bake a new one. Consume more wood. A memoriser is a living person of unimpeachable integrity, one who cannot be bought. In addition, you have to teach somebody how to write contracts. Memorising contracts is the least of what a bard does."

"Scribes do more than scratch contracts," Bhargava said. "In Pitr-vihara-naad,[74] the history of a king's rule is written on the walls of his tomb."

"Yes, yes, I am sure they do. Then they shut up the tomb and nobody can go in. What use is such a written history? Can they sing what is written? Does it make a good story? A poem? Something else? Does everybody understand what is written? Does anybody read it? How does a reader compare to a bard in terms of telling a story? Ask anyone, 'What makes a story-teller interesting?' It is the creative use of intonation and stress, and spontaneous annotation that a skilled bard brings to story-telling."

"Bard, you are expecting too much from a single reader. The potential of writing is not *just* to replace story-telling."

Vaishampaayana glowered at Bhargava. Bhargava glared back. A vendor of mead[75] had just pulled his cart to the edge of the entrance of the tent. It was filled with jars smelling of the

---

[74] *Pitr-vihara-naad* is the translated version of the name of Egypt. It means *The Land of the Temple of Ancestral Spirits,* one of the ancient names of Egypt. See Endnotes.

[75] The drink which I have called "mead" was most likely a mildly alcoholic drink made from a solution of water and honey heated with spices (ginger, lemon and lime, cinnamon, lime flower-buds, and wild berries, such as cherries, strawberries, blackberries, and juniper berries) and fermented with a locally available yeast. It is one of the oldest alcoholic drinks known, believed to be tens of thousands of years old.

sweet-and-sour mead. He watched the excitement grow and while they talked at each other, he came over with a cup of mead for each of them.

"How much?" Bhargava asked as he took the warm cup in his hand.

"Whatever you can afford, sir," the vendor said.

"Two shells per cup?"

"Yes."

"Good."

The mead-vendor handed a cup to Vaishampaayana who shook his head. As the mead-vendor turned away, Bhargava said, "No, no! Don't go away." Then turning to Vaishampaayana, he said, "Please, oh bard! Be my guest and accept this cup."

Vaishampaayana took the cup. It was warm in his hand and was a relief from the chill of the rain. Bhargava took a drink. After a brief pause, Vaishampaayana followed suit. The mead warmed the throat as it flowed down, leaving a strong flavour of the jasmine honey common around Hastinapur.

"Keep it coming," Bhargava said to the mead-vendor. He turned back to Vaishampaayana. The intensity of their mutual glares had dissipated in the glow engendered by the mead. He smiled at Vaishampaayana and said, "You may know that I am Bhargava, of the Mūlamāhuri family." He pronounced it *Bāgoā*.[76] "Who may you be, bard?"

Vaishampaayana gestured at the mead-vendor. "You see how simple it is to make an oral agreement. Thank you for the mead. My tongue gets dry when I work in the market. I am Vaishampaayana of the Vasishtha-gotra."

Bhargava's eyes brightened.

---

76 *Bagoa* is pronounced "Baa-go-a(h)". *Bhargava* would be pronounced "B^{h}ar-gov-aah", with an aspirated 'B'.

"Famous family. Our families originate in the same land, on the Sindhu south of Suvastu."

"That's interesting. That was a long time ago, for my ancestors have lived in Hastinapur from ancient times – we believe we were present at Janamejaya's Nagamedha campaign. If I ever go to Takshashila, I will pay a visit to the area we originated. I gather you don't like the simplicity of the oral agreement."

"Takshashila is the most beautiful city in the world. You'll see when you go there. Come sit with me. I'll show you why you are absolutely wrong." They drained their cups. The vendor had two more cups ready and at Bhargava's gesture handed them each a cup.

"Listen," said Bhargava. "What I just did with this vendor was a market transaction – the barter is finished, here and now. I will give him eight shells before I leave. There are no questions about promises. No questions about contracts. We only discuss the bartered items. A contract is what makes a trade happen – a registry is bureaucracy. You need a contract for trade, not a registry; you only need a registry to control the marketplace."

Vaishampaayana said, "Hun-hun…it's merely a matter of degree. The trade has to be registered and remembered. If it is on a clay tablet, an accidental drop could shatter the tablet. Then, where's your contract?"

"A bard can die. A trader will take good care of any tablet that describes a contract."

"Ah-ha! So, it can happen. It isn't that easy to kill a bard. On the other hand, a clay tablet? You know how easy it is." Vaishampaayana tossed the mead cups towards one of the many holes that had been dug out for trash. It broke into pieces. He walked up to it and picked up some shards. "See. You can't even put a clay cup back together."

"A trader takes care of what is owed to him!" More mead came and they took it.

"So you say. There is an even bigger problem," Vaishampaayana said. "These written contracts breed dishonesty."

"What? You are joking. How?"

"Not at all. Here in Hastinapur, you can come to an agreement with anybody. People here are so used to how contracts work that nobody would even contemplate cheating the other. After all, there is a true version memorised by a sworn-to-tell-the-truth bard. What would I do if I knew that your copy of a tablet is lost or broken, or that an item was described incorrectly? I might be tempted to cheat you. Even if I would not cheat you, what if we both die and our heirs, who inherit these muddy agreements, may not be so inclined?"

"You are just making unwarranted assumptions."

"Not so," Vaishampaayana insisted. "The Kavi Sangha occasionally gets asked to adjudicate contracts that only existed as tablets. Invariably, one or the other party is taking advantage of the 'lost' contract."

"What can you do? There are cheats everywhere."

Vaishampaayana laughed. "You know that traders from Bhaaratavarsha are considered extremely honest. Your family benefits from the reputation that Bhaaratavarsha has."

Bhargava smiled at that. "That we do. That's a small victory for you."

Vaishampaayana pushed his advantage.

"There's more. Writing will create people who cannot think for themselves. They will no longer memorise and internalise a dialogue, a chain of argument. It will impoverish their minds for they will no longer need to know anything. Wisdom will be lost, for we will no longer value the wisdom of the older man that he can express whenever desired – instead, the readers, and perhaps even the listeners will say, 'What is written on the tablets? Let us consult the tablet storage,' and they will be as children, knowing little but certain of a lot. Their opinion will change with every new tablet they read, for they will only have a vague memory of the previous ones they read."

"Whoa! Hold it. Now you are exaggerating. That has not happened in the West."

"How can you judge that? Don't they call Bhaaratavarsha the land of peace? Maybe we are wiser. You know what? That isn't all – we have more fun."

Bhargava laughed. "You should not drink so much mead, my friend. It's talking through you! *More fun?* That is preposterous, a completely unbelievable claim. What does that have to do with contracts, oral or written?"

"It is not entertaining to be part of an audience at a *reading*. That is what the West has. *Readings*. We have *tellings, story-tellings*. The bard knows well what he recites and is sensitive to the audience. To the reader, every word in the text is novel, needs to be assimilated. A reader, who barely understands the text seen for the first time, is supposed to express its truth to the listeners? I recall the time I was at a reading by a trader from Hava-satya.[77] He had come by sea to the port of Dwaraka and from there had come through the region of Malwa to Mathura. It was the eighth day of the month, devoted to the Krishnaavatara, celebrating the god Krishna, the Dark Lord, who founded the city. I was visiting along with other Kavi Sangha apprentices. The trader sat next to us at a story-telling event. He became increasingly excited and finally he dashed to the podium. He said that he was considered the best reader of stories in his city and he would be delighted to share

---

[77] The name "Ethiopia" would be spelled H-B-Sh-T, in the Egyptian/Semitic form without vowels, and pronounced "*Hava-satya*" by inserting preferred vowels.

some of these stories. With much hesitation, it was approved. It was certainly an unorthodox act, allowing a Mleccha – a *Mleccha*! – join the community in praising the Lord Krishna.

"The trader went up on stage with a heavy basket. We watched as he took out a clay tablet and began declaiming rhymes in the language of the Kaamatis.[78] His eyes were fixed on the tablet and he did not look up or around. His body did not move. His voice was dramatic for it ranged over three octaves. He was certainly a talented vocalist, with a pleasant singing voice, but the words were in an unfamiliar language and he did not stop to explain. Then he was done with that tablet and he put it back in the basket and took out another one and continued. The audience was polite and so were the organisers of the story-telling event. I think they were in shock, at least for a brief period. They allowed him to go through five tablets, for more than a ghati. The audience was restive. Were these strange songs in honour of the Lord Krishna? If he had been an inexperienced local bard, perhaps an apprentice, his guru who would be constantly apologising the rest of the day, would have quickly escorted him off the stage.

"You see the problems – the audience could not ask for clarification; the reader could not digress to another story that might engage the audience; the reader could not relate to the audience in the same way that any bard would. The listener is not permitted to *listen* – they hear, disengaged, for they quickly learn that they cannot change the course of the reading. They sit passively, waiting for the reading to end."

Vaishampaayana sipped of the mead, and continued, "The trader was upset when he was asked to stop and leave. It was pointed out that nobody understood the language of his declamation. He protested that he had intended to translate after he was done with one story, but he had not been given enough

[78] *Kaamati* is one of the many ways they would have pronounced the Egyptian word k-m-t, meaning either "The People of the Black Land", or "The Black People", another ancient Egyptian name for themselves.

time. After that farce was over, the trader had the gall to ask if he could *write* down the stories of the other bards in that festival. No bard would ever ask that – it is considered rude to memorise a story as it is being told to the public, except with the explicit permission of the bard. A guru might give such permission to his student who was being trained by him to perform it. The gall of it... memorise, by writing, another bard's performance? Especially after such a travesty of a performance. The trader did not live it down; his business suffered and he left rather suddenly."

"Is that why all traders must enter a story-telling venue through a separate entrance?" said Bhargava.

"Yes. Traders from the West are the only people who try to cheat and steal a story told by a bard. The guards ensure that they are not carrying any tablets."

Bhargava laughed. "That is the most ridiculous thing I have heard in a long time! Do you really have guards checking if Western traders are carrying tablets?"

"What's so funny? It's been done, though I do not know of any trader objecting."

"I certainly hope so. Did any of them know what they were being checked for? Have you had reports of anybody dying of laughter?"

"I get the point."

Vaishampaayana reached for his clay cup but it was empty. The mead vendor handed him another cup. Bhargava, who had been drinking all through Vaishampaayana's tirade, said, "My turn now. You drink."

Vaishampaayana took a long drink of the fresh cup of mead. The mead was sweet to the tongue and flamed as it went down the throat. It warmed him inside and the two of them continued talking and drinking while the mead vendor willingly continued to supply them.

900 B.C.E

Bhargava continued, "None of these things you describe have happened in the West. Your Kavi Sangha here knows that it will lose power in the cities if bards are ever replaced. Do you think that the common city-dweller cares whether you are telling a story from memory or because a god is whispering it into your ear or because you see it written in the air in front of your eyes? They have come for the show, to be entertained. I understand that one trader did not know how to perform. Maybe he did not know how to translate either. That must have been an awful experience. In Moolasthan, we are proud of our readers who keep audiences engrossed. Your bards are an expensive luxury."

"Bhargava, the bard who has lived with the memorised story does more than recite – living with it will inform the bard's every action during the recital. An expensive luxury, you said? That simply is not true..."

Bhargava wouldn't let him finish.

"Do you know why only three guilds are left, of all the guilds that used to exist? The traders' guild could not be broken up because we are spread all over the world. We only trust those with whom we have had mutually profitable dealings. Even within a family we are cautious. Maybe here in Kashi, the centre of this empire, we can let down our guard and trust your memorisers and archivists. It is *our* guild. Only the guild keeps us honest year after year, decade after decade, and in some families, over centuries. That is why the guild of traders will never vanish.

"The warriors' guild did not break up. Even in lands where they tell you that there is no warriors' guild, there is one. Warriors do not need an organised guild. All over the world, warriors become rulers. Even here, in Bhaaratavarsha, your land of eternal peace. The warriors in the guild make sure that their own children are trained first and best – call it their apprenticeship from birth. When times are good, there is no need to induct new families of mercenaries. When times are bad, even non-warrior survivors will have military skills and so recreate the guild with new members.

"Lastly, there is the Kavi Sangha. It contains and controls the ancient guild of bards so that only people it approves of, like you, can join..." He stopped and looked askance at Vaishampaayana.

"You stopped drinking. Are you done? You barely drank anything."

"Yes, yes. I did. Quite a lot. Truthfully... I must stop now."

Vaishampaayana had drunk more than he was used to. Bhargava gestured to the mead vendor and said, "More." The mead-vendor hesitated – Vaishampaayana was going to say something when Bhargava laughed and clapped the mead-vendor's shoulder.

"Don't worry, my man. You'll get paid."

"Sir, the two of you have drunk almost a rice-barrel-worth of mead. How will you pay? I don't see a rice-barrel."

"I'll pay tomorrow."

"Sir, excuse my lack of trust. How can I trust you? You are not from Hastinapur."

"You don't trust me? Then come with me to my home and I will pay you there."

"Sir, I cannot leave my cart and bull here – the market police will charge me with abandoning my goods. I must be paid now or I will notify the guards."

Bhargava looked at Vaishampaayana.

"You don't have a barrel of rice, do you?"

Vaishampaayana shook his head and did not say anything. It was his first day on the job, and already... he would be imprisoned for cheating and that would end any hope of advancement in the guild.

Bhargava said, "I have an idea!" He looked at the vendor and continued, "You see my friend here – he is a bard and a True Witness. I'll acknowledge my debt to you of a rice barrel and promise to pay it by tomorrow, and he will register it. If I don't pay you tomorrow, you have a basis for complaining to a judge."

The mead vendor looked at Vaishampaayana – he had seen the young man working as a memoriser, but the sober young man of the morning was a good bit less sober now, if not as intoxicated as the trader. Vaishampaayana stood up, squared his shoulders, and said, "There is no difficulty. I can register the agreement."

The tone of assurance in his voice convinced the vendor. Bhargava acknowledged the debt, and promised to deliver the rice-barrel the next day. Vaishampaayana registered both contracts. The proposed price – a rice-barrel – was highway robbery, but as Bhargava said, *I am a caravan trader, I am used to that*. Neither Vaishampaayana nor Bhargava convinced the other, but they ended the debate as friends. The only drawback arose when Bhargava said, "I am a Vaishya, a member of the guild of traders. I'll consider you almost as good as one, because you are a Vais." It was silly, and Bhargava was drunk; Vaishampaayana could not see a joke in it, but Bhargava thought this insight a work of genius. Over the years, Vaishampaayana found that being called Vais reminded him of their first meeting, which made him smile and relax. After all, he had won that argument and saved Bhargava from being detained by the market guards and bringing shame on his family. But…

***

Kaushambi/Hastinapur
circa 850 B.C.E.

The silliness was pleasant and Vaishampaayana's slow smile gave way to the steady breathing of a relaxed sleeper.

900 B.C.E

Vaishampaayana's Morning

Kaushambi/Hastinapur
circa 850 B.C.E.

Vaishampaayana woke up feeling refreshed – that was a relief. He had escaped the flood, but every night his dreams had been of his lost friends and other kavis. *I must let them go, so that they get relief. So that I get relief!* Ghosts followed him everywhere and that was how a doctor would diagnose his melancholy – by not releasing their memories and allowing them to detach from his emotions, he was reflecting the melancholy felt by these ghosts on leaving the world with all its variety, all its joys and sorrows. That night a different sort of ghost had helped him – the living ghost of his old friend had yoked sleep and allowed him some rest.

It was just before dawn. Vaishampaayana stepped out of his house. There was still a light fog over the water, but higher up the mist had cleared. The eastern sky was tinged a very faint orange and from that colour, the sky transitioned to a greyish blue overhead to deep dark black to the west. He finished his ablutions just in time to see the thinnest edge of the sun become visible. Vaishampaayana bowed to the eastern sun, and thanked the twelve Adityas for the coming day and invoked the blessing of the goddess Sarasvati for the day's task. By the time he finished, in about twenty vighatis, the complete disk of the sun was visible.

His two apprentices, Surya and Savitr,[79] were just returning from a walk. Their names brought a smile to his face. *I've just finished invoking their namesake, and here they are!* They had come with his morning tea, ginger root ground with the juice of lemons in warm water, flavoured with honey. He warmed his hands with the cup. For the next six ghatis, he went through the daily memory exercises that the Kavi Sangha taught all its members – he would announce the name of the exercise and if his apprentices knew the exercise, they would follow. The initial

---

79 *Surya* and *Savitr* are both names of the Sun, one of the Adityas.

exercises were *shlokas* recited in a variety of meters and they fell in with his rhythm and copied him. The later exercises focused on the activities of the previous day, enhancing the memories for some and helping others fade away and be forgotten – they had their experiences and he had his. The apprentices finished sooner than he did and kept visitors away.

Visitors were ubiquitous – if he allowed them, they would come before sunrise and not leave even after sunset. The press of visitors had declined since the flood showed that he was not superhuman, but there were still visitors looking for wisdom rather than influence with the city council or with other eminent persons. He would have preferred to focus on the writing project, but without a scribe, it would go nowhere, and he did not expect Bhargava to come at daybreak.

One of Bhargava's apprentices came by about five ghatis after sunrise.

"Sir, the Master is delayed. He does not know how long it will be. He is profoundly sorry. He assures you that he will come as soon as the unexpected task is done."

Vaishampaayana said, "What happened?"

"I do not know, sir."

The boy looked left and then right and lowered his voice. "He went to the marketplace early in the morning and has been preparing to welcome a caravan. He is worried because the advance messenger has not come."

"Isn't it a bit late for caravans?"

"Yes, sir. The Mistress received a messenger yesterday while the Master was with you. She has also been very busy."

There was nothing to be done. Vaishampaayana sighed. The grace of the Goddess was not his that day. There were other tasks to be completed – he could visit the temporary school that had been established for the children who did not have tutors hired by their parents and see if any were suitable as apprentices. It would be something to occupy his mind.

He was back in about eight ghatis. It was not yet noon. The sun was high and bright, and every mundane thing was sharply outlined, from the green trees to the white jasmine and yellow marigolds that grew everywhere. His apprentices had picked a bunch and placed them in a mound by the side of Pashupati's niche. In Hastinapur the Goddess received flowers as her daily offering, but here in Kashi the gods were very different. In Hastinapur, he was used to the quirky Ganesha, known for his pranks, and the benign Sarasvati, the goddess of learning, who had migrated from the west and settled in Hastinapur a thousand years ago. It was easy for a kavi to bring them to life during a recitation. Here, the people of Kashi worshipped Pashupati who wandered as he pleased and only came to the city on the days that his spouse Parvati would escape from her father's home to meet him in his most favoured city. Ganesha was a bit strange, but Pashupati could be wild. Even the best kavis found it difficult to recreate a god who matched the energy of the audience. The winter solstice celebrations invariably got out of hand – it would be wise if they could return to Hastinapur by then.

Bhargava was waiting for him. He was wearing a brilliantly coloured *angavastram*[80] and *panchagam*,[81] very obviously new, and the scent of fresh marigolds came in with him. He was seated, but when he saw Vaishampaayana, he stood up. He moved his mat to be alongside Vaishampaayana's mat, facing the river. It had been a long time since Vaishampaayana had seen his friend so nervous.

Vaishampaayana said, "What's this special day about? Why, you look prepared to welcome the New Year – you know it is not coming again for another six months."

---

80 The *Angavastram* is the upper robe used to cover the torso and shoulders.

81 The *Panchagam* is the lower robe used to cover the body below the waist.

"It is a special day for me, not necessarily so for others."

"Why?"

"My son finished his apprenticeship with my first cousin Vijaykartha in Takshashila. My wife got a message that his caravan would arrive today. She would not let me do anything else – I had to be at the city gates to welcome him. He wanted to surprise me and my wife tells me that I must be surprised when he turns up. He has graduated as an accomplished Master Trader; he is qualified to manage a caravan. Not only that, he is a Scribe. He never told me that he had signed on with the Guild of Scribes in Sumer when he was stranded there for a whole year by the war with Haltamti.[82] He is not just a Journeyman Scribe, he attained Master Scribe as well."

"Congratulations. That's interesting. He'll see your nice new robes and know that you were not surprised at all."

"Darn, you're right. His mother insisted that I wear this – she does not want him to be welcomed by a father who looks like he needs new clothes. 'It is a bad omen,' she says. Now, don't act disinterested – you should be more than interested, my friend. He is a far better scribe than I will ever be – he can take over from me."

"We'll see about that. So what are you doing here? Go meet your son."

"He's not coming today."

"What happened?"

Bhargava pursed his lips and shrugged. "I don't know what to make of it. The Master of the caravan, my cousin, sent me a confused message. Apparently they had not received word of the flood and they had gone to Hastinapur – they lost a day. He blames me for it!"

---

[82] *Haltamti* is the Sumerian name for Elam, which lay between Sumer and Panchnad.

"Why?"

"In his message, he says that I should have sent him a message! Ha! A thousand travellers would have told him of the Hastinapur floods. Even if he did not get the information directly from a traveller, he should have suspected something when many of his correspondents in Hastinapur did not reply! What kind of Master Trader is he, if he does not keep one ear to the ground? What is he teaching my son?

"Then, he sends another message: *I will come to your home, on such and such a day* – that was last week. He follows up with: *Disregard all previous messages – I am going to Mathura first and then I shall come to Kashi.* So now it will take even more time."

Vaishampaayana said, "That is good, isn't it. It gives you time to get ready for him. Do you want to rest a bit from my work?"

"No… My house is getting very tense. Yesterday, my wife got a message from my son – it must have been a delayed letter, as he did not know about the floods. He said he would be here today. That's why I was waiting by the gates. Everybody is on tenterhooks; my wife is unhappy. There is nothing for me to do there when I am not actually preparing for or sending off a caravan."

"You've had no rest."

"Not at home. What we are doing – it takes my mind off these things. This is most restful."

"So, we can work today."

"Yes."

"Excellent."

"I have a few questions about what we did yesterday."

"Please ask."

"Vais, it may not seem so to you now, but I am overwhelmed with the importance of what we are doing now. Writing down the oral history of the greatest empire of the last thousand years – can't you feel it? We are surely making history even as we are writing it down."

Vaishampaayana did not know how to respond. He knew that Bhargava had been coerced into doing this project. Now he was calling it the most important project. What Bhargava did not understand was that he, Vaishampaayana, had to be coerced into it too.

It all began when the Vyaasa had asked the city for ten apprentices to be assigned to the Kavi Sangha to replace the members who had died in the flood. The ten apprentices would be between eight and fifteen years old. It would take between three and ten years to train them as bards – to memorise and to recite to order. During that period, they had to be fed and supported. Without them there was no hope of maintaining the city's historical archives, which were already at risk.

The council was shocked. What had happened to the Kavi Sangha, one of the most powerful guilds in the city? The city council had not realised the true state of affairs.

The Kavi Sangha was not wealthy, in Hastinapur or elsewhere, even if it was prestigious and powerful. Apprentices used to be supported by their master, but many of the masters were gone. The contract registries and other tasks requiring memorisation supported the masters; readings at festivals provided public support. The area of the city occupied by bards had been one of the worst hit by the flood and the bard's guild had suffered the greatest loss in both people and their wealth. The flood, moreover, had dislocated Hastinapur and long-distance trade had come to a halt. The most profitable of the Kavi Sangha's sources of income, the registering of oral contracts, was all but dead. The Kavi Sangha in Hastinapur was bankrupt – its savings gone and no surplus income to support apprentices even if they could get them. It would soon collapse and disappear unless something was done. In addition to the allocation of supported apprentices, the Kavi Sangha needed that many years of support for these apprentices.

The Kavi Sangha was popular, because of the entertainment the bards provided, but it had enemies in the council who opposed any support. *The losses caused by the flood were an omen,* they said. The bards' quarter had been closest to the river and those houses had been the first ones to be destroyed by the wave of water that had come down from the hills. *The flood was a signal from the gods. This indicated that the bards should not play any role in a future Hastinapur. It was a sign that the Kavi Sangha must dissolve itself.* The Vyaasa had been barely able to contain his anger, but the council room had resembled a war zone as his allies and his enemies quarrelled, with many curses and threats. Ultimately, cooler heads prevailed.

The council reconciled all these concerns and offered to help him with the most important task – to save the archives. They could not support any more apprentices, especially since trade was dead, and all their resources were devoted to rebuilding Hastinapur. The Vyaasa had protested –how could he save archives that were normally maintained by almost fifty of the most skilled memorisers? There was an answer from the council – for many years, traders from the farthest lands had offered documents *written* on clay tablets from their sponsors in Sumer and Elam and asked for similar tablets to take back with them. The tablets were like the accounting tablets that caravan traders used for tracking inventory – they consisted of a *written* body whose authenticity was validated by the marks left by a seal pressed into the clay before firing. The seals were small but highly detailed and difficult to copy – they could be verified by comparing against previously received versions. Once fired, the tablet could not be changed.

"Write it down, then you won't need more people," they said. The proposal was a surprise. The Kavi Sangha had no writers. Nor did any other citywide organisation. The only people who wrote were the foreign traders who used clay tablets as an immutable permanent token of an agreement, and palm-leaf for the temporary ones. Like Bhargava many years ago, the traders acquiesced with reluctance in the memorisation procedure that Bhaaratavarsha required them to use for registration. They still used their own clay registers with writing as well. *How am I to use a means for tracking trading accounts to archive a peoples' history? They are not being reasonable.*

Vaishampaayana had argued against the use of writing. He claimed that writing was a poor and miserly substitute for memory. Writing worked for traders maintaining their inventory, but did it have the complexity to direct a recital? An accounting tablet did not have to evoke complex emotions in its readers or listeners. A bard's recitation ignited the nine *rasas*[83] in an audience that required the bard's manipulation of intonation and emphasis. The unfeeling reading of a written document could not do that. He repeated ad nauseam, *the Kavi Sangha has no writers or readers and it will take time to create them.* He did not claim that memorising was traditional and writing wasn't, nor did he say that writing was a risk and memorisation was not.

The city councillors cited the cost of memorising – many, highly skilled bards were needed. Hastinapur owed a huge debt to the people of Kashi who had organised the rescue and resettlement of the homeless. The more they debated, the more Vaishampaayana withdrew into a shell in which he thought of his dead colleagues – Jayakumar as always, but also of Padmanaabha who had suffocated in a water-sealed alcove with a roomful of apprentices because they could not swim. Vaishampaayana found himself replaying these thoughts obsessively and barely listened to the council. He had finally accepted the city's meagre

[83] Ancient South Asians identified nine basic, "atomic" emotions, that were the foundation of all emotional expression, in real-life as well as in drama and other fine arts.

offer when the city persuaded the trader Bhargava of Kamboja, known to be his old friend, to be the scribe. *He will bear witness to the sincerity with which I address the problems. He will bear witness to the inadequacy of writing to bear the burden of an oral archive. He will bear witness to the failure of this project.*

When Bhargava and Vaishampaayana had first met to determine how to proceed, they had both assumed that the other supported the idea of the project. To a certain extent – Bhargava viewed the issue as a trader – he had always sponsored a shift from oral registration of contracts to written registration. Being pragmatic, he was wary of assuming that writing would therefore be good for archiving history. If his old friend Vaishampaayana was willing to do it, he, Bhargava, was willing to help. Meanwhile Vaishampaayana was slightly relieved, thinking, *At least he is my friend and he will listen to me even if he is limited by his own biases.*

Now Bhargava seemed to have changed overnight to a person overwhelmed with the significance of what they were attempting. Why did it matter?

"Bhargava, my friend, perhaps this is as significant as you think it is. Maybe it isn't. What difference can that possibly make to our work? Is this about the benediction – do you want the benediction to refer to this earth-shattering event?"

"Vaishampaayana, my brother! The dedication is a trivial matter. I am overwhelmed by the historical significance of putting into this form a work that has only been transmitted by recitation for a thousand years. I may be a Master Trader, but as a scribe, I am an amateur show-off. Somebody far abler than me should do this job. That is why I brought up the question of my son – if he is available and if he agrees, you should work with him. This occasion is too important to be left to an ignoramus like me."

The occasion is the destruction of my city. Vaishampaayana had not conceived of an occasion at which the *Itihaasa Purana* of

Hastinapur would be read in its entirety. He had not thought about providing an all-purpose benediction. He did not want to celebrate the destruction of Hastinapur. Bhargava seemed to demand an immediate answer to his proposal. His brain moved like molasses in response to Bhargava's question. He delayed answering.

"The occasion for the benediction?"

"Not the benediction. This, what we are doing, is far more important. Commemorate the writing down of the history of the city. Surely this is a landmark event that will never be forgotten."

No, that was fantasy. Bhargava was being carried away. "No. Writing is a defeat, not a victory to be commemorated."

"Find a victory here that you can celebrate. If writing is not that victory, maybe the act of reading the written text is one. When do you think this written history will be read?"

How was that any different? Could Bhargava not see the obvious? He was just taken up with the idea of writing. Vaishampaayana said, "The true answer? When they can no longer find a bard to recite from memory. That will be the end of the Kavi Sangha. When that will be, I do not know. It could be very soon."

Bhargava was sorting through the pile of palm leaves near him. His head jerked up at that sentence. *I've been oblivious,* he thought.

"Vais – don't revisit the decision. It has been decided. If you consider it calmly, you know they had no choice. I know that you know it, for you gave in easily. My proposal is simple – you can keep the recitation of the *Jaya Itihaasa* a sacred event by limiting how a reading happens. That can be under your control."

Details like these were still being debated between the Vyaasa and the city council. If it were left to the city, the council would replace the bards at all the recitations during all the annual festivals throughout the year with readers. *Bhargava was right, though,* Vaishampaayana thought. *He had to put up a better fight even if he did not believe that he would or could win.* This development struck at the very foundation of the Kavi Sangha and its popularity – the entertainment provided by the bards. It would be a revolution. *Where would it end?* Vaishampaayana did not wish to contemplate it. *How to maintain control over a concept that has become an object?*

"Bhargava, the only way I can control when a reading happens is if I have the document and control it physically. You realise that every time it is read, it comes into the public, and there is a risk of losing control."

"Then limit the number of days it is read."

"Many people will be unhappy."

"On the contrary. By making it a rare event, you will make it more precious and the occasional reading will draw the audience like a flame draws the moth."

"Hmmm…" Vaishampaayana said. There was the germ of an idea – he would have to think about it.

"Let go of your doubts. What do the other cities do?"

"Every city that was part of the ancient empire of Bhaaratavarsha with its capital in Hastinapur arranged to tell its own founding story during the spring festival. In Hastinapur itself, the *Jaya*, the story of the Great War, was the prologue to the story of the city. The stories are told on the nine evenings before the full moon day after the equinox, and on the nine evenings that follow. Our *Jaya* is too long to be recited and recounted to an audience in a mere eighteen days, so we only recite selected parts. This suffices for most cities, except Mathura, Kashi, and Hastinapur.

"In Mathura, they tell the story of Krishna the Yadava who established the city at its permanent site. They say that this is the same Krishna who, as Arjuna's friend, helped to capture Devavrat the Terrible. Mathura celebrates Krishna the Yadava as a young man bewitching the sixteen thousand stars of the Ocean of Milk who come to him as milkmaids – in exchange for one day of fulfilment these milkmaids deliver a year of divine grace. Neither fulfilment through the god Krishna nor the god's divine grace made Mathura the great city it became later – rather, the protection provided by an empire conceived of by Devavrat, constructed by Devavrat, and through Krishna's efforts ruled by the descendants of his sister Subhadra and the Pandava Arjuna.

"In Kashi, they tell the story of the birth of Kartikeya, the general who made Kashi the imperial capital it is now. He is proclaimed the son of the great god Shiva, born of all six Krittikas, the six mothers of creation. The story of Hastinapur is irrelevant to them, even as Kashi seems irrelevant to the *Jaya*, for there is no mention of Kashi. Instead, in the Kashi cosmos, Shiva's dance destroys the previous age in a great war of a scale never to be seen again. After centuries of chaos, Kartikeya knits together the fabric of an urban society centred on Kashi, the holiest city in the world, which sits on the tip of Shiva's trident as the world trembles on the edge of an abyss, the abyss of universal Chaos.

"I have been told that neither Kashi nor Mathura accept wholly the story told by us in Hastinapur – for in our telling, the empire that we live in, ruled by Mathura once and by Kashi now, was not made by Krishna, the Supreme god of Mathura, nor was it the aftermath of Shiva's dance of destruction that destroyed the previous age, but the result of an earthquake that re-routed a river."

"This characteristic is common – these three cities, and a thousand others besides, use the eighteen days to tell their stories. All the attendees are happy and waiting to be awed and entertained."

"We must make the Hastinapur *Itihaasa* the most precious of these. Mathura and Kashi recite their *Puranas* four times a year – you should read it once in four years!" said Bhargava.

850 B.C.E

"Bhargava, that might make it precious, but it will also ensure that it is forgotten. If the written version is the only memory, it can be lost or stolen. It can be appropriated by a king or stolen by an emperor. Whoever gets a copy will lose respect for it for they will be able to read it when and where they please."

"Vais, that is completely under your control – you must not permit anyone to make another copy. Make sure that your one copy is the only one that will exist. When you bring it out for reading, make a mystery of it by transporting it to the stage in a closed carriage. Put the reader behind a curtain. Make a mystery of it."

"Will the city council go along? After all, they are the ones paying and they will want control. Why won't they ask for a hundred copies?"

"Vais, do you think scribing is easy? I am only going to provide a scribe for one copy as a courtesy. Extra copies will be charged at the full cost of production. The city council will collapse with shock when they see the cost."

"Bhargava, we have spent long enough on this subject. Let us move on for now. If your son can help us, I will gladly accept his help."

"Thank you my friend. Shall we resume now?"

"It's time for lunch. We'll get to it after lunch."

The Geography of Jambudvipa

Kaushambi/Hastinapur
circa 850 B.C.E.

Vaishampaayana looked at the boy who approached him. He was the new apprentice who had been assigned to help him that day – it was considered an honour to spend a day with the Vyaasa and every few days a different boy came by. Before the flood, this task was restricted to the most senior apprentices and it might have been half a year or more before a specific apprentice came back;

but now, there were so few of them they were sending children who were still in basic training. *He must have just graduated from the elementary programme.* The boy brought him some water in a rough clay cup. *I am failing in my responsibilities to my apprentices and to the Sangha – I should spend at least five ghatis every day with the boys assigned to me. Otherwise I am treating them as servants.* He took a drink of the water and said, "Son, is this your first time here? What is your name?"

"Panini, sir. I have just entered the middle programme. Guru Samudrakavi said you would test me today to place me with the right teachers."

"Hmm… it doesn't look like that will be possible – I expect to have little free time today. I won't test you today. Go back to your guru and tell him to give you some more lessons."

The boy's bright eyes dulled. Vaishampaayana was reminded of how he had been at that age. *The boy must have been looking forward to a session with the Vyaasa.*

The boy said, "Sir, I am happy to stay here. Guruji says I have a good sense of rhythm – he asked me to practise memorising the conversations I hear and setting them to the gayatri[84] meter."

Bhargava turned his head sharply to look at the boy. The boy looked at Vaishampaayana. Vaishampaayana looked at Bhargava and then looked at the boy. Bhargava started to say something and then stopped. Vaishampaayana thought, *I am allowed to change my mind.*

Vaishampaayana said, "Good. Then you can stay. Remember to practise forgetting as well in the evening."

"Yes, sir," said the boy whose eyes had regained their brightness. He returned to his post by the door of the Vyaasa's

[84] *Gayatri* is a rhythmic pattern used in Vedic poetry that consists of twenty-four-syllable verses organised in lines of six syllables.

house. Those eyes reminded Vaishampaayana of the many bright-eyed children who no longer came to serve him. He shivered – there was no wind but he felt a chill creeping up his spine and freezing his warm cheeriness. He turned to his friend.

Bhargava's forehead was still furrowed. Vaishampaayana said, "My friend, you have a question?"

"Yes, yes. I hope he forgets all he hears? Devavrat explains the geography of the earth during the Third Age. He also implies that the Third Age was over. Is there a significance to this?"

The apprentice had come with lunch. "Let's eat," Vaishampaayana said, "I'll explain that after the meal."

"Good," said Bhargava, "I am certainly hungry."

Lunch was flatbread and roasted plantain served out on a plantain leaf. Sun-dried clay cups were filled with water. Another cup was put down – the apprentice brought a large bowl of soup and poured it into each cup. The soup was a lukewarm weak *rasam* – Bhargava stirred the soup with his finger, but nothing solid emerged from the bowl.

Bhargava knew that the Kavi Sangha was frugal. *Will I survive a month of lunches like this? Will my son? It was... alarming.* After the food was served, Vaishampaayana gestured to the boy.

"Come, Panini, sit by my side and eat with us."

"Sir, my guru will not..." said the boy.

"Don't worry, I will not tell your guru."

The boy looked around, as if checking that there was nobody spying on him. Then he set a third plate and served for himself and sat down.

They ate silently using their fingers as was customary. When Vaishampaayana was done, he rinsed his hand out with a little water and took a drink. Bhargava followed his example. Then the boy brought a betel leaf in which was nestled a small piece of a sweet made of curdled milk and condensed mango juice.

Vaishampaayana said, "Good. I was hungry. What did you think, Bhargava? I asked the boy to make soup today as an extra."

Bhargava considered what to say. He took a deep breath and said, "You know… Vaishampaayana, why don't I arrange for lunch tomorrow?"

Vaishampaayana laughed, "My friend, I wanted you to see the way we eat. Yes, life among the poets can be bleak indeed. Our work helps – it is a good way to stop thinking of food."

Bhargava nodded, though he did not agree. *Work was inherently tedious, eating well was an art – food was a good way to stop thinking about work.* He said, "Vais, I know that the Kavi Sangha lives very frugally. Two of your apprentices cost less than even one of mine. We eat well, I grant you. That's why we succeed in so many varied places – people share over food. Sharing is good for business."

"OK, Bhargava. Do what you want."

"Great! I'll have my boys bring lunch tomorrow."

Bhargava continued, "The geography you've laid out is a bit strange – did the regions of the world change as well when the Third Age was over and the Fourth Age began?"

Vaishampaayana said, "The Kavi Sangha's geography of Jambudvipa is more poetical than accurate. It centres the world on Panchnad and provides mere hints of the world that lies far from that centre. When necessary, the description is embellished with wonders. You, Bhargava, have travelled much and can add valuable detail."

Bhargava said, "Yes… I've travelled a lot. I've gone as far west as Egypt and stared at the sea of sand that is the western boundary of life. I've crossed the Eastern Sea to the Kamboja settlement that is the greatest source of tin in the world. Every city that I have visited has its own version of the geography of the world, placing the city at the centre and depicting the path from the world of the gods to that central city. I commend your Kavi Sangha for one thing – you are more comprehensive and cover more of the world than any other description I have heard.

"East of Moolasthan, every city uses a variant of Lomaharshana's geography that you just recited. From Moolasthan to Kaushambi, over a hundred yojanas, the geography is said to be that of Jambudvipa. The bards of each city sing of Jambudvipa. Every one of them is a little different, some more fanciful than the others. Even so, they all describe this imaginary island, Jambudvipa.

"Why imaginary? Many reasons – one, there is no Mount Meru beyond Himavat[85] that towers over all the other peaks. The inhabitants of Kashyapura,[86] that jewel-like city set on the banks of the most beautiful lake in the world, have told me that from the peaks of the northern mountains one cannot see the grasslands of the Shakas or the plateau of the Bo. You only see more mountains – is one of them Mount Meru? They could not tell me, for the name had no meaning for them. Nothing else. Second, Jambudvipa is not an island at all. Why call it an island? Could it be the faded community memory of a great flood?

"In Kashyapura, there is a legend that all of the land was a vast lake and the divine sage-father Kashyapa, drained it by cracking the natural dam at Varaha-moola,[87] *Boar's Point*, exposing the sunken valley of Kashyapura to settlement and creating the Sutudri, the Yamuna, and the Ganga. In the middle of this lake was an island paradise blessed with a thousand jambul trees –

85 *Himavat* means "White Mountain Range" and refers to the Himalayas. We will use "the Himalayas" in later references.

86 *Kashyapura* would be modern-day Srinagar on the shores of Dal Lake.

87 *Varahamoola* is the ancient name of the town of Baramulla in Kashmir.

this heavenly island, they said, was the original Jambudvipa, the Paradise created by Brahma for his own pleasure. When the waters drained, the island became an unattainable peak of mythic beauty and size. That story is fanciful enough, but it at least refers to a land that was once an island.

"One thing I must say for the rest of your list of the people and the lands around us – I have been there and seen some of them. They exist. Some of your names are legendary – Dilmun for one, is famed in legends of the West as the doorway to a land of incalculable wealth. My banker in the capital of the Assyrians called it a myth. The Bo plateau still holds the Bo people. Su-wa-Xia is completely unknown, the traders I meet who come to Takshashila from the East call their country Shunk-wa[88] – they say it means, the Central Land.

"Third, I am intrigued by your description of the guilds. There were only seven? Didn't they have *jaatis* – we have over a thousand! I only know of two jaatis that act like the guilds you describe, and control admission – your own guild of bards, and my guild of traders. All the others are hereditary – one is born into it and one can neither join a jaati nor can one leave it. The flood has shaken up your guild of bards – you may blame the flood, but the guild of bards was dying even before the flood. Already you restrict your traditional training to the promising entrants. The guild of warriors no longer trains its members – entry into it is by inheritance or by force, and exit by massacre or death. The guild does little for its members, and the members do little for the guild."

Vaishampaayana said, "It has been over a thousand years since this story was composed. I am not surprised that some peoples have disappeared, that others have changed both practices and names. I am surprised to find any that are completely unchanged!

---

[88] Both Suwaxia (modified version of Huaxia) and Shunkwa (modified version of Huang and Wang) are names of China or of parts of China at different periods in its history – Huaxia from about 1500 BCE and Shunkwa from the eighth century BCE to the third century BCE.

"You asked about the survival of the trading guild and the guild of the bards while the other guilds disappeared. As you surmised correctly, jaatis replaced the other guilds and now we have over a thousand jaatis. Why did only the guilds of the traders and the bards survive as guilds? It is a perceptive question. The answer has to do with power. The answer has everything to do with the story of this Great War. For all those changes happened after the War when Devavrat's empire came back to life under Pandava rule.

"Now, let us return to Devavrat's report on his childhood."

Bhargava said, "Should I include this conversation we just had?"

Vaishampaayana said, "The story of the Ages and what they mean is belief, not events. It does not belong in a history of the past, if it had no influence. It did not. This story does not belong. You should only write down the words of Devavrat or others from that period I recite about. The discussion between you and me is not a part of this history."

"That's emphatic enough, my friend. What's the matter?"

"I've just spent time explaining something that does not belong."

"Isn't that what a good story-teller does? Take the story in the direction that the audience is interested in?"

"My friend, you don't understand. Should I make this so interesting that people will prefer to read rather than listen? That will be the end of bards and poetry!"

"I see," Bhargava said as he frowned and mulled over the implications of Vaishampaayana's statements. *I wrote all of this, and now it will go to waste? We'll see about that.*

Bhargava continued, "Let us return then to Devavrat's words."

850 B.C.E

Vaishampaayana said, "When we stopped, Devavrat had just finished describing the Panchnad way of life and the absence of war. He will then describe how and why Hastinapur came into existence. These are events that occurred long before the time of this *Jaya*[89] that we are writing down."

Bhargava picked up a palm-leaf and a stylus. They both sat down. Vaishampaayana began,

"Devavrat said..."

"Hold on," said Bhargava. "I see my apprentice coming up the path."

They waited until the boy came up to them. He was breathing hard.

"Sir..." he began and then stopped to catch his breath.

"Yes?" Bhargava said.

"The Mistress wants you to come right away, sir."

"What happened? Is something the matter?"

"I don't know, sir. But a courier came a short time ago. With a message – written on a tablet. She sent for me and asked me to read it, but I could not. Nor could anybody else."

"What do you mean, you cannot read it. Make the sounds."

"We did sir. All of us there agreed on what the sounds were. But when we read the sounds, the message made no sense."

Bhargava contemplated the boy who stood a little stiffly. *What language was the letter in?* He turned to Vaishampaayana and said,

"Vais, I have to go."

---

89 A *Jaya* is a commemorative lay composed for the victors after a battle or war. Samvarana would commission the first *Jaya* when he defeated Panchala and recovered Hastinapur. The Great War described in this novel is the only one that is referred to as '*the Jaya*'. Later, many *jayas* will be composed, but this *Jaya* is considered the greatest of them.

Vaishampaayana shrugged. *Why does everybody want me to be the one who accommodates?* He said, "Come early tomorrow, Bhargava. I hope it is good news, and you will come relaxed and happy."

***

The next day Bhargava came early. Almost two ghatis early. Vaishampaayana had just finished his ablutions. An archivist needed a ghati every morning to practise *nishkamsmaranadharanam,*[90] but he had not even started when Bhargava came. They exchanged pleasantries and then Bhargava said, "Yesterday's message was nothing urgent – my son will be here today. After lunch. I will leave then and spend the day with him and my family."

"Of course, I understand. Take him to his mother and feed him whatever he has missed these five years.[91] If you have time, come by later with him."

"I will. Could we start now, even though it is a bit early? It will help me stop worrying."

"Bhargava, I appreciate your thinking for me. Yes, we can start right away. Where were we?"

"Devavrat had just finished with a history of Panchnad."

"Yes, he continued then to his own life."

---

90 *Nishkamsmaranadharanam* means "holding on to memory without attachment", constituted a collection of mental exercises and practices, that a bard used to erase unneeded memories while retaining the necessary ones. See Endnotes.

91 Panchnad used a calendar based on the moon, but traders used solar years as that determined the schedule for long-distance trading – caravans left or arrived by the cycle of seasons that were aligned with the sun.

CHILDHOOD'S END

THE PANDAVA CAMP
CIRCA 2000 B.C.E.

Devavrat said, "Out of boredom with my teachers in the guild of traders, I had joined the guild of bards in their classes. I began as a precocious learner in listening – less than thirty moons (over two solar years) into my education, I could report conversations lasting as long as a ghati; I could memorise lists of words exceeding one hundred; I could identify over a hundred sounds. I had arrived at the level of expertise expected of an eleven-year-old apprentice bard ready to enter a period of intense study under the tutelage of one or more Gurus. I was still a child – I thought my parents knew of this precocity, but, in retrospect, perhaps they did not. Many of my interactions were with servants and teachers who reported remarkable progress that my parents must have immediately discounted. When they quarrelled, they seemed unaware of my presence. A normal eight-year-old would not have understood their conversations; I certainly did not, but I memorised them and retrieved the memory later, at a time when I did understand.

"Why is this relevant, you ask? I was an eight-year-old with the memorisation skills of a much older boy. I spied on my parents, and what I heard went into some dark corner of my mind. Over the years, I came to understand those words better through replaying these conversations in my mind. I finally understood the events of that year, when my mother died."

It struck Devavrat that something had changed in Yudhishthira. He had come in abruptly without the usual polite excuses. His eyes frequently darted to the entrance and when they came back to focus on him, they seemed to have lost their brightness. *Was he even listening? What was the hurry?* He would have to solve that puzzle. In the meantime, Devavrat did not want to change his narrative. Whatever hurry Yudhishthira was in, that hurry could wait.

"May I continue?"

Yudhishthira's forehead was furrowed, as he tried to grasp what Devavrat had said. He summarised in his mind – Devavrat's memorisation skills were not public knowledge, and he did not display them. The rulers of Hastinapur no longer trained to be anything other than warriors. They trained to be warriors and nothing else.

"Yes, of course."

Devavrat went on:

"I listened to all the conversations that went on in my house and memorised them. I was young and had not developed the moral yardstick by which to judge people's actions – whether they were my parents or my teachers or even the staff with whom I spent most of my time. That is the power of these skills – the past is not a closed book from which all learning has been squeezed out.

"One day, I was about to enter my mother's private chambers – that morning she had gone to the river-side cottage that her father lived in and I knew she had returned when one of her maids ran out to fetch water to moisten the *kusha* grass screen and to fetch the fan. I heard my father's voice and stepped back. There was an edge to his voice, of pleading – he sounded like I did when I wheedled a sweet from the cook. I stopped and listened. I automatically memorised what was said, but I only understood some of it. That I did not forget testifies to the skills I learned from my teachers.

"My father said, 'Gangu, Gangu, Gangu! Why can't you understand?' I recognised the signs of a major breakdown – my father called my mother Gangu only when he was aroused or overwrought. 'We face a crisis! For fifty years, from the time of my grandfather, we have been struggling with this problem. We chose to be generous to the refugees as they came here. Everybody agreed to make the sacrifice – that is what makes us great. What's the use if we cannot...? We have become poorer. Our enemies grow stronger. Every day I hear about some Panchala demagogue who wants to create a new army to liberate our Nagas. We need to be more practical, more pragmatic. You know that the Kavi Sangha felt that we were being too kind – they had proposed exiling all refugee families that had children, or killing their new-borns. That would encourage them to go further east. I demurred – they would be going into a wilderness with no support from us. I said... we said, *No, we must all bear the burden,* and softened the law that the Kavi Sangha had formulated. We made the law that each family would be allowed one child to replace each adult in the family. We applied this to everybody! We stopped referring to them as refugees and called them immigrants. We voluntarily treated them as our equals, even though we were the overwhelmed hosts and they were the desperate and impoverished guests. We all took a risk – all we need to do now is survive this drought and the threat of famine. We will survive, and in a few years, when the crisis is past, we can repeal these laws. If not me, it will be my son – Devavrat will repeal the laws!'

"My memory is perfect and that is exactly what he said, but I have often wondered at those words – that I would repeal those laws? Much is lost in this recitation. Was he proud that I would do this? Was he chagrined that he could not? What else was hidden in those words? I had learned to memorise speech in a single hearing, but inner meaning had not figured in that feat. Nor did the elements that conveyed emotion. It was the first time I had put a learned skill to use, and there was something magical and wonderful about it. I stood there memorising my father's words even as he spoke, even as in my mind I observed myself memorising, full of wonder at my ability. The sounds came in and were transmuted into the parts of a giant tree, in my mind, an awe-inspiring banyan tree that provided the framework for that memory. With loving care they seemed to be deposited, one on this leaf, another on that branch. Some made their way onto the hanging roots and clung to them like butterflies. Others fluttered about for what seemed an absurdly long time, tiny jewelled hummingbirds refusing a perch, until the right one was found, and they too transmuted into butterflies. As the tree filled up with sound that created a background chorus, the butterflies would sparkle and light up, providing hooks for unravelling the chain of a melody. The shortcomings that I complain about are afterthoughts – in hindsight the most magical acts become mundane and tiresome. Meaning was in the melody, and it had to be played, or as in this case, replayed, to extract content. The incomprehensible beauty of it overwhelmed the child that I was – it was a long time –years –before I understood the words. That required rehearsing the words, and that is what I did – not just this, but many other conversations that I chanced to overhear – until I finally understood them, and then they lost the sparkle of wonder.

For a long time I felt that I had committed a crime – that if I had understood this dialogue that I had memorised with such pleasure, I might have been able to protect my mother. There were days that I searched desperately through the stock of remembered conversations searching for more evidence of my culpability, rehearsing each one. Most of them revealed little that was worth saving forever – however, I found the mundane exciting for it revealed details of lives that as Regent I would never experience for myself, and the memory would return to its assigned spot in the banyan tree of my mind. Then I recalled a few that showed the repeated conflicts between my mother and my father – I had memorised much that could only be retrieved by re-invoking the feelings of the time. Even as I grasped the meaning of some significant narrative, I discovered that some of them seemed to become lost and were forgotten. The act of rehearsing could result in forgetting these highly charged memories – that is one of the methods classified under *nishkamsmaranadharanam*. Luckily, not all of them vanished, and I stopped. They were depressing to review in this manner – but despite that there were days when I would return like an addict to rehearse just one more leaf and then one more and then another until I hit one of the dialogues between my father and mother and when that memory faded I would react with self-accusation and vow never to do it again."

Yudhishthira said, "Grandsire, are you saying that what I have asked you to do risks being lost forever from your mind? In that case, I should…"

Devavrat said, "I am dying, and these memories will be of use to nobody. Let me judge for myself what memories I wish to die with and those I wish to hand over. If you win this war, they may be of use to you."

"Your death will be a burden I must carry."

"Such are the unique burdens that only a ruler can carry. If my memories are to be of any use, Yudhishthira, you as the King must carry this burden."

Yudhishthira took a deep breath. *Yes, I do want to understand this past.* He nodded.

Devavrat continued, "In any case, I listened. I had three choices – I could leave, but I did not have the desire to do so. In the beginning I felt that this conversation made sense and revealed secrets to me that I did not know. I could go in and interrupt a quarrel that I did not fully understand. I could stay and listen to the conversation. Much of that conversation was new to me. We had been suffering a crisis since the days of my grandfather Pratipa – I did not know that! There were refugees – I wondered: who were they? How could I identify a refugee, and what made them different from non-refugees? My father had said *We...call them immigrants now*. I knew about immigrants, they lived in the immigrant quarter of Hastinapur. I did not know that they did not belong there, that they were not just another guild that provided a ghetto for its members, but people who were guests at first, and whom now it was difficult to feed. More worrying statements: *We have become poorer. Our enemies grow stronger*. What was this crisis and how was it that I knew nothing about it? Then, that the Kavi Sangha had proposed a harsh law. I knew about the Kavi Sangha. They were the intellectual bulwarks of the Kuru family ever since Guru Vasishtha, the founder of the Kavi Sangha, had taught King Samvarana a new way, the way of the warrior. Every day a Kavi Sangha member would be a guest at our dinner ceremony. A brief session with the King would be followed by the recital of poetry. Dinner would follow. Occasionally, the Vyaasa Parashara came and told stories while the children of the palace ate dinner. Once I had asked him what he did when he was not telling stories. He said that he wrote poetry. I had asked him what the Kavi Sangha did and he said they told stories and remembered everything. They were especially good at memorising and repeating stories. Knowing my own ability for memorising, I had asked him if I should join the Kavi Sangha. My mother had frowned, but the Vyaasa had smiled and said, 'Yes, of course. You will be a great leader who will do great things.'

"I digress. What had my father said? That they had proposed applying a much harsher law restricted to the immigrants just to encourage them to go east. I knew about 'going east'. That has been the Kaurava mission since the founding of Hastinapur. Every year at the Spring Festival, the directive of the Namegiver, Hastin, would be recited and it talked about the historic role of the Pauravas to keep the culture alive, of the Bhaaratas to spread it in all directions, and the particular mission of his own descendants to populate the East. The only descendants of Hastin who had whole-heartedly accepted this mission were Kuru's descendants, the Kauravas. The others had been killed by the Panchalas, or had abandoned Samvarana, or like my uncle Bahlika, accepted the offer of leadership elsewhere. There were many other directives, but this was the strangest one, for in those days settling in the East was an unthinkable fantasy. 'The Kauravas cannot go east from here.' The last assertion was by my mother's father, a man who said little, and what he said was difficult to understand. My father disagreed – neither the Naga nor the long-term settler could be coerced, but the immigrants could be. The immigrants had to go east and relieve the burden on Hastinapur. My father just did not know how to make it happen.

"The Nagas and the immigrants were a study in contrast. The Nagas moved often, but did not want to migrate; the immigrants had migrated but did not want to move. Once a month, the King and I would make a trip to the Naga temple that was at the centre of the city. To get there from the King's mansion we had to drive a bullock cart through the newly formed immigrant quarter and then to drive through the Naga quarter. Sometimes I would sit with the carriage driver, a family fixture named Bakakula. Bakakula had a pithy description – the immigrant quarter looked like the residents had come to stay, while the Naga quarter looked like the residents were passing through. I don't know whether Bakakula was trying to impress me with his wisdom or reciting a common observation.

"At other times, I would sit with my father and as we exited the immigrant quarter, my father would make his observation. 'Compare the immigrant quarter to the Nagas,' he would say. 'We, the city dwellers, love the immigrants – they keep everything so neat and tidy, unlike the Nagas. Take note, however, that it is the Nagas who go into the forest to hunt, it is the Nagas who cultivate crops, no matter how inefficiently, and it is the Nagas who will forgo neatness and control in order to work with the jungle.'

"It took me many years to realise that my father and the driver were not disagreeing with each other – the Nagas are the ones prepared to settle a new frontier land, while the immigrants hope to join a developed culture, and this can make all the difference.

"Such statements left me confused. What did father approve of? He would get upset if the house was not maintained meticulously, occasionally calling the house manager in for a lecture on some shortcomings – cobwebs in the corner, dust not swept off the hearth. This upset everybody, beginning with my mother, as she was the one who gave the orders to the house manager. My father's intervention would then lead to a private discussion between my father and mother, where she would call his actions unbecoming of a chief. At these sessions, I would be a lamppost, listening, saying nothing, etching those discussions in my memory.

"This time there was a difference. My mother's voice had piqued my interest because she punctuated her words with sniffles – she must have been weeping. She sounded sad, not angry, and I had rarely seen this. My father's voice was also different – not the low bass that he used when talking to his ministers, but a voice that pleaded, almost a whine in the beginning, then transitioning to the bass as he became more confident and assertive. He had mentioned my name, Devavrat, and I took that as a cue to enter.

"I ran in breathing a bit heavily as though I had been running. I look back in wonder at my ability, even at that age, for dissimulation. I used to mimic my father talking to his ministers, my audience being the driver and the cook, and it was only a short stretch from an act to a pretence to a lie. I stood there breathing heavily as though I had been running and said, 'Father! You called for me! Does that mean you will play with me now?'

"My father did what he would always do when he wanted to distract attention – talk. 'Yes, glorious youth!' he began. You and your generation, Yudhishthira, are used to this kind of speech, but it is a new thing, a style that the Paurava immigrants brought to Hastinapur. Complimentary adjectives that meant little, but added little flowers of grace to conversation. I had not yet been taught to speak formally, the language of the court, but already in my father's time, the fashionable speech had evolved to this elaborate decorative form. My father could never use it with a straight face; so when he addressed me formally, I felt I was being mocked. It made me want to squirm, to scratch an itch that could not be reached. I had to stay still as he was the King even though he was my father.

"He bowed and smirked, 'Yes, glorious youth! And what is your wish this time?' I wanted the fight to stop, and the best way would be to draw him away from my mother's quarters. We used to play a game in which I would shoot magic arrows, *astras,* like the ones in the stories of the gods and demons that were performed on festival days. I would shoot Agni's *agneyastra,* and father pretended to put out the fire. I would fire Indra's *indreyastra,* which casts a web of illusion on its targets, and father would pretend to be snared in an illusory world. When I wanted to stop playing the game, I would shoot Brahma's *brahmastra,* the weapon that would destroy all of Brahma's creation, not just the material world of the senses, but the immaterial world of consciousness as well. Yudhishthira, you are smiling, but when I was a child, I wanted to believe in them, though I knew these weapons were fantasy.

"I said to my father, 'You will be the target and I'll shoot a *brahmastra* at you! What will happen this time?' I was concerned that this was a transparent attempt to distract him, but my mother intervened.

"My mother said, 'Dev, go outside and play!'

"That made the decision for my father.

"Father said, 'Let him be!' Then added, 'I'll fall to the ground and gibber like a monkey.' This was to me.

"Mother was displeased. 'This is what you do when I talk about my concerns. You can do what you wish to your clan. Why kill my sons like this?'

"Father said, 'Dev, go outside and play.' He took my hand and took me into the back garden. He pointed to a tree. 'See if you can hit it at fifty paces with your arrow.' He went back inside.

"I waited a vighati or so, hoping he would return, then sat down on the stoop by the closed door and rested my chin on my fist. That was what Sanghamitra, the cook, did when he was thinking about a recipe or contemplating a taste. He looked like he was in deep thought, lost in an ocean of self-realisation. It seemed an appropriate pose. I contemplated the *tulsi* bush and listened.

"My father's voice came through clearly. 'We have sacrificed a hundred children like them. Do I only kill the daughters of the immigrants? That was the Kavi Sangha's recommendation! I rejected that option. What was I supposed to say to the people – apply such laws only to the immigrants? Are we Yavanas with one law for visitors and a different one for residents? Are we Mlecchas who enslave captured women for their own entertainment? Are we like the Sumerians who say that boys are better than girls? Are we? Are we?'

"That day I did not understand anything. Now I understand everything. What is the use of hearing if one cannot understand what is heard? Once something has been said, it can never be repeated with the same meaning. Ah! That startled you, Yudhishthira. Isn't that a thought to contemplate? That even though the pupil is first taught to memorise, even though the crowd is displeased if a bard changes a story by as much as a word, even though our word for knowledge is memory,[92] we cannot reproduce the past even in speech – it is truly lost time.

"My boy, you are impatient with my digressions. I can see that. The point of a story is its interpretation, isn't it? You shake your head. No matter. I will get on with the story.

"What did I understand – that the Kavi Sangha wanted to kill all the children? They were talking about Uncle Vyaasa! He wanted to kill all the children – how could something so frightening be true?

"My mother said, 'You counter criticism with this story you made up, about these dead children being your nomadic forefathers, the Vasus, re-incarnated to bless your enterprise. Your poets spread this ridiculous story that every dead child, boy and girl, is a god or a goddess.'

"She continued, 'I have to do something. The banks of the river are dotted with small mounds of dirt commemorating these dead children. When this is over, we will know exactly what it has cost us. I know what it cost me. I would have been happy just to hold them for a few days. My arms longed to cradle them, my breasts longed for their lips, my eyes longed to smile back into their eyes.'

"My father replied, 'Shall I change the laws and make it apply only to daughters?'

---

[92] *Shruti* means both "*knowledge that has been revealed by hearing*" and "*memory of orally revealed knowledge*" (revelation was considered to be more like hearing than like seeing). Such a concept of knowledge would characterise an oral, pre-literate culture, like Panchnad in 2000 BCE and Hastinapur in 850 BCE. Contrast this with "*Smriti*" which means "*remembered knowledge*", but what is remembered was not what was "revealed", i.e., not "Shruti", but rather knowledge gained through the *experience* of the person recalling it.

"My mother said, 'No. What if my next two children are girls? I'll kill myself if you change the laws again. I would look forward to my next baby. But not with you for a husband...'

"My mother was going to kill herself? Why? Because of laws that my father had enforced on the advice of the Kavi Sangha. That did not make sense either. What did she mean? The distracted thoughts would have made me miss the rest of the conversation, but my autonomic training helped.

"My father asked, 'Are you expecting?'

"Mother replied, 'Yes.'

"He said, 'Let's hope that it's a girl.'

"At that my mother stayed silent. Their voices went low, and I could not hear them anymore. After some time, it became obvious that my father had forgotten his promise and he was not coming out to play with me. I did not want to go in, so I left through the outhouse gate and wandered down to the river where I often spent my time.

"Yudhishthira, I am telling this to you in the hope that you understand. My earliest memories are coloured by this crisis. All our solutions to the crisis subsequently have been traumatic."

"May we not create our own solutions?" said Yudhishthira.

Devavrat reflected on his grandnephew's words. *Yes. Every generation demands the right to repeat mistakes.* It was a fruitless debate.

"You say you have a solution. You are shaking your head. You disagree with me? I don't claim to have a solution anymore, but your solutions will be no better."

He could feel frustration build up. He had to be careful that he did not gesticulate and move the arrow. That would kill him. *I'll finish the story I have started.*

2000 B.C.E

"Days passed," Devavrat said. "I could not talk to anybody about this. Not Bakakula, the cart and carriage driver, however close he might have become to my father after his many years of service. Not Sanghamitra, the cook, he would withdraw at the first sign of criticism directed at Father or Mother. I could not see any way to talk to my parents about this – they would be upset that I had overheard them. I fretted for a few days, watching Mother carefully for signs that she might kill herself. Nothing happened. What signs was I looking for anyway, and how would I recognise them when they showed up? Mother was as cheerful with me as ever, nor did Father change. The words did not increase in meaning when I rehearsed them; rather they began to look more ordinary and forgettable – one of the known hazards of the bard's profession, as I told you, is that too much private rehearsal of memorised oral events can result in forgetting.

"My education continued along the same two streams – physical training to be a warrior, and mental training in memorising, calculation, and reporting observations, to work as a trader. The increased emphasis on the military training was Guru Vasishtha's contribution – he had taken a trading clan and created warriors out of them – a clan ever prepared for battle. The physical training focused on the use of arms, the effective use of armour, accuracy with the bow and arrow. We are no longer traders – neither you nor Suyodhana have been trained to trade."

Devavrat paused in his telling. Lomaharshana leaned towards him and brought a small jar with water to his mouth. Devavrat took a sip – the cool water felt sweet on his tongue. Even so, it did not wash away the bitter taste of the memories he was dredging. *This is another slice of history you do not know, Yudhishthira – your father is to blame for the appalling way he educated you, without understanding why the Kauravas bear arms while the rest of the civilised world hires mercenaries.*

Devavrat said, "My mother then became ill and was confined to her quarters – I know now that she was pregnant but I did not know it then as I was kept ignorant of her pregnancies. She wanted the child to be a girl. I've learned that the general belief is that if a woman does not see a man during her confinement, the baby will be a girl. It does not always work that way, but the failures can be explained away – if a baby is a boy, she must have encountered a man, and if a baby is a girl, she did not encounter any men. If some man did visit, she must not have seen him. If a man visited and she saw him, maybe some as-yet-unknown factor prevented the man's inherent influence. Please note – the proof of what the mother saw is the gender of the child! That is no way to think. There is a mystery worth solving – how can one determine the gender of a child in the womb?"

Yudhishthira frowned. Devavrat looked at him and smiled. *Yes, yes, I see that you do not care about this particular puzzle. Maybe, it will intrigue you later.* Devavrat continued:

"Days passed and became months; by and by the emotions faded, except for the memorised conversation that I could reproduce if asked. Nobody did. My life continued. My mother came out of her confinement, but without a child. She acted as if nothing was amiss, and so did my father, so I did not see anything amiss."

Devavrat paused. Lomaharshana moistened his lips again. "A little more water," he said. Lomaharshana looked to the nurse who shook his head; Devavrat said, "I've barely eaten anything – a sip of water won't make me sick." Lomaharshana let him sip the water for a short time, about half a vighati. Then he took the cup away. Devavrat sighed.

"I'll continue," he said.

TRAGEDY ON THE RIVER

THE PANDAVA CAMP
CIRCA 2000 B.C.E.

Devavrat continued:

"Years passed. Over the next three years my mother must have become pregnant, gone into confinement, and come out without a baby, and I only realised something was wrong later. I was over eleven years old –almost twelve. I had gone into Mother's garden with some sweets that the cook had made. I wanted to surprise my mother. She was sitting by the side of the garden that faced the river, a winding path sloping gently down, flanked by jasmine and *tulsi* bushes along the edge, *ashoka* trees providing shade with their densely packed leaves, their shade keeping at bay the shadows of depression, and further away from the path, mango trees planted for their shade as well as their fruit. Mother was looking down at a small pool that had been constructed by the gardener and his staff – he had built an underground canal that brought water from a rainwater-holding tank. The rainy season had just ended and the world was a glistening green, the scent of jasmine blown in by the breeze from the river. Mother's pose and the cast of her face and lips were incongruous with that setting.

"'Why are you crying?' I asked her. I am not sure exactly what I said – I find it very difficult to memorise my own words in a conversation. I could either talk or memorise, but I could not do both at the same time with any competence.

"She shook her head. 'You look hurt,' I said, 'Should I bring Father over?'

"Mother shook her head again. 'No, please, Dev, don't do anything. I am not feeling well.' Those were her exact words. I've played this one out in my mind many times.

"I said, 'You've been sick for a couple of months. Does Father know? Has the doctor been in to see you?'

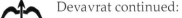

"Mother replied, 'I saw the doctor a few days ago, Dev. This problem… she cannot help me. Your Father is busy. I must decide on my own.'

"I asked, 'What did the doctor say?'

"Mother's eyes glistened and her voice was calm and low. 'She cannot help me, Dev.'

"I was at a loss – this was the first time I had seen her like this.

"I turned to her attendant, who had just come out with a small cup. 'Chaya, did the doctor prescribe anything for my mother?'

"Chaya said, 'Yes, Prince. She suggested that the Queen eat only yoghurt made from fresh goat's milk, for three days. I've just brought her some.'

"I cried out in exasperation, 'Mother! How will that help you? The doctor prescribes goat's milk yoghurt for everything. Maybe Father should call another doctor for you, a better one, with more experience. If Father is not doing it, I will.'

"My mother said, 'No, don't call anybody. Come, let me look at you.'

"She did not say anything, but she pulled me close. Her eyes looked steadily into my eyes, then above them, then the rest of my face. I looked back at her, unblinking. Then she looked at my eyes again, and her gaze was soft but with such intensity that I thought she would weep. I felt the tears that seemed about to burst from her eyes well up in mine. 'Don't cry, son!' she said, her arms around me in a tight hug that loosened as she slowly let me go. I did not want her to let go.

"She said, 'You are not like him at all. You look like my father.'

"I don't know what I was expecting, but that was not it. I blurted out the first thing that came to my mind. 'Mother! Father says I look like his father.'

"She looked away and faced the pool. 'It doesn't matter. Go play with your bows and arrows. Goodbye.'

"'Go, play.' That was what she said. It was a strange thing to say. I would have done as she said, but my legs had turned cold and solid like the ice that we see in the northern mountains and those petrified legs could not move.

"'Why did you say goodbye? Are you going someplace? When? Where? Can I come too?'

"Questions tumbled out of me as my mind raced while my body stood played Statue.[93] I must have dropped the sweets.

"My mother smiled faintly, 'Don't worry, darling. I'll be with you no matter where I go. Tell your father that. He knows how to take care of you. You should take care of him too. Go, play!' and she put her hand to my back and gave me a slight push.

"Those were her last words to me. Yudhishthira, she said, 'Go, play', and with that my childhood ended. I left the garden and went to find the cook to get some more sweets to give Mother when she was in better spirits. Sanghamitra heard me out.

"He said, 'You go and fetch the doctor right away. Don't worry; she is one of the best doctors here. I would go, but I have to finish preparing the afternoon meal. Take the doctor directly to the Queen.'

"Two ghatis later I was back at the mansion, this time with the doctor. The garden was empty. I could hear the chatter of her maidservants down by the riverbank. The curtain closing the entrance to Mother's chamber was pulled open. We went in, and I looked around the unlit room. There was nobody there. I came out.

---

93 A version of 'Tag', possibly one of the oldest games played by people.

"'Mother! Mother!' I called. 'Chaya! Anybody! Where's Mother gone – she was here just a short time ago! Mother! I've brought the doctor.'

"There was no reply. Chaya, one of my mother's attendants, came in from the garden. I asked her, 'Chaya! Have you seen Mother?'

"'Yes,' said Chaya. 'She went out through the back door. She said she was going to the river.'

"I was puzzled. 'Why?' I asked, but Chaya shrugged. I went out of the door and gestured to the doctor, who had hesitated outside. 'Come, let's go to the river.'

"We went down the path. The slope was such that, at some turns, one could see the riverbank where the path ended. Mother was at the edge of the water. I was excited. 'There she is! By the edge of the water!'

"'Mother! I've brought the doctor,' I shouted.

"I cannot say that she heard me – I was only twelve, and my voice was yet to break. My mother seemed about to do something. I was too far to see what she was doing, but I had stopped and was trying to figure it out. Meanwhile, Mother finished whatever she was doing and walked into the river.

"I stood uncomprehending. Then I turned to the doctor who was squinting at the river.

"'Do you see that? Do you see that?' I said, and the doctor stepped back at my vehemence, but kept quiet. I do not know what, if anything, she made of the situation, but I knew what I wanted her to think.

"'She can't be going for a bath at this time of day. Something is wrong. Doctor, you must come with me.'

"The doctor stayed silent. The she said, 'Prince, the Queen might not be happy to see me. I'll wait here.'

"I was not going to put up with that kind of behaviour. 'You come with me right now. Do you see what my mother is doing? She's walking deeper into the water. It gets dangerous there.' The doctor followed me, hesitating at every step. I could not bear to go that slowly. I ran.

"'Mother! What are you doing?' I shouted as I ran down the path. The workers in the garden looked at me, puzzled. Then the Queen's maidservants tried to stop me – it was the women's area of the river and men were not allowed – but I was considered a boy even if on the verge of becoming a man, so they did not try very hard. I ignored their entreaties and kept running. They followed me.

"By the time I got to the river bank, my mother had walked out about a hundred steps – the river bed sloped gently but at that distance from the bank, the water was deeper than her height. I thought I saw her head bobbing up and down, which meant that she was trying to keep her nose above water. I shouted again, 'Mother! Mother! Come back. Somebody help her. Bring her back.'

"At that point I understood only one thing. My mother's last words came back to me – she had said 'goodbye' and fobbed off my questions. It hit me now, what she meant. She had intended to kill herself! I was not going to let that happen. I screamed, 'She's going to die! Go bring her back! Now! Bring her back!'

"Their faces were blank. They did not move. Even now, this distant memory brings a lump to my throat. If it weren't for this arrow, I would face away from you. What is the worth of an old man's tears? You do not need to see my eyes flooded."

Yudhishthira looked away. *Am I asking too much? Granduncle could die from remembered grief.* Memory was a double-edged weapon.

Devavrat continued:

"The inactivity of the attendants aroused my fury, and I exploded with a burst of vertiginous energy. I ran back up the path, picked up my bow and quiver of arrows that I had left in the garden, and came running back. Nobody seemed to have moved, further feeding my frenzy. To the left of the beach, the kitchen staff had been constructing a fish weir along the curve of a bend in the river. Rope made from *sisal* was wrapped around a roller – this was the rope used to create nets in the fish-trap. I grabbed one end of the rope and tied it to an arrow. I pulled and freed a long length of rope. It looked long enough. I shot the arrow out over the water, but the weight of the rope held it back, and it only reached halfway to where I had last seen my mother.

"I had failed my mother. The memory of that conversation from many years ago tumbled out and my mother's words, *I'll kill myself,* seemed to echo in my head and heart. I had known of this threat for so many years and done nothing. I looked around, and nobody was moving. Nobody. It was up to me and only me. I had to keep trying, nobody else was.

"I pointed to one of the maidservants who were standing around paralysed. 'You. Help me with the rope. I must get it to my mother.'

"The maidservant, a young girl named Usha, said, 'Sir, are you sure you saw the Lady go in?'

"If I had been the Great God Shiva, she would have been ash. My forehead throbbed. 'Yes, I did. Believe me! It was the Queen!' I was surrounded by fools.

"'I don't know, sir.'

"*Why was she so cool about it?* Her lack of urgency enraged me. I raved, I ranted, I pleaded. I cursed.

"'Please. I need a boat. Help me find one.'

"Nobody moved. I turned to the doctor. 'Did you see my mother enter the water?'

"She said, 'I am not sure, Prince. My eyesight is not as keen as yours. If you saw her, it must have been the lady of the house who entered the water.'

"I looked around for support. There was none – all the maidservants shook their heads. The watchman had come on hearing the commotion, but he did not enter the women's area and; he looked blank. Where did they imagine my mother would be? The doctor had made her best effort to pacify me – if I said it was so, it must be so. If I wanted any more action from them, I would have to order it.

"'Go find my mother.' I faced them all. 'If you find her somewhere else, let me know. If you want to stay here, get me a boat. Otherwise get out.'

"The watchman left. The maidservants collected and muttered to each other and then they left. The doctor shook her head and said, 'Prince, you should not have threatened them. They work for your father. You will need their help.'

"I was not mollified. 'Don't talk to me about helping. You were supposed to help her, and all you did was give her weak tea. Along with a scoop of yoghurt.'

"'She was pregnant. The baby was born, a boy. By the orders of the Kaurava, it was taken away.'

"This was news to me. I was oblivious to some things. However, this was irrelevant – there was nothing I could do. Now, I had to try to rescue my mother. That was it – there was nothing else more important. I stared downstream in the direction the watchman had gone. I stamped my feet. I did not know why it was taking so long. Finally, a boat appeared around the bend – one of the two rowers was the watchman. The watchman said, 'Sir, tell us where you last saw your mother.'

"I started to get into the boat, but the doctor and the watchman spoke together, 'Sir, you cannot be on this boat while we conduct this search. If you too have an accident, your father would have our heads.'

"I asked, 'Who will revive my mother when she is found?'

"The doctor said, 'We will. I'll take the watchman with me – point us to where you believe your mother disappeared. If she is there, we will find her.'

"'I'll swim,' I said. 'I can save her.'

"'Son,' said the doctor, 'I know you can swim. That is not enough. Your mother is a grown woman. Unless you are an expert swimmer practised in saving people, you will be unable to bring her back to shore. That is assuming you find her body floating rather than sunk in the bottom of the river. Let us do our duty post-haste.'

"She was right. I could barely swim – I told myself that I could have learned to swim earlier, that I could have practised at saving drowning people from the start, that I was to blame. I should have been able to save her. I knew, rationally, that this was not a reasonable belief, but it was how I felt. Now you understand why I made sure that your cousins learned to swim. If your father had not taken you away, you too would have learned to swim.

"I watched the boat with the doctor reach the place I had pointed to. They were a little too far to the left, and I signalled with my hands. They seemed to understand. I heard a footfall behind me, and turned – it was my father's Chief Minister, Sashidhara. A well-fed man with a smooth, oily brow who listened carefully to my father but did whatever he thought expedient. He bowed very low – you could tell the rank of any person in a hall by the depth of Sashidhara's bow.

"He said, 'Prince, salutations. I was told that you were angry and distressed. I came right away for the gardeners were incoherent and could not explain what had made you so angry.'

"I answered, 'With my own eyes, I saw my mother walk into the deepest part of the water and disappear underwater. Nobody else was paying attention to her, as though she were invisible.'

"He bowed again. 'I will investigate promptly and report to you. Surely the Queen is safe somewhere else.'

"I answered, 'You do not need to investigate anything. What I need from you is an explanation – the doctor tells me that my mother delivered a baby boy and my father had it taken away?'

"I expected some response but Sashidhara's face and eyes did not change. He waited a moment as if to understand my question and then said, 'Yes, the baby was subject to the laws of our city. I am sure the King and Queen intended to tell you soon. I regret that the news came to you from the doctor. She will be chastised. Where is she now?'

"I said, 'The doctor has gone out in the boat to look for my mother. There! Look the boat has stopped, and they are waving their hands.'

"He peered. 'They seem to be shouting. I cannot hear them clearly. My eyes do not see well – what do you see?'

"I said, 'They are pulling something out of the water.'

"We continued watching. Time crawled by. The boat headed back. I walked back and forth in front of the Minister, stopping to look at the boat, and then continuing. As the boat approached the shore, the watchman shouted to me.

"'Prince, it is the Queen. We were too late.'

"That was not the answer I wanted or could accept. 'Why isn't the doctor doing something?'

"The Chief Minister became solicitous. 'Son of Shantanu, please do not blame the doctor.'

"The boat hit the shore. Some of the maidservants had heard the shouting and had come to the riverside. They collected around my mother's body. It was limp, with her wet robe wrapped around her upper body. They lifted Mother and carried her ashore. We heard a commotion behind us – it was my father, the maidservants creating a path for him.

"He saw the body being lifted and rushed towards it. When he recognised Mother, he stopped. The group brought her gently and laid her down near his feet. The doctor could barely speak – she was shivering with the wet and the cold. The fear that she would be held accountable for failing to revive the Queen may have paralysed her tongue.

"My father stood unmoving. When nobody else said anything, he spoke. 'Devavrat! What have you done? Why? Why?'

"I tensed up at the strangeness of his charge and replied with equal vehemence.

"'You mad King! See what you've done to my mother. She died because of you.'

"My father turned to his Chief Minister. 'Sashidhara, arrest my son! He will explain himself, even if I have to drag it out of his throat.'

"Sashidhara shouted, 'Everybody! Leave, now! Take the Queen to her bedroom. Leave me with the King and the Prince.'

"In retrospect, I admire the Chief Minister's skill at being slow in following direct commands while doing something else that seemed like action. The bustle of activity satisfied my father's urge to do something immediately. In a short time, the riverbank was cleared. Then the Chief Minister addressed both of us.

"He said to my father, 'Sir, do not act hastily – the Prince is not responsible for the Queen's death.' He then turned to me. 'Prince, it is not appropriate to address your father in this manner.'

"My father said, 'The guards told me that the watchman had seen the prince go mad and drown his mother.'

"I said, 'He saw nothing. Nobody believed me when I said that Mother walked into the water. He jumped to a conclusion.' Nobody was obliged to believe me, an eleven-year-old child.

"I attacked my father with words that day. He, abashed that he had accused me, said little when I accused him of being mad. I attacked the Chief Minister as a liar who would say anything on my father's behalf, I attacked the Kavi Sangha as a criminal organisation, I attacked the culture of the Kauravas as a bankrupt one that made all its members slaves to immoral laws. The Chief Minister heard me out patiently. I do not think my father heard me at all, for all he did was stare at the river shaking his head while I ranted and raved. The Chief Minister responded to my attacks with soft words, pointing out that my father was grieving and in shock; that the city needed to see its King and his heir together in their grieving; and, finally, that my mother would have wanted my father to take care of me. The words meant little to me, but his voice, soft and low, slowly quenched my anger, and then he put his arms around my father's shoulder, almost like my father was his son or a favoured nephew and whispered to him until he, too, relaxed. The Chief Minister then went over to the huddled maidservants and held a quiet, almost a whispered, conversation with them. He came back and with his arm around my father's shoulders, he took him away. I stayed there, staring across the river at the spot where I had last seen my mother. My mother's helpers loitered, hesitant to come to me. Nobody spoke. As the evening came, the breeze from the river got cooler and cooler until it was uncomfortable. I got up to leave, and the maids followed me, keeping me within sight until I retired for the night."

At this point, Devavrat sighed and grew silent as though he had reached the end of that chapter in his life.

***

2000 B.C.E

Yudhishthira waited silently. One, two, then three vighatis passed and Devavrat continued to be silent as a frown gradually built up on the brow of the usually quiet, usually tolerant, usually polite King.

"You are sad that your mother died when you were a young boy?" said Yudhishthira. "Is that all there is to this story? Why tell it to me? Did you try to change your father's policies? Did you oppose the Kavi Sangha? Are you looking for sympathy? I have no time for that. I understand that, after all these years, you are not reconciled to the manner of your mother's death and blame your father. So what? I too have a story of loss, as do my brothers. We lost my father when I was fourteen – you exiled him when I was born. Do I blame you? My father invited people, all people, Nagas, Hastinapuris, immigrants, even Rakshasas to join the settlement he established on the banks of the Yamuna – one of many branches that had developed an ox-bow lake. When Bhima and I were toddlers running through his settlement, Father barely found the time to hug us – he was away dealing with crises every day. Then Arjuna was born and miraculously the next three years saw a flowering of the settlement as trade along the Yamuna with the Nagas and the Yadavas flourished. Arjuna played on the knees of our father. He knew him as a father while Bhima was too big and I was too old. When Nakula and Sahadeva were four years old, cracks started showing up between the members of the settlement. The relaxed founder and leader of the settlement vanished and so did the unworried father of five. Four troubled years followed for father as he tried to keep Indraprastha together. The circumstances of his death are questionable. Arjuna walked around in a mute daze for days. Do I blame you for that death? The mother of the twins, Nakula and Sahadeva, died as well. The settlement broke down. My mother, convinced of a conspiracy, took us and fled to Hastinapur, to your shelter. I am grateful that you took us in.

2000 B.C.E

"However, the story of our childhood does not explain the principles we hold dear. Why was this story of your mother's death relevant to the policies you've followed?"

"Yudhishthira," Devavrat said, "When the Kavi Sangha helped Samvarana, the ancestor of the Kuru family, become the dominant power in Hastinapur, they also established the precedent that the King's laws were the final law of the land and could be enforced by the King on both Nagas and Panchnadis in Hastinapur territories. It was easy to enforce in the city, but outside the city it was easily ignored. The immigrants accepted the law as the prerogative of their hosts, so the opposition outside the city bemused them. The city residents, ever-conscious of hostile Panchala, needed the army – so they accepted it grudgingly as a short-term option, but became increasingly unhappy as time went on. The Nagas in the city were often the ones who had become 'rogue' – becoming traders in Hastinapur gave them a new and valuable role in their own culture and so they accepted the short-term solution.

"The death of my baby brothers scarcely caused a ripple – there were so many other deaths. I am not seeking sympathy as you think – we were raised in different eras – as I grew older, I came to understand that even if I could not accept the law like an immigrant, I could not react like a city dweller. I was going to be the King and the sole legislator of law in a new political framework. I had to suppress my anguished reaction, just like my father had suppressed his."

Devavrat continued: "The law that my mother died to protest was not repealed, but its enforcement weakened. When my father married again, his wife demanded changes – these changes crippled the law and over time got rid of it."

Yudhishthira said, "I see. Let me tell you how my father explained it to me so many years ago. The traditional, consensus-based framework under which families policed themselves in

Panchnad no longer held in Hastinapur. Vasishtha and the Kavi Sangha created the first military state of Panchnad to ensure Kuru hegemony. This old political framework was replaced with one in which the King had absolute power. The clan became powerless and citizens had to petition the King. The King received hundreds, sometimes more, petitions – too many to be considered carefully. The only way to get a petition addressed was to draw attention to it by organising public support to express outrage. That brought the King's standing army out to maintain order. The army's violence, state-sponsored violence, became an easy option. This is exactly why my father wanted change – to create a form of government that was closer to the old Panchnad form. Unlike the Panchnadi towns, your government was established and maintained by the army.

"I have one question though – you've mentioned that your brothers were killed to satisfy a law that the Kavi Sangha proposed. My father never told me what it was – he refused, saying that the exact law was not important. Exactly what law was this?"

"The region around Hastinapur is not as easy to cultivate as Panchnad had been," Devavrat said. "The Nagas did all the agriculture while the city dwellers were manufacturers and traders. The standing army established after Samvarana did not grow or raise food. When the immigrants started coming, we had to grow more food or import food from elsewhere. The standing army also grew in response to the increase in the population. Importing food was out of the question for the whole world was going through a drought. We asked the Nagas to increase the size and number of plots that they burned for planting, even for the coming season. We assured them that it was only for a short time until the immigrants could return to their earlier homes. Easier said than done – a Naga band typically only managed one plot of a size appropriate for the size of the group and the effort that it could muster. There was no simple way to change age-old practices. We made other attempts, to improve the production of food – both grains and cattle, but failed in the face of the Nagas' inflexibility and the immigrants' reluctance to settle down as full-time farmers.

"A few years later, the Kavi Sangha noted that many tracts of land surrounding Hastinapur were over-worked and projected that in a mere two hundred years all the arable land would be unusable. There were more and more immigrants from Panchnad, and the birth rate had increased. If this continued, the land would be unproductive in sixty years, not two hundred. If the birth rate could be controlled, they would have a hundred and twenty years during which to do something. If immigration could be controlled, it would help.

"To address this, the Kavi Sangha proposed a rule that a family of a husband and a wife could only have one girl child. Female children beyond this would be handed over at birth to the state. The Kavi Sangha argued that controlling the number of girls was the most effective way to controlling population growth. Restricting the number of boys would have a short-term effect, and that was good, but restricting the number of girls would pay off in the next generation.

"This form of the law was difficult for Shantanu to accept – most Panchnad cities were still matriarchies and blatant discrimination against female babies would be opposed. As a trading centre Hastinapur maintained good relations with other lands as a matter of policy – he did not want the remaining Panchnad cities, however weak, to consider him an enemy. To decrease that opposition, the rule was extended to both boy and girl babies – every person could have one child of the same sex as themselves and no more.

"After I was born my parents wanted a girl but my mother kept delivering baby boys. Shantanu set an example by obeying his own law. Oftentimes he had to use the military police to enforce it in Hastinapur, if needed. The children were taken away and handed to the Kavi Sangha."

2000 B.C.E

Yudhishthira said, "What did..." and stopped. Devavrat looked at him. Yudhishthira's face had frozen as though set in stone.

How was he to explain to Yudhishthira that Shantanu was not a monster? Devavrat felt the urge to defend his father, but he did not have many options.

"They took great care to put the babies to sleep by feeding them sweetened milk mixed with essence of *datura.*[94] Death would follow. Then, once a month, they would hold a funeral for all the babies."

"My father used to say that the Kavi Sangha was the only body he knew that was both ruthless and kind."

Devavrat said, "The Kavi Sangha is the only organisation that could have done it. The Sangha is not a monolith – it consists of two parts – the bards who perform at festivals and the archivists who save the memories of a reign. They maintain histories, both financial and of events, provide witnesses for contracts, and so on. The bards keep the Kavi Sangha popular. Even in the best of times, performing for festivals only breaks even, for the bard's compensation is at the mercy of the *yajaman,*[95] the sponsor of the festivities, or of the audience. The archivists bring in wealth, for the contract archiving business is critical to running the economy. The result is that the archivists run the Kavi Sangha, and it was the archivists who performed the culling. The bards could never have done it, but they went along. Laws were enforced by archivists. The bards made life bearable with their stories that explained everything."

---

[94] *Datura* is the Indian Thorn Apple (*Datura metel*), first documented in ancient Sanskrit literature, traditionally used as a painkiller, a narcotic and a poison.

[95] The *Yajaman* was the sponsor of a ritual sacrifice (*yagna*) – he paid for it, he received from the priest conducting the ceremony items blessed by the ritual, and he redistributed these items among friends, their families, and other attendees.

"I did not know of this aspect of the Kavi Sangha," said Yudhishthira. "Perhaps this explains my father's opposition to the Kavi Sangha. I understood his other reasons for opposing you, but his opposition to the Kavi Sangha puzzled me. King Shantanu tried to be fair by expanding the law to apply to everybody, not just the immigrants?"

"Yes. That attempt at fairness did not make him any friends. The people watched as he applied them to his own family. While the immigrants accepted it, the residents did not. Unrest increased slowly; along with that, the size of the military's standing army increased."

"I understand. Earlier I thought that you were digressing and telling us the sad story of your mother's suicide. It was surely that on the surface, but the deeper story was the role of the Kavi Sangha. You know that now you are seen as the foremost supporter of the Kavi Sangha."

"Yudhishthira, my son, it is not so simple. At one time, the Kavi Sangha and I were united in all policy issues. Our interests meshed – I was their foremost supporter; they have been the bulwark of my regency."

"How did that come about? For after your mother's suicide, you must have been completely opposed to your father and to the Kavi Sangha. What changed? I am surprised at your father's behaviour, not befitting a ruler – how did great-grandmother Satyavati get him to repeal the law? What was the Kavi Sangha's reaction?"

Talking about his stepmother had never been easy for Devavrat – a direct question about her role made him choke, broke his voice. He moved his arm to indicate disagreement with the question. That moved the arrowhead, and a wave of pinpricks washed over him, a hundred long needles plunging deep into his body. He felt faint and closed his eyes. Yudhishthira became solicitous.

"Are you tired?" he asked. "Would you like to rest now?"

Devavrat nodded. Now he couldn't speak, even though the pain had stopped, for it left behind a fog that slowed his thinking. Speech was impossible. He closed his eyes, hoping the pain would stop.

"I'll come back later," Yudhishthira said. He carefully adjusted the position of his granduncle's hands and turned his face and shoulders a little so that the pressure on the arrow was relieved. Devavrat's eyes fell on the mattress that had held Shikhandin's body, and the memory pulled the corners of his mouth down, making him look like a mourner at a funeral.

Yudhishthira noted the change of expression and the loss of colour and said, "I'll make sure that that bed is moved out of here. There is no reason for you to see where your enemy lay."

You do not have to do that! Devavrat commanded his mouth to speak, but it refused. He struggled to get the words out and failed. *I am like one of the lakes I've constructed that suffered from a collapsed dam.* All his power had drained out.

Yudhishthira waited for a few vighatis. Devavrat's eyes were closed, and despite himself, he began to sleep. He was only dimly aware when Yudhishthira got up and left the tent.

THE WAYS AND WOES OF THE KAVI SANGHA

Kaushambi/Hastinapur
circa 850 B.C.E.

They had stopped for lunch. One of Bhargava's apprentices had come from the trader's kitchen with a lunch consisting of a soup with pieces of fish floating in it, a dish of charred eggplant, a few pieces of flatbread, and mead. Bhargava forestalled Vaishampaayana's questions, saying, "I thought you might like to eat like a trader."

Vaishampaayana contemplated the food – his own apprentices ate so sparingly, they were as slim at fifteen as they had been at ten. He gestured to his boys, Surya and Savitr, to come closer. He gave them the bowl of soup and their eyes lit up when they saw the fish. They had been apprentices for over two years. Since they joined the bards, fish – any kind of meat – was a luxury they rarely experienced. These had been difficult years – after two years of disciplined eating, two years in which they had made friends, they had lost those friends in the flood. Now they had spent almost a year in mourning. *I've not yet found support for the few we have left, let alone for another two.*

Vaishampaayana's thoughts cycled obsessively back to such statements.

"No wonder you're so thin!" Bhargava said. "You give the food away."

"I'll eat the rest," Vaishampaayana said. "It's enough for me."

"Isn't it much better than your meal yesterday – what was it? Weak *rasam*, invisibly-thin flatbread, and roasted plantain?"

Vaishampaayana shrugged. *What did it matter what I ate?*

Vaishampaayana took a bite of the flatbread dipped in the soup. Usually he did not eat such rich fare. Then, suddenly, he had been served two rich meals – the debate yesterday with the city elders about the cost of transcription had been over a lavish dinner, and, now, this meal – both memorable. *I, too, am easily impressed by good food.* The city leaders had assumed that he would easily agree with their proposals. Instead, the food had energised him. *How could they splurge like this during such a troubled time?* A good meal had sharpened his conflicts with the city council.

The Kavi Sangha, from the highest levels down, was frugal, almost ascetic. Vaishampaayana had adapted over many years to a spare diet often prepared by an apprentice. They had subjected Bhargava to it the previous afternoon. Bhargava had eaten it. *The look on his face!* Vaishampaayana felt like grinning at the thought, then felt chagrined. *That was not a nice trick. From the first day I met him, food has been important to him – how he had guzzled that mead. I should have merely threatened him with a meal like that – it would have been enough to tease him.* Vaishampaayana wished he could have served that frugal meal to the council – he had pleaded with them for more apprentices, arguing that a Kavi Sangha apprentice consumed far less than any other guild's apprentice, but his arguments had been ignored in the city's calculations. Thinking about council meetings depressed him.

Bhargava interrupted his reverie.

"Should I assume that the Kavi Sangha was supporting both sides in the conflict?"

"No, no, no! The Kavi Sangha was centred in Hastinapur and it maintained the archives of the city. As you know, the Vyaasa Shukla, also the brother of the Queen Mother Satyavati, King Shantanu's second wife and Devavrat's stepmother, wanted, or at least would have preferred, that the Pandavas return to Hastinapur. He thought they would be easier to manage if they stayed close by, in Hastinapur. Now, Suyodhana's intransigence on the one hand, and on the other, the alliance the Pandavas made with Hastinapur's ancient enemy Panchala, forestalled any compromise. It looked like a foregone conclusion that the Pandavas would lose. Eliminating Devavrat Bhishma introduced some uncertainty, but he still did not see the Pandavas winning the war."

"Then what were the kavis doing in the Pandava army camp? Why would they be trusted? Why were they allowed there in the first place?"

Vaishampaayana said, "Ah. Good question! The Kavi Sangha stayed on in Hastinapur – there was no point archiving events on the Pandava side. That the Kavi Sangha had a team in Indraprastha was chance. Dumb chance. The archives of the Kavi Sangha explain how that crisis came to be memorised from the perspective of the ultimate winners and not only from that of the losers."

"What do you mean by dumb chance?"

"When the Kavi Sangha, and for all practical purposes, that means the Vyaasa, decides to archive history-in-the-making, it will appoint an Archivist. The Archivist was expected to interview key persons in the beginning and debrief them regularly thereafter. The people involved rarely dissented for they knew that this was a rare honour. There was little experience with a bitter enemy, but one would not expect such an enemy to welcome an Archivist. Even if they did, they would place restrictions on the Archivists that served as a barrier to spying. The Pandavas were on the run, unlikely to win. The rebellion was historic and the Pandavas were expected to lose. The Vyaasa appointed an Archivist in Hastinapur to memorise and organise the history of the Kuru family. No Archivist was planned for Indraprastha, nor sent to the Pandavas. It was a miracle that they had one.

"The miracle was that there was an Archivist in the forest with the Pandavas. Many years earlier, when the Pandavas had been allowed to re-establish the settlement of Indraprastha, the Kavi Sangha and its then newly elected Vyaasa Shukla, had offered Archival support to the Pandavas (Hastinapur and Indraprastha were not enemies yet). When war broke out, the bards and archivists of the Kavi Sangha in Indraprastha were suspected of spying for Hastinapur and not allowed to leave Indraprastha if they knew of Pandava planning. The Pandavas' advisors, many from Panchala, had recommended imprisoning the kavis. Some proposed killing them – feelings against the Kavi Sangha ran high in Indraprastha. The Kavi Sangha had been Devavrat's ally in the policies of the empire he was building, which were anti-Naga in effect. As for the Panchalans – they viewed the Kavi Sangha as the instrument of Panchala's defeat so many generations earlier.

"Yudhishthira rejected the advice and allowed the members of the Kavi Sangha to leave, if they wished, or, if they were willing, to stay and continue to archive. Two of the oldest senior members left, leaving behind only four kavis, including Lomaharshana. They stayed on – being with the losing side, it was difficult for them to communicate with their leaders and get approval from the Vyaasa, but they stayed on. They would do their job, with or without the Vyaasa's approval for every little step. It was some time before the Vyaasa was able to convey his approval and commendation. *Do your job – memorise. You will never be asked to become spies. If asked, pledge loyalty to the Pandavas.* In later years this policy, of loyalty to the host of the archivists, would become part of the ethos of the Kavi Sangha.

This small team initiated the Pandava archives as an extension of the Hastinapur archives. The expulsion of the Pandavas from Indraprastha was followed by a quiet period during which Hastinapur forces hunted for the Pandavas in the forest. Meanwhile, the Pandavas stitched together their coalition and re-built their army from unhappy Nagas and older residents who felt displaced by immigrants. During this quiet period, Suyodhana declared that any contact with the Pandavas was betrayal and even the Vyaasa felt constrained not to visit the Pandava camp openly.

"Since Shantanu's time, the Kavi Sangha had admitted many Nagas. This began during Parashara's term as Vyaasa, and continued under the next Vyaasa, who recruited Shukla. When Shukla became the Vyaasa, he continued the policy. Shukla recruited Lomaharshana, the Archivist who memorised and organised the Pandavas side of this history. Even though very young, Lomaharshana had already built up a reputation as an Archivist. Suyodhana had demanded that this recruitment of Nagas stop, further alienating the Nagas from his rule. The Kavi Sangha deployed its Naga kavis outside Hastinapur. Lomaharshana had been sent to Indraprastha to be Archivist for the Pandavas. He was more than an expert memoriser. He was a skilled elicitor of facts – the events, conversations, actions that had happened in recent days. He was a poet and a storyteller with a keen sense for what had to be archived."

Bhargava said, "Vais, hold it! I should be writing this down."

850 B.C.E

"Be calm, my friend. That was not part of the narration, and you do not need to waste any palm-leaves with your scratches. It is about the kavi Lomaharshana who preserved the history of the Pandavas. It is not about the Great War or its causes."

"I disagree, Vais. The story of the Kavi Sangha is central to the story of the War."

"The Kavi Sangha will maintain our archives in our own way – we prefer not to cloud the archives of the city with our presence. We will stay invisible."

"Invisible and forgotten. Is that your goal?"

"So be it," Vaishampaayana said.

They finished the rest of the meal in silence. By the time they finished, it was three ghatis past high noon. The ficus provided welcome shade but there was no escaping the heat. The warm afternoon breeze from the land to the river kept them dry even if hot. Still, a thin sheen of sweat formed on Vaishampaayana's back and face when he shielded himself from the wind. Vaishampaayana found himself getting sleepy. *I am not used to this rich food.*

He had not told Bhargava the whole story of his meeting with the city council. It was the first one after the transcribing had begun. He had reported the slow going, but expressed optimism that it would speed up. Now, he thought it might take six months. The council meeting became heated. Some of the councillors had expected much more progress. Nine days – that is what they considered reasonable. Writing, they said, should go faster than expounding on the stage with all its attendant delays – there should be no such delays. Vaishampaayana's estimate of six months floored them. None of them knew how to write – their experience of writing was limited to the occasional report by the customs inspector on the inventory of a caravan. He would read from clay tablets in cryptic notation maintained by the trader's factor for the trader's family and submitted to the city. That report, of hundreds of tablets, took less than a day – nine days seemed more than enough. Six months was excessive – why was the Vyaasa proceeding so slowly?

Vaishampaayana had tried explaining, that writing down a syllable took the same time as speaking four or five syllables; that corrections were inevitable; that the scribe needed to rest; that he, Vaishampaayana, needed to rest; that comparing the task to that of the customs inspector was ludicrous (though he had refrained from saying so explicitly). He had left the meeting, his mind whirling with untoward possibilities, and a sense of vertigo gripping his stomach. He had no idea what he should do – he should talk to Bhargava, but what should he tell Bhargava?

"You're not used to this food, Vais. You look like a python that has swallowed an antelope."

"Bhargava, a short nap after this lunch and I will be fresh once more."

Bhargava pointed to a man walking swiftly in their direction. "There's my assistant Master headed this way – I think my son's caravan must have just come in. His mother has not seen him for six years; I've not seen him for four. His letter from last year said that his next trip would be his first time as Lieutenant to the Master (all of the responsibilities with none of the share). He thought to surprise us, but I'll surprise him."

"Go meet your son, Bhargava. Take him home. Shower him with a father's love. If you can, let's meet in about ten ghatis for a short session before the evening meal. I'll take my nap."

"Yes, I'll come as soon as my wife permits."

Bhargava left. Vaishampaayana went back into his house, to the cooling dark of his room, where he lay down on the rope-strung bed. The bed was one of the few luxuries that had survived the flood and come to the new site. He fell asleep immediately.

850 B.C.E

Bhargava's Son, the Expert Scribe

Kaushambi/Hastinapur circa 850 B.C.E.

Nine ghatis later, Vaishampaayana woke up, almost exactly on time. *It's my special genius,* he would tell his disciples, and they would laugh to humour him. He could go to sleep for a specific period and wake up as planned. He was not as accurate as the Samavedins[96] who could go to sleep at a set point in a recital or ritual, wake up at another precisely set point of the recital, and pick up the recitation. *That's a trained skill, mine is an unasked-for gift.* He cleaned his mouth with cold water from a plain red ceramic jar, spitting into another plain red ceramic jar set into the ground. He washed his face and hands, and then drank a cup. He felt refreshed. His stomach had stopped complaining. He came out of his house and his eyes fell on the line of bricks that formed a foundation for the walls. *Those bricks are crumbling. It has only been a few months – in Hastinapur last year, and maybe even in Panchnad of a thousand years ago, they would be discarded as shoddy work.* Temporary though his unit was, he was beginning to feel proprietary about it.

He went outside. Bhargava was sitting under the ficus with a young man who looked exactly like him.

Bhargava smiled at Vaishampaayana, "Welcome, my friend. You've met my son before." He beamed as he gestured to the young, lightly built man who had stood up with palms joined. "Can you believe this? Look at him – look at my boy, Chandrasekhar. Doesn't he look amazing?"

"Of course, I have and I remember the meeting well. Chandrasekhar, you've hardly changed, still as handsome as your father was when I first met him," Vaishampaayana said.

---

[96] A *Samavedin* was a bard specially trained to use chants to keep accurate time – they were the "chronometers" of Panchnad (in 2000 BCE). This is not the conventional Sanskrit meaning of Samavedin, and I have taken some liberties by creating this meaning. In later times, a Samavedin would be a priest who could recite the Sama Veda, and *keep track of time during rituals.*

Vaishampaayana smiled as he said this. Bhargava had brought the boy, barely sixteen years of age, to Vaishampaayana to register the contract that would apprentice him to his uncle from Takshashila. Vaishampaayana did not know if he should be insulted or honoured – being asked, at his age, to register a contract. That was what young bards did. He had obliged Bhargava. Then, a few months later, the caravan left Hastinapur with the boy – Vaishampaayana had been invited to the send-off party and had brought mango wine from the Kavi Sangha's brewery. The boy drank too much of the sweet poison. His mother had been very upset.

Vaishampaayana continued, "Yes, it's been a long time. My wife still berates me on my poor judgement in pouring wine at your leave-taking."

Bhargava scowled and the young man grinned.

Chandrasekhar said, "You remember! Of course, you would, you are the lord of Kavis, the king of Vedins. I just saw mother today, it has been five years since I left with Uncle's caravan. My apprenticeship ended today!"

"Did you get the release registered? Please do not ask me to do it!"

"No, sir. I will do that later, but Uncle has not come with us. Instead we signed a written version."

Vaishampaayana's head rang with the implications of what the boy had said.

"A written release?" It seemed to Vaishampaayana that the drumbeat of change that had been haunting him through all these meetings with the council had just become louder. "On clay tablets?" *Is he oblivious?*

"Yes, sir. I wrote up the release contract, and Uncle Vijayakartha pretended to grumble when he signed it with his seal."

850 B.C.E

Chandrasekhar reached into a shoulder bag and brought out a cylinder. He unrolled a faintly yellow sheet that he passed to Vaishampaayana. "Look."

"What is this?" Vaishampaayana asked, fingering the sheet lightly. It felt like cloth, but thick and rough. One side of the sheet was covered with black scratches in long lines. *Writing! I hope my moist fingers do not erase the marks. How fragile this is!* This was not a palm-leaf – that was what Bhargava was using. This sheet felt more like felted cotton. *How long will this last? Will it last five hundred years?* The Kavi Sangha had archivists still memorising archived agreements from five hundred years earlier, land contracts that were still relevant. *I cannot conceive of using this for those agreements.*

"It's called pa-pie-raha. Along with baalasuryaa[97] and trapu,[98] it's our biggest import into Takshashila. It has become very popular among the Western Panias of the Egyptian Sea.[99]"

Bhargava was a Vaishya, part of a greater Pania community spread out over the entire face of the earth. That was the Panias' claim to fame and immortality – they covered the earth. *Who could verify such a claim other than another Pania?* The Panias of Takshashila traded heavily with the West – Takshashila prospered as the hub of trade in all directions, and the great university of ages past was no longer there. Kashi and Mathura were the centres of learning now.

"Is papyraha better than the palm-leaf we are using?"

Bhargava said, "Absolutely – it's lighter and easier to write on."

"How long will it last?"

---

97 *Baalasurya* is Lapis lazuli, a deep-blue semi-precious stone that has been prized since antiquity for its intense colour.

98 *Trapu* is tin or tin ore, used to make bronze – by 850 BCE, bronze had been replaced by iron for weapons, but it was still considered decorative, used for statues and domestic utensils.

99 *The Egyptian Sea* is the Mediterranean. The *Western Panias* are the Phoenicians.

"I don't know. The traders who bring it say that the tombs of the ancient kings of Egypt, from more than a thousand years in the past, contain virtually unchanged papyraha."

Vaishampaayana looked at Bhargava. "If Chandrasekhar is right, shouldn't we be using it instead of palm-leaf? Especially considering the difficulty of keeping a palm-leaf document safe every time it is read in public."

Bhargava chuckled, a sound that came out like a horse neighing. *He's nervous,* thought Vaishampaayana. *Why?* Bhargava's genuine laugh was a full-fledged ho-ho-ho from the belly.

"It's too expensive," said Bhargava.

"What do you mean?"

Chandrasekhar said, "Takshashila imports it from a great distance. We don't know how to make it – it is from a plant we do not know of. We've tried to copy it with other plant fibres – coconut palm, banana leaf, even mango leaf, and failed. Each papyraha sheet costs fifty times an equivalent palm-leaf."

Vaishampaayana fingered the papyraha. It was ridged like the reed mats they were sitting on. The ridges had been smoothened out, but they could still be seen. It felt like the matted cotton used as body armour by warriors who could not afford copper or bronze plates. Unfortunately, any colour put on felted cotton spread out like dye and coloured the whole piece – you could not "write" on it. This papyraha was covered with drawn pictures drawn with thin lines like scribbles and nothing had spread or smudged. *It's beautiful. Why can't we make it ourselves? The plant can't be the secret; there must be something else.*

"So, you have the most expensive release contract in this city?"

Bhargava laughed, still nervously. He had had to sit down to calm himself when his son had told him how much it had cost to write the release contract on the papyraha. The boy had returned home with expensive tastes.

"He has the only written release contract in the city. Ignore the cost, my dear friend; it is worth it to have my son come back" He leaned forward, almost whispering. "He can take this job over from me. He would love to do it. He'll be much faster. You will finish sooner."

"Your fingers hurt that much?" Vaishampaayana had never before worked with his old friend and he had begun to look forward to their daily sessions. *Have I underestimated how hard this job will be on the scribe?* He recalled Bhargava's complaints the previous day. *No wonder he is nervous – he is afraid that I will refuse.*

Bhargava grimaced as he clenched and unclenched his right hand. "Yes."

"Can I afford your son's rates?"

Chandrasekhar said, "May I say something?"

Vaishampaayana and Bhargava nodded.

"Uncle, I am stuck here for at least two months waiting for the next caravan to be assembled. That's when I will become too busy to scribe. Until then let me do this. It will be good practice in scribing. I will not charge anything – just feed me lunch. Try me for one day."

Bhargava shook his head slightly when he heard "feed me lunch", but he did not say anything.

"Can you write on palm leaves?" said Vaishampaayana.

"I've done it. I am sure I can."

Bhargava let out a quiet sigh. Vaishampaayana looked with hooded eyes at Bhargava. *He was concerned that his son only knew to write on the papyraha. That explains the nervousness.* Vaishampaayana said to Bhargava. "He does not know the story up to this point. He will be confused and not understand."

Bhargava said, "We'll read what I have written this afternoon. Tomorrow morning he will be ready."

I should have expected this – it was not a spontaneous offer from the boy. The father had planned it. Bhargava had not expected the papyraha and the possibility of being stuck with importing it had made him nervous. If his son could only write on the expensive stuff, he could be a ruined man. I'll have to check him out – I want Bhargava to take credit for our success. I also want to work with my old friend. Vaishampaayana felt his thoughts were jostling and disordered – he had to get them under control.

Vaishampaayana said, "Go back to your mother tonight, my son. Convey my respects and blessings to her. Thank her on my behalf for making her husband and now her son available to me – it is an enormous sacrifice. I'll see you tomorrow. Bhargava, no scribing this afternoon."

Bhargava said. "Vais, don't worry. In exchange for a lost half-day, you will get someone who will write much faster than me. If you continue with the narrative of the morning, I'll watch and I'll help. I will not leave and will resume with you if you decide that Chandrasekhar cannot do the job. I'll even read his work every day and make sure that there are no errors. I'll do that every day of the project."

Vaishampaayana bowed to the inevitable. Writing so much and at such a pace was hurting Bhargava. If he refused the offer, Chandrasekhar might leave on some short trade mission and not be available even if Bhargava was unable to continue. The boy seemed competent and eager to help his father. The scratches on the papyraha looked neat and organised.

"Make sure he is ready tomorrow."

"Of course, of course!" Bhargava said as he left with his son.

The next day Chandrasekhar and Bhargava arrived in the morning, three ghatis after sunrise. Vaishampaayana had just finished his morning rituals and had sat down on the mat under the tree. When his apprentice saw two people arrive, he ran indoors and came back with a mat just in time for Chandrasekhar and Bhargava to sit down. Vaishampaayana smiled at him – the boy was one of the many apprentices whose parents, also bards, had died in the flood. *I've unfinished business with the council – they have not identified the two apprentices they promised me, so we have to find suitable candidates.* The Kavi Sangha was now this boy's home. His response to the arrival of two guests showed that he was conscious of what needed to be done and would do it with alacrity – he had the potential to be much more than a bard. Vaishampaayana's smile faded as he contemplated the sorry state of affairs in Hastinapur and how it might become impossible for the Kavi Sangha to even support the few apprentices he had left.

Bhargava said, "You look sad, my friend. What has happened?"

"Nothing new, Bhargava. I felt touched by the future just now, and it drained hope from me."

Bhargava leaned forward and took his friend's hands in his. "My friend," he said, "To the extent I can, I will help you. Immerse yourself in activities that are useful, and you will cheer up."

Vaishampaayana nodded. "Yes, of course. Are you ready, Chandrasekhar?"

"Yes, Uncle, I certainly am."

Vaishampaayana said, "Yesterday, we stopped after Devavrat told Yudhishthira a brief history of Hastinapur: how it was settled by Hastin; how Samvarana was driven out of the city by Panchala; how Guru Vasishtha and the Kavi Sangha helped him regain his city by creating an army; how his mother killed herself after many years of living with the one-child-per-person[100] law. We also indulged in a digression from the story being told

[100] Strictly speaking, "one child of the same gender as a parent to replace that parent." We will refer to this as the "one-child-per-person" law.

by Devavrat, to events at the Kaurava court that comes from the Archivist in Hastinapur. With this narration, the bard had introduced the Kaurava chief Suyodhana and his close friend Karna, both chafing to continue the hunt for the Pandavas. Having won Indraprastha, Suyodhana and Karna had become confident that they could handle the Pandavas. They could not convince their own council, which remained cautious and preferred to consolidate a victory rather than support a continued hunt."

Chandrasekhar said, "What will they do when they find out that he is a prisoner of the Pandavas?"

"We will get to that. The bard will leave the audience with questions. In the meantime, Devavrat talks to the Archivist Lomaharshana."

850 B.C.E

PART 3.

The Crown Prince

DEVAVRAT REFUSES TO SPEAK

THE PANDAVA CAMP
CIRCA 2000 B.C.E.

Shikhandin was gone.

When Devavrat woke up the next day, he had been moved. He could no longer see the opening to the tent. *Where is Shikhandin?* He thought. Everything else in the tent was as it had been. Shikhandin was absent. The last traces of his stay were gone. Yudhishthira had done as he promised. *My fate,* Devavrat thought, and was surprised when the frog that had lodged in his chest squeezed his heart – he couldn't breathe and tears flooded his eyes. *Self-pity –I thought I had conquered this emotion years ago.* He turned his head the other way but gasped at the fiery blast of pain that caused his stomach and neck and legs to spasm and his heart to beat louder – that reminded him that the arrow was still stuck in him. He turned back and a bolt of lightning slashed its way from his armpit through his heart to his left abdomen. *I am fainting*. When he opened his eyes, Yudhishthira was leaning over him.

"Grandsire! Wake up! Wake up! Ah, good!"

Yudhishthira and his brothers had been raised in exile and had not known what to call him when they were brought home. The memory of that return made him smile. They had called him "grandfather" which had made Satyavati's courtiers giggle nervously, then look around to see if Satyavati was around before admonishing them not to do so. He was their granduncle not their grandfather. Satyavati wanted to make sure they knew that. Over time, they learned to call him grandsire or granduncle like everybody else.

Yudhishthira must have been waiting for me to wake up. That was one more difference between him and his cousin Suyodhana. Yudhishthira behaved as if he cared. Suyodhana behaved as if he was the King, and was above caring.

The Archivist was sitting a short distance away. Yudhishthira gestured towards him and said to Devavrat, "You've met Lomaharshana the Archivist."

"Yes," said Devavrat.

"You're feeling rested? Have you had a morning meal?"

"Not yet," Devavrat said. "I am not feeling hungry."

Yudhishthira frowned at the Archivist. Lomaharshana said, "I'll get him a meal, sir." and left.

Yudhishthira said, "What I got from yesterday's narration was that your disagreements with your father began very early. Were these disagreements the cause of your father's decision to disinherit you? Why did you agree to his outrageous request? What role did Satyavati play in it – she was young, a girl, barely a woman. How did she manage to convince Shantanu to make her son the *yuvraj?*"

Devavrat looked out of the door. The flap was blowing in the wind – the season when cold winds blew down from the Himalayas had begun. The flapping merged with the beating of his heart. *Why do I have to tell this story?*

2000 B.C.E

"Yudhishthira. There was no estrangement between my father and me on policy. The policy I implemented in later years was the policy that my father and I agreed on."

"He still demoted you and denied you the kingdom. Why?"

"It wasn't over policy."

"Then, why?"

"I don't want to talk about it."

"Your father's action was the most controversial of his reign. People still talk about it – the injustice done to you by your father. Some people even claim that it is the cause of Hastinapur's problems. We are suffering as punishment for the injustice done to you."

"Yudhishthira! I do not want to talk about it."

"It is possible your father had good reason for it and I just do not know. I cannot believe that it was mere whim. Why not tell the world your side of the story?"

Devavrat could feel his heart beating faster, much faster than the fluttering of the door-flap. *Why was Yudhishthira persisting in these questions? There was only one thing to do.* He tried to turn his face around, but his shoulders would not move, and the wound protested with sharp shocks. He closed his eyes.

"If it wasn't policy, what could it be?" Yudhishthira said to the silent Devavrat.

Devavrat's eyes remained closed.

A sound from the door showed the Archivist with a ceramic bowl of soup and a small plate of seasoned rice with yoghurt. He looked at Devavrat who had his eyes closed. Yudhishthira was frowning.

The Archivist said, "What happened, sir?"

"He just stopped talking and closed his eyes. He did not want to answer my question."

"What question?"

"Why he gave up the kingdom to Satyavati's children."

"Hmm…" Lomaharshana put the food down next to Devavrat. He stood up and walked out of the tent and gestured to Yudhishthira to follow him. When they were both outside, he whispered, "The Vyaasa is coming this afternoon. Ask him."

"The Vyaasa? Why haven't I been told of his visit?"

"It is not a public visit – he does not want the news broadcast. I don't know if he would know why, but I hope so."

Yudhishthira squinted in the sunlight. "Hmm… I must have angered the Regent. You are right, the Vyaasa should know if anybody does. I would be unhappy if the Regent stops talking because of me."

"I'll see what I can do, sir."

"When the Vyaasa comes he may be able to talk to him as a friend."

Yudhishthira left and Lomaharshana went back in.

Devavrat looked away when the door-flap opened. He did not give Lomaharshana a chance to speak.

"I am tired today. Leave me alone."

"The Vyaasa will be visiting us today. He expressed a desire to see you."

Shukla and Devavrat were old friends, but communication between them had become infrequent. As Shukla became more influential in the Kavi Sangha, finally becoming its head, it became harder to meet as they used to – every meeting was fraught with meaning to the people around them. *It will be good to meet without all that.* There was a hitch – what was Shukla doing here in the enemy camp? The Kavi Sangha supported Devavrat's plan – *had that changed? Were they double-dealing? Why?*

"Shukla? Here?"

"Yes, sir."

"It will be good to see him. Wake me up if he wishes to see me."

"Yes, sir." Lomaharshana stood up and bowed with joined palms. "By your leave, sir," he said, as he left.

***

Kaushambi settlement, circa 850 BCE

Chandrasekhar said, "I am confused – what happened? Why does Devavrat refuse to talk?"

"Be patient," Vaishampaayana said. "It will all be explained."

"It's an unexpected development. How are you going to explain this sudden change? The change in Yudhishthira is also surprising. Who else could know about Devavrat's life? What could evoke so much anger or pain?"

"Well, Chandrasekhar, that comes next."

Vaishampaayana smiled at Chandrasekhar, who grinned back. *I've missed narrating stories ever since the flood – it feels good when the audience gets engaged,* Vaishampaayana thought. *Bhargava's son is responding well.* He sipped water from the small earthen jar by his side, and resumed his discourse.

Shukla's Visit

The Pandava Camp
Circa 2000 B.C.E.

Lomaharshana could not sit still. He stood in the shade of the banyan tree that towered over the north entrance of the camp, the entrance formed by tying to one side the roots hanging from the canopy. It was mid-afternoon and he had been waiting for the Vyaasa. The Regent had shut up, for the day he said, and had refused to listen, much less to talk. The guards looked at him as he paced around the tree – they knew who he was so they left him alone.

What he was planning to do was a break in normal protocol. The King would expect to be the first person to meet the Vyaasa. The Vyaasa was not just another head of a guild – as the head of the Kavi Sangha, he wielded tremendous influence on the marketplace, and as the intellectual descendant of Vasishtha, he was the chief advisor to the rulers of Hastinapur. The Vyaasa was close to the Regent, believed to be a close, even only, friend. The capture of the Regent could change many things. *Why had the Vyaasa sent word to cooperate with the King?* It was the first time that the Vyaasa had used the renegade group of Kavis in the Pandava camp, and that could be interpreted as approval. From that point of view, the Regent's refusal to talk was a disaster. *Did I make a mistake in leaving the King alone with the Regent? What had happened while he was gone? The Vyaasa will hold me responsible. He could withdraw his tentative approval of our work.* Lomaharshana had to talk to him first.

There was a flurry of movement at the gate as the guards came out and opened the small gate. The Vyaasa came in. He was by himself. Lomaharshana had expected the Vyaasa to come with the usual entourage of helpers, and onagers[101] drawing carts. There would be a small circus enacted by the guards of inspecting everything and chatting with the driver and the cook – that would have allowed Lomaharshana to talk with the Vyaasa without interruption. The Vyaasa was late and he appeared to have come by himself. *Had he walked?* Lomaharshana wondered. *All the way from Hastinapur? There would be no circus. He would not have much time to present his problem.*

[101] The onager is a species of wild ass found from West Asia to India – it was one of the first equids domesticated for hauling carts.

Lomaharshana went up to him and bowed, his palms joined, "Welcome, sir!"

"Ah, Lomaharshana. It is a pleasure to be welcomed by you at the gate. Is the King not well?"

Lomaharshana looked towards the leader's tent, and his face darkened. The King himself was coming towards them – there was no time to explain.

The Vyaasa interpreted Lomaharshana's quick look. "Difficulties with the King?"

Lomaharshana nodded. The Vyaasa smiled as Yudhishthira came up to him.

Yudhishthira said, "Welcome, sir. You visit here after a long time. We are grateful for your years of advice, even support. The Council awaits you."

"Thank you for the welcome, my boy. I would like a quiet visit without any public acknowledgement. I will meet only the very few. I want no ceremonies."

Yudhishthira sighed and then pursed his lips. Worry lines flashed across his forehead. He said. "I'll give instructions right away, sir. We'll cancel all the public meetings – none have been announced, as we did not know the exact time of your arrival."

"Thank you, that is excellent," said the Vyaasa, squelching any hopes that Yudhishthira might have had about changing his mind. "I heard that the Regent might be a prisoner here."

"Yes, sir."

"Is he alright? Has he been injured?"

"The doctors say it is a fatal wound that they can do very little to heal. In any case, he cannot move. I'll take you to him right away, sir."

"It is late today. I'll see him tomorrow morning."

2000 B.C.E

"Yes, sir. We have prepared a tent and a bed for you." Yudhishthira led the Vyaasa to the tent prepared for him. It was large, unusually so for a tent that had just one occupant. The land sloped slightly from east to west and the entrance therefore was at the western end. A trench had been dug all around a rectangular floor about ten hastas[102] across and eight hastas deep. Three rows of poles were embedded into the ground, the outer row of poles in the trench and the two inner rows being slightly higher. The poles were tied at the top to crossbars that created a rigid framework for the roof with a slope from the front down to the back. In addition, ropes of sisal extended from the middle poles to the outer ones and cross ropes created a web. The web was overlaid with large felted cotton squares that were tied to the ropes. The walls were made with cloth or felt hanging from the ropes. The floor was rammed earth, a luxury that came about because this camp had been occupied for many weeks – a temporary tent that was disassembled every night would not have such a floor. In addition, it was covered with felt, a luxury extended to the Vyaasa. The trench was a traditional feature – the permanent houses in Panchnad had a similar trench for sewage. It could help deal with the rare rainstorm. The trench was not intended to be rainproof – it was customary not to go to war during the rainy season, so that was not seen as necessary. One corner served as the toilet. A hole had been dug in the ground and a ceramic pot with a number of drainage holes in its bottom placed in the hole. The dug out soil was mounded to the side, with a small wooden paddle stuck in it, used as a scoop to cover sewage and other trash. A small bucket of water was nearby with a large flat round paving stone that provided a place to wash face, hands, and legs – the water drained into the trench. A luxury prepared for the Vyaasa was a low bench with a tile

---

[102] *Hasta* is the same as the cubit (the length of the arm from the elbow to the tip of the middle finger, approximately eighteen inches). A more exact definition is needed when used as a standard as each person will have a "personal hasta" measure. See Endnotes.

top that covered the hole. This was short-term accommodation, and if they moved on in an orderly manner, the pot would be removed and emptied into a field trench, and the hole filled. The trench around the tent would also be filled.

The tent contained a sleeping area along the side furthest from the toilet area. The sleeping area had a few more pieces of felt. A roll made of cotton cloth sewn along the long edge and stuffed with cotton was a pillow. The Vyaasa's tent had a wooden slab cut from the trunk of a tree of approximately two cubits in diameter polished on both sides – this served multiple purposes for it could be a seat for a visitor, a table to eat off, or plan for a campaign. Near the toilet area was a bucket of water. A flat rectangular paving stone provided a hearth. The Vyaasa washed his face and limbs and lay down for a brief rest – Yudhishthira would want to talk during the late afternoon break.

Rest eluded him. He had heard that Devavrat Bhishma had been wounded badly and was dead; then he heard that he was alive but on his deathbed; and then, that he was dead again. In his mind, there was not a single person, but two – he had come here in the hope that he could confirm that Devavrat was alive, but he could not shake off the feeling that Bhishma's death would be convenient. In his heart he wanted Devavrat alive. What of Bhishma? Did he want Bhishma dead? Bhishma's death would free the Vyaasa from the debt he owed Devavrat, debts he could not ignore. Now he found Devavrat to be still alive but fatally wounded and not likely to last more than a few days. That Devavrat was still alive meant the Vyaasa could see him one last time. In recent years their interactions had become formalised, and he missed the informality they had enjoyed as young men – he could share this feeling with Devavrat, however much he may have become Bhishma.

It was not as though they did not have strategic issues on the table. His last interaction with Suyodhana and Karna had been wasted effort – the two behaved like a pack of hunting dogs that had cornered an injured doe and would not be pulled away. If Devavrat were no longer around, Shukla would feel less of an obligation to Hastinapur. Right now, he owed a lot to the Regent of Hastinapur and little to Indraprastha and its allies.

Lomaharshana, the chief Archivist for Indraprastha and leader of the small group of bards in the Pandavas' camp, had broken protocol to find some time to talk to him – he was worried and needed reassurance, some guidance, and if possible, better direction. That group was an unexpected treasure that was paying strategic dividends at no cost. If Hastinapur lost this unnecessary war, the Kavi Sangha would survive as the advisor to the Pandavas; if the Kavi Sangha survived this war, it would need leaders like Lomaharshana. All they had to do was survive.

Sleep was fitful and Shukla felt barely rested when he woke to the sound of the bells hanging outside his tent, but as was usual with him he sat up fully awake. It was Yudhishthira.

"Come in, my son. Come in," he said.

Yudhishthira pushed the flap aside and came in with joined palms, "Jaya! We seek your blessings, honoured Guru."

"Live long, my son! You have them a thousand-fold."

"Are you comfortable, sir? Is there anything I can do for you?"

"You've done very well, Yudhishthira. I am comfortable – there is nothing that should concern you. I have not had a chance to see your brothers – are they doing well? What news of your wife, the Queen of Panchala – how is she?"

"Honoured Guru, your concern for my brothers and wife is much appreciated. My brothers are doing well – I see them every day. They have enquired about you, and I hope you get a chance to see them. Panchaali, of course, we don't see everyday. We send messages as needed, but it is a risky venture getting through

Suyodhana's troops and Dushasana's spies. They patrol all the paths leading from the old city that come towards us. Please share your news with us, sir – how is it with you and your sister, my grandmother Queen Satyavati? Tell me how my mother fares? My uncles Dharmateja and Dhritarashtra – are they well?"

"I am glad to hear that all of you are well. Come closer, Yudhishthira; do not stand so far away. Sit here. Near me, so that I need not be so loud. I will talk to you as an advisor, not as your master – I am not the King, you are."

Yudhishthira came in and sat facing the Vyaasa, who sat up to look at him.

The Vyaasa said, "Now tell me what this is about."

"It's regarding Granduncle Devavrat. He agreed to work with the Archivist to memorise his story. Then, when I asked him about something, he stopped and has refused to cooperate."

"What did you ask him?"

"To explain how Satyavati became his stepmother and convinced his father to disinherit him. Why did he accept the decision? Were there other differences in policy? He said there were no such differences. He refused to provide any further detail. His answers were terse, and his attitude was brusque. Finally, he refused to answer any questions. When I insisted, he stopped and told the Archivist to come back the next day."

"Hmm... why did you insist?"

"There are so many questions to which only he can provide answers. What was Shantanu's plan, and how did it differ from Devavrat's actions? Did the crown make a difference – if Devavrat had been the King, would he have followed different policies? What led my father to disagree to the extent of giving up the crown and exiling himself? These differences and what they meant – we must understand them."

Yudhishthira stopped.

"Do you want answers to these questions? That I can give you."

"Answers without context are useless, sir."

"You are right. Your father's differences with Devavrat were many and deep, but it was before I became the Vyaasa. I spent much of that time in Takshashila. But between King Shantanu and Prince Devavrat – I can assure you that there were no differences in policy between them. Not even when Devavrat became Regent after Shantanu died."

"How do you know, Guruji?

"I was there. Satyavati is, after all, my sister. Devavrat became my friend when Satyavati married Shantanu; I know why he declined the crown. I had a small if unfortunate part in it. I could have kept aloof; instead, I added unnecessary and unfortunate complexity to what might have been a simple life. I am not proud of my role."

"The reason or reasons he declined the crown – how did they influence policy, if they did?"

"They did, but not the way you would expect. My advice to you – avoid this matter with the Regent."

"Skip the story of his disinheritance completely?"

"No, you do not have to do that. Just do not ask Devavrat. I will tell you, and the Archivist can listen and include it in his archive. Let me get ready. Ask the Archivist to come here – I would like to speak to him."

Yudhishthira gestured to one of his guard. "Go tell the Archivist that the Vyaasa is ready for him." Then he took his leave of the Vyaasa.

The Archivist arrived in half a ghati.

The Vyaasa came directly to the point. "The Regent Devavrat will not willingly tell of what led to his vow and of

Queen Satyavati's marriage to his father. I played a small part, so I am familiar with it," the Vyaasa said. "It would have been best if the Regent's story had been told in his own words, but I do not expect that he will do so. You will supplement the Regent's narrative with this story that I will narrate."

"Where does it fit, sir?" asked the Archivist.

"It is about the marriage of Satyavati and Shantanu and of Devavrat's vow."

"I am ready, sir. When should we start?"

"Shortly, I will go to a meeting with the King's closest councillors. The King is eager to get started on that meeting. I expect it will last most of the afternoon. Most likely, we will have two ghatis before the evening meal."

Lomaharshana bowed and turned to the door. As he was stepping out, the Vyaasa said, "You have done very well, Lomaharshana. Your team, too."

Lomaharshana turned and bowed again and left. *Praise from the Vyaasa was a rare thing.* He felt lighter as though a burden he had been bearing had miraculously transported itself.

When the Vyaasa returned from the meeting, he found the Archivist waiting for him. It was past time for the late-afternoon snack – the cook's assistant from the camp kitchen had brought a bowl of fruit lightly mashed with mead, lime, and water, and it was sitting untouched by his bed. The Archivist waited as the Vyaasa carefully picked out the bobbing crab apples out and placed them by the side.

"Lomaharshana, you will get real apples when you are sent to Takshashila. If this war ever ends. They almost rival the mango though they are very different experiences. For now, enjoy these small tart cousins."

The evening meal was announced. Even as he got ready to visit the kitchen, a meal was brought to him and the

Archivist. "The King's order, sir," said the meal carrier. It was a traditional light meal of rice and salty buttermilk. They sat outside the Vyaasa's tent as the sky turned dark. A bright band of stars spanned the sky – it was the eleventh day after the full moon, and the moon would be rising closer to daybreak. It would be a dark night, one for reflecting on the stars. An attendant came by and lit a small fire in a pit a few feet from the entrance of the tent. A few sprinkles of citrus oil would keep insects away.

A couple of vighatis later, Yudhishthira, the King, came by.

"Lomaharshana tells me that you will be narrating the story of Devavrat's renunciation. I thought I would like to hear it first-hand."

"Yes," said the Vyaasa Shukla.

The Disaster and the Terrible Vow

The Pandava Camp
circa 2000 B.C.E.

"'I renounce my rights to Kingship…I will not marry, I will not have children, I will not make love to any woman.' Those were the words by which Devavrat created this world– he set in motion a chain of events that led to this war," said the Vyaasa Shukla.

"The fires of Devavrat's anger were stoked by a woman and a king. The king was his father Shantanu; the woman was his stepmother-to-be Satyavati; the public cause was the King's willingness to circumvent his own laws to satisfy his desire for Satyavati; of private causes, there were many. It is likely that if the King had not made those laws in the first place none of these consequences would have come about."

"Guruji, I am puzzled," Yudhishthira said. "What did the King's laws have to do with this renunciation?"

"Everything," Shukla said. "That is what I will explain."

"If the laws were so responsible – responsible for everything as you said, I must know why they were made in the first place. Otherwise the narrative is incomplete."

Shukla nodded slowly. "I was hoping to finish in a couple of ghatis – but the story of the laws is long, for it is the story of the Disaster. We will need most of the day tomorrow to satisfy your request."

"That is acceptable. Begin with the story of the Disaster."

Thus, in answering the King's question, Shukla narrated the history of the Disaster:

"The Disaster took place in multiple acts. The first act was the shaking of the earth. Prithvi shook. It was in the time of Pratipa, great-grandson of Arugvat, the grandson of Kuru. Some said that such shaking showed Prithvi's anger with humanity. The truth of this accusation was incontestable for there was always something that could have angered Prithvi – the Earth is a capricious mother who will hug her children on one occasion and turn against them in an instant. That must be what happened here. The earth shook and it changed the world.

"The star-gazers have their own language – the quakes, they said, marked the end of the Age of the Bull and the beginning of the Age of the Ram. They pointed to a starry outline in the sky – that is a bull, they said; then next to it they point out the outline a ram. If a wise man is one who can see through obscurity, the star-watchers certainly qualify as wise. I frequently wonder, why these two animals and not any other? Do not all animals have a body with four legs, a head and a mouth? If you can see one animal in the sky, why would someone else not see a different animal? No matter, it is their mystery. They will tell you that the change of Age denoted by the stars is a subtle observation first made by a Samavedin and verified by the other Samavedins. Samavedins are bards who specialise in maintenance of clocks – managers of time, if you will. All bards study the Samavedins' art, but only the most skilled with the greatest fortitude, patience, and focus, go deep into that art. A sad consequence of their training is that many, many Samavedins go mad as they age – obsessed by incessant measurement they become even more obsessed, they become counters who see numbers in everything. The Samavedins say, and there is no cause to disbelieve them, that this cosmic observation has taken centuries to make and it could only have been made because Samavedins, too, maintain archives of their observations. When asked about the significance of the transit from the Age of the Bull to that of the Ram, they defer to the astrologers who see future history in the stars – the Samavedin measures time, not history. In any case, the heavens moved from one Age to the next and shook the world; the world changed.

"It is the case though that neither the priests nor the philosophers, neither the star-gazers nor the star-readers predicted any particulars of the Disaster. The shaking of the earth surprised everybody.

"Prithvi shook. The river Yamuna, the great tributary of the Sarasvati withdrew her blessings from the people of Panchnad, turned away to flow east at the northern ridge of the Aravalli range. The river Sutudri, which split into a hundred streams on the way to join the Sarasvati, abandoned those channels. It no longer went south after it emerged from the Himalayas – it turned sharply to the west to join one of the tributaries of the Sindhu many yojanas away. Kàalindini, less than a yojana away, lost its water supply and in time would be abandoned. The River Drishadvati, rain-fed from the western slopes of the Aravalli range, flowing south of the old Yamuna continued to flow as it did and arrived to the meeting place with the Sarasvati to find that it had been abandoned. It could only bequeath to the Sarasvati a fraction of the water that great river once enjoyed.

Other tributaries flowing down with the monsoon rains that fell on the Aravalli range continued to feed the Sarasvati. It was not enough. The die had been cast and showed *kali,* the losing throw.

"The consequences in the east were tremendous. That year the east was flooded. The southwestern corner of Kuru territory, once called Khandavaprastha, which had been arid scrubland in the rain shadow of the Aravalli range, became a wooded swamp. The Yamuna's water flowed along the eastern foothills of the Aravalli range until the Sahyadri range was visible and the land sloped up to the south. The Yamuna then turned to the east (many yojanas south of the Ganga at this point) and entered forested regions populated by new Naga settlers along the banks of previously monsoon-fed rivers now overflowing with the snow-fortified Yamuna. The floodwaters then continued parallel to the Ganga until they reached the Charmanavati River emerging from the Vindhyas. The Yamuna-augmented Charmanavati followed its old bed until it merged with the Ganga at the place we call Prayag. Nowadays this stretch is called the Yamuna. For many years there was no fixed riverbed in the upper reaches of the river – it was a flood plain and the situation was very unstable. Over the years, as the river made its way through the Naga-occupied forests a stable bed was created. The occasional depression collected water to become a pond; some of these ponds grew larger to form lakes. For many generations, though, the Yamuna remained an unstable rogue river.

"The Kauravas continued to call the river by its old name, the Yamuna. The first region that was traversed by the new Yamuna had few inhabitants, mostly a small number of Naga bands. The Nagas dealt with the new situation as they had always done when displaced by floods or other natural threats to their settlements – they moved to a new location, burned a new clearing for their plantings – started afresh. Their biggest problem was that they might not have food stores that would help them through a new crop cycle. In this case, the availability of water in an otherwise arid region would increase the arable land, but only after the river settled down. In a few years dormant seeds sprouted, grass and reeds appeared, followed by tadpoles, insects, small fish, and then, finally large fish. When the fish became plentiful, the river dolphin, a gift of the mother-goddess, would appear and it would be time for the Nagas to return. Many Naga bands on the banks would switch to fishing, like the Meena-Nagas in the northeast of Jambudvipa who lived by rivers.

"Downstream from where the Yamuna merged with the Ganga, a few yojanas from our settlement here in Kaushambi, the increased flow almost doubled the width of the Ganga. Much of this widening was towards the flat northern bank as the southern bank sloped up to the Vindhyas. This was the territory bordering Rakshasa country that saw conflict when Naga bands expanded into this area and met Rakshasa bands doing the same. Both sides traditionally avoided such conflicts by turning away, so a sparsely occupied no-man's land extended from this juncture to Laghu Nagapura where a river emerging from the plateau, called the *Hiranyaganga,* joined the Ganga. From that point on, Rakshasas were found on both sides of the river, but the added water of the Yamuna split Rakshasa society into two – one on the north side and the other on the south side of the Ganga – they found it harder to get together and interacted much less. The settlement at Laghu Nagapura flooded and was moved to higher land.

"Back in the west, the Sarasvati dried up slowly, its waters disappearing into the sand at its southernmost point just before the point at which it used to split to form a delta to the sea. A slight ridge about five yojanas from the sea had created the last of the Sarasvati lakes. The water would flow over the ridge and find multiple paths to the sea. When the water level in the lake fell permanently below the ridge, the saltwater of the sea moved into as much of the delta as possible but was still a long way from the lake. The land in between was dry and salty, and would become a salt-water marsh in the rainy season. The lake itself dried up slowly as the Sarasvati brought in less and less water.

"The other lakes that had dotted the river's path to the sea also received less and less water and slowly dried up. The southernmost lakes dried up first; then the other upstream lakes that dotted the Sarasvati also dried up as the stored water evaporated and was fitfully replaced by monsoon water. The southernmost settlements were abandoned first. Some émigrés went north towards other Panchnad towns, where they were initially helped but as the magnitude of the disaster became clear, they were asked to move on. Some went to the northwest towards the towns on the Sindhu, in particular the great city of Moolasthan, but here too they only received temporary help as the northwestern towns struggled to cope with their own floods and shifting rivers. Those émigrés kept going northwest through the passes that lead to the Kubha River, where they stayed and settled. Some émigrés went south to Saurashtra and then proceeded down the shores of the Western Sea.

"The émigrés who went north past the other Panchnad towns reached the place where the Yamuna and Drishadvati once joined – now there was only the trickle of the rain-fed Drishadvati. The Sutudri used to flow through innumerable channels – its swift flow prevented it from depositing silt but also left shallow beds covered with rocks and gravel rather than soil. The Drishadvati, though slower, did not bring down much silt. Agriculture was not feasible. The emigres then went east towards Hastinapur, expecting help but worsening the situation there. Having come that far they stopped, as the prognosis was poor – the land on either side of the Ganga was clayey, difficult to till; they also would have to become pioneers opening up untested lands, which they considered a drop in status; and some of the land was occupied by Nagas who would object to losing their land. The Panchnad refugees did not want war and nor did the Nagas – they were not eager to start a war as they did not know what armed conflict might bring.

2000 B.C.E

"From Saurashtra a large faction went north along the eastern side of the Aravalli range. In the beginning, there was a belief, a hope, rather, that the Yamuna would return to its original bed and the Sarasvati cities would regain their wealth and power. That hope faded as the years passed. Moolasthan and the cities on the Sindhu were not in a position to help the Sarasvati refugees – the Sutudri's water had increased the flow in the Sindhu significantly and all along the river, embankments had overflowed, and the river had moved to a different channel. The disruption was small in comparison to the lot of the Sarasvati settlements, but the Sindhu towns could not be of much help.

"Notwithstanding all the differences between the older Panchnad towns and Hastinapur (militarised with a standing army, patriarchal, ruled by warriors not traders, and so on), there had always been a substantial faction in Hastinapur that thought of the city as an outpost of Panchnad – many citizens still considered themselves the children of Bharata or the children of Puru, who settled by the Sarasvati, and not merely the children of Kuru who had secured the power of Hastinapur on the Ganga. The Kauravas, who ruled Hastinapur, and their leader Pratipa, recognised that the cities of Panchnad were collapsing and were concerned that Hastinapur would collapse along with them. At this point, the Kavi Sangha concluded that the changes in the Sarasvati were permanent and the Sarasvati settlements were doomed and would never return to their former greatness. Hastinapur was already their stellar success – they made a critical decision to abandon Panchnad and move to Hastinapur and begin the process of recreating an urban civilisation.

"First, a key action was felt necessary – Pratipa[103] was persuaded to justify his name and formally declare the independence of Hastinapur from its Kaalindini parent and from the Puru homeland; independence too from the Sarasvati,

---

[103] *Pratipa* means "rebel" or "adversary" (among other meanings).

to be replaced by a permanent commitment to the Ganga. The significance of that declaration was that he was formally reneging on the implicit promise to support the parent settlement in times of need, or to follow their ways of conflict resolution. He would be free of commitments to submit to a matriarchy. As such, this made it possible for Hastinapur to treat the refugees differently from its own population and the Nagas. Though supported by the Kavi Sangha, Pratipa's declaration was not welcomed and caused much debate – ultimately he compromised by postponing complete emancipation, leaving it to his son to complete the break-up.

"Of Pratipa's three sons, the oldest, Bahlika, objected to the Kavi Sangha-inspired decision and he decided not to accept the leadership. He led a batch of refugees to the Northwest, crossed the Sindhu and entered Gandhara via the Kuberakuta[104] road. They intended to return to the old tradition of rule by traders rather than warriors. His group of emigrants crossed the Kubha River into a plateau north of Gandhara. There they discovered that collapse of civilisations was not limited to Panchnad – all over the West, drought and famine had devastated ancient trading networks; wars had become ubiquitous; the people they were expecting to settle with were themselves impoverished by the changing climate and the collapse of trade. Further migration west would have to be postponed by a few generations. They went as far west as they could and named their settlements and themselves Baahlika. They sent word back of this discouraging development – this only made Kururashtra look like the only alternative to all of Panchnad.

"Pratipa's second son Devapi was declared *Yuvraj,* heir apparent."

It was getting very dark. The fire would need more wood if they intended to go on for longer. The camp security captain

104 *Kuberakuta* meaning "Kubera's Fort", is the Khyber Pass. See Endnotes.

had already come by once reminding them that their fire might give the enemy some hint of where they were – this was a mock threat for they were well within Yadava-controlled territory and any approaching force would be marked long before it was close enough to see their little campfire.

"I will continue again tomorrow morning," Shukla said "After the narration, I will visit my friend."

With these words, they went to their separate tents.

Hastinapur and Mathura

The Pandava Camp
circa 2000 B.C.E.

The Vyaasa Shukla had just finished his morning rituals when the bells outside his tent jingled. It was Lomaharshana.

"Excuse me, sir," he said. "The King has asked that we meet in his tent. I have come to lead you there, when you are ready."

"That I am, my son," Shukla said.

A few vighatis later, they were seated around a wooden board set into the ground. A cup of water and one of jambul juice was placed at each place. The Vyaasa took a sip of the water.

"I'll continue where I left off yesterday. Do you have any questions?" he said.

"A few," said the King. "I'll ask them at the end, for they have to do with how the Kavi Sangha develops policy."

Shukla smiled, then sighed, "Hard questions, undoubtedly."

The Vyaasa continued, "In less than a century after Samvarana's return to Hastinapur, with the creation of Hastinapur's standing army, a patriarchal government and patrilineal inheritance of power was entrenched in Hastinapur. Pratipa's declaration of partial emancipation from Panchnad, followed by the use of the army to control the behaviour of immigrants, extended Hastinapur's rule – it became universally recognised as the hegemon of the stretch of land from the western bank of the Ganga to the fluctuating eastern bank of the Yamuna and from the northern foothills of the Himalayas to an undefined boundary with Naga allies to the south. This region came to be called Kururashtra. Trade had been disrupted during the first part of the crisis, but people expected that when the crisis was over, trade would rebound, and normalcy would be restored, with Kururashtra in full control of trade between the east and the west.

"The Panchnad towns were emptying and a million people were migrating in all directions. To the north and west were other cities that shared their culture, but the earthquakes and great changes in the flow of the Sindhu had hit them hard as well. The émigrés who went south established themselves in Saurashtra where the rivers Narmada and Tapti made the land productive. Further south, along the coast of the Western Sea, they established ports and cities that could attempt to continue the commerce that had once been the life-blood of Panchnad.

"For all its promise, Saurashtra was suffering from many years of drought. Being monsoon fed, the water in the Narmada River varied between extremes, but it had a large watershed and potentially would be rich land. For the time being, it could not support a large population. Many migrants, led by the Yadavas[105] of Panchnad, went northeast along the eastern slopes of the Aravalli range in the direction of Hastinapur. The land here was hilly and unpromising. Where it was flat, there was not much water. The Yadavas continued north and east between the Aravalli range to the left and the Sahyadris to the right into the valley of the Charmanavati. They then followed the Charmanavati River into the Gangetic plain to the meet the new River Yamuna. This land, receiving both rainwater and snowmelt, looked like promising territory.

105 *Yadava* means "a descendant of Yadu".

"Since the river was unstable, the Yadavas tried to go upstream as well as downstream in search of a place appropriate for settlement. Upstream, the river was still not stable and the situation looked bad. When they tried to go downstream, they met and conflicted with the Nagas near the river and with Rakshasas in the forest. They compromised as well as they could. They wanted to establish a city, to be called Mathura, the "City of Honey".

"The Yadavas made many attempts to establish Mathura. The river's constant shifting was only one problem – opposition from Nagas and Rakshasas never ended.

"The last group of emigrants from Panchnad was from the upstream cities. The population classified themselves into the Pauravas, the most numerous, the most ancient and the poorest clan; the powerful Bhaaratas who ran most city councils; and a small sprinkling of Kauravas who were largely up-and-coming traders. These refugees could go north along the old bed of the Yamuna past the point where the Yamuna's course had changed and cross it closer to the Himalayan foothills. There was an ancient bridge, but the bridge had been damaged during the earthquake. The local Naga fisher-folk, also called Meenas (or Meena-Nagas), ferried the refugees over in exchange for textiles, weapons, ornaments, and jewellery. Then, going east, they would first come to the Ganga and continuing southeast along the right bank they would reach Hastinapur, where they would request refuge for they were family. The familial relationship meant that the request could not be refused. The declaration of emancipation was intended to do that, if enforced.

"Pratipa's son Devapi[106] did not have the stomach to deny refuge to the wandering refugees. The Kavi Sangha suggested a tough stance. Hastinapur did not have the resources to support all the refugees, so a bad situation was becoming worse. Reclusive to begin with, Devapi became more isolated when he

---

106 *Devapi* means "friend of the gods" or "beloved of the gods".

rejected Kavi Sangha help. Increasingly, he attempted to solve all problems by himself and failed. The common opinion was that Saturn, the Lord of Suffering and the Arbiter of Fate, infected him at an early age. This could have been true for he was often melancholic and pessimistic.

"One day, Devapi's clothes were found abandoned by the edge of Khandavaprastha. The King was nowhere to be found. A message had been left with an attendant – the King had abdicated. He did not want to do it publicly as he knew they would try to dissuade him. He wished his brother well.

"The third son of Pratipa, Shantanu, became the leader of Hastinapur. Shantanu realised the magnitude of the refugee problem and sought the help of the Kavi Sangha."

"Why did the Kavi Sangha not propose actions that had worked in the past – create settlements on empty land, grow their own food, look out for themselves?" Yudhishthira said. "Why invent new policies, especially dire ones?"

"This was well before I came to Hastinapur as a young man," Shukla said "The Vyaasa before Parashara was Bharadvaja, who was considered a pragmatic realist – he responded to the disinclination of the refugees to perform the actions you describe by proposing positive and negative inducements."

"Pardon me, sir," Lomaharshana said, "what do you mean by disinclination of the refugees? What did they refuse to do?"

"Everything! There were many, many reasons for their not wanting to be pioneers."

"Everything? What does that mean?"

"It was the people, the land, and knowledge. That covers almost everything. By 'people', I mean their view of themselves; by 'land', I mean the refugees' unfamiliarity with the land and its attributes; and, by 'knowledge', I mean their skills as pioneers and the tools they used."

2000 B.C.E

"Please elaborate, sir. This provides only a glimmer of understanding."

"Yes, I can elaborate on the reasons for the failure of the policy.

"First, the people. They felt they were being asked to displace an existing population. The existing population, the Nagas, consisted of nomadic, loosely allied bands that did not build permanent settlements and occupied central and eastern Jambudvipa, that is, the plain of the Ganga from the foothills of the Himalayas and points south. These bands were matriarchal, very much like the Panchnadis had been – the matriarch ruled as the leader of the band with the help of the other women. The band members were other women and the children as well as a number of men who had been invited to join. The men who were organised in bands called themselves the 'Snake people', which became *Naga* in the Paurava speech of the west. There was fear that the Nagas would not allow any settlement on *their* land.

"Second, the land. Even if the Nagas were amenable to sharing their traditional lands, the methods of farming known in Panchnad could not be used in the new land. The land of the Ganga was heavily forested and the Ganga was the year-round source of water, but irrigation systems would have to be constructed to sustain agriculture far from the rivers. In Panchnad, with the many lakes on the Sarasvati, it was easy to irrigate farms. The situation was different in Kururashtra. The Aravalli range, which started at the eastern end of the Saurashtra peninsula and went northwest, paralleled the Sarasvati along its east bank. As it went north, the range tapered to a ridge where it met the Yamuna. At that point, the Yamuna turned west to join the Sarasvati. The south and east side of the Aravalli range was protected from the monsoon clouds that came from the southwest in the summer. The monsoons were the sole source of rain in all of Jambudvipa. As a result the eastern foothills and hillside of the Aravalli range made for a wretched land, eternally dry and unproductive.

"The Aravalli range also made it difficult to communicate from the eastern foothills of the Aravalli range to the Sarasvati settlements on the western side. A new settlement on the eastern side could only be reached from Panchnad by entering Paurava territory north of the ridge, and then heading south. The water from the Sarasvati could not be diverted to the eastern foothills of the Aravalli range. This prevented the natural growth of the Sarasvati settlements from the west to the east of the hills. Even if a settlement came to exist, the distance to the hub of Panchnad life and civilisation seemed to be far off and this was unacceptable to these migrants.

"With all these obstacles, the task of pioneering seemed difficult, and uneconomic to boot.

"The third element was knowledge, that is, of appropriate technology. There had been past attempts by individual Panchnad adventurers to settle along the banks of the Ganga. These failed because the work was hard and the returns meagre. They would begin by exporting lumber from forests cleared, as a prelude to sowing. Trees were cut down– clearing the dense forest was hard work – and the lumber would be prepared for export to Panchnad. The lumber trade was, has always been, transportation-intensive – there had to be roads on which carts could be driven. When the Yamuna or Drishadvati was reached, the lumber was floated down, either on rafts or as logs. In the spring and summer, the Yamuna was full; in the summer and fall, the Drishadvati was full – the lumber could be floated. After the rains had stopped and the summer harvest was done, the level of water in both rivers fell and floating the logs became difficult. This continued through the last two moons before the solstice and the two or three moons following the solstice – an occasional spell of warm weather might allow limited traffic, but it would be difficult.

"Nowadays we mark and number the trees and make it a crime to cut down any income-producing tree like the mango, but in those days, the value of a tree was its value as lumber for building or as fuel for furnaces. After much of the forest had been clear-cut, it would be time to remove the stumps and prepare the ground for planting. At that point, the settlers realised how hard it was to work the clayey soil, very unlike the loose and rich soil of Panchnad. This soil was good for pottery and bricks, but not easy to till. An easy solution was to burn some of the lumber (that they had prepared for export) to create a layer of ash – thus they re-invented the Naga practice of slash-and-burn agriculture in tandem with manufacture of pottery and bronze castings. They discovered that slash-and-burn agriculture was not productive enough to support the Panchnad manner of living, in solid houses of brick in a permanent settlement."

***

Kaushambi/Hastinapur
circa 850 B.C.E.

Vaishampaayana stopped. The cup of water was empty – he had not even been aware of drinking while telling a story. Panini brought him another cup of water. He took a sip and continued.

***

THE PANDAVA CAMP
CIRCA 2000 B.C.E.

The Vyaasa Shukla said, "Panchnad, before that oath, was a troubled land. Peace was a way of life; and so, despite the troubles, there was no war. The Sarasvati had begun drying up in the time of Pratipa, Devavrat's grandfather. Pratipa wanted the Pauravas and Bhaaratas in the oldest parent settlements to work together and restore the Yamuna's flow to the west. He offered all the help that he could – this was limited as the Yamuna's sudden appearance in the east was radically transforming the Gangetic plain as well.

2000 B.C.E

Hastinapur itself was not in the path of the flood as it skirted along the boundaries of Kururashtra. Naga and Rakshasa bands had suffered the brunt of the flooding in the beginning, but now they were responding to the opportunities created by the new river. Naga bands in the heartland were moving up the Yamuna with new settlements. Rakshasa bands further to the east were preparing to move into the no-man's land that separated them from the old Naga boundaries to exploit the new source of water. The only opponent Pratipa faced who might choose war were the Panchalas who had not been touched by the change – Pratipa had his hands full keeping Panchala from crossing the Ganga again in a reprise of their ancient confrontation.

"The Pauravas and Bhaaratas were traders first, and builders second – they could not see the need to undertake, at current cost, a huge project with no immediate return. There was no profit to be made. It was possible that the monsoons might make up the difference. The river might return to its previous course on its own. The Pauravas dithered and while the impasse continued, migrants from further south overwhelmed the Puru towns. Faced with a population crisis, the Pauravas were unable to afford such a project. The Bhaaratas reprised the Pauravas' experience; they considered action only when the Paurava cities failed to handle the refugees, but it was too late and the Bhaarata cities succumbed to the exploding population of migrants as well. Pratipa could see the juggernaut building up and wanted to stop it before it arrived in Kururashtra; but he did not control the Yamuna upstream where the problem could be solved. Pratipa felt helpless and failed to take decisive action. In the first years of Shantanu's reign, more refugees turned up at the Kuru borders seeking help. These refugees included Pauravas and Bhaaratas who had abandoned their settlements as the drought spread north.

"Shantanu took counsel with the Kavi Sangha and its Vyaasa (Bharadvaja, before Parashara) on developing a long-run strategy to deal with the refugee situation. Something had to be done immediately that would choke the flow. The refugees imagined an unpopulated land with a bounteous river like the Sarasvati on whose banks settlements could be raised. The reality deterred them, but by that point, they were already in Hastinapur and had no place to go. Hastinapur itself had to become unattractive. The broad outlines of the strategy were to recreate the Sarasvati-centric way of life of Panchnad on the banks of the Ganga and the Yamuna; to change the pattern of use of arable land from slash-and-burn to permanent settlement (again, as it had been on the Sarasvati), even if it meant that the Nagas would have to change or would have to leave; to encourage the refugees to be the pioneers in settling the new land; to police the roads from the west along which the refugees came and control their entry; and to oppose the work breakdown that the guilds enforced in the old Sarasvati settlements; to slow down the growth of the population to match the rate at which new settlements were established. The democratic organisation of the old settlements would have to be abandoned and a unitary state like the empires of the West that traders described (such as Parsaka, Sumer, and the land of the Blue River) would have to be established.

"In the short-term, this required that, first, Shantanu maintain and expand the army so that it could deal with the societal unrest that might follow while watching the Panchalas and, second, that the population growth in Hastinapur and in the camps be tightly managed. The first and immediately contentious result of those plans was the 'One child per person' policy. This provoked unrest that had to be put down by the ever-expanding army. The reported suicide by Shantanu's wife magnified the unrest."

CHANDRASEKHAR'S QUESTION

Kaushambi/Hastinapur
circa 850 B.C.E.

Vaishampaayana paused and drank some water – as before Panini came and refilled his cup. Bhargava stood up and walked towards the path and looked down – he was expecting something. Chandrasekhar also stood up and stretched his legs. He then went through the complete sequence of the Welcome to Dawn *adavu,*[107] and then crossed his fingers and stretched them out. He sat down and said, "Sir…"

Bhargava came back. "They are bringing lunch – I was getting hungry. Vais, that was a very long stretch. I was almost fainting with hunger. Don't do that again."

Vaishampaayana pursed his lips and looked at his friend who was standing and gesticulating. "You could do with some hunger, you know."

Chandrasekhar grinned when he heard that but kept his head down. Bhargava darted a sideways glance at his son,

[107] A prescribed sequence of moves from one pose to the next, used during training by dancers and martial-artists. See Endnotes.

looked back to Vaishampaayana and said, "First my wife, now you. Let me eat my lunch in peace."

Vaishampaayana said, "I've arranged for my own lunch, the meagre one. Your rich food is keeping me awake."

Panini was carrying a small basket. Next to him was a much larger boy carrying a correspondingly larger basket. Bhargava rubbed his hands and smiled. The boys started getting ready to serve lunch.

Chandrasekhar said, "Uncle, I have been wondering about something all morning. Could I ask you a question?"

"Yes, my son. Of course. I hope it did not distract you from doing a good job of transcribing."

"I did my best, sir. My questions: Who is being trained to read this epic? Will it be soon? How are you training them to read? What will be the test of success? A few more in that vein, but you get the drift, sir – it is about how your people are getting ready to use this."

Vaishampaayana frowned. *There is something wrong with that question. What is it? Darn...*

He had always assumed that the city council no longer wanted the Kavi Sangha to recite the *Jaya* at the festivals. So who would it be? Not some fly-by-night trader who knew how to maintain caravan accounts on clay tablets. Once the question was formulated, the answer was obvious. The council would come back to him and ask him to train readers. What guild would the readers belong to?

Even if the Kavi Sangha only trained the readers but did not make them guild members, what kind of training was it to be? Memorising would no longer be necessary, so they could skip all the early training that so distinguished the bard from the rest of the world. If the trainer were not a bard, he would not know beforehand the things the bard knew – the feelings that were associated with the poem, how they were to be expressed in tone and delivery – *abhinaya*[108] was a skill necessary to the bard; the associated skill of expressed empathy would be necessary for the reader.

"Chandrasekhar, what do you suggest?"

"Sir, first, you will have to train to read people who already know how to recite the *Jaya*– thus you will determine what is missing and how it is to be fixed."

Chandrasekhar stopped, expecting Vaishampaayana to say something, but Vaishampaayana was silent. Chandrasekhar waited for about a vighati, then continued.

"Second..."

"Chandrasekhar... wait! I need to understand what you just said."

Vaishampaayana rubbed his moustache and beard, a white fibrous roll that ended in a point about four *angulies* from his chin. After about a vighati, he said, "I am bothered by what you just said, Chandrasekhar. What do you mean by 'what is missing and how it is to be fixed'? What do you think is missing? Have you been able to write down all I have said?"

"Uncle, I wrote down everything you said. The difficulty is that people, and perhaps that includes you, have the impression that writing creates a finished product. They see the trader keep track of inventory and think, *that is so easy – he makes marks corresponding to numbers and, similarly, he makes marks corresponding to objects. Then he signs it and, there, it's done.* That is a myth. Writing by itself does not make a finished product. Moreover, most certainly not, when used for creating something other than an inventory. For instance, writing a narrative down will not make a history of it. There are no letters indicating

108 The techniques used by a poet to express emotions (classically, nine) while reciting or narrating a work. See Endnotes.

emotions; there are no letters for variations in speech or in accents or dialects; there are no letters for emphasis. And so it goes."

"What do you propose?"

"A reader reads what has been written and a senior apprentice of the Kavi Sangha listens and corrects as needed."

Bhargava said, "No! No, that doesn't work."

Vaishampaayana said, "Why not?"

"I can't afford it!"

"Why not? Before your son's coming, I had imagined that we would verify your transcription – you and me. Now, your son shows me that it is not so simple, that we will need more reviewers and there is likely to be additional work."

Bhargava said, "Vais, You don't know what you are asking for. As it is, I am donating my time. I expect Hastinapur to recover and prosper again – when that happens I will have friends who remember that I helped save your archives. I hoped that we could replace me with a young scribe, but with these additions, the project is too complex. Now we are using the best scribe in the land, my own son! If my guild finds out that I have been providing his services, even if they are not trade-related, for free, they will make me a laughing stock – I cannot afford to add apprentices to this project. Especially senior, almost fully ready members of the guild, which is what will be needed because the reader must read exactly what is written and the listener must understand what is being recited, deeply, with nuance and all."

"Then, it will have to be you reading to my apprentices. Or Chandrasekhar."

"No, no, no. Look at my son – he is sweating from sitting in the morning sun. You are wringing him out like a dirty washcloth. He will become a mere husk, an empty shell, drained of everything. All my investment in his training will be wasted."

"Bhargava, my friend, calm down! Chandrasekhar is young – do not worry about him. The written text must be verified. Who will do it?"

"You say you have apprentices – let them do it. You should start training yourselves in reading and writing. Now, not later. Then you can read, you can verify, and maybe even correct."

"Is that reasonable? How long will it take?"

"A few weeks for reading, a little more for writing. It depends on how much time they can devote to practice."

"That, Bhargava, is too late – we may be done by then and you will want Chandrasekhar to work on your own projects."

Bhargava sighed. Vaishampaayana felt guilty – he had missed the council meeting during which Bhargava had been persuaded to work with him. The council had assured Bhargava that it would not take much time, maybe as much as two weeks. Bhargava was experienced in writing up accounts, but not for taking dictation. The council had made it sound easy. Bhargava had estimated that if the digressions could be kept under control, the whole project could be done in four weeks. *If I had been there, I would have fixed their errors in estimation right there. Instead, here we are, a few days later, still struggling to begin, let alone progress at a steady pace.*

The city council could have asked any Western trader, for the same script was used for accounting from Panchnad all the way to Egypt. There was only one reason for pulling Bhargava in for unwanted recognition – he was known to be a friend of the Vyaasa. Was it possible that they knew that once, many years ago, Bhargava had tried to teach Vaishampaayana to read? Vaishampaayana had thought it was their mutual secret. It was also their mutual secret that the brilliant genius Vaishampaayana had been unable to learn to read. He had faltered at the simplest meaningless convention. Why was the character called "aleph" pronounced "ah" in one place but "ay" elsewhere?[109] Why was it the first in the list of characters? Why did the character have a name, anyway? Shouldn't its pronunciation be its name? Why were the vowels not placed next to each other in the ordering? What was the significance of the order of the symbols? What was special about these symbols? Why could they not have a different symbol for each consonantal sound instead of an idiosyncratic way of composing symbols to express different consonants? The questions showed no sign of ceasing. Vaishampaayana had been an impossible student and Bhargava had given up trying to teach him.

They sat silently looking around, a bit embarrassed by Bhargava's outburst. Vaishampaayana could see that Chandrasekhar was grinning, stifling a laugh. The apprentices looked alarmed. It looked like these two old men were about to fight – what should they do if that happened? Were they expected to come to their masters' support?

Vaishampaayana lowered his voice and said: "Bhargava, we should approach this calmly. We should have our solution in place before we say anything to the city council."

"I agree," said Bhargava.

"No matter what we decide, we need a baseline measurement of the quality of the writing, good or bad. That will help us come to a decision."

"Yes, that is true."

"Let us have our apprentices spend half a day, not less, not more, on validating what they can. One of your boys will read what has been written. Two or three of my apprentices will listen and stop, question, and correct, as it seems appropriate.

---

[109] The script that Bhargava knew was derived from an ancient "Script of the Sea-people". The Sea-people were Phoenicians who were considered "Western Panias" by Jambudvipans. All the other alphabetic scripts of the Middle East were derived from the Phoenician.

They will begin verse by verse and if the going is smooth they can speed up. Each side, readers and listeners, will assign one person who will not participate but just records the meeting. I will assign an archivist for the listening side, and Bhargava, you should do the same for your side."

"I agree. I will ask my son to record for us. When can we start?"

"Good. I have an archivist in mind – if he is available tomorrow, we can perform this test tomorrow morning."

Bhargava turned to Chandrasekhar. "How about it? You think we can get a group together?"

Chandrasekhar said, "It's easy for us – we only need to bring a reader and me. Uncle will have a harder job finding people."

Vaishampaayana said, "I'll deal with it – I will know by sunset who can come tomorrow."

Chandrasekhar said, "Shall we start tomorrow morning?"

Vaishampaayana said, "Yes. In the meantime, let us continue."

They finished lunch – the food that had been ordered by Bhargava for his friend was shared among the three apprentices. Vaishampaayana stuck to his own diet.

Vaishampaayana felt refreshed after lunch. The meals of the last two days had made him drowsy, but not today's meal. He said, "Good! Let's continue for another fifteen ghatis before we stop for today."

Shukla's Confession

The Pandava Camp
circa 2000 B.C.E.

"One shameful act by an ambitious young boy made me what I am. It led to Devavrat's renunciation. It also led to my sister's unhappy life."

The Vyaasa's words confused Lomaharshana.

"What do you mean, sir? What ambitious young boy?"

"I was that foolish boy. This is my confession, meant only for your ears, Yudhisthira, and the archives of the Kavi Sangha," said Shukla.

"Sir, am I the right person to whom such a confession should be directed?" said Lomaharshana.

"Yes. I have had a long life. I may not have the time to submit this confession to other senior members of our Sangha, to be judged, the way my predecessor Parashara was. I do not have the courage to accept that kind of punishment if I live much longer."

Shukla took in a deep breath and exhaled it slowly. Then he continued: "We, Satyavati and I, come from a family of

Meena-Nagas, called 'Matsya' by the Panchnadis.[110] Hah! You look surprised – yes I am a Naga and so is Satyavati. You have a question, Lomaharshana?"

"Sir," Lomaharshana said, "surely you will have more to say about the imperial and militaristic strategy designed by the Kavi Sangha and Devavrat, but on the face of it, it is unfair to the Nagas, our own people. You were not the Vyaasa when the first steps of the strategy were enforced. Yet you supported the policy. Why?"

The Vyaasa said, "I was not the Vyaasa, but I have watched the strategy develop and as the brother of the Queen, received a hearing – I feel I have had a hand in shaping it from almost the very beginning. You wonder how I could support a strategy that was unfair to the Nagas?

"I had to think long and hard before I concluded that this policy was in the best long-term interest of the Nagas. Like all such policies, much is left to an honest and sincere implementation, even though we know that the implementers are human, error-prone, and corruptible. The Pandavas would undo everything on the altar of fairness; Dhritarashtra's sons serve only themselves; the immigrants are desperate but not desperate enough to change; and, the Nagas are shortsighted and unwilling to compromise. Devavrat's memoirs will illustrate this well. Ask me this question again when the war is over. I have been as self-serving as the sons of Dhritarashtra, as unswerving in my goals as our insufficiently desperate immigrants, as shortsighted as the rest of the Nagas.

"When Shantanu married my sister he abandoned one element of the strategy. He backed away from the short-term plan to stop population growth by limiting family size. Individual decisions like that have created problems

---

110 *Meena* is the Naga word for "fish", while *Matsya* was the Panchnadi word.

for the plan. For instance, I have mentioned that Satyavati's grandson, King Mahendra opposed it – he exiled himself from Hastinapur in protest, and spent the time with his wives, Kunti of the Bhojas and Madri from the Madra clan. Now his children oppose Devavrat's plan, without even knowing most of it.

"Look at the alliance the Pandavas have cobbled together to oppose Hastinapur. Panchala is in it. Panchala has been against Hastinapur from its founding as a trading outpost. The Yadavas are in it – their leader Krishna keeps his own counsel but weaves a path to a Yadava empire that would rival a Kuru empire centred on Hastinapur. Though the Yadavas, descendants of Yadu, are cousins to the descendants of Puru, Yadu's brother, their imperial plans will not mesh with Devavrat's goals. They are inimical to Yudhishthira's goals. Add to this incongruous mix, the southern Nagas represented by their army chief Virata, who styles himself King of the Matsyas, that is, the Meena-Nagas. The Meenas may be Nagas but their interests diverge from those of Panchala. They have fared well under Hastinapur's policies, so why do they oppose Hastinapur? All they see, like you, is the unfairness of the policy.

"Creating a fair world is a fantasy – I will narrate the story of Shantanu and Satyavati's marriage, and you can decide what would be fair. My father played a part in that drama, for reasons that are easy to understand."

***

Kaushambi/Hastinapur
circa 850 B.C.E.

Vaishampaayana paused. Sweat glistened on his brow. "Another hot day. It's making me thirsty." Then, a little louder, he said, "Panini? Can you get me some water?"

Panini was nodding off after that unexpected lunch, but Vyaasa's words aroused him and he rushed to fetch the water pot and pour a cup of water for his guru. Vaishampaayana took a sip, but the sip was not satisfying and he kept drinking and drained the cup.

Bhargava said, "Well, friend, what is the Vyaasa's secret? What sin is he confessing?"

"I'll get to it!"

Shukla's World

The Pandava Camp
Circa 2000 B.C.E.

Shukla said, "Lomaharshana, you are a Naga, but not a Meena-Naga. We Meenas are a bit different from you, even though we are still Nagas. The last fifty years have seen much change, for the Nagas as well as for the Meenas. I will describe the world my sister and I came from.

"My father's sister was the matriarch of our small band of five families. That made us part of the first, the ruling family. My father, the matriarch's eldest brother, was the head of the band's warriors. Unlike Panchnad, we had no guilds. We do share with the Panchnadis an obsession with the number five. You've seen often enough how Nagas like to see groups of five. Five is considered a fortunate number. The size of a band like ours can vary, but the number of families in a band will be a multiple of five; large bands will often be composed of five smaller bands which may be similarly structured – we have had bands with over a hundred families.

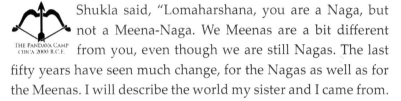

"Unlike the other Nagas the Meenas do not move for land – we move for water. We establish our settlements on the edge of the river at a place where a small pond or lake could be formed. Such lakes are often created naturally at a river bend, but then the downstream channel would silt up, followed by the upstream channel. The depression would be cut off from the river – the Meena-Nagas specialised in restoring such lakes. The depression had to be suitably small, but not too small; it had to be large enough and not too far from the changed course of the river. A number of Meena-Naga bands would get together to dig a new short channel from the river to the depression and a longer straight channel downstream back to the main flow. The channels were designed to cut the speed of the swiftly flowing river, which slowed down erosion. It was hard work, but when finally ready, such a lake would support many Naga bands.

"The Meena bands could not settle down yet – it would take a few years for grasses and other plants to sprout, followed by the appearance of insects and tadpoles. The next season, small fish would appear, followed by bigger fish. Lastly, the river dolphins would enter the lake – they are the vehicles of the Goddess, signalling plenty and giving us permission to settle on the lake. The calm lake provided a home for fish, including river dolphin and trout. The construction of such a lake was a major investment that we did not easily abandon. A fish weir could be constructed, though we only did that in preparation for hosting the clan's *potlatch*.[111] The houses by the water might be on platforms held up by stilts, while the houses further back would be on earth. Once a band settles down, it can establish a garden for root vegetables and herbs close by.

"Our band had settled on the banks of such a lake, near the southern border of Hastinapur – the city-dwellers had occupied land that Nagas had left fallow, for their ceramic and metal furnaces. When this happened, the Naga bands had grumbled, but since no Nagas were in occupation of that land, there was nobody to rally around. In those years, the Nagas avoided conflict by moving elsewhere. They did that for many, many years. The Naga chiefs were sensitive to the changed balance of power created by Samvarana's return – Hastinapur had become an armed capital city, not just a trading entrepôt. The Hastinapuris abandoned their foundries when the chaos of the

---

[111] The word *potlatch* is borrowed from the term for a redistributive feast held by the Trobriand Islanders of New Guinea. See Endnotes.

immigration crisis had cut the eastern trade for ore. The land to the north of us was a sorry, blighted presence, but we assumed that this was how the city-dwellers left land fallow, and that they would return to use it when it was convenient.

"I was fascinated by the Hastinapuris and spent much time with them. Noticing my interest, Parashara adopted me as his protégé. This was before he became the Vyaasa. He had come to our settlement to assess how the city-dwellers and the Nagas could cooperate rather than fight each other. Refugees were coming in from the west in steadily increasing numbers. The Kavi Sangha hoped to help them establish new settlements rather than overwhelm Hastinapur. The Nagas' cooperation was essential – the immigrants could learn from the Nagas and the Meenas how to live off the land and river.

"Parashara spent a lot of time visiting us. He was freely available to me as a teacher. I did not know then the reason for his frequent visits, but at that time, I was excited about city life. It made my life by the lake seem monotonous and boring, in addition to feeling useless. He sponsored me into the Kavi Sangha and enrolled me in the school of bards even though, at ten, I was much older than the six-year-olds around me. I was excited and engaged; I did very well, so much so that in less than two years I caught up and was among the bards of my age who were considered the most skilled at memorisation and storytelling. In that skill, I was the equal of Devavrat, who had established extraordinary performance records when he had studied with the Kavi Sangha apprentices.

"In the meantime, my sister Satyavati, a few years older than me, became pregnant. A pregnancy unacknowledged by a father was not considered remarkable among Nagas. The same held true in ancient Panchnad, matriarchal Panchnad. When Samvarana regained Hastinapur, it should have become a matriarchal settlement like the others in Panchnad, but it did not – it continued to be ruled by a head trader and succession was to the trader's son.

Fatherhood became more important. The Kavi Sangha also thought it knew everything about fatherhood – they had rationalised the change as being in line with local hegemony enforced by a standing army. In recent years, the focus on fatherhood has become more intense. I do not know why. Suyodhana and his brothers are particularly obsessed with establishing paternity, and, as they call it, 'the purity of the mother.'

"I digress – the situation was not so extreme when Satyavati delivered Parashara's child. Parashara asked us to be circumspect among city-folk. We were puzzled but followed his advice. That year he became the Vyaasa. His visits stopped. Unfortunately for Parashara, the leaders of the Kavi Sangha came to know that Parashara was the father of a child with a Naga woman. I should mention that in ordinary times, this would have barely caused a ripple but these were not ordinary times – the Vyaasa's credibility as an observer and memoriser of Naga customs and an advisor with respect to policy towards Nagas was compromised. His secretiveness about it made his behaviour seem underhanded and unwise. That the woman's father was the chief of the Naga band raised more questions. The senior members of the Kavi Sangha, its governing body, determined that Parashara should be penalised.

"Parashara realised that he had compromised his role as an advisor to Hastinapur and the Panchnadi refugees – from that point of view his actions had been either wrong or unnecessary and unwise. He agreed to a penalty. The Kavi Sangha determined that he should take a two-year vow of silence, a particularly harsh sentence for a bard. Parashara decided to spend his two years of silence on an island near our lake. In Panchnad, his responsibility to his child would have been to ensure acceptance into a guild, and I do not know what he thought was right in this situation, but he chose to stay close to us. The mother, my sister Satyavati, was also upset, first about the secrecy that she had been asked to maintain, then about the public fuss. Faced by the concerns of the Kavi Sangha, Parashara's questionable judgement, and Parashara's fickleness, she decided to raise the boy herself and refused to allow Parashara any significant role. Thus Parashara's efforts to be near his child came to naught, but he was still my Guru and my mentor within the Kavi Sangha."

Lomaharshana said, "The great Parashara was penalised? While he was the Vyaasa?"

The Vyaasa Shukla said, "Yes."

"But... but... such a punishment is not mentioned in any of our archives."

"The entire episode has been kept unknown outside the highest circles of the Kavi Sangha," Shukla said. "Hastinapuris were given the impression that this was a vow taken by Parashara for his own personal spiritual reasons. Even Shantanu was not informed – it was felt that his trust in the Sangha would be tested. He was not inquisitive by nature and he accepted Parashara's story.

"My sister named her child Dvaipaayana[112], meaning 'born on an island', to acknowledge his obscure parentage. His skin colour led to the nickname Krishna, partly in contrast to my name Shukla because I was so light-skinned. He looked like his mother and had the family hallmark – the full upper lip that curved down. He was a chubby, playful boy whose presence cheered my father.

"My world was a peaceful world. It had been peaceful for many years. All of that was turned upside-down by the events I am about to describe. I was not present at the beginning, but my father and sister were. I picked up bits and pieces of the events which I have woven into a narrative – even in those days, long before I heard of the Kavi Sangha, I would delight in creating and telling stories. I would have been a natural candidate for membership at a young age if I had lived in the city. I have

112 *Dvaipaayana* means "born on an island".

thought over these events so many times, in the hope that I can discover a prefigured destiny that would give meaning to the rest of my life. This is what happened one day in the life of my father and sister, and what I did that day."

Lomaharshana said, "Sir, you are the head of our Sangha. I am merely a fledgling, a child. I ask you once again – is it appropriate that you confess this to me?"

Shukla said, "My confession must stay secret – my punishment would have to be at least as rigorous as Guru Parashara. I cannot risk it. After the war, perhaps..."

The King Comes a-Courting

The Pandava Camp
circa 2000 B.C.E.

Shukla continued: "It was about a hundred moons[113] after Devavrat's mother had killed herself. That day my father was outside his house playing with Krishna Dvaipaayana, who was then three years old. I was away, collecting wood in the forest, and heard about what happened, much later, from my father. Satyavati was sitting on the steps watching them play. A stag burst out of the forest to his right, and stood by the riverbank, panting. It continued along the bank and then entered the forest on his left.

"My father was quick. 'Hunters! Satyavati, go in.' She did, leaving my father by himself when, a few *vighatis* later, four men came out of the forest on the right. They were armed with bows and they followed the trail of the stag. They stopped when they saw my father. One of the men walked towards him. After some hesitation, two of the men followed the first man, while the fourth stayed behind. My father knew the first man– he was Shantanu, the King of Hastinapur. He came up to my father, held out his arms, and embraced him.

113 Almost eight solar years.

"Shantanu said, 'Rajah! I rejoice to see you. How is your land here? Does your family flourish? Does this mighty river provide enough for you?'

"My father was relieved but taken aback by the friendliness. He tried to respond in kind.

"'You are welcome, brother, to my small home! The goddess has treated us well. We flourish, too, in the shadow of your protection. What cause for worry could we have? It has been many years since you came this way. How are your Queens and your children?'

"'My dear wife passed away many years ago. This is my only son, Devavrat.'

"Shantanu gestured at the man who had not come forward – he did not respond. He was the youngest and slightest and was engrossed in shining his bowstring with a piece of leather. One of the other men went up to him and nudged him – he looked up, flushed, and stepped forward. He struck my father as much younger than the others, but his bow was strung more tightly than theirs and he had more arrows in his quiver.

"Devavrat bowed to my father who raised his hands in blessing.

"Shantanu said to my father, 'How are your children? You had two, as I recall, when we last met. Are they still with you or have they joined other families?'

"'My children, Satyavati and Shukla, are still with me.'

"Meanwhile Satyavati had put the baby Krishna down inside and had started rolling up the pads we slept on. Krishna did not like being put down and he showed his displeasure by crying. Without thinking, Satyavati went to the door and said, 'Appa, can you …'

"She froze when she saw the men, then she flushed and looked away, but she finished her sentence: '…give me his toy elephant?' even though her voice dropped until it was almost inaudible.

"At the sound of a woman's voice, the men looked up. Devavrat, who had returned to working on his bow, put it down and looked at her. All the men stared at Satyavati, as if they had been frozen by a spell, as my father picked up the toy and gave it to her. She went back into the cottage, and my father watched as the group slowly unfroze. Devavrat was the last one, but the King had already asked my father a question:

"'Is that charming lady your daughter?'

A thousand thoughts went through my father's mind. Ever since Hastinapur had established itself as the dominant power by dint of a standing army, Nagas had learned to be cautious around the city dwellers, especially the fighters. Some, like Parashara, were friendly, but there was the occasional arrogant one around whom the caution was merited. He put aside his fears to answer the King:

"'Yes, sir. That is my daughter, Satyavati. She is taking care of Guru Parashara's son. As you know, he has retired to a nearby rest house while he is completing his vow of silence, but his wisdom shines through the vow of silence. Please come in and grace my home. Stay for a meal.'

"My father hoped that by mentioning Vyaasa Parashara, he would mitigate the risk posed by the arrogance of the Hastinapuris. The invitation to a meal was a calculated risk – it was not yet time for a regular meal and hunters usually did not like to abandon their prey if they were not hungry. These men did not look as if they had ever been hungry.

"Shantanu looked at his men – they seemed ready to leave. He said, 'Thank you, but not now. We will resume our hunt. Some other time, perhaps. You did see a stag come this way?'

"'Yes, sir. The stag passed by a short time before you arrived. It went that way,' said my father pointing west.

"Some days later, the King's messenger came with presents from the King. The messenger explained that the King wanted my father to consider a future for his daughter in the Kuru family.

"My father thought that they were talking about Devavrat. The boy was young and manageable and my father was comfortable with the notion that he might court Satyavati. The city-dwellers did not have the same customs as the Nagas, and the city women were less forthcoming than Naga women, but in matters of love, all men and women were similar. He recalled the wandering soma-peddler from a few years ago, the one who consumed as much of his drug as he sold and was in a perpetual semi-trance. He claimed he had gained spiritual powers from the spirits in the Himalayas. On seeing Satyavati, he proclaimed that she would be a great matriarch and her progeny would rule the greatest empire in the land. Everybody laughed – she had five cousins who were in line to be matriarch – for they all knew that Satyavati was an unlikely matriarch. My sister was not in line to be the matriarch of our band – the way she would become one was by spinning off a daughter band – and our band was itself newly formed and still too small. It made perfect sense if Satyavati married Hastinapur's King and became matriarch of Hastinapur – why, Hastinapur was the only candidate for any kind of empire within a hundred yojanas.

"His response to the request was, 'The boy can come himself and persuade her – Naga women make their own choices.'

"Later that day Devavrat approached my father asking permission to court his daughter. *I am the King's son and heir. I will be King after him. The people of the city will treat your daughter with the greatest respect. You need have no fears about her wellbeing.* My father encouraged Devavrat to court Satyavati himself. He said, 'Naga families do not arrange marriages. Feel free to approach her directly. However, remember, she is as free as you. Any Naga woman would be delighted to be invited to be the matriarch of a band.' My father did not understand Kuru customs and he tried to make sense of them in the light of Naga practices – he thought that marrying the King's son would elevate her to the status of a future matriarch.

"With that, Devavrat left to find Satyavati.

"In the meantime, the messenger came back and clarified that the King wanted to marry Satyavati himself. My father realised that there could be trouble and his family would be in the thick of it. He rushed to abort any possibility that Devavrat and Satyavati would meet and be mutually attracted. He managed to cut short the first meeting between Devavrat and Satyavati – they only managed to speak a few words. Unfortunately, I was again away that day. If I had known all that was happening, who knows if I would have acted as I did; things may have turned out differently. As it happened, I returned just before Satyavati.

"When Satyavati came home, she said, 'Why did you call me away, Father?'

"My father looked at me – I thought he was going to ask me something, then he turned away. He said, 'I have something important to discuss with you.'

"Satyavati said, 'I'll listen.'

"'Satyavati! The King comes to visit us today. He wants something from me that is not mine to give. What am I to say? I am troubled by strange dreams and visions. I do not know how to express what I am feeling and thinking.'

"Satyavati said, 'Don't worry, father. I know what he wants.'

"'You do?'

"'Yes. I hope you told him that among us the boy takes the lead.' She smiled as she said this.

"I found out afterwards from her friends what had happened – that Devavrat had come across her when she was with her friends – he had been tongue-tied and awkward, while her friends teased him. He had made hurried excuses and left. It had been, she told her friends, very sweet of him. The 'boy' she referred to was Devavrat.

"That got my father's attention. 'What did you say?'

"'I know why he came.'

"'I cannot tell the King how to act – a King does not expect to behave like a commoner. He does not know our customs. It is dangerous to run afoul of the Kauravas, especially a powerful chief like Shantanu.'

"I did not know what my father was talking about. Nor did my sister.

"'What's the danger? What are you worried about? It is not up to you to say no! I am the one to decide. As should be the case right now. I see no reason to say no. You've raised me from childhood, father, and you know me well enough. You cannot decide for me.'

"My father continued his puzzling behaviour.

"'Satyavati, my dear. This had gone beyond my simple powers of explanation and understanding. I will let the Kaurava do what he will and you what you must.'

"What did he mean by Kaurava? Why was he talking about 'the Kaurava' as though there was only one such person?

"Satyavati said, 'What is the matter with you father? I've not seen such behaviour before. You worry needlessly. We haven't heard anything bad about him, the King, or the King's men. I am sure he is an honest, caring, and earnest boy, and there is nothing to be afraid of.'

"My father mumbles when he is confused. 'If only your mother were here. Oh, what am I saying, even she could not have helped me. How do I explain this?'

"Satyavati tried again. 'It would be nice to have a father for Krishna. You've told me so yourself. We are fisher-folk, not city-dwellers with their ridiculous laws. Following our custom, the boy approaches me. That is as it should be. Why should I worry?'

"'The Kauravas are not Nagas. You cannot stay here – they will expect you to go with them.'

"I listened silently to the dialogue between my father and Satyavati and I was excited to hear that if Satyavati married a city-dweller, she would have to go live in the city. It would mean that I would have a safe place in the city from which to achieve my ambition. This is where I joined the conversation.

"I said 'Father! Satya! Your friend Gauri told me that the King came here! You should have called me! You know I want to move to the city permanently – I could have asked him.'

"They ignored me. They stood, looking sad and unhappy, Satyavati pouting and sniffling while my father was walking back and forth mumbling inaudibly. I persisted – this was not an opportunity to be missed.

"'Isn't that what you are talking about – Satya going to Hastinapur. I can go with her. Will they let me stay in the palace?'

"Satyavati looked piqued. 'Oh, Shukla! Is that all you think about – your future in the city? Maybe you'll be jester in the King's court.'

"'I'd take that. Dad! What is going on? Why are you both looking so upset?'

"My father said, 'The King wants to marry Satyavati and take her to Hastinapur.'

"Satyavati said, 'Father is against this. So he says; only, he won't explain why…' and then she stopped when she comprehended what our father had said. We both said, simultaneously, 'What?'

"My father said, 'No, no! I made a mistake, I was just mumbling. It's nothing, nothing at all.'

"I said, 'Great! You won't be lonely; I'll go to the city with you! This is great!'

"'The King! Marry the King? I won't, Father, please, tell him no! Why should I not marry Devavrat? I'll kill myself. How can I bet he King's wife?'

"'That's why I don't know what to do! ... what did you say? How do you know about Devavrat? Did you meet him?'

"'We exchanged a couple of words. He seemed charming and shy. I just thought...'

"My father interrupted her. 'What did he say?'

"'I know he came to see me – my friends told me that. We hadn't said much, then you were shouting for me and he ran away. Maybe the King is coming on his behalf?'

"I finally understood what Satyavati's objection was. *She did not want to marry the King. She wanted to marry somebody else, somebody named Devavrat.* That I could not understand.

"'You don't want to marry the King? What kind of silly idea is that? Are you worried about your baby? The King can certainly be his father. Who is Devavrat, anyway? Sounds like a citified name, not a Naga.'

"My father said, 'The King will have my head!'

"Satyavati said, 'What did you tell him?'

"I said, 'I hope you said yes, right away.'

"Satyavati looked at me and rolled her eyes upward. Her voice rose to a higher pitch.

"'I hope you told him no, right away.'

"My father and I were familiar with that higher pitch, which suffered no opposition. We both spoke up.

"'Please, Satyavati, don't start now.'

"My father said, 'We are not a wealthy and powerful band. The King courteously calls me Rajah – he is being polite, for it is merely a courtesy. If I say no, he will destroy us.'

"I said, with the conviction of youth, 'This is my only chance to enter the city as an equal and not a supplicant.'

"Satyavati said, 'I don't care. If my life is to be destroyed, why should I care about you, and you? Father, please don't let this happen. I'm depending on you.'

"My father held his head in his hands. 'Satyavati! The matter is beyond my control. If you refuse, the Kaurava will destroy us and you will be his property. If not, you will reign as the Queen, and we will survive.'

"I added to the objections. 'I will have a glorious career as the councillor to the great King Shantanu.'

"Satyavati said, 'If he knew that I love his son, he might change his mind.'

"That was when I finally got it. *Devavrat was the King's son.* My voice went to a higher pitch.

"'His son?'

"'My father said, 'I cannot do that. Suppose he does not accept that. As far as he knows you've never met his son.'

"I got my voice under control. I was still flabbergasted.

"'His son! Oh...'

"Satyavati said, 'He can ask his son.'

"I was in two minds. Either option sounded fine to me.

"I said, 'Why would you want to marry the son when you can be Queen with his father? Fine, all right, you love him; you don't love him, whatever... you get what you want. And that's what you want... you can be Crown Princess and I'll be famous as the advisor to the glorious Samraat Devavrat.'

"Satyavati went and held our father's hands. 'Yes, that is what I want. Don't tell him about his son. Tell him that I will not be Queen. That I am not trained for it. That I will disgrace him in public and his people will be ashamed to see me.'

"'Satyavati. I'll do as you ask. I expect he will answer those objections. You can be trained. You won't disgrace him. What if he says all this and accepts whatever demands you make? Will you marry him and forget the son?'

"'Never. Tell him something else. Help me. Shukla, stop thinking about yourself. Help me.'

"I was intrigued. 'Hmm… King Devavrat. I wonder what he will do if you marry his father?'

"'I don't know. Don't ask me these questions. He'll run away. Maybe kill himself. How do I know?'

"'You're sure?'

"'Yes.'

"'I don't think so. Let me tell you how they do it in the West, in Sumer and Parsaka. Traders from there tell stories of heirs who rebel against their fathers. Their father orders them to debase themselves in apology for some insult to him, under pain of death. The desperate heir refuses but does not allow himself to be killed. He is angry, not with the king, but with the person he blames for the falling-out, oftentimes a stepmother, a brother or a sister, even someone who may have been trying to help him. He will exile himself and bide his time. When the king's named successor tries to take control, the exile will return, to fight and kill his rival. Most court officials will desist from taking sides, as it is a risky business.

"'Devavrat will follow that example – he will go into exile. When the King dies, he will return and become the Chief. Then, he'll kill you. That's how they do it in the West.'

"My father said, 'Shukla! Are you mad? Don't come up with these grotesque scenarios. Help us come up with a plan. What do we do?'

"I said, 'Father, this is my proposed plan. Demand that your daughter be crowned the matriarch of Hastinapur, with her husband as the King – that would be unorthodox for a Panchnad city but Hastinapur is not a Panchnad city. This practice can continue – the matriarch's eldest daughter will be the next matriarch, and her husband will be the King. While the matriarch is unmarried, a regent chosen from the qualified nobles may perform the King's rituals. Secondly, demand that the King's laws about the number of children you can have do not apply to you – your children should not be killed by the King.'

"'What? I don't get it. I do not want children by the King.'

"I was ready for that. 'Look, Satya! The king cannot have any more sons because of his own laws. That's why his first queen committed suicide. This plan does not require that he break his own laws – his daughter will inherit. However, Devavrat is a danger to this plan and he cannot simply exile or kill Devavrat. That would lead to civil war because the Crown Prince is popular. The plan puts pressure on him to do something against the son he loves. The King will have to give you up. Later, after the dust has settled, and he comes to his senses, for you are so much younger than him, his son can marry you.'

"'Why won't he just kill us and take her?' said the father.

"'Make the demand in public. Tell him that an astrologer foretold at her birth that her descendants would be kings.'

"'You think he'll believe that nonsense? How does that allow me to marry Devavrat?'

"I had come up with the idea in an instant. It was so obvious that I could not see any problems with it. I knew how it would work. I knew why it would work. I said, 'The King will give up the idea of marrying you. In a few years, Devavrat will ask to marry you and it will be seen as fulfilling the prediction. The King will have forgotten this instant infatuation. He will realise how much more suitable you are as a daughter-in-law.'

2000 B.C.E

"My father said, 'I don't like this. What will Guru Parashara say about this?'

"'Don't worry. He has been observing a vow of silence. I am the only student who understands his signals. I'll provide his advice.'

"My father's fear of retribution was far greater than his worries about making up a story about a prophecy."

Lomaharshana said: "Sir, were you not afraid of Guru Parashara exposing you?"

Shukla said, "I do not know, Lomaharshana, where I got the gall and the deviousness to plan this trick. This is the first I have talked of it."

For a few vighatis they were silent. Shukla's shoulders slumped and his eyes were downcast. His hands began to tremble. He brought them together and interlaced them tightly. Shukla glanced briefly at Lomaharshana's face but it looked blank, almost as though he were practising the *nishkamkarnarpana*[114] discipline. *Why does he not judge me?* Shukla found that he could not guess what Lomaharshana was thinking.

Lomaharshana's mind had been whirling. *How am I going to keep this a secret? Why is the Vyaasa confessing at this point, why to me? I cannot forgive him, his Guru must.* He tried to keep his emotions off his face, but the effort was not easy and the stress of the demand made him enter the nishkamkarnarpana trance-state involuntarily.

Shukla continued: "We waited half a day for a query from Shantanu. My father was unable to perform his usual tasks – the fish line did not get pulled up and the fish harvested; he did not go to the men's hut where he was expected. Satyavati also hung

---

[114] *Nishkamkarnarpana* was a trance state in which a bard would listen without judgment and without attachment to what was being heard. See Endnotes.

around, a haggard look on her face. Nobody ate. I asked my father to explain what had happened and that is how I know all these details. Of course, I am a storyteller and I have added the necessary rhetorical elements to make a story out of a collection of events.

"Shantanu's messenger returned about eight ghatis later. I went up to him and offered him some lunch. He demurred. 'I am in a hurry,' he said, 'Do you have a message for me?'

"I said, 'Yes, I do. This is what my father says – these are his own words. To my brother and great King, Shantanu, greetings. You can be assured of my deepest respect and regard for you. Your offer does us a great honour. That my daughter Satyavati came to your attention is surely a sign of the good fortune that comes her way. However, she is concerned, as am I, about the great rift, the abyss that yawns between our customs and yours. We are different people who live different lives – far be it for me to judge what is best for your people, your family, or your King. My daughter is born to be a great queen – so said Guru Parashara when he first beheld Satyavati. Among the Meenas, she might become a great matriarch of an influential band. What would she be among your people? There is no matriarch in Hastinapur. Will she be another one of your wives? Will that fulfil her destiny to be a great queen? Further, the fortune-tellers say that from her womb will be born a dynasty of great rulers. How can that come about, when by Hastinapur custom, your older children will take precedence over hers? Your son, Prince Devavrat, is the *Yuvraj* and next in line to be King. Lastly, your law limits every family to one boy and one girl. You already have a son. Any sons born to Satyavati would be surrendered and killed. Only one daughter will be allowed to live. If she does not have daughters and is not permitted to have sons, she cannot establish a dynasty with you. She cannot accept marriage under these conditions.'

"The message continued, 'As Satyavati's father, I do not intend to bar the fulfilment of your mutual desire. These are my conditions: Satyavati will be your only wife and Matriarch of Hastinapur; all of Satyavati's children must be allowed to live; her daughter, if she has any, and only her daughter must be the next Matriarch of Hastinapur, and the matriarchy shall continue through that daughter. If Satyavati only has sons, one of them or their progeny, and no others, must be crowned King of Hastinapur; the King's wife shall be the matriarch, and their daughter will continue the matriarchy. Neither Devavrat, nor any of his descendants, nor any other descendant of yours who is not also descended from Satyavati can be King. Satyavati's dynasty cannot be allowed to die with her. Satyavati's promised future must come to be. These are all my conditions, there will be no others.'

"Shantanu's messenger took this response back to his master."

The Chief Minister Reconstructs a Memory

The Pandava Camp
circa 2000 B.C.E.

Shukla said, "Many years later, Shantanu's Chief Minister retired. He had been ill with a disease that was robbing him of his energy and the doctors had given up on him. I went to visit him and a chance remark by him to the effect that he should not have supported Shantanu's exploitation of the Prince's generosity to his father aroused my curiousity. When I asked him to clarify, he said it would take too long as he got tired very easily. My duties to the Kavi Sangha were not onerous; my position as the brother of the Queen meant that my movements were not questioned or subject to review. I paid many visits to the Chief Minister and that enabled me to reconstruct the events that took place after Shantanu received the message from Satyavati's father.

"Sashidhara, the Chief Minister, was an extraordinary actor – it is a curious act of fortune that the Chief Minister for Hastinapur came from the guild of performers. This goes back to Hastin's time, when Nagapura was founded as a caravan site. Caravans go on trips lasting months. Even though every day requires work, the tedium can be extreme. All caravans carry one or more performers who provide entertainment. Sometimes, a performer might become a close friend of the head trader. The guild of performers had always been one of the core guilds in Hastinapur.

"Shantanu was not trained to be King – he had two older brothers Devapi and Bahlika, and even if one died the other would be likely to succeed. When Shantanu became King, he was not ready to play the role. Shantanu had rejected the advisors suggested to him for the role of Chief Minister – they were much older than him, closer to his brothers, and he felt patronised. Sashidhara was a friend he trusted and he trusted his ability to read people's faces. He insisted that Sashidhara attend all meetings and all events alongside him – his friend's presence increased his confidence. Later, Shantanu insisted that Sashidhara be his Chief Minister, but the situation was not a happy one as Sashidhara lacked essential knowledge. Finally, Pratipa's old minister decided that it was best to accommodate the King – he took charge of Sashidhara's training and made a chief minister of the former actor.

"Sashidhara had been present when Devavrat renounced his inheritance. Despite the passage of time and Sashidhara's illness, he had never forgotten the events that led to the scene when Devavrat renounced his inheritance. He was able to recall these events with exceptional clarity, and able to portray, with his skills at *abhinaya*, what the participants felt as portrayed by their posture, their behaviour, their actions, and their words.

"Sashidhara was a skilled actor – he performed for me Shantanu's reaction when he heard the messenger; then as he narrated other events he performed other parts. It was a tour-de-force of the craft of *naatya*. Sashidhara told the story as though an invisible spectator had watched the staging of a play. What I will tell you now is Sashidhara's version of the events of that day as narrated to me.

"When the messenger came up to Shantanu and announced that he had come from the fisher-chief, Shantanu began to smile. The messenger asked for forgiveness if his message caused consternation – this prologue was unexpected and Shantanu's smile became fixed and his face darkened a deep brown. When the messenger had finished delivering the message, Shantanu's hands were shaking. There was no smile as he said to Sashidhara, 'This is preposterous. I can't be expected to comply – I cannot disinherit my son. Nor can I change the law just for my own sake, for I will be rightfully condemned as a hypocrite. Send an answer to the fisher-chief that his message hurts me.'

"Having said that the king walked out of the council chamber and entered his own quarters in the mansion. He did not come out for the next several days.

"Over the next few days the council did not meet at all as the king was absent. He would send a messenger after the morning meal to announce that he, Shantanu, was not well and did not wish to leave his quarters.

"Sashidhara did not send the fisher-chief the message that Shantanu had called for. After a few days, he came to the King's private quarters. He said, 'Sire, you do not need to fall ill in this fashion. These requests from Satyavati's father can be addressed.'

"'You are doing it again,' said the King. 'Trying to cheer me up by being optimistic. You can stop it. Or else…' He stopped as the meaning of the second sentence sank in.

"The King continued, 'How?'

"'Thank you, my lord, for listening to me. I do not offer a foolish optimism. All of Satyavati's requests can be accommodated, at least for the immediate future. First, you will announce that people can transfer their rights to a child to another person. Some transactions like these have already been reported, we would just be permitting something that people already do. I will then arrange for a number of volunteers, both men and women, who are willing to give up their rights for your sake.'

"'Surely that is not enough. What about my son Devavrat? What of his right to inherit the rule of this city?'

"'Sire, it is your prerogative to name Devavrat your heir, not his to assume by right. You can promise Satyavati that when a son is born, you will simply make Devavrat's rights subordinate to those of your new son.'

"'That does not change anything – we will still deprive Devavrat of his birth-right.'

"'Yes, sir. That path is strewn with conditions. Satyavati must first give birth to a son. Maybe sons. Those sons must then grow up to be crowned. For that matter, Prince Devavrat himself must survive until you die. This issue may never need to be settled.'

"'I will not lie,' said the King.

"'There is no need for you to lie. Nor will the Prince – I will talk to him about this.'

"Then Sashidhara approached Devavrat with a request. He said, 'Dear Yuvraj. The King, your father, wishes to make a request of you.'

"'My father is always welcome to ask, for his request is like a command,' said Devavrat.

"'King Shantanu would like you to relinquish the title of heir apparent.'

"Devavrat said, 'Relinquish my title as *heir apparent*? Is there something I have done? not done? I fail to understand. Is this a punishment? If so, why request it – the King has the right to withdraw this boon at any time. It is not a request, it is a command. I will comply. Tell me one thing, if you can… Why?'

"Sashidhara said, 'Your father, the King loves a woman and wishes to marry again. His wife-to-be has demanded that her son should be the next King. Only a descendant of both the King and the new Queen can ever be the ruler.'

Lomaharshana was jolted out of his trance-state, when he could not understand this proposal.

Lomaharshana said, "Sir! Please stop – I am confused. Satyavati had not demanded that."

Shukla said, "Good! Good! You get the point. I knew that matriarchs ruled the Panchnad cities – this was very much like the Naga settlements. Only Hastinapur was different. I thought that the Hastinapuris would not find a matriarch all that unusual. If I restored the matriarchy with Satyavati as the matriarch, her children would be rulers, and maybe they would even be the great rulers foretold by the wanderer. I modified the rule of inheritance slightly – even if my sister did not have daughters and a patriarchy was reinstated, the inheritance would only go through her descendants. I asked for her daughter to be matriarch and for her son to be the next King. The patriarchal Hastinapuris focused on the second part of this demand, that the son of the matriarch would be the King. In their minds, this was the important requirement – but in the mind of a Naga, the matriarchy would have greater importance. The two positions could even be reconciled in practice by requiring that some future matriarch marry a male descendant of Shantanu and crown him king."[115]

115 The Pharaohs of Egypt followed a rule of inheritance that could have developed from matrilinearity along similar lines. See Endnotes.

Lomaharshana said, "I understand the intent. What happened?"

"I thought I was being clear," said Shukla, "Unfortunately, I was not understood, and there was much confusion. That was not my intent. Some of that confusion has undoubtedly played a part in the disputes of today. However, the confusion of how this inheritance works has been a problem all along. As you know, this was a moot point, but yes, this error did play a role in what followed."

Shukla continued with the story he had been told. "Sashidhara had conveyed the request to Devavrat and Devavrat had fallen silent. It was a long silence. As the vighatis flowed by, Sashidhara wondered if he should have taken a more subtle approach. Then Devavrat said, 'This is good news! My father has been lonely and needs a Queen by his side. She would be my mother and my life is hers to command. A title is a little thing – I can easily give it up. Is that all she wants? Is there anything else I should give up?'

"Sashidhara said, 'That is a true observation, and wise, *Yuvraj*. This is all she asks. Your father will appreciate your generosity and greatness of heart.'

"'Nothing else?'

"'Yes. Nothing else from you.'

"'Who is she? How long has my father kept his wish a secret?'

"'He has not known her long. He has asked that this desire to marry again, as well as her identity, stay a secret for some more time.'

"'If he wishes that, I will certainly obey him.'

"'Your leave, Yuvraj!' said Sashidhara and left."

Shukla paused and took a sip of water.

Lomaharshana said, "Sir, may I venture an opinion?"

The Vyaasa smiled, "That is not expected of an archivist. The best archives contain fact not opinion."

"Sir, it is a Kavi Sangha principle that one person's fact is another's opinion."

"Tell me," said the Vyaasa. "What is this opinion you would venture?"

"This is an emotional mess. You expect me to convert it into a coherent story?"

The Vyaasa stared at Lomaharshana. Nobody said anything. As the silence lengthened, the seed of fear that he had overstepped, threatened to overcome Lomaharshana and he started shivering. Suddenly the Vyaasa laughed.

"Lomaharshana, courage is another attribute of a good archivist, for falsehood must be confronted. You have done well. I agree. The Chief Minister's story is difficult to understand. Simplify it if you can."

"I'll try."

The Vyaasa said, "Now, let's get back to Sashidhara's narration. My age is showing; what was I saying?"

"Sashidhara had been telling you the events of that day. He had just informed Prince Devavrat that his stepmother-to-be wanted her sons to inherit the throne and he had agreed to it with barely a moment's thought."

"Ah, yes. Sashidhara continued narrating the events following that conversation.

"The next day Prince Devavrat heard a proclamation in the centre of Hastinapur. I made the mistake of asking Sashidhara the question that popped into my mind. 'How did you know that Devavrat heard this?'

"Sashidhara's eyebrows went up and he stopped talking. It was a silly question – Sashidhara had a thousand spies reporting on the public actions of the Prince and the rest of the ruling family.

"The King's herald proclaimed, 'Attention! Attention! O People of Hastinapur! Attention! The King has issued a proclamation!'

"Devavrat was in a class being conducted by the Kavi Sangha when the announcement was made. The class was conducted under a banyan tree in a small garden off the central square of Hastinapur and the crier's voice could be heard in the class, loud and clear. One of Sashidhara's many spies guarding Devavrat reported that at first, Devavrat turned towards the source of the cry and there was a smile on his face.

"The crier continued: 'The King has decided to heed the call of his people. A market in which men and women can buy and sell their right to have a child will be established. His son, Prince Devavrat will be the arbiter. The Prince will deal with all questions. He will be personally responsible to the King for his decision on every purchase.'

"The spy did not expect what followed. They had not been given any specific directions, just to keep the Prince from coming to harm, so the Prince's behaviour was simply inexplicable. As the announcement ended and its meaning sank in, the Prince jumped up and shouted, 'No!' It was apparent that the announcement might have been a surprise for the Prince. The other students and the teacher had turned to stare at him but he was oblivious to their stares. He looked around as though he was lost; he may have been looking for a way to run, but he did not. Instead he headed for the tree and the other students parted to clear his path; he sat down hunkered against it, his knees folded against his chest and his head bent down. Everybody was silent. Later, the Chief

Minister met with the teacher and the students to persuade them to be silent about the Prince's reaction. The teacher, a kavi who had a fondness for simile and metaphor, described the Prince as a man who had walked off a cliff and his feet were flailing as they sought purchase. They cooperated and news of the episode never spread.

"Ten vighatis passed. Devavrat's head came up. His eyes were dull and seemed to be focused far away. He stood up and without looking at anybody or even acknowledging the teacher, he walked out of the class. The spy followed him – Devavrat went to the council chamber where his father was in a meeting with the Chief Minister.

"He said, 'Father! Chief Minister! I just heard your town crier announcing the new market for buying child-rights. What is this? When did you decide this? When did you decide to name me as the arbiter?'

"Sashidhara said, '*Yuvraj*! Were you not informed? This plan was discussed at an emergency meeting this morning. Your servants told us that you were away by the river.'

"Devavrat's eyes were cold and distant as he turned and stared at the Chief Minister, as though his presence was an unfortunate accident. Devavrat said, 'Please do not explain why you did not tell me. I know why you did not tell me. I want to know why you are creating a market for these rights at this time.'

"The Chief Minister said, 'Yuvraj, you know yourself that the law we have created is a harsh law. We need it because of the crisis. The Kavi Sangha expected that the law would discourage the refugees from coming to Hastinapur. We hoped that those who did, would go past us to the newer settlements further south along the Ganga where the law would not apply. Within Hastinapur, the law has fallen most heavily on people who are poor and do not have the resources to adjust to the crisis. This has been a source of unrest.'

"'We have known this for a long time,' said Devavrat. 'What is the difference now?'

"Sashidhara continued, 'In celebration of the King's wedding, we thought that we could soften the law. Every year, some people try to circumvent the law and the result is unhappiness. We could address that problem, for every year a number of childless persons die, forfeiting their right to a child. They could transfer their rights. Some of these people die of illnesses that require special care or for which the only cure is in a foreign land, Takshashila for instance – if they had some property or other wherewithal, they could arrange with a merchant or trader to take them there in exchange for this right. Their right to have a child is the only valuable property they possess.'

"The Prince was not mollified. He said, 'Your spy service needs to be re-trained, apparently, if they cannot track the pregnant women in Hastinapur at any one time.'

"'I will certainly deal with that deficiency, *Yuvraj*. Your advice is most welcome. Meanwhile some residents of Hastinapur desire another child. We asked the Kavi Sangha whether it was wise to let such people buy the child-right of another. Initially the Kavi Sangha opposed such changes – softening the law would gut it. During the morning's discussion that you missed, Yuvraj, the question that came up repeatedly was the seller's reasons for selling off their child-right. The Kavi Sangha representative suggested the reasons we came up with. For my part, it felt less than legitimate – one sold one's child-right at the risk of injuring one's ancestors, whose spirits rely for sustenance on the food we eat. The ancestor with no descendant is doomed to starve in the world of ancestral spirits. However, I did not wish to oppose the Vyaasa's counsel.

"'The Kavi Sangha added one minor condition. They wanted Shantanu to encourage the seller to migrate to one of the frontier settlements where the right to children would be restored. This would encourage younger, more flexible men and women to be pioneers while the older immigrants tried to make their living in the city.'

"Devavrat said, 'Kavi Sangha proposals have never been acted on hastily. How was this proposal approved in one short meeting? Was the Vyaasa consulted?'

"The Chief Minister said, '*Yuvraj,* you know that Guru Parashara has taken on a vow of silence. He does not speak. It had to be this way.'"

The Vyaasa Shukla said to Lomaharshana, "The Chief Minister would recall his faux pas vividly in later years. The only decisions that were described as 'it had to be this way' were ones that the King had already made, ones for which the council approval was *pro forma*. As the head of the Kuru family became increasingly regal, his expressed wishes had become commandments. What followed was a direct consequence."

Shukla continued, "The Chief Minister reported this as one of the most dramatic confrontations he had seen between Devavrat and his father. Devavrat turned to his father, 'Why now?'

"Shantanu could not meet his son's gaze. He looked away, and then down. His hands shook and a slight flush crept up his face. 'It had to be now.'

"Devavrat said, 'Your new wife wants children and does not want to be bound by your laws!'

"The King's voice was a whisper. 'Yes.'

"'You've already asked me to give up my right to the crown. Why did you not ask me to give up my right to a son to you so that you and the Queen can have a boy as well as a girl child?'

"Shantanu's eyes scrutinised a spot on the ground. He said, 'Err... I am sure we would not want that...'

"The Chief Minister said, 'We know, *Yuvraj*, how devoted you are to your father. I advised the King to be cautious. There are so many problems: the new Queen may be barren. She may only have daughters. Who but you could be King?'

"Devavrat looked at his father and then at the Chief Minister. As the implications of the Chief Minister's statements dawned on him, his face changed – anger had turned it red, shock made it lose colour; his eyes which sparkled with rage, turned hooded and dull; his full cheeks lost their tone and turned grey like a slab of unpolished granite."

The Vyaasa Shukla said, "Recalling how Devavrat changed colour, the old Chief Minister's voice shook and became a whisper. I had to lean very close to hear him.

"The Chief Minister told me, 'That was one of the times that I watched the Prince closely and I felt I was looking into a soul in pain. He resembled his father in so many ways, except this one – the King never seemed to have suffered any kind of deep, exposed damage. The manner in which Devavrat conducted himself was also revealing. He was a young man with a well-toned physique and was impressive when he held himself straight. His father had looked the same way when he had turned twenty. His neck turned pink and if his upper body garment (*angavastram)* had not been there, it would have been seen spreading in all directions. I watched as his face regained its colour. His fingers were shaking. If he was anything like his father, he was going to explode with anger. I signed to the guard, for prince or no prince, he could not be allowed to injure the king. He finally spoke, in a low bass voice that came from a mouth framed by lips that curled down, topped with a nose that flared with every stressed word.' I was struck at the vividness of the old man's memory and memorised his exact words from that point on. He continued with his narrative:

"Then the Prince said, 'This is how you begin your new marriage – with a lie and a promise? You tell her that her children will be King, that she can have as many as she pleases. My mother died for your plans. My brothers were killed as babies. Now you want me to arrange the buying and selling of child-rights for your new love?'

"The King looked up briefly and was about to say something. Sashidhara thought that such an act would not be wise, no matter what the King said, so he patted the air with his hand, palm facing down, signalling the need for patience. Fortunately, he said, the King saw the motion and kept quiet, not saying whatever he had intended to say. He let his eyes drift back to the ground. Devavrat did not stop his rant and the words continued without a break.

"'You did not want to ask me to offer the logical sacrifice now. Just in case there are no sons there would be no need to deliver on the sacrifice you would have to demand of me. You even created a new role for me – chief broker for buying and selling children.'

"Sashidhara tried to intervene – he said, '*Yuvraj*...'

"Devavrat turned to him, his face livid, 'Don't call me *Yuvraj*! I am done with that title. You chose this... this is your solution.'

"That was the last time the Chief Minister called him by that title. He said, 'You make it sound complicated.'

"Shantanu's face sagged and looked grey. He said, 'Son, please do not be angry. I want her to be my Queen. I think of her constantly and am unable to do anything else.'

"Devavrat's voice did not change. 'Take me to this paragon. I will renounce my rights to Kingship there.'"

Shukla said, "The demand froze the King and the Chief Minister – they stood still like blocks of ice cut from the eternally white heights of the Himalayas. Sashidhara said that he intended to suggest a quiet meeting in a more private location, but that Devavrat forestalled him. Devavrat was in no mood to wait. Sashidhara often wondered what would have happened if he had succeeded in preventing the ensuing drama. The world might have been a different place.

"Devavrat called in a louder voice, to the doorman, 'Call Bakakula, right away.'

"Sashidhara heard the King say, 'Stop! Don't do this', but the words came out as a gruff mumble. Sashidhara did not want to go either, but when the cart came, they followed Devavrat into it silently.

"Devavrat said to the Chief Minister, 'Tell him where to go.'

"The Chief Minister looked at the King, but there was no help there. The King seemed to be struck dumb, almost as if bewitched. Devavrat made a sound, a groan that sounded as if he was about to rant again. The Chief Minister said to Bakakula, 'Take us to the fishing village – you know the house.'

"Bakakula nodded and they set off. Nobody spoke for the entire ride. They rode past the village and that is when I saw them. The way they sat in the cart struck me as strange and I did not know what to make of it. I thought it might have to do with my sister, so I followed right behind them, and as I expected, they went to my father's house. Sashidhara looked at me, but at that time, I was just another Naga boy, and he did not even recall it.

"Devavrat had been sitting, unmoving, as though he was completely oblivious. When the cart stopped, his forehead furrowed. I heard him ask the driver, 'What are we doing here?'

"The driver said, 'This is the lady's house, sir.'

"Devavrat shook his head as though he did not believe him, but he did not move.

"My father must have heard the noise they made when they stopped, for he came out of the house. I could see that he was nervous – he rushed down the steps and stood by them as if prepared to stop anybody. He saw me and waved at me – he wanted me to leave, but I did not obey his signal. He was not smiling, but his mouth was in a fixed grimace, a replacement for a welcoming smile. In all my life I had never seen him act as strangely as he did that day. The Chief Minister whispered something to the King, but the King's countenance did not change and he showed no sign that he had heard or understood what Sashidhara said. Later, the Chief Minister told me what he had said – *Be careful; he looks likes a scared man and in his fear, he may go berserk. We should act to reassure him.*

"I think the Chief Minister's reading of my father was wrong. My father glanced at me again and frowned – he really wanted me to leave. I did not. He made a sign with his hands. I could not believe it – it was the *reversed pataka* sign, used to warn people of the presence of a deadly predator, like a tiger. I did not leave. He frowned but then it was time to attend to his visitors. Later he would tell me that he was concerned that the King might kidnap Satyavati and kill anybody who opposed him. He was unhappy and worried when I did not leave, and he had done his best to hide that.

"My father said, 'Welcome, sirs. We are overjoyed at your visit to this humble house. We cannot compare to your palaces and mansions, but please accept our hospitality.'

"The King and the Prince were silent, gazing into the distance. The Chief Minister said, 'The King and his son wish to see your daughter Satyavati.'

"Devavrat turned sharply when he heard the name. A glow returned to his eyes even as his brow furrowed.

"'My dear daughter is inside. She will be delighted, I am sure, to see you. Please come in.'

"The King and Chief Minister came down from the cart. Devavrat did not move. The Chief Minister made a gesture, inviting him to step out. Devavrat remained motionless for a vighati or so, and then came off the cart. They went into the cottage and I followed, despite another frown from my father. The baby was in a hammock hanging from the ceiling a short distance from the door. Satyavati was pushing the baby back and forth in his hammock. Across from the hammock a number of clean, unused banana leaves had been set in front of seating pads – they were preparing to eat lunch.

"When the visitors entered through the door, Satyavati rose and spoke, palms joined in front of her. 'We are honoured that you come to our simple house. Please come in. Please sit here,' she said, pointing to a low seat next to her.

The Chief Minister spoke while both the King and Devavrat stayed silent.

"'Namaskar, Satyavati! The King would speak with you.'

"Satyavati's eyes were wide and she smiled. She looked perfectly composed. I knew there was turmoil in her mind; how she managed that smile, I do not know. Despite his anger, I could see Devavrat respond, the lines of anger in his face disappear as he drank in her soft brown eyes, and a reflected smile began to form in his eyes and lips. Satyavati had been looking at him, but she then turned to the Chief Minister. I think that was when the significance of the Chief Minister's words must have hit him, for the smile vanished; the strangeness of the situation, his father's presence, and the exchanges he had had with the Chief Minister, conspired to drag that smile away. His eyes became slits and his forehead wrinkled; I could see his throat moved as he swallowed saliva, usually a sign that somebody is preparing for some action.

"Satyavati said, 'With me?'

"The King seemed to be having second thoughts. Then he asked a strange question. 'Is it true that an astrologer has predicted a bright future for your descendants?'

"Both Sashidhara and Devavrat's faces were studies in puzzlement, eyes moving upward, brows furrowed.

"'I don't know, sir, but that is what some people say.'

"Her father said, 'Sir, forgive a foolish man's credulity – I should have known better than to tell people of the astrologer's ravings.'

"'No matter,' said the King. Their words had given him the time to compose himself. This time, he spoke plainly. 'You have demanded that I marry only one wife, namely yourself. That I will assent to. You also said that you would only marry me if my laws did not kill your children and if your sons would be King after my death. These are difficult demands. Tell me, are these your wishes?'

"Devavrat was standing aloof from his father – he snapped his head round to face his father when he heard his father's words. I watched Devavrat all the while; his eyes had a faraway look, he was swaying slightly, as though he felt the floor was collapsing below him.

"I had not anticipated this path. I did not know where it would lead. My sister was on her own and would have to navigate by herself.

"Satyavati said, 'Yes, sir. Those are my conditions.'

"*Don't say that!* I wanted to say, but 'No' led into a fog of uncertainty.

"Shantanu said, 'Your demands have created a storm in my family.'

"Satyavati glanced at Devavrat, glanced away, and was quiet. When Sashidhara was describing this to me, I told him of what had transpired between Devavrat and my sister – it was the first time he had known of their mutual infatuation and he now believes she was waiting for Devavrat to say something. I was too inexperienced to make that deduction, so I do not know that I could have done anything. Neither Devavrat nor Satyavati said anything. I regret that they did not – if only they had... if only they had...I regret that I did not do something, anything, that would have stopped what happened."

Shukla stopped. He turned his face away from Lomaharshana and stared into the far corner of the tent. The wrinkles on his forehead deepened and his eyes retreated into the shadow of his eyelids. Lomaharshana waited. *There is no hurry,* he thought. *This story has been simmering for a long time and we can wait a little longer.*

Shukla turned his head and stared at the Archivist. *I hope he survives this test of faith. The war between the Pandavas and the Kauravas has done much damage to the Kavi Sangha. Now, I've laid out my contribution, my corruption, and my regrets. If only that were all – there is more to come.*

Lomaharshana said, "Are you feeling ill, sir? We can continue later."

Shukla said, "Thank you for your patience. I have much to atone for. I don't want to stop, I would much rather finish this."

"As you wish, sir. I am ready if you want to continue."

Shukla said, "After that exchange between the King and my sister, everybody was quiet. The King, Devavrat, Satyavati, my father, and Sashidhara stood still as statues. Nobody paid attention to me. The silence went on and on. I glanced at Devavrat, whose eyes were glazed and unfocused as if sightless. Satyavati did not turn her face to his. Devavrat's head must have been spinning. Two vighatis felt like an eternity. Then Satyavati said, 'My conditions are just and honourable. My children would not be subject to death if I were to marry anyone else, in my band or even in other Naga bands – why should I make them subject to your arbitrary culling. As a mother, I shall want my children to prosper and not be subject to anyone. My descendants will be free if they rule. It would not be honourable to plot such a succession after we are married, so I make this condition clear in advance.'

"Shantanu said, 'I accept your conditions.'

"Then he pointed to Devavrat. He said, 'This is my one and only son, Devavrat.'

"When he said that, Satyavati's head snapped around to look at Devavrat, who was now looking at the ground, as though hoping that it would open and swallow him.

"Shantanu continued, 'He has been my heir since he came of age and expected to rule after me. Today, he renounced this inheritance. As a condition he desired to see you and to hear your conditions directly from you.'

"My memory of this moment is of unmoving statues. Sashidhara's version was dramatic, especially after he learned of Devavrat's nascent feelings for Satyavati. The walls imprisoning Devavrat would have collapsed when the King said these words but Devavrat would not achieve freedom thereby. He raised his head to look at Satyavati but he could not meet her eyes. I think in these last minutes he lost hope that she might prefer to be with him rather than his father, and that doubt held him back from speaking. He hung his head and only looked at her feet. His eyes were dull, like the eyes of a newly released lifelong prisoner. Devavrat would only have seen boundaries and restrictions no matter where he looked.

"Then, breaking all the rules that Sashidhara believed governed human behaviour, Devavrat raised his head and stared directly at Satyavati. Satyavati flushed at the implied challenge and her own anger at the world that was being constructed around her surfaced.

"Satyavati said, 'I am touched by your son's desire to satisfy his father at the cost of his own interests. The Prince is always welcome to visit me and to ask me any question.'

"The King glanced at Devavrat, trying to comprehend his son. Devavrat stared at Satyavati as if he wanted to read her innermost thoughts. This time, Satyavati looked away, her eyes dull and blank. Sashidhara modelled their looks for me, a look that showed a man who feels betrayed to the core, and the look of a woman who had lost faith that her life could be salvaged, that somebody could do something to stop a runaway cart. They were silent. The silence stretched for one vighati, then another, then a third. The Chief Minister coughed.

"Devavrat stirred. His eyes were looking at something far in the distance. He said, 'My father has announced that I will manage a market in which people can buy and sell their rights to have children. He expects that he will be able to buy as many child-rights for you as you desire. I am no longer his heir, I am the supervisor of the barter of children.'

"Satyavati said, 'That is not what I asked for–'

"She could not finish the sentence for Devavrat continued to talk.

"'I will not be party to such trades. My father desires you and you want your children to rule. Your demands...'

"'But...'

"'Rather, your wishes shall come true. I hereby renounce all my rights to have children, and give them to my father.'

"'Prince, but...'

"Shantanu interrupted her. 'Devavrat, what are you saying?'

"Devavrat bowed deeply to his father, palms joined. 'Father, our ancestor Yayati demanded a year of youth from his son Puru. As it was for Yayati, so must it be for you – your desires too must be satisfied. To you, I yield my birthright. Lady, I see a woman mad with the desire to be mother to kings. My mother asked me to promise that I would take care of my father – I see no way to stop this mutual lunacy without violating that promise, and causing pain to you, my living father. You will not need a market for the trading of children and I do not have to create one. This is my vow – I will not marry, I will not have children, I will not make love to any woman. O King, my father, my right to father a male child is yours. Welcome, O Queen, to the Kaurava family.'

"Tears came unbidden to my sister's eyes. She said, 'But...' and stopped, for Devavrat had turned away and was walking to the door.

"Devavrat turned just outside the door to face Shantanu. 'I will not run your child-right exchange, Father. Be satisfied with what you have obtained here.'

"Shantanu followed his son down the steps. The Chief Minister followed him. Satyavati too followed them and I was close behind her. Shantanu said, 'Son! Why did you do that? You don't need to swear an oath. Not such a terrible one. Chief Minister, say something to stop him. Bring him back. What a terrible vow.'

"The Chief Minister said, 'Do not worry, my dear friend. This storm will pass. You have what you came for.'

"He repeated this last nugget of advice, appealing to the King as the friends they had once been, his voice a whisper. Meanwhile the King mumbled his plea to Devavrat, his voice slowly losing strength. They did this repeatedly. Finally Shantanu stopped, turned to Sashidhara, and the whisper got its hearing.

"The King turned back to Satyavati and said, 'Satyavati! Your demands have been met. I assure you that I will do whatever it takes to ensure that your children will live. Your son will be King after me.'

"Satyavati stared at Devavrat who continued to walk away towards the hunting trail. She had not stopped her attempts to say something, but only managed to get to 'But…' as she was interrupted each time. This time it was the Chief Minister.

"'Great lady, I take your leave! Let your father know that he should prepare for the wedding.'

"With those words he left, following the King, who was following Devavrat."

Shukla said, "That was the end of that climactic scene as the King, the Chief Minister, and Devavrat walked away from my childhood home. The King and Chief Minister entered the cart and sat down; they watched as Devavrat walked off into the forest."

Lomaharshana said, "So the most dramatic moments in this are the imaginings of an actor?"

Shukla smiled and said, "Shush, boy! I was there and what happened differs only in suspense from Sashidhara's take. His memory for the conversations match mine exactly – I had some training in the Kavi Sangha schools so I think I can be confident that it happened that way."

Shukla continued, "I had kept quiet during the march down the steps. I watched as the cart holding the Chief Minister and the King disappeared into the forest. As soon as they disappeared, I ran to my sister and hugged her. I said, 'You did it! You did it!' repeatedly, while she stood stiff in my arms like a tree trunk that refused to budge. Even now, after all these years, I can feel the smile that broke out on my face.

"I said, 'You are to be the Queen of Hastinapur! That's marvellous! That's the best thing that could happen.' I looked at my father who was also standing stiff and unmoving. I remember thinking, *What's the matter? Why aren't they happy too?*

"Satyavati said, 'I am lost. I will kill myself.'

"My father said, 'Shukla! See what your mad plan has done. The King agreed to all her demands – now she must marry Shantanu.'

"I had watched the Prince earlier when he approached my sister; now, I had seen his extraordinary overreaction to the King's acceptance of the demands. *What kind of man gave up so easily,* I wondered. *He is a weakling, not one who would create an empire. If there is any truth to the fortune teller's predictions, he is not fit to be her husband.* I occasionally recall that judgement, and how wrong it was, how grounded in ignorance and arrogance – the memory serves to curb my own sudden groundless enthusiasms.

"I said, 'This is the best alternative – the Prince is a young man who does not know his own mind. He loves her now, but that can change with the next beautiful woman he sees. Now she is destined to be the Queen and our band will gain protection from the city.'

"'I'll be the Queen, the dead Queen.'

"Our father said, 'Satyavati! Please do not speak like that.'

"'It doesn't matter,' she said. 'I might as well be dead.'

"'If you kill yourself, our band and other Meena bands will suffer at the hands of the King. You cannot do this.'

"'I might as well be dead.'"

Lomaharshana had been looking confused – it seemed to Shukla that he looked increasingly uncomfortable.

The Vyaasa said, 'What's the matter, my son?'

Lomaharshana said, 'Sir, excuse me, I understand the Queen Mother's reaction. The Chief Minister's story, ending with the King and the Prince departing in different directions, makes no sense. What happens next?'

The Vyaasa grimaced and said, "Lomaharshana, I am reporting the Chief Minister's memory of an old conversation. I was there and all I remember are the words but not the feelings. I did not know Devavrat those days, and even though we became friends later, there were certain subjects that were never talked about. I don't think he knew that I knew of his loss. I did not know then why and how his mother died or what he had been through. He should have hated his father, but he was in his late teens and I was a few years younger. When we were together, we were occupied with other things; I was not privy to his innermost thoughts.

"There is one additional vignette to narrate – following Kaurava practice, Shantanu visited Parashara, as the head of the Kavi Sangha, to get his blessings for the marriage. My father had secluded himself saying that he was not well; my sister pleaded the ages-old malady of women, the monthly period of rest and seclusion; I went along as the only person in the village who could interpret for the Vyaasa. Sashidhara did not know of this expedition – I suspect he would not have been as easily deceived as the King.

"Shantanu did not know that the baby in the house was Satyavati's son by Parashara – young children in Naga bands had many caretakers and he assumed that the baby Krishna was just another child. He did not know that Parashara had once been my sister's lover

"Shantanu informed Parashara of the proposal wedding and asked for the Kavi Sangha's blessing. I could see conflict writ large in Parashara's eyes but Shantanu did not. Parashara controlled his feelings and gave his blessing. If only Shantanu had stopped there, I would not have guilt hanging over me.

"Shantanu saw fit to ask about the prediction that Satyavati would be the mother of great kings ruling an empire. Over many years, and despite my father's feeble attempts to correct it, the prediction by a wandering traveller became ascribed to Parashara just before he had stopped speaking. Shantanu chose to ask Parashara about the prediction.

"Parashara signed that he knew nothing of a prediction. I kept my voice low as I translated and told the King that the prediction was real. Parashara may have taken a vow of silence but his hearing was acute. He signed some more, demanding that I tell the truth. I translated these new signs, constructing a revised version of the prediction. Parashara became increasingly disturbed and tried once more – I continued my dissimulation.

"Lomaharshana, you might wonder at my younger self's actions. I was playing a dangerous game, one hanging by gossamer threads woven by an invisible spider. I hoped Parashara would not break his oath for I had seen him hold his tongue when my sister exiled him. I also banked on Shantanu's love of my sister – the King would be angry at me if I were exposed, but he would stay his hand. For a few moments, it was touch and go as Parashara struggled with his dilemma -- to my relief, he did nothing. He sat still for a few vighatis, signed again, and then left abruptly.

"'What did he say?' asked the King.

"I had to say something. 'He warned me to stay close to my sister for she would need my protection as well as yours.'

"In this manner, I assured myself a permanent place in the entourage of the ruling family.

"I discovered that life in the palace was mostly tedious and only the Kavi Sangha's meeting halls provided a stimulating environment. Devavrat would also be there and I was only a bit younger than he was.

"'I think that Devavrat welcomed the loss of kingship – in those early meetings with the Kavi Sangha, Devavrat was sometimes subversive, questioning the Kavi Sangha's wisdom. Since he was not a guild member and was a prince, he was not vulnerable to pressure.

"There are two parts to the puzzle of *Yuvraj* Devavrat as he was then known. Only he knows what happened between him and his father Shantanu in the years following his mother's death.

He had blamed his father and the Kavi Sangha for the death of his mother. The Chief Minister said that he took the young Devavrat under his wing. The Chief Minister was empathetic and allowed Devavrat a free rein to express his feelings over his mother's death and determine how to deal with it. He pointed out how dependent his father was on the Kavi Sangha and how the Kavi Sangha used the King to execute its plans. In the ordinary scheme of things the guild of bards was a useful organisation; it had acquired great power with great potential for evil and the Vyaasa was directly responsible for using this power.

"The thesis that his father was manipulated by a powerful Vyaasa impressed the young Devavrat. The Kavi Sangha archives reveal how often this happens, from Samvarana onwards. Yes, Vyaasas sometimes bite off more than they can digest. Even the founder, Vasishtha, could be said to have over-played his hand when he established a standing army. The Vyaasa Bharadvaja, who proposed the one-child-per-person law and was the Vyaasa at the time of his mother's death, passed away a few years later and Parashara became the Vyaasa. One of Parashara's first acts as Vyaasa was to come to Devavrat and express sorrow at the death of his mother. He also promised to work at changing the law, but before he could do that, he was surrounded by controversy and sentenced to his vow of silence. Parashara's intervention enabled Devavrat to grudgingly accept that his father was not responsible for his mother's death, and he recollected the many conversations in which his father had expressed sorrow and contrition at what had to be done. Much blame could be attached to Bharadvaja, the most conspiratorial Vyaasa in history. The Chief Minister considered the reconciliation between Devavrat and Shantanu his own greatest achievement.

"Sashidhara was in a nostalgic mood. The floodgates of reminiscence lifted when I told him of Devavrat's feelings for Satyavati. It explained so much that had puzzled him. In his opinion, Devavrat could excuse his father for falling in love with

Satyavati – it was human nature, Satyavati was beautiful, his father was weak, one who gave in easily to his desires. Devavrat did not extend that forgiveness to Satyavati herself – her actions were not a result of a Kavi Sangha plot gone awry, but those of a deeply deceptive and dishonest person. She had deceived him, if not with her words, then with her eyes. The demands she had made of the King showed her for the ambitious woman she was – one determined to be Queen and Matriarch of a dynasty. He would have suspected even the Chief Minister, Sashidhara thought. As Chief Minister he had displayed his chicanery – he had played a trick to persuade Devavrat to give up the throne. The Kaurava family had become rotten at its core – the thought of establishing a market for the rights to have a child would have made him feel that he was in a creek carrying sewage and other decaying matter – Sashidhara had an actor's felicity with words. Devavrat would have said to himself that he was glad that he had forestalled the rot by vowing celibacy. If Satyavati suffered because of his vow, she deserved it. Everybody around him was flawed and only Devavrat had held to the truth – he would gladly give up the throne if it would make his father happy. He would be happiest if his father obtained release from the deadly embrace of the Kavi Sangha.

"I questioned the Chief Minister closely about this interpretation of events. 'Experience is the mother of all knowledge,' he said. He pointed to his belly just below the navel. 'I understood Devavrat here, in my gut,' he said. 'Devavrat was *quick to judge, quick to act, and quick to forgive.*'

"Whether accurate or not, this assessment of Devavrat did not describe his actions with respect to my sister Satyavati. She was judged in the blink of an eye; the consequent acts made in the next instant; but, of forgiveness, there was none extended to my sister.

"Satyavati became the cup-bearer of all Devavrat's anger at his mother's death, at the Kavi Sangha's mistakes, at his disdain for my sister's ambition, as he saw it. I could not tell him of my role in devising the disastrous strategy. Nor could she, for he so clearly lusted for her, perhaps even loved her, and that option had closed forever.

"I observed him closely during the days immediately after that dramatic vow. If he was angry about it, he did not show it. He avoided the subject of Satyavati, his new stepmother. He avoided her – if she was in the palace, he would be elsewhere, if she were headed to the marketplace in the centre of the city, he would go hunting in the forest.

"The only subject he seemed to care about was the refugee crisis and how it could be managed."

The Uncertainty of Support

Kaushambi/Hastinapur
circa 850 B.C.E.

Vaishampaayana was tired. Reciting these verses made the dry autumn days seem longer and the warm breeze hotter. Chandrasekhar was flexing his fingers and wrists, rubbing down the muscles of his arm, a grimace twisting on his face. *Was writing that hard? It didn't look like it needed any effort.* The only person who seemed energised was Bhargava – he'd done nothing but listen. *That is strange – a half-day's work as a contract witness and registrar in the marketplace used to leave me dazed. The thrill of memorising was followed by a fog that obscured one's identity. Purpose would seem absent.* On very busy market days, the Kavi Sangha would send out off-duty members to make sure that the bards registering the contracts made it back home. He'd been on both sides of that transaction and now, he felt like he had been wrung dry like a wet *angavastram*.

Bhargava, however, looked unaffected.

"Do you recall anything I said?" Vaishampaayana asked.

"Sort of," said Bhargava. "I like to absorb the emotions I feel when I listen to a story. This story arouses much emotion, it makes me quiet."

"Silly of me. I thought you were sleeping."

"I don't need to memorise it, brother. My son here is writing it all down. If I ever feel the need to know exactly what you said, I'll fetch the written account and, there you are! I can re-experience those emotions once again."

Bhargava continued, "Don't worry. I heard you. Let me show you that I was paying attention. I am going to guess that at the end, Satyavati kills herself. Why is Devavrat silent? Because thinking about the loss revives his grief?"

"So, you *were* sleeping. That's it for today. I am tired. How lucky for you that you aren't."

"How can I ever be tired listening to you?"

Vaishampaayana smiled at the flattery. He could not find the energy to continue. He could not find the energy to argue.

Instead, he said, "Ah-ha! Flattery. So you say you are interested. That's all right, go on pretending. I should know better than to tell stories to ignorant foreigners. Any Hastinapuri audience would know why Devavrat couldn't speak. I would not have to explain anything."

Bhargava had not heard his friend make a remark of this kind before. "Vais, that's unfair. You yourself said that I should ask for clarifications. That's what I am doing. So, tell me – does she kill herself or doesn't she?"

"Tomorrow. I will see you tomorrow."

Chandrasekhar said, "Don't fret, Father, I'll read the story out this evening."

The next day, when Bhargava and Chandrasekhar came, Vaishampaayana had moved his mat to the side of the alcove in the ficus tree outside his house. He glanced at the two of them for a moment, then continued what he was doing, apparently cleaning the hole in the tree. A small fist-sized and almost conical stone daubed with red was on his right and a smaller stone covered with *vibhuti,* sacred ash, was next to it. Bhargava waited, while Vaishampaayana went about the task methodically. *Too methodically,* Bhargava felt, as the waiting stretched. His son Chandrasekhar seemed to have learned patience if nothing else during his apprenticeship. He was glad that his son had learned to be a scribe, as it allowed Bhargava to help his friend out. He had watched him scribe the previous day – *what a useless skill writing was, good for accounting and inventory management but a waste for everything else.* He wished Vaishampaayana would finish what he was doing so they could get started. *If this were a barter being discussed, I would lose the exchange.* Finally, he coughed and said, "Vais, can we get started?" Vaishampaayana put a small reed mat to mark off a sitting area in the alcove. He picked up the larger stone and touched it to his eyes, first the right, then the left, and placed the stone into the hole. He repeated with the smaller stone. Then he turned to Bhargava and said, "Those idiots have refused my funding request!"

What idiots? Bhargava was going to ask, but he realised he knew the people concerned. *They aren't idiots -- it's your own fault.* That's what he wanted to say. He knew that it would have made no difference, would have been worse than useless. Vaishampaayana was on the council – he was, perhaps, even the most respected member of the council. If he made his request with authority, the others would fall over themselves to give it to him. Vaishampaayana's attitude and behaviour in this situation struck Bhargava as obtuse. Whenever one of his proposals was for the benefit of the Kavi Sangha, Vaishampaayana would send another member of the Kavi Sangha to plead on their behalf and recuse himself from the council. If I stay, *they will approve it for me and not for my arguments in its favour.* Vaishampaayana had explained to Bhargava. There was more, though – if the council were evenly divided, Vaishampaayana would vote against his own proposal. The city elders must have balked at whatever new estimate of time and effort Vaishampaayana had given them. It was a mammoth task, no doubt. Just in the last few days, Bhargava and Chandrasekhar had gone through an impressive number of palm leaves. This was easily the longest document Bhargava had ever seen – he had never seen so many palm leaves in one place. They had gone through a small part of the story, less than a tenth, Bhargava estimated. Why, Devavrat was barely an adult. *The story has to go on until the hero dies, doesn't it?* That thought raised another unexpected question. *Was Devavrat the hero?* He realised he did not know.

"What did you ask for?" Bhargava said.

"Nothing much. I asked them to provide support through next winter for ten bards and two of your readers."

It seemed a little excessive to Bhargava. Granted, it might take that long, but only a few apprentices could help with this task at a time. *Ten apprentices? What was Vais thinking of?*

"What have they offered?" He realised that getting involved was going to cost him. *I'm going to have to pay to finish this project.*

"They've cancelled the support I asked for your boys. In addition, they've restricted the support they promised me – now it will only be until next spring. The coming spring! Even if we work night and day, we will not be done. How am I to feed you and your apprentices as well as mine? This was their project, not mine. They wanted it written up, not me. All I wanted was to rebuild the Kavi Sangha in Hastinapur. I tell you, they have no shame! The last straw was the cut in the budget for palm leaves. How do they think we will abbreviate the archives? 'Drop unnecessary stories,' they said. 'Drop anything that has not been requested for a long time.'"

"Accept their offer," Bhargava said.

850 B.C.E

"Accept it? That will stop our work dead in the ruts along the road. What will I finish the project with?"

"Don't let it be known, but I'll make some food available from my trading partners. That will allow you to stretch the budget the council has given you. Perform something at the spring festival and get the public on your side. Then ask for an extension. Even if they don't, I'll help you finish this project."

Vaishampaayana smiled broadly at Bhargava – he stood up and hugged him. "I knew that Siva and Ganesha would come through."

"Good," said Bhargava, disengaging himself. "Now, let's continue from yesterday."

The Marriage of Satyavati

THE PANDAVA CAMP
CIRCA 2000 B.C.E.

"I might as well be dead."

The Vyaasa Shukla continued his narration with Satyavati's desperate response to the sudden turn of events.

Shukla said, "Satyavati's announcement resounded like a drum made of lead. My sister thus announced her indifference to death. My father and I were familiar with Satyavati's proclamations, but there had never been anything as unusual as this situation or announcement as extreme as this one. *I might as well be dead.*

"I recall thinking, *Yes, the situation was a bit extreme. You could even say it had gotten out of hand.* However, she was going to be a Queen – what's the big deal who she married? I look back at the young Shukla and am appalled at his insensitivity and selfishness. Was that me? Are all children like that at that age? I could not imagine why my sister would wish herself dead over a marriage. After all, there had been no drama when, at the age of fifteen, she had welcomed Parashara to her bed. He was handsome, clever, fit, and devoted to her. I was barely ten years old and did not pay attention to most of the social interactions that went on around me, whether romantic or otherwise. Unfortunately, he was even more devoted to the Kavi Sangha. When he asked us to keep his parentage of Krishna Dvaipaayana a secret, she had gone along and asked us to honour that request. There had been no drama, no morbid resignation. She finally informed him that he was not welcome to visit, but it had been a calm and reasoned decision.

"Parashara's request, by itself, shows how far apart we Nagas were from the Hastinapuris. Parashara's belief that the baby Krishna Dvaipaayana was his son and his son alone, and not another man's child by even a tiny bit, seemed to us a peculiar fixation. Satyavati went along in the beginning. She was unhappy when he told her that he had to stop visiting her for he was going to be the Vyaasa, but she accepted his decision – the Nagas allowed both men and women the right to make such decisions. When he then returned, as the leader of the Kavi Sangha punished with a vow of silence, she found that he was no longer the man she wanted but a stranger and she did not welcome him again.

"With her startling announcement, my father and I were uncertain about what Satyavati might be capable of and we tiptoed around her. Fortunately, my sister Satyavati did not commit suicide. She did not even attempt suicide.

"Devavrat disappeared – first he secluded himself, and then one day, before the wedding, he left Hastinapur and walked to the site of the first settlement he had created – Varanavata named after his ancestor, Samvarana. He did not come to the wedding. Shantanu took this to mean that his son was not completely reconciled to his loss. The rumour mills of the city churned with news of a rebellion in the making. It came as a surprise to most people when Devavrat returned to Hastinapur a few months later. Only three people knew exactly what he had lost – my father, Satyavati, and I.

"Do not judge Satyavati by Hastinapuri standards. The Kauravas had already started down the path of walling women away from power. Satyavati is and was a Naga woman – if she had stayed with the Nagas, she would have founded a band as matriarch eventually. She would have been a powerful mother-ruler, caring and terrifying to her children. She did not know what she was getting into when she married Shantanu. For that matter, I did not either. We did not understand how patriarchy worked and the ways in which it had changed the Kauravas. The return of Samvarana, a trader by training, to Hastinapur as a king leading an army, had replaced the core leadership with warriors. Kuru, who came immediately after Samvarana, was a hybrid – a trader-cum-warrior, but he was still a trader first and warrior second. That changed. Even though the city was renamed after Hastin, a trader, and the ruling family took Kuru as their dynast, the later generations trained to be warriors first and traders second.

"Devavrat's vow became publicly known in a modified form. His mother's suicide was believed to have been a protest against the one-child-per-person law and she was revered as the goddess Ganga to whom the culled children had been dedicated; his renunciation of his birthright on the occasion of his father's marriage gave notice that his mother was not forgotten and her issues were his issues – some people called him *Gangaputra.*[116] When Shantanu finally repealed the law as a failed enterprise, Devavrat was credited with making the change, though it was Satyavati's demands that were instrumental in persuading Shantanu.

"I visited my sister often. I was a few years younger than Satyavati and still considered a boy. My time with Parashara had made me eager to live in the city and I was ready to abandon any Naga constraints. I was already studying with the Kavi Sangha and that, along with my sister's place in the ruling family of

---

[116] *Gangaputra* means "Son of Ganga".

Hastinapur, would let me enter the most powerful cliques that I knew of. I also knew that I would never be chief of my own band even if I wanted to (my father's sister was the matriarch, so her daughter would be the next matriarch and her son, if any, would be the next chief). I now regret that I had not completed the adult initiation ceremony to join the fraternity of Naga men. Now, I would never be -considered a 'real' Naga man.

"Occasionally if a Naga matriarch had no brothers, a band would look for a chief directly related to her – her cousins who were sons of her mother's sisters. If the chief died, his brothers were next in line; if he had no brothers and no acceptable cousins, the band would look for a trusted chief outside the band not directly related to anyone in the band. This was rare. If Satyavati had founded a Naga band, I would have been her obvious choice for chief, but she left to go with the Hastinapuris. She expected me, nonetheless, to come with her. I wanted to, so it was an easy decision.

"I was in constant terror that Parashara would denounce me when he returned at the end of his penal term. I could not take it and one day went to Parashara and apologised profusely. I do not know what I was looking for, but Parashara's countenance did not change. I cried. I demanded to be punished. I vowed that, like Devavrat, I would give up all pleasures, but Parashara remained a stony visage. A few months later Parashara died, still observing his vow of silence – that is when I understood what he intended to convey with that stony face. He must have known that he was going to die and he no longer cared about the success or failure of the activities of the Sangha.

"The court that I had so longed to join was a meaningless façade for power. I was a mere spectator, its inner workings unknown to me. Daily there were reports of disorder in the refugee camps, rumours about Panchala. Where was the imagined centre of the kingdom where powerful individuals congregated for animated discussions over important issues?

The most excitement was generated when a caravan arrived with news of the western world. It took a long time, but somewhere in the stories which Parashara used to recount to the children of our Naga band were stories of the grand courts of the Kings of Paarshava and Sumer. These were the stories that had fired my imagination. I also realised that at least some of the stories were made up – one of the more amazing stories was that they were the inheritors of an ancient world with a single culture and language that had perished when they created a giant brass tower or needle in order to pierce the veil of heaven. Why would such a greatly advanced people have bothered to import the tiny bronze figurines from Panchnad or the cotton textiles that the Yadavas specialised in? Other stories, which mentioned gigantic buildings that rose high and from whose top the Great Father (one of the titles of the ruler of Egypt, the greatest of the western lands) could survey his whole empire and command obedience, sharpened the difference between us and the rest of the known world.

"I began spending more and more time with the Kavi Sangha. As a Naga, I was not raised to be a member of any of the Panchnad guilds. I did not have to join one, but I participated in all the lessons of the guild of bards. Despite my late start, I did well. That is how my life became entwined with Devavrat's life, for he too, had begun to spend more and more time with the Kavi Sangha.

"In Devavrat's case, he was avoiding Satyavati. He avoided the sections of the palace that she could move around in. By not joining the court, he avoided seeing her sit next to his father. Just like me, he found his vocation in the Kavi Sangha.

"In the beginning, this made Satyavati unhappy and angry. Matriarchs of Naga bands learn a style of speech, a command voice, used to control and manage the men who enter the band, whether children born in the band, or older male members, or adult men who visit some of the women. The men learn to obey a matriarch's command voice. It did not work that way in Hastinapur. She expected me to obey her and I did – it was a habit for both of us, and to this day she will command me to do something trivial – 'Bring me that pillow,' she will say, and I will do it. It is only the complex demands that are deliberated over and analysed. She expected that others would obey her, and they did, but not because of her command voice. They obeyed her husband with greater alacrity.

"Satyavati also found that, unlike Naga matriarchs who worked just like the other women except when in a formal role, she had very little to do during the day. When she tried to do something, some maidservant or other would jump up to do whatever Satyavati was attempting. Her role in court was to sit next to Shantanu on formal occasions; Shantanu would try to dissuade her when she wanted to attend private meetings alongside him. When he finally relented, Satyavati found that Hastinapur was, all said and done, still a trading town and much of the private discussions were about shares in caravans, dangers avoided during trips to Laghu Nagapura, the dramatic drop in trade since the refugee crisis began, and so on. This contrasted with the life of a Naga matriarch – in daily life treated as any other member of the band, but the ritual head of the twelve festival days of the year – the first day of spring, the feast of the mango, the feast of the burnt sacrifice, the ceremony of planting, the blessing of the waters, the day of waiting, the ceremony of the first harvest, the ceremony of closing the harvest, the day of decorating the earth, the return of the sun, the hunting ceremony, the gleaner's day. For four of these, the matriarch was the focus of celebration. The Kuru traders had nothing like this and what they did have was centred on the safety of the caravan. In a ritual sense, Hastinapur was still a caravan lead by men, and women had only a small part in it.

"Satyavati had found a mission that she could lead, the formation of a women's tradition in Hastinapur. It was a gallant effort and over many years she created a meaningful way of life for the women, a cycle of annual celebrations that gave meaning to daily life. This war has brought everything to a halt and threatens to undo all that she has done."

Shukla stopped. For a few vighatis he was silent and appeared thoughtful. Lomaharshana extended a small bowl of water to Shukla. He drank, almost absent-mindedly. *Was he done?* Lomaharshana thought. *Has he fallen asleep? Should I interrupt his train of thought?*

Shukla stirred and focused on Lomaharshana. He said, "I wanted forgiveness from Parashara but did not receive it, for he despised me. I wanted forgiveness from Devavrat but never asked for it. I wanted my sister's forgiveness but she refused to think back on the events of that day. My father, who died of a broken heart soon after Satyavati left our house, forgave me on condition that I stay around to take care of my sister. That condition has constrained my choices all along. I have done my best to take care of my sister.

"Lomaharshana, Satyavati's actions and achievements, both good and evil, deserve their own separate treatment. The changes introduced by Satyavati made her presence ubiquitous and Devavrat felt haunted by that presence. He wished to leave the town and go elsewhere, but Shantanu would not hear of it. Shantanu was being cautious – even if Devavrat was loyal, he could change and regret his decisions.

"Our activities in the Kavi Sangha had proceeded in parallel and we were companions through much of our education. He acted disinterested and maybe he was, but he would always ask me to meet with him after my visits to my sister. We became friends and together we came to understand the Kavi Sangha and we came to understand its projects and appreciate its way of thinking. Despite this improved understanding, in his heart he could not reconcile the logic of empire-building and the sacrifice of his infant brothers.

2000 B.C.E

"After Parashara died, Devavrat persuaded the next Vyaasa that the one-child-per-person policy had been ill-advised – it had not taken into account the response of the common people and Shantanu's small modifications had not made it any better.

"This is the story that Devavrat has never revealed to anybody. I know it because I witnessed the events and saw what happened to him. He did not know of my shame and chagrin over the advice I gave that created so much unhappiness. We never talked about those days, no matter how deep our friendship."

Yudhishthira had listened silently as Shukla told this story. He now spoke. "Guruji, I understand. We will not question him about Satyavati or the circumstances of his disinheritance. He has closed us off completely. Please persuade him to change his mind."

"It is late tonight. I will visit him tomorrow before I leave. We shall see."

The next day the Vyaasa Shukla was up early. The sun had not risen when he stepped out of his tent and a slight fog had crept up overnight from the river to the campsite. The camp was on a slight rise north of the Yamuna. As Shukla gazed over the river, a few fingers of dawn appeared to the east. As it became lighter and the veil of the fog dissipated, the river emerged out of the haze – it moved swiftly past the camp, slight eddies of white marking the place where it flowed over rocks visible near the bank. It was not like the placid lake that he recalled from his childhood and it was not the Ganga – despite that, he felt at home. *Hastinapur is never like this,* he thought. *Despite the many years I've spent there, I do not feel calm when I am there.* Telling the story of his sister's unfortunate demands had made him think of her as he went to sleep. He had woken up still thinking of her – she had been an inadvertent victim of his own ambition. Now he would have to convince Devavrat, another victim of that same ambition, to plunge into that past to retrieve... *Retrieve what? What will he find in that desolate land of lost time?*

2000 B.C.E

The camp had been up for some time. As Shukla prepared himself for the day, a bearer came by from the kitchen with a warm cup of almond milk coloured yellow with turmeric, and a few slices of guava sprinkled lightly with salt and pepper. The light meal satisfied him, and as he finished it, Yudhishthira and Lomaharshana came up to his tent and escorted him to Devavrat's tent.

Yudhishthira said, "Guruji, we will stay outside until you ask us to come in."

Shukla nodded assent and rang the small bell before he stepped inside the tent.

Swapping Tales

The Pandava Camp
Circa 2000 B.C.E.

"Devavrat, my friend."

The familiar voice cut through the fog that Devavrat had drawn around himself. *It was a bad dream,* he thought, and opened his eyes. He was still in a tent and his legs and one arm were tied to support poles. *Was he expected to attempt escape?* It was as he had imagined in the dream. It was not a dream and he was not free; his shoulder was sore and hurt, there might well be an arrowhead in there, and then he remembered that he was mortally injured. The voice was Shukla's voice. *What was Shukla doing here? He had left him back in Hastinapur.* Maybe he was on the brink of death. Maybe it was still a dream and he was imagining a visit from an old friend. *Was this how I will die? With all my friends flashing in front of my eyes?* He was lucky he had so few friends – he would die quickly. But not if, like these conjured-up memories of friends, they talked so much.

He turned his head but stopped when the flashes of pain in his shoulder became continuous. He was determined to control the pain and not let it control him – so he closed his eyes, but then his face set in a grimace that betrayed him, and he opened his eyes again to look at his friend.

"Shukla, my friend," he said. "What are you doing in the enemy camp?"

It had been over a year since Devavrat had been able to meet the Vyaasa in private. Public meetings in Suyodhana's court were exercises in formality once war had broken out with the Pandavas. Suyodhana did not trust the Kavi Sangha. Even though the Kavi Sangha supported Hastinapur and had supported Hastinapur for many generations, even though the Vyaasa had called for the Pandavas to make peace on Suyodhana's terms, even though there was no reason for the Kavi Sangha to change its mind, Suyodhana remained suspicious of Kavi Sangha activities. The Kavi Sangha had told him that he should be gentle with the Pandavas if they surrendered.

Shukla said, "I too, am a prisoner at home."

"Are you? I've met the Archivist here. He says your whereabouts are secret."

"Ah. Yes."

"He predicted yesterday that you would come today. You must keep him. He seems to know when you are not in your prison."

Shukla laughed. "There's no need for sarcasm – the Kavi Sangha has its ways to communicate. An army, Devavrat, does not imprison me. More than anything, my body betrays me and holds me."

"As does mine. I have an arrowhead in my lungs. I am to die of it."

"I, too, will die very soon. My doctor says it will happen, he just cannot say when. Soon."

"What does the doctor know, Shukla?"

"He says my urine is a sweet dish for ants; that my waning eyesight is a warning sign; that the aches and pains in my arms and legs are a prelude to the final days."

"Is this why you came here? To join me on this deathbed?"

"No. I came for many reasons. I had hoped to archive your memoirs in Hastinapur under more pleasant surroundings. Now that will not be possible, so I ask you to work with the Archivist here. Before your capture, a Hastinapur victory in this unfortunate war was inevitable – now it is not. Suyodhana and Karna are impetuous, strong-willed, and wrong-headed – only you could have restrained them and focused their attention. You knew that too. I was not in Hastinapur when you decided on this expedition. You are the most senior commander – what could have possibly tempted you down this foolhardy path?"

Devavrat grimaced. "Shikhandin offered us a chance..."

"Shikhandin? Of Panchala?"

"Yes. You know of him? He came to Hastinapur on a secret mission, a proposal from the disaffected leaders of clans within Panchala."

"He convinced you?"

"Yes."

"How did he do that?"

"I know now what I did not know then. I was inclined to believe him. He revived old memories."

"Amba?"

"You knew?"

"Did I suspect it? Yes. Not with any certainty though. Some Kavi Sangha members visiting Panchala returned with news of events in Panchala. I had asked them to assess Panchala's preparation for war – you recall how the chief Drupada used to issue challenges to Hastinapur every few years to meet Panchala on the field of blood. They reported that nobody was preparing for war – the spear and arrow makers were idle, and the smiths were lackadaisical as usual in preparing for the harvest festival. The challenges were just fuss and bluster.

"I see. Does it mean that you've suspected that Amba was alive all these years?"

"All these years? No. This is recent knowledge, only a few years old."

"You must tell me more."

"I will. I want to trade though. You must help us with your memories."

"Why now?"

"I told you. I am old. I will not have many more chances to reconcile warring factions. Consider it a plea from my death-bed."

"You know what they want me to tell them."

"Yes. I have relieved you of a painful narration. I told them of the events – Yudhishthira and the Archivist know of your first meeting with Satyavati. I have told them all about it. You do not need to recount it. Go beyond it – start with the death of Shantanu."

"Why is this memory a part of your archives? You tell me that it is a part of your story. I am not convinced that what I felt or what happened to me matters. Is it not enough to tell what happened and let my sorrow be private and forgotten? You already know how the world has changed – make it your story."

"Let the Kavi Sangha be the judge of that, Devavrat. There is more to the life of a culture than dynasty-lists and the inventory of monuments."

Devavrat sighed. *Why did it have to be the story of my life that he wants to add?*

2000 B.C.E

"You think that that the 'more' you seek is the story of my life?"

"Among others. I plan to interview Dhritarashtra, Kutaja, Kunti, even Suyodhana and Yudhishthira, young though they are. They have to stay living and stay healthy. I'll wait for them just like I wait for you. Why, if I can get to them, I will even listen to the Queen of Panchala, Krishna the Yadava, and others."

Devavrat said, "Good luck to your waiting."

Devavrat was silent. A few vighatis passed in silence. Then Shukla closed his eyes.

"How long will you wait here?" Devavrat said.

Shukla opened his eyes. "Until you agree," he said.

"Hmm… what if I refuse?"

"That is not an alternative."

"I could choose to die."

"Then you will not know what happened to Amba."

Amba's story. That was the only story he wanted to know. *Did Shukla really mean 'agree to tell it now or die'?* He did not understand the sinking feeling of despair that engulfed him when he thought about Amba – he had failed her and he was desperate to know the extent of her suffering. He needed absolution – he had been responsible for Amba's pain. She had raised Shikhandin on her own. Shikhandin had died in his arms – he wanted to tell Amba that her son had felt his father's touch at least once in his short life. How could he tell Amba that he understood her pain if he did not know what it had been? Her suffering was his suffering and for that to be true, he had to know what the rest of her life had been. Even the bare bones would be better than nothing.

What was Shukla offering? He wanted to take their story and make it public. It would become another story used to titillate the public, stories of the clay feet of great men.

2000 B.C.E

"The Kavi Sangha performs historical story-telling every year at festivals here and in Panchnad. Will this memoir be part of every recital?"

Shukla smiled. "You don't need to worry – there will be none based on this archive for many years. The Kavi Sangha will only recite archival histories after seven generations have passed. All living persons will be dead before this is made public. Not every story makes it to a recital – the stories that do are always more than entertainment."

Devavrat considered that assertion. Was it good enough? He did not want to be reassured – he wanted a commitment he could believe.

"What about him?" Devavrat indicated with his eyes the Archivist standing quietly.

"You know the drill," Shukla said. "You considered becoming one yourself when it seemed that your position in the city was precarious and it appeared that your brother, the King, would imprison you if not kill you. Joining the Kavi Sangha would have preserved your life."

"The King? You mean Chitrangada, Shantanu's and Satyavati's son," Devavrat's voice fell.

"Tell me about him," Shukla said. "Tell me how he died. Satyavati says a gandharva killed him, that you were there when he was killed, and you were too cowardly to bring his body back. Did you tell her that? If so, what was the truth? Gandharvas, magical beings who sing as they fly, do not exist."

Devavrat had made up a story that would save Satyavati grief, but the lie had not satisfied her, and now it had caught up with him. It had been a hastily conceived lie, built on memories of stories told by an imaginative twelve-year old Chitrangada to his five-year old brother, of a king with magical powers named Chitrangada. Now her brother was asking for the truth. *Can*

I trust him? The answer would have been trivial if Satyavati had been anybody but Shukla's sister. As it was, it was not easily answered. Shukla was neither a trader, nor a warrior – a trader habitually keeps secrets, a warrior learns not to obsess over scenes from a battlefield. *Is the value of telling the truth of Chitrangada's death greater than the value of letting it die with me?* Questions like these clouded his mind.

It is a good thing that I am dying, Devavrat thought. He had never bothered to find out Satyavati's side of the story. He did not want to know it either. *We have stayed aloof for so long, what was the point of cutting open an old wound to check on its healing?*

The story of his life after Shantanu and Satyavati married was like a story that had been told and retold in public. Devavrat had concentrated on projects that took him away from Hastinapur. Two years passed. Satyavati had a son, Chitrangada. When Chitrangada was seven, his brother Vichitravirya was born. Whenever Devavrat came to Hastinapur, Shantanu would be playing with Chitrangada. The toddler looked like his father, a toy Shantanu, except for his eyes and the pouting mouth, which broke into a broad smile when he saw his older brother. *Anna,* he would scream and come running. Shantanu was almost fifty years old, and not inclined to play on the floor with his son, but Devavrat could. Chitrangada would mimic Devavrat. He would run when Devavrat pretended to be angry and chased him round and round the room without catching him. Chitrangada would climb up Devavrat's body onto his shoulders and then jump off while Devavrat held his hands. As Vichitravirya grew older, he too joined in their games, but the first and strongest tie was between Devavrat and Chitrangada. Despite the hint of Satyavati in Chitrangada's features, or maybe because of them, Devavrat came to love his brothers.

The bond between Chitrangada and Devavrat did not fix the relationship between Satyavati and Devavrat. Occasionally, Devavrat noticed his father's puzzlement at some convoluted interaction between his son and his wife, but he was, mostly, oblivious to the tension that existed between them. It was possible that he also chose to ignore it. It took many years, but slowly Devavrat and Satyavati settled into a routine that allowed them to appear next to Shantanu in public. In private, they avoided each other.

Shortly after Shantanu's death, Shukla had persuaded Satyavati and Devavrat to meet in his presence to resolve a conflict – it had been an awkward disaster in which neither proved capable of initiating a discussion or following up on Shukla's leads. *It was good advice, maybe just premature,* Devavrat thought. They were both unwilling to try again, and never did.

Then Chitrangada went on a fateful expedition. Devavrat was too late to save Chitrangada from death. Lies had been made up to spare Satyavati the details of her son's end.

Everything I love turns to dross. Devavrat's stomach sank as memories of his brother rose.

Devavrat was silent again. A few vighatis passed. Shukla looked at Devavrat with concern, "Are you alright?"

"Yes."

"You became silent and your eyes looked far away."

"I was thinking about Chitrangada's life and his coronation,"

"His coronation?"

"Yes. A lot started with that coronation."

"I want to know about his death."

I am a trader and here I am, freely giving away this story. Devavrat laughed at the thought of payment – he stopped as the shoulder sent its shooting message across his chest. *I can get stories out of Shukla! A bard habitually tells stories.* He returned to his earlier questions.

"Do you really know what happened to Amba?"

Shukla slowly turned his head away, but not before Devavrat saw his eyes lose focus. He waited for almost three vighatis and then tapped his legs against the tent pole to get Shukla's attention. The tent shook, but it did not seem to affect Shukla. A short time later, Shukla turned back to him.

"Are you alright?" Devavrat asked. "Am I not allowed to question you?"

Shukla smiled. "You would want to know about Amba, wouldn't you? Here, let's play your game – let's trade. You tell me about Chitrangada's death and I will tell you about the events that followed Vichitravirya's death."

He does not want to talk about Amba. Why? Hadn't any reason for secrecy come to its end in the last few days? Was there more? Devavrat found the questions multiplying.

"Can the Archivist memorise all that?"

"Oh, much more than that."

"Amba's story has three parts," Devavrat said. "The first part I know and will tell you. It's the story of how I met Amba. The second part I do not know – why she left and what she did. Do you know that part? The third part, I think you know – what happened to her, how she ended up in Panchala, and how she raised Shikhandin as a warrior?"

"I don't know everything. Yes, your meeting and involvement with her is a mystery. If you fill that in, I will have the boy recite how and why Amba escaped Hastinapur and hid from you. I'll tell you what I know of Shikhandin and how he was raised. I still do not know exactly how Amba ended up in Panchala."

Devavrat was struck by the words. Once again, he had said that Amba escaped! Escaped from what? From a person, perhaps – who could it be? It seemed to be a fair exchange.

Devavrat felt exhausted and needed rest. *Not now. I cannot take this in now.*

"I am tired. After the midday meal," Devavrat said. "I will start with Shantanu's death and how Satyavati and I became co-regents; then, the story of Chitrangada's northern misadventure; finally, I will tell you of my affair with Amba. You will then tell me of Vichitravirya's death and what happened to Amba after she disappeared from Hastinapur."

"Yes. Only what I know."

"No drama then. Good. Now, go away. Let me rest."

Shukla said, "Stay strong, old friend," and left silently.

Shantanu's Sunset

What Next?

Kaushambi/Hastinapur
circa 850 B.C.E.

Lunch appeared at the gates as planned. It was a little early, but Vaishampaayana could see that it was a welcome break for Chandrasekhar. His scribing had kept pace with Vaishampaayana's recital, but this morning's episode seemed to have bothered him. It had certainly bothered his father.

Bhargava waved the lunch crew away and took a deep breath. He let it out slowly while he brought his hands up to his head and slashed down with them. He said, "Dash it, Vais! I am disappointed. He avoids her! Is that all? For how many years? Don't they even meet by mistake? Pass by on the street? Doesn't she see him when he visits his father? All this emotion and drama, resolved by Devavrat refusing to meet Satyavati's eyes, except by mistake.

"Nor do I understand Satyavati. She says that she might as well be dead. Then, what? Why does she go ahead with the marriage? What happens between Shantanu and her? Does Shantanu not realise that she does not love him? I find it hard to imagine her life."

Vaishampaayana said, "Bhargava, my friend. This is the story that has come down to us. It is history, not melodrama. Even if those events you just speculated about happened, they must have been of no consequence – otherwise they would have been included. I can speculate about Satyavati's reasons for going ahead with the marriage – she was ambitious – and she thought she was going to be the matriarch in Hastinapur. She knew that Hastinapur differed from the Nagas in the primacy of the men in governance but she may not have been prepared for the extent of male domination – there were no women playing senior roles in the state, something unthinkable in Naga bands. All she could be in her new role was the founder of a dynasty. When Devavrat met her and impressed her, she was just beginning her transition from a young girl and early motherhood to adult. She wanted to die, but she was a pragmatic woman – she might have realised the silliness of her announcement and did not act on it. Devavrat's impulsive vow was similarly silly – it would have impressed her as extremely foolhardy, if not foolish, and she was amazed when nobody attempted to dissuade him and the seriousness with which he followed it. She had compromised and found other reasons to live. He should have found other reasons to back away from his vow. She had not asked for celibacy, she had not asked that he never make love to another woman, just that he not have children who aspired to be Crown Prince. Even then, as Queen, she would have managed the expectations of any of his children if he had had any.

"Consider your own response, my friend. You question Satyavati's decision to live an admittedly difficult life, but you do not question Devavrat's impulsive and frightening vow. Nor do you question his father's behaviour – if your son behaved dangerously, would you leave on a trading caravan? What does

Shantanu do – he almost treats the vow as ordinary business to which he pays no further attention. Maybe later in life he feels a bit guilty. You want the short-lived interaction between Satyavati and Devavrat to have cosmic and romantic consequences, but the dangerous and destructive actions of Shantanu and Devavrat do not arouse you emotionally."

"Fine, I admit to my faults. Still... that's the story? The romantic Devavrat lived a long, lonely, and embittered life? The ambitious Satyavati goes on to become the mother of kings?"

Vaishampaayana said, "Yes, indeed. Excellent summary, my friend. A master of the art of summarising, I salute you. Allow me, if you will, to tell the longer version!"

"Yes, yes, O master of the art of sarcasm. Please go on." They smiled at each other.

Vaishampaayana said, "It all begins with the premature death of Shantanu."

Shantanu's Death

The Pandava Camp
Circa 2000 B.C.E.

"He is going to kill me and then my children."

His spies had told Devavrat that this was the first thing Satyavati said when Shantanu died. *She means me.*

Devavrat had fallen asleep after Shukla left. The continuous narration was not physically tiring, but every word that he uttered felt like he was losing a piece of his soul and that was emotionally exhausting. Each word came with its memories, some ringing with joy, but most of the words cut off the sunshine, putting the darkest monsoon-cloud to shame. Some memories he had worked to forget were returning, an alarming thought to one trained to remember and trained to forget. He woke up later that morning with Satyavati's words *He is going to kill me and then my children,* echoing in his mind. *It's only a dream.* That thought was comforting for a short time, barely a tenth of a vighati, until he recalled that it had been real and not a dream. Shantanu had died and Satyavati had barely waited for the funeral ceremonies to be completed – she had rushed off with the children to Varanavata. This was what he had to tell Shukla and Yudhishthira. His father's death, his stepmother's panic, his own deep conviction that he should not be the ruler, the co-Regency and how it worked. This was not a dream, it had happened, and Shukla was coming with Yudhishthira to hear his version of events.

The sounds of the camp increased during the midday meal. A nurse had to take care of his every need and Devavrat found that uncomfortable. In any case, he had lost his appetite and only ate a small amount under the nurse's urging; he still needed the occasional drink of water, just to keep his mouth moist as he talked. With the water came gurgling sounds from his empty stomach. Hunger by itself was not a problem – every trader or warrior encounters a time when meals become irregular. The occasional day or two with no meals because of an error of judgement – the wrong turn at a fork, or haste making for an unsteady bow while hunting deep in the forest. Hunger wasn't the problem – thinking about it and thinking about food made him queasy. He waited uneasily for the meal sounds to end.

Shukla came in with Yudhishthira and the Archivist. They complimented him on his ability to look powerful and healthy despite his injuries. *Did they have to be so unrelentingly positive?* It only reminded him that he was trying hard to ignore the pain, but his visitors insisted on bringing that elephant back into the room.

Shukla said, "Devavrat, let's get started."

Yudhishthira and Shukla sat down cross-legged facing Devavrat while the Archivist took his place behind his head so that Devavrat could not see him. *That was a good idea.* Devavrat considered asking Yudhishthira to position himself similarly, out of sight, but… a reasonable request of a host but not of his jailer, however considerate. *It might be easier talking about these events if Yudhishthira were not here.* What could the story of Amba, of Chitrangada's death, or a host of other Kuru family secrets mean to Yudhishthira, who had been a stranger to that family much of his life.

Yudhishthira spoke first.

"The Vyaasa tells me that you have much to talk about. There is also much I want to know. My duties call and I have to leave, but the Vyaasa assures me that the Archivist will reproduce all that you say without any error, and I can listen to him. You will not have to do this again. If I have questions, I'll be back. Meanwhile, I am available."

Shukla felt cheerful. He enjoyed the only-too-rare experience of listening to fresh stories, anecdotes that he did not already know. Most often, he was expected to be the originator of tellings. In addition, it had been difficult to meet Devavrat in private – a meeting between Devavrat the Regent and the Vyaasa of the Kavi Sangha was a political event, fraught with consequences. Suyodhana would come by with questions and not accept the answers. Under that tension, his friendship with Devavrat from their youth threatened to dissipate, the bond as frail as a spider's web holding on to a hummingbird – small enough to be caught, too big to be eaten. A meeting was long overdue; it was a pity that they had waited until Devavrat was dying.

***

THE PANDAVA CAMP
CIRCA 2000 B.C.E.

He is going to kill me, and then my children. With these words, Satyavati gathered her sons and made her way overnight to the town of Varanavata.

Yudhishthira and Shukla were sitting in the late afternoon with Lomaharshana. They were on a grassy patch at the highest point of the sloping land that the camp occupied – the slope crested a short distance away and there was a freshwater pond fed by a small brook that emerged from the Himalayan foothills. A channel for the overflow led down to the river. This was an ideal location for a camp – it was not on the river, so water had to be carried a longer distance – longer but downhill from the pond, not uphill from a river. They could see clearly in three directions. The lake and the larger river far to the south contributed to a steady north-south breeze all day that swept smoke and other odours away. If it had not been for the camp this would have been completely forested – as it was, the camp had slowly used up the nearby trees for fuel, leaving a few that were considered sacred, like the banyan and the ficus.

Yudhishthira said, "Have you been successful in making my granduncle talk about the aftermath of Shantanu's death? What did he say? You have been working with him for a week."

Lomaharshana said, "The Vyaasa asked me to compose it in shlokas. That was a challenge for the time period covered was the time of some of the Regent's greatest successes, and often he had to be stopped and asked to slow down. His patience, though, is remarkable. Let me start here.

"I am Lomaharshana, the Archivist chosen to remember the story told by the great one. He began it with his stepmother Satyavati fleeing the city on the death of his father. It seems like a simple story of a new ruler getting rid of other claimants. I wish it were that simple. The Regent Devavrat has lived a long life, and early in his life trained with the Kavi Sangha, but he does not know how to narrate a story. I would not care to recite his dry narration – there is nothing to hold the attention of the listener or of the raconteur in a story told so straight. My teacher, the Vyaasa sympathised with me – with his help I have made a story out of the Regent's words. Here it is, close to the Regent's own words, but re-formed to be sung. The name *Bhishma,* 'The Terrible', was earned in the course of the events described here, for his given name Devavrat, *a god's oath,* did not strike terror in anybody. Here is the story of the Regent Devavrat.

2000 B.C.E

"During the Regent's narrative, both the King and the Vyaasa interrupted the Regent to ask questions or express opinions. I have retained these where they added explanation to the primary events of that time."

Shukla said, "Wait a vighati. I was closely involved in this composition. I'll let the Archivist tell the story without my supervision – I will be back soon." He rose. So did Yudhishthira and Lomaharshana. Shukla took his leave and the King and the Archivist sat down.

Lomaharshana began the story told by Devavrat.

Devavrat said, "A few years after the birth of Vichitravirya, my father fell ill and the right side of his body was paralysed. Then his organs failed. He had complained of a headache, mild at first, but increasing every day, despite the doctor's ministrations. Then one morning, he could not get out of bed. I was visiting Hastinapur from the extended waterworks projects that kept me busy and out of town. I had asked to meet with my father and the Vyaasa Jaimini about problems posed by the Meena-Nagas, Satyavati's people, who were expanding their range up the Yamuna into the land called Khandavaprastha. The king's illness precluded this discussion and at the Vyaasa's insistence, I stayed.

"I spent my time playing with my brothers – there was nobody else in the court I wanted to meet and nobody wanted to be seen meeting me, for that might arouse Satyavati's wrath. My father was young, in his early fifties, Chitrangada was eleven and Vichitravirya was about four. I was in my early thirties. Nobody expected Shantanu to die, but he became weaker and weaker. Some days he was delirious or seemed to be living a different life in some other world. He talked to his first wife, my mother, calling her 'Gangu' as he had many years ago. He would be animated whenever I came to his sickbed and said anything – he would recognise my voice, and try to sit up and respond. He spoke clearly and did not mumble, but his words made little sense.

"If there was a theme to the fantasies it was guilt and sorrow. One of the more comprehensible statements was about the one-child-per-person policy. *They welcomed me into their midst. 'Who are you?' I asked. 'The children you killed,' they said. 'Now we are immortal. Come join us.' There were so many.* If I were asked to explain that, I would have said that he was dreaming a nightmare about being surrounded by dead children.

"Another understandable theme was that he had deprived me of something. *I failed you – Gangu was supposed to kill all of you.* This was strange indeed, given that the order to kill had come from him and my mother had nothing to do with it. He went on to say that I could have been in heaven like my dead brothers, but had to suffer here. He offered to fix that so I could be with them. *I can make you immortal, just like me. From heaven all is possible.* Of what he had truly deprived me, there was not a word, so this was another nightmare not a message from dead spirits.

"He conversed with his absent brother Bahlika. *I told my brothers. 'Come back to Hastinapur. We will honour and welcome you.' They would not listen. 'Where are our children?' they said.* Bahlika had left with his family long before Shantanu became King, with the plan to go as far west as he could. He might have imagined that they too had died. It is said that dead men without progeny suffer eternal hunger, so that belief may have been the source of his hallucinations.

"He dreamt that his brother Devapi was dead. *Devapi, my brother! Forgive me for making you leave. I should have stopped you that day.* His brother Devapi had taken off his clothes and walked off into the woods leaving behind a wife, but no children. This was the first time I had heard that my father could have stopped Devapi from leaving. He had seen him leave. What if Devapi had children – wouldn't they have inherited Hastinapur? However, Devapi had had no children, his wife had been barren – she continued to be present in Hastinapur, a ghost, sad and invisible, until she died. Now he felt guilty that he had not tried to find Devapi. Initially, he had not wanted to find him; later, he thought it would make relations with Satyavati even more fraught with untoward possibilities. It was news to me that he and Satyavati were unhappy with each other. When my mother was queen, the entire story of her relationship with my father was a loud whisper, like the ones made by street actors. He had felt so clever then – convincing his brother that he was cursed and that he could not have children and should abdicate. He had not expected him to run away or possibly kill himself. It was *karma* – his actions in depriving his brother of his birthright were the cause of him making me lose mine. He was sorry that he had made me give up my birthright. He had a boon for me. *You can choose the time of your death.* A strange boon. My father was delirious when he talked to me. His idea that Devapi had children was disconcerting – if it was not a delirium-induced nightmare, it would add to the chaos around us. I took it seriously – I sent trained searchers to likely places, but they found nothing.

"A few other people aroused the King – Satyavati would come with Chitrangada and Vichitravirya – I would leave when I was informed of her coming. I never found out what was spoken between them.

"After a few days, I thought he was getting better and said so to the doctor. The doctor shook his head in disagreement – this disease was well known to mimic health just before the patient's death. It fooled caregivers often. A skilled physician knew what to look for. 'He smells sour and I cannot change that,' the doctor had said. That kind of pronouncement left me unmoved. *What did he mean? He smelled sour? Why would his smell, probably caused by drinking spoilt milk, indicate any disease?* The doctor had no explanation; rather, the one he produced in public was gobbledegook about mystical influences entering through the mouth. In private, he would explain that the smell was an indication that the body was consuming itself and that indicated only one disease. There was no cure for that disease. When this happened there would be periods when the patient would appear to get better, but this was a side effect of the body cannibalising itself. The king daily appeared more active and the delirium stopped. He was more in control of his mind if not his body. One side was still paralysed, but his mind seemed to be intact.

"Of course, the doctor was proved right. One morning, I had come to consult Shantanu about the Vyaasa Jaimini's proposal to stop using the army for civil construction. Shukla was there. I did not see his sister around, so I assumed Shukla was there on some private matter. He deferred to me, but expressed interest in my issue. Jaimini had become the Vyaasa just before Chitrangada was born and he had worked at coming up with alternatives to the plan that had been developed when Bharadvaja was the Vyaasa.

"Bharadvaja's plan entailed the use of the army to suppress opposition. Lakes and waterworks were to be constructed and would be owned by the state. Immigrants would settle newly irrigated lands. Nagas would not be allowed to return with their slash-and-burn practices. With the immigrants leading as the advance guard, the empire would expand south by a sequence of waterworks defining the boundary, creeping south every generation, and slowly eliminating the Nagas from their current range. When Parashara became the Vyaasa, he wished to change the emphasis from exclusion to inclusion – his penalty cost him influence and subsequently, death cut short his tenure. That brought in Jaimini. Jaimini was not a revolutionary, but nor was he enamoured of Bharadvaja's imperial solutions – he could not support a waterworks empire that catered to one group and destroyed another. I agreed with him, but thought that he lacked pragmatism – in his search for the best and fairest solution he ignored what was happening on the ground with the help of the army. Slowly but steadily, the boundary between Hastinapur-irrigated land and Naga territory moved south.

"We were in the King's room discussing the Vyaasa Jaimini's proposal to withdraw the army from frontier construction projects that Shantanu was directing. The King was walking around – he felt the need to keep his legs in shape with some form of exercise. At one point he stopped pacing around. He looked thoughtful and complained of excruciating pain in his left arm. He sat down, his mouth set in a grimace. Even as Shukla and I considered calling for the doctor, he said that his chest hurt, and collapsed. We picked him up, but he had lost consciousness, and felt limp in our hands. We laid him out on the bed for the doctor. As we waited for the doctor, I listened for a heartbeat but could not hear one. Just as the doctor entered, the smell of urine and waste filled the room. The King was dead.

"A messenger was sent to Satyavati immediately. She came back with him, her children in tow. I could not bear to meet and commiserate with her. I left the room and retired to my quarters.

"The Chief Minister came to see me that night. He said, 'You must take charge, Prince Devavrat. There is much confusion all over the city.'

"'Why?' I said. 'The Queen is in charge. I will support whatever action she wants to take.'

"'She has left with the princes for Varanavata.'

"'What happened?'

"'She was heard to say, *He is going to kill me and then my children*. It appears that she is uncertain of your intentions.'

"I did not want to rule. I had said so but it appeared that such a statement was mere talk. Even the Chief Minister, Sashidhara, standing in front of me, seemed uncertain of what I would do. *He has known me since I was a child. Despite that, he, too, is sceptical. What can I do if after all these years, I am not trusted? Nor am I understood.* In the last few days I had begun to imagine that my father would agree with me about the imperial plan. *Was that also a delusion?*

"When I expressed these confused opinions, Shukla asked me why I thought the Chief Minister did not understand my intentions. I replied, 'He did not respond appropriately to Satyavati's fears – whether he agreed with her or not, a loyal minister would have reassured her that I had no such intention. It is only if he himself were uncertain that he would hold off.'

"I know now that I was naïve. The decisions of the last decision-maker, if truly based on bringing together many streams of information, will sometimes appear opaque to the other who could only see part of the information that influenced the decision. This was normal. This was why, even when following the Kavi Sangha's policy, Shantanu contrived to look unpredictable to some of the participants in the process.

"Looking back, I think that the Chief Minister was being properly cautious. However, it could have backfired for it made me unsure of his behaviour. If I intended to get rid of my brothers, I would also suspect the Chief Minister's loyalty. As it was, I felt that my father had left the task of implementing policy concerning the immigrants to me, and I had no major disagreements with my dead father and King about that.

"I found myself receiving information that usually only went to my father and it helped me understand how much he walled off his differences from me. My father could partition off implementation of this policy from his personal life, and I could not. After the trauma of my mother's death, Shantanu maintained a strict separation between his own wishes or desires and the Kavi Sangha policies that he implemented – I could not do that. When I gave up the kingdom, it had been with the expectation that I would never rule and therefore never face the dilemmas that my father encountered. As I waited for the flurry of activity caused by my father's death to subside, I had a nebulous idea of withdrawing from public life and leaving it to my brother to implement the long-term agenda of Shantanu and the Kavi Sangha. My brothers were too young to understand why I would do such a thing, so I had to reassure Satyavati. I would have to meet her and it could not be a public discussion. Yet, I did not want to meet her in private.

"The thoughts made me postpone any actions with respect to Satyavati. Instead I arranged to meet with the King's council, my father's old council, in her absence. When I entered the council chamber, I could feel the excitement ripple through the room, like a warm and wet summer breeze blowing in from the river in the late afternoon. The members of the council and the attending citizens were standing – they bowed low to me as if my face was too bright to behold. The Chief Minister seemed to have lost something – the smiling group that usually formed around him were just a little further away from him and they were not smiling. The Chief Minister himself stood, his upper body erect and tense, a pose I had never seen him take.

"They expected that I would declare myself King. I walked slowly, glancing at every one of them as I walked by – nobody met my gaze, but they looked to the ground and bowed. The throne was on a stage reached by three steps. It consisted of a section of a ficus tree trunk about four feet in diameter and about a *hasta* tall, its top covered with cotton padding. On top of that was a pillow. My usual place was on the floor to the left of the throne, marked by a single pillow. To the right of the throne was a place similarly marked by a pillow – if Satyavati had been there, that is where she would have sat. I sat down at my usual place – I felt a sigh make a second ripple through the room.

"In the past, when the King was absent, Satyavati would call the meeting to order. As it was, I initiated the meeting, even though I did not want to do so. The people present acted as if this was perfectly normal and it was merely a matter of time before I moved over to the next seat. I asked the ministers to summarise the state of their departments and report on what had been done that year and what else needed to be done. They responded with much alacrity and little substance – they abandoned any attempt at providing the summary I had asked for or describing the state of their responsibilities. Instead, they devoted their time to extolling my praises. For instance: *they had always been impressed by my deep understanding of past discussions; I had brought reasoned thought and a keen intellect into the discussions. They were awed by the wisdom I had shown even as a young boy.* Unfortunately, in the past, they looked to Shantanu and Satyavati for direction and my ideas only received the respect that my father bestowed on them in public. '*Now we see how right you have been, sir,*' they said. I wondered if my father had felt like this. I wished I had not called the meeting.

"After half a dozen hagiographic reports, I stopped the speaker and said, 'The next speaker who avoids reporting and uses the time to praise me will be expelled from the council and from his post.' The room became very quiet – all the extraneous sounds, the ripples, if you will, that make a collection of people alive, died. The unfortunate councillor who had begun his report, a polished and sophisticated urbanite, an early immigrant from Panchnad, stumbled through the rest of his very short presentation and returned to his seat. The session moved very quickly after that. Then it was my turn and by now, some life had returned to the group, for I had not punished anybody.

"I said, 'My brother Chitrangada was anointed as the Yuvraj by my respected father when he lived. My father's wishes were clear and we should announce that in accordance with his wishes, Chitrangada will be crowned King when he comes of age. In the meantime, his mother, the Queen Mother Satyavati, will be Regent.' I then announced that I would go to Varanavata to attend on the Queen Mother and Regent, and bring her back to Hastinapur along with my brothers, for the formal investiture.

"The silence that followed rivalled the earlier quiet. Nobody moved. I could almost read their minds: *Is this a trick?* I wanted to shout from the highest mound: *This is what I want.*

Unfortunately, I don't think that anything would have been credible. The last part of the surprise: some of the listeners smiled and glanced at each other and bowed even deeper than before when I passed by. *They expected this?* The announcement should have been a surprise, but they acted as though it was routine. They had interpreted my statements for deeper meaning and found what they were looking for. I wondered what I could have said that would not be twisted on reinterpretation.

"Satyavati received reports of this meeting. I received reports of these reports. *Your stepson Devavrat has pretended to obey his father's wishes. His speech was a transparent attempt to convince the councillors of his intentions, but nobody was fooled.* The report inserted an implied threat into every sentence that I had used. When I came to Varanavata and requested a private meeting, she refused. Her messenger said, 'Come to my public hall ten ghatis after sunrise. There will be others asking for an audience. There, in public, I will certainly listen to you. I expect you to hold to your oaths.'

"I had decided that no matter what happened, I would do as she wanted. I had promised that I would ensure the inheritance of the kingdom by Satyavati's children. When that oath was demanded, my first impulse had been to refuse. I expect that I could have refused – my father would have felt humiliated in public. To avoid further conflict I would have left Hastinapur.

"It does not take much to insult a king. A king cannot swallow insults, either. This is one more difference between the old Panchnad cities and Hastinapur. A matriarch's rule is not threatened if somebody refuses to obey – a king's rule cannot survive if such disobedience is tolerated. At that point I felt a deep empathy for my uncle Devapi's decision to abdicate and disappear. My vow prevented me from doing that. It meant that I stayed and created the institutions that would keep the country under the control of Hastinapur. If I walked away, I would allow some usurper to eliminate my weak young brother and my father's wife. *That* would be breaking my promise."

At this point Shukla re-joined them. Lomaharshana stopped.

Shukla said, "You should continue – where in the story are you?"

Lomaharshana said, "The King is dead and Prince Devavrat has gone to ask Queen Satyavati to return to Hastinapur from Varanavata with her children, to rule as Regent."

Shukla said, "Ah, yes! She left for Varanavata without waiting for me to come to Hastinapur. When I found out, I followed her to Varanavata. Things happen when I cannot be there to calm my sister down. You may continue."

Lomaharshana said, "I've written the shlokas as though narrated by the Regent."

Shukla said, "That's an interesting choice."

Lomaharshana said, "Yes, sir. It allows me to create a simpler story – I do not have to explain how the narrator knows what is being told about the episode. In addition, I can explain the narrator's feelings and thoughts."

Shukla nodded his head. Yudhishthira, who had taken the interruption to stretch his limbs, said, "I am ready. Pray continue."

The Archivist said, "The story continues in the Regent's words. Devavrat said: 'I did exactly as Satyavati asked me to – I came to her public hall as a supplicant. In the public court, I beseeched her to return to Hastinapur as the Queen Mother and Regent for the future King Chitrangada. I don't believe Satyavati expected this. Her eyes gave away her feeling that this was a trap. I saw fear in her eyes when I looked up. *She is driven by fear. I must reassure her now, otherwise this fear of me will continue forever.*'"

Lomaharshana said, "When I related the story of this meeting, that is, my first version, to the Vyaasa Shukla, he said that in the Queen Mother's narration to him, she had looked in

Devavrat's eyes and seen calculation; in her words, *the cold, hard calculation of a man plotting the best time to take revenge on me."*

Shukla said, "My sister has a talent for that."

Lomaharshana continued with Devavrat's narration.

Devavrat said:

"Satyavati's brother Shukla, not yet the Vyaasa, advised Satyavati. I was grateful for that. At his suggestion, Satyavati made a counter-offer – she and I would be joint Regents. She would keep control of the city and any part of the army within the city, and I would administer the rest of Kururashtra. Her first entry into the city would be after I left. She would announce that she had invited me to be co-Regent – it was her gift to honour my loyalty to my father and to her. She had rules that I was required to follow: I could only return to the city after she had taken control of the army. She would tell me any other rules, as and when it became necessary. She named her purpose – she was doing this for the safety of her son, the true heir to Shantanu. She wanted me to repeat my oath that one of my brothers would become the future ruler of Hastinapur. Thus, she and I would bring peace to a city that was on the edge of bursting into civil war between her supporters and the malcontents who were against her because she was a Naga.

"I accepted her proposal – I would have accepted anything that would erase the fear in her, the fear that I had finally recognised. Satyavati had taken into consideration the possibility that the city might not accept a Regent of Naga origin. There was still much anger among the city dwellers and so she had made a calculated decision to ensure that I would cooperate, by sharing power.

"Satyavati did not return immediately. Her absence, coupled with disbelief in my announcements, began to weigh on the various families that had settled in Hastinapur along with the Kauravas. A second public embassy led by her brother

Shukla was sent to invite her to return. She returned to a grand welcome that I organised, even as I left the city before the event.

"This was the problem – my avoidance of Satyavati did not lead to increased trust. Satyavati had feared me and even though I had abased myself and begged her to return, she continued to fear and distrust me. Our agreement that I would stay outside the city while she stayed inside was unworkable – she needed to go out, if only for pleasure, and I had to come in for meetings with other administrative officials, including their ministers. We modified the agreement, but it continued to be difficult to manage. It was stressful and irritating to me that I had to constantly monitor my actions so as not to violate some element of the agreement. The core of the agreement held – Satyavati became co-Regent and Queen Mother, and took care of her babies, Chitrangada and Vichitravirya; I was co-Regent and managed all the internal affairs of Kururashtra. We shared responsibility for collecting taxes and authorising expenditures – the Panchnad model that mandated standard taxes and standard expenditures was already in place and did not change. Monarchies spend in order to glorify the ruler, but in the absence of a ruler, the revenues could support minor luxuries for a principal family.

"Satyavati raised the boys by not withholding anything from them. They were self-willed and stubborn, and nobody chided them. Left to their mother they would have learned nothing. I worked with the Kavi Sangha to arrange teachers for them in history, economics, trade, martial arts, and strategy.

"Meanwhile, the Kavi Sangha and the Vyaasa Jaimini worked to create a state that maintained order in the face of chaos, while preserving what was best in the abandoned cities. As the Vyaasa Bharadvaja had observed many years ago when he convinced Shantanu to allow Panchnadis into Hastinapur – chaos destroyed knowledge even when it did not kill the bearer. '*Knowledge*,' he said,'*in an urban civilisation like Panchnad did not just reside in the minds and bodies of individuals – it also resided in the relationships between people that characterised urban life. Knowledge was lost when the smith who knew how to smelt metals went south while the craftsman who knew how to construct the moulds for a graded sequence of cast weights went north – the system of standard weights that supported an honest oral trading infrastructure would be lost. Similarly, if the last brick-maker who could make high-quality bricks of a fixed shape, size, and strength was lost, the engineer who knew how to make buildings with those bricks would no longer make solid structures. The bricklayer would struggle to lay bricks with irregularly shaped bricks and would create a pastiche wall, ugly to view. In an urban civilisation, knowledge nestled in all kinds of niches, waiting to be exploited.'* The Kavi Sangha could preserve knowledge as long as the rest of the world functioned well enough – destruction of knowledge threatened in every riot, every clash between immigrant and Naga, and every conflict over scarce resources.

"Chaos was unavoidable – it streamed in steadily from outside. The solution was to channel its energies. During the last years of Shantanu's reign, I had begun building dams to create small lakes and ponds along the paths of the Ganga and the Yamuna. The Kavi Sangha suggested (and I agreed with this assessment) that the settlement of Varanavata would be the model for new settlements. Varanavata was the camp where Samvarana had spent his years of exile. It was on the banks of a constructed lake on the Yamuna and over the years, it had become a pleasant agricultural community. Canals and irrigation channels brought water to the fields where it was used. The plan was to create more agricultural settlements in the land between the two rivers north of the ridge where the Yamuna had changed direction. The Nagas had only expanded slightly in that direction, and there were only a few bands to be dealt with. Immigrants could settle this land. Rainfall was low and water had to come from the two rivers."

"By that time, we had stopped enforcing the limits on the number of children in a family. A limit on the number of children is easier to enforce in an urban setting. Not so in a rural setting. The need for limits did not go away. We were left only two ways of managing the growth – not let in any more immigrants or make them move to the borders of the land we controlled and could use. We were not prepared to turn back the refugees, at least not yet. We would have to settle new refugees on the border. They would have to farm the land. The massive dislocation of people had made the trading network unreliable, so they would first aim to produce the food they needed before producing for export. The fine pottery and ceramics for which Panchnad had been famous could no longer be made and exports to the West collapsed. In Panchnad, the land to the south had been extremely fertile while the land to the north was good for crops only in a small band on either bank of the river. As a result, Panchnad had two kinds of towns – the northern ones that focused on manufacture and the southern ones that produced the food. This model could not be reproduced here – we had many northerners and few southerners. We tried to make the Nagas our 'southerners' but that was misconceived. Most of the southerners of Panchnad had gone south into the unknown territory of the Southern Peninsula. Every lesson that we learned took our best efforts, but worse, it took us years to absorb. Meanwhile we were sending the refugees to these half-built and half-baked northern settlements."

Lomaharshana paused and took a drink of water. It was almost a ghati after the sun had disappeared, and dusk was falling fast.

Yudhishthira said, "We must continue tomorrow so that I finish hearing all this."

Lomaharshana said, "Sir, the Regent stopped at that point. Tomorrow, I will ask him to finish his narrative and I can summarise for you, if you wish."

Shukla said, "Yudhishthira, you choose – do you wish to listen to the Regent or to listen to Lomaharshana's summary?"

Yudhishthira shook head, "We should continue tomorrow with the Regent. I will attend from the morning until I am called away. Anything I miss, the Archivist can summarise for me."

With those words they adjourned.

King Chitrangada takes Charge

The Pandava Camp
circa 2000 B.C.E.

The next day King Yudhishthira, the Vyaasa Shukla, and the Archivist Lomaharshana came together to Devavrat's tent after the morning meal. The entrance was closed with a curtain of felted cotton. The nurse came out and said, "Excuse the delay, sir. The Regent is not yet ready."

After about a ghati, the nurse invited them in. Devavrat was lying on his side, his eyes closed and his mouth set in a thin line. As they entered, he opened his eyes and said, "Come in. I regret to say that I can no longer control my body. Give me death."

The King said, "Grandsire! We regret to trouble you in this manner. We cannot heal your wound, but nor are we ready to kill you when you are in this state."

Devavrat said, "Should I attack somebody or strive to escape? Then you will kill me?"

Yudhishthira said, "Sire! As a fatally wounded prisoner, I do not believe you can harm anybody. An attempt at escape would be met by a search to find you and bring you back, not to kill you. An attempt by you to kill somebody is unlikely to succeed and anybody who responds to such an attempt by killing you would be punished, at the very least, chastised. I have ordered that nobody is to attempt to kill you."

Devavrat said, "Then you do not hold out any hope for me. Am I to continue in this undignified manner?"

"I've asked everyone here to treat you with respect. They will do so."

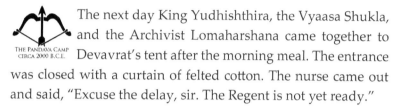

"You are here for your purposes – why should I care?"

"Because we have the same goals – how to create a country that works for its people. The Kavi Sangha wants to record your life. Both of us seek to honour your life and your work. You have done much and even if I do not agree with what you have done, I still wish to understand it. If only to keep from repeating it."

"Is that the consolation you offer me? You will remember me for my errors?"

Shukla intervened. He said, "Devavrat, my friend. We have known each other for a long time. You will die soon. I will die soon after. You can be remembered for all you have done, both successes and failures, errors, if you will. Alternatively, you can be forgotten completely. Which would you rather have happen? That choice I can offer you as the Vyaasa. Forgive Yudhishthira – his father's ghost, your nephew, drives him. Tell him what he wants to hear, so that your brother's son may rest in peace."

The three of them contemplated each other in silence. Devavrat considered what had been said. He had given up so much in his life. Was this to be the ultimate fruit of his sacrifices? He had killed his own son; Amba had attempted to kill him; the people he had sworn to protect had died, his brother Chitrangada, his nephew Mahendra, the host of others who had opposed him. Shukla offered him oblivion or fame – Shukla did not realise that he cared for neither. The only person in recent days who had expressed sorrow at his condition was Yudhishthira, who had little reason to be kind to him. If he owed anything to anybody, it was Yudhishthira, who empathised with him when no one had for many years. It would be an act of kindness to satisfy his request and it was the only one within his power to grant.

"Yudhishthira, my child! I'll do as you wish. Come, Archivist, sit near me and listen to me talk. Yudhishthira, is there any question you want me to answer?"

There was nothing else to be said. Yudhishthira said, "Lomaharshana ended yesterday saying that refugees were directed south into hastily made homes in territory that Nagas had left fallow. What was the reason for that?"

Devavrat was silent in response to Yudhishthira's question and stared at the ceiling of the tent. It looked like he was about to say something, but then he stopped and continued staring. They waited for ten vighatis. Then he closed his eyes. Yudhishthira did not move. Lomaharshana could not wait.

Lomaharshana said, "Forgive me, Lord. Could you continue with your narrative?"

Devavrat's eyes opened and he looked at Lomaharshana. So did Yudhishthira and the Vyaasa, causing the young man to cringe.

"Yes, I will," said Devavrat. He gazed at Yudhishthira. His father used to have the same stubborn look of conviction. *Memories are lost in time and we lose ourselves in them.* Yudhishthira did not appear to have changed and was looking at him with the same concern that he had the day before and the day before.

Devavrat said, "Yudhishthira, I will answer your questions when the time comes. At this time, I will speak of Hastinapur after my father married Satyavati.

"As I said yesterday, Satyavati and I established a co-Regency. A few years passed, Chitrangada came of age and was crowned King. He died fighting Shakas in the north."

Shukla said, "This is a point that has created much debate. My sister was told that a gandharva, also named Chitrangada, challenged him. Well... we know that gandharvas are imaginary beings and do not exist. Whoever told Satyavati that had not told the truth. Now you say Shakas killed him?"

Yudhishthira asked, "What exactly was the Queen Mother told?"

The Vyaasa continued: "I learned from her that Chitrangada had set out on an expedition to the northern border and that Devavrat followed him to stop him. Devavrat's men came back with a story of a gandharva killing Chitrangada. At that time, I investigated on behalf of Queen Satyavati. I questioned Devavrat's soldiers and they all had the same story – Chitrangada was already dead by the time they arrived, the gandharvas had vanished leaving behind a small contingent of their allies, the Shakas; the ensuing battle with the Shakas lasted longer then expected, there were more casualties than expected, but Devavrat's army had finally prevailed. Many Shakas were captured and following their own practice, they were enslaved. The Panchnad settlements do not have slaves, but they could be easily sold to the western countries that clamoured for them. The Shaka slaves were shipped off via the port of Tripura on the Sindhu delta. You cremated Chitrangada's body because in a few days the body had begun to decompose and could not be carried safely."

Devavrat said, "Yes, gandharvas do not exist. I made up that story in order to spare Satyavati the details of her son's death. I also wanted to spare the people of Hastinapur those details."

Shukla said, "The bard reciting the story knows what to include and what to exclude for the audience dictates the telling. However, the bard must know it all, for the choice is made at the time of telling. You've already told us of the death of your father and the co-Regency that you set up with Queen Mother Satyavati. What happened after that? What led to your brother's death and to another co-Regency"?

Devavrat said, "That I will cover. Recall that my second brother, your grandfather, died some years later, leaving two pregnant Queens with the not-yet-born Mahendra and Dhritarashtra. That was the third co-Regency. When Mahendra exiled himself, he left behind his blind brother Dhritarashtra – a blind person cannot be crowned King, so

Satyavati, Dhritarashtra, and I formed the fourth co-Regency. For whom were we holding the seat? When your father died, one faction wanted you, Yudhishthira, son of King Mahendra, to be crowned King. Dhritarashtra kept quiet when Satyavati objected, but it was clear that the suggestion to overlook him because he was blind had offended him. He supported a second faction that wanted to make his son Suyodhana the King. This was considered radical and against custom – the custom among caravan masters was that a son could supplant his father as Master only if his father died or was mentally incapable. This was intended to prevent a caravan from being hijacked by a coup. Hastinapur had never been a matrilineal matriarchy – the Master was called King – Suyodhana could not become King while his father was alive and in his senses. Your father was dead – you could be made King, if we agreed. A compromise was reached – Dhritarashtra gifted your father's forest back to you. When you accepted the offer, you gave up your legitimate claim to be the King of Hastinapur. We mutually agreed to call Dhritarashtra the King, for it pleased him and did not affect anything.

"Sending you away did not resolve Suyodhana's problem. He could still not become King. He could not kill his father because that would not sit well with Queen Satyavati, or, for that matter, with me. He could declare his father incompetent and prove it by a public demonstration of his father's dementia. Satyavati would not countenance such an act and I could not, either. However, Suyodhana's faction dominates the councils and the city, so Suyodhana now rules in the name of his father, the co-Regent. I am the other co-Regent, along with Queen Satyavati, but almost everybody obeys Suyodhana's dictates as though he were already the King."

Yudhishthira said, "You have been co-Regent for Hastinapur many times. What can you tell us about these co-Regencies?"

Devavrat said, "As Shukla said, I have already covered the death of my father and the establishment of the first co-Regency. Next I will present the short reign of my brother Chitrangada, his northern misadventure, his death, and..."

Yudhishthira said, "Excuse me, Grandsire! At another time, I would have urged you to tell me all about my granduncles. Today, I want to know the forces that motivated your imperial decisions. Chitrangada ruled for a very short time; I've been told that Vichitravirya showed little interest in governing. Neither of them could have affected policy in any significant manner. Whether in retirement or not, you ran the country. What does the foolhardy death of my granduncle Chitrangada matter if they did not affect your imperial plans?"

Devavrat pursed his lips and nodded. His brother's death by itself meant nothing; the chain of effects from that death was significant. Chitrangada had been suspicious about the Kavi Sangha, a trait he derived from Satyavati who considered the Kavi Sangha evil, even as she used its volunteers to do tasks that she wanted done. Chitrangada had suspended all cooperation with the Kavi Sangha – his death had restored the Regency and reinstated the agenda of the Kavi Sangha.

Devavrat said, "My son, Chitrangada's reign and his death forced the Kavi Sangha and me to change, to expand substantially the scope of our imperial plans. His younger brother Vichitravirya was young, but in addition had not been raised to rule – he showed no desire to act as King and ruled only because he had to and because his grandmother wanted him to. Vichitravirya enjoyed life with his two wives; his unexpected death and the subsequent late birth of his children allowed us, the Kavi Sangha and me, to collaborate with Satyavati and set many irreversible changes in place. The events leading to and after Chitrangada's death changed many things – that death was a critical decision point. The co-Regency after Vichitravirya's death lasted eighteen years until Mahendra ascended the throne."

2000 B.C.E

Devavrat paused. *Only I know how my brother died. Amba does, too. That's how I met Amba.* These thoughts added to his melancholy.

He continued, "Shukla, my friend. I have one wish."

Shukla nodded.

Devavrat said, "You must tell me what you know. You said that you knew how Amba reached Panchala and her life there and of her son Shikhandin – that is all I wish to know. You must tell me of Amba's life."

Yudhishthira said, "Does this need to be a part of this archive?"

Shukla was silent as he considered his answer. *Why was Yudhishthira, who had been so solicitous earlier, showing signs of impatience?* His father Mahendra had disagreed with Devavrat over policies – the result was that Mahendra deliberately withdrew into self-exile. Telling the story of Devavrat's life in such detail postponed the explanation of that decision. Given Devavrat's condition he might never get to that point. Devavrat's life outlined the framework on which Hastinapur had tried to address the crisis created by the refugees of Panchnad. Some key events in Devavrat's life corresponded to shifts in policy – Devavrat's mother's death resulted from Shantanu's first attempt; Shantanu's marriage to Satyavati heralded a change in policy that was given to Devavrat to develop; Shantanu's death and the division of labour defined by the co-Regency meant that Devavrat focused on solutions outside the city; Chitrangada's death had led to an alliance against the Shakas; Vichitravirya's death gave Devavrat sole control of policy, and it was not until Yudhishthira's father came of age that Devavrat's power began to diminish. Yudhishthira must think that the story of Amba and Shikhandin was a distraction that postponed any discussion of those differences.

When the silence had continued for many vighatis, Devavrat said, "I don't care whether Amba's story is included in the archive, but if you do not tell me what happened to her, I will no longer cooperate."

Shukla said, "Yudhishthira, listen! The archive is not solely a repository of how the city was governed and the stories relevant to that. By creating stories that can be recited and that will hold the attention of an audience, you give life to the history of the city. Perhaps you wish to get to the causes of your father's self-exile. I guarantee you that we will get there."

It was Yudhishthira's turn to ponder. Finally he said, "So be it. I shall stay patient."

The bell at the entrance to the tent rang. A Panchalan soldier came in and bowed to the King. He said, "Sir! The night's reconnaissance teams have just come in. They have requested a meeting with you and your brothers."

Yudhishthira grimaced and considered his options – they had successfully executed the ambush and captured the Regent, but the war would not end so easily. If it were a troop movement by Hastinapur, it would be valuable to get the Vyaasa's input as well. Meanwhile Devavrat was cooperating well with the Archivist, recounting what Yudhishthira wanted to know, and that had to continue.

Shukla interrupted, "Yudhishthira! Lomaharshana is a master of memorisation and archiving – he will do a perfectly good job even without our presence."

"Guruji, I am not concerned about Lomaharshana's skills. The Regent wants to narrate the history of events that led to the deaths of my grandfather Vichitravirya and his brother Chitrangada. Your presence and mine are the only guarantee that the Regent will narrate the histories we wish to know. You and I are the ones who can decide if a digression should be pursued or should be dropped. How can Lomaharshana make that decision?"

"You are right," Shukla said, "You are the best person to elicit the knowledge you seek from the Regent. However, we both know that you cannot be here all the time. You have the opportunity to tell Lomaharshana what you are looking for. I will have Lomaharshana summarise for you this evening and he can be asked to fix any shortfall the very next day, when memories are still fresh."

Yudhishthira hesitated. I am the King, he thought. I should...but I am the King and there are many other tasks to be addressed. He knew what he had to do.

Yudhishthira said, "Lomaharshana, listen! Grandsire, this is what I seek. My granduncle Chitrangada and my grandfather Vichitravirya ruled for a very short time. Yet you seem to place great importance on their short lives. Why? Battles were rare in those times – over two thousand moons since Samvarana was restored by violence. Yet Chitrangada died in battle. My grandfather Vichitravirya became the ruler at a young age and died young. I am told he died before his sons were born – their birth was described as a miracle. I am eager to hear of them, even though my mind is pre-occupied with this war. What was grandfather's life like? What did he accomplish? His death must have been a shock to the Queen Mother Satyavati."

Devavrat said, "Yudhishthira, your granduncle, my half-brother Chitrangada, was eager to show off his skills as a warrior. I had trained him and I believe he wanted to impress me even as he charged me with treason for not handing over the full army to his command – his mother had handed over control of the troops stationed in the city, but Chitrangada wanted to command all the troops including the ones protecting all the things I had been building – dams, canals, roads, and settlements."

"Why did you not give him complete command of the army?"

"He was impetuous and inclined to quick action without thinking through its consequences. I asked him to command the army through me, but very quickly he realised that I was slow to respond to demands for urgent action. He could not see how often a threatening crisis would pass without requiring any response. Unfortunately, he did not learn the futility of action from these episodes.

"I also kept control of the secret service – I told him that this was the traditional practice, so that the King's reputation and character were not sullied by contact with low and despicable persons only fit to be spies and provocateurs. After that bit of dissimulation, it was a relief that he never found out about his mother's secret agents – he might have confined her to her home to prevent further damage to her reputation!

"Despite my best efforts, I had to hand over control of the army to the King. I retained my personal guard, almost a hundred men, but I did not use them to guard me. They guarded the projects I had in progress throughout the region. I also created a border police force to augment the guards used inside the city – they would help manage the flow of immigrants and keep them from conflicting with the Nagas."

Yudhishthira said, "You told us earlier that the official story of his death was false. Do you know the real story?"

"To the best of my knowledge, there are no gandharvas – they are mythical beings. I do know the manner of his death – I've kept it a secret for so many years. I used to think, *when I die, it will die with me*. Even the Kavi Sangha's archives do not contain that truth."

"It is not appropriate that nobody in the family knows the truth about his death. As long as you were alive, you could reassure yourself that somebody knew the truth. It is incumbent on you to tell the story to somebody. If there is cause to keep it secret, let the burden be mine. Lomaharshana, do you understand what I would like to know?"

The Archivist replied, "Sir, the best test is, as Guruji said, for me to memorise and compose a narrative, then give you the chance to review it. I am open to correction."

Both Shukla and Yudhishthira stood up. Shukla said, "Good luck, my boy! You must take the King's place."

Lomaharshana turned to the Regent Devavrat. "Sir, shall we continue?"

PART 4.

Interlude

THE SCRIPTING PROBLEM

Kaushambi/Hastinapur
circa 850 B.C.E.

It was late evening. Vaishampaayana repeated Lomaharshana's words, "Shall we continue?"

Then he said, "This is a good time to stop for the night. I'll continue tomorrow."

As they got up to leave, Bhargava said, "You will tell us the story of Chitrangada's death, won't you?"

Vaishampaayana said, "As I just narrated, even at that time, there was debate over this question. Fortunately for you, the debate has now been settled and the story is part of the archive. Yes, I will begin with that tomorrow."

Chandrasekhar said, "Sir, I had agreed to meet with your apprentices and ours to review the work that has been done to date. We had planned to meet tomorrow. My apologies – I was planning to mention this earlier. Should I cancel my meeting with the apprentices?"

Vaishampaayana said, "Chandrasekhar, I am pleased that you reminded me. We will have to continue our narration after your meeting with the apprentices. You can report on it first."

He continued, "Bhargava, don't make a face – at our age, it isn't amusing. We will continue the next day."

Two days later, Bhargava and Chandrasekhar came in on time as usual. Bhargava did not stand as he usually did as the mat was laid down, but walked around, staring at the long morning shadow of the ficus tree. Vaishampaayana came and sat; so did Chandrasekhar and one of the apprentices he had brought along. Bhargava was slow to sit down. Vaishampaayana waited. Finally, Bhargava did sit. Chandrasekhar had prepared his palm leaves and was waiting. After everybody had been seated and had prepared for the narration, Vaishampaayana said, "Today, I shall continue from Yudhishthira's assent to the plan that the Vyaasa Shukla had laid out. But before that, we have to discuss yesterday's session held by our apprentices."

Bhargava said, "I have a request about today's plan. You mentioned that Devavrat earned the name Bhishma when Chitrangada died. Can we know how that happened? You should surely cover Chitrangada's death. Please don't skip the story of how Devavrat earned the name *Bhishma*."

Vaishampaayana said, "It is an episode we usually skip during recitals. Devavrat's vow of celibacy seems awful enough to most listeners that we explain the name *Bhishma* as a response to the earlier vow."

"Why skip it?"

"Hastinapur is our city. Devavrat Bhishma is Hastinapur and Hastinapur is Devavrat Bhishma. The details of how Devavrat came by the name Bhishma – the act was shameful and we do not wish to dwell on it. Devavrat is the founder of an empire – he made this city a great city, a capital city that ruled for many centuries. That empire is gone, replaced by two splinters – the eastern ruled from Kashi and the western ruled from Mathura; the eastern ruled by Pauravas and the western ruled by the Yadavas; Shaivas in the east and

Vaishnavas in the west. Hastinapur has not been the capital for many years. We have fallen far and with this flood, we have hit bottom now.

"The one and only time I recited this episode, the Chief Councillor called on me. 'It is bad enough that the people of Mathura and Kashi call us decrepit. We do not need to broadcast the shameful deed of the founder of the empire as well.'

"Now, we are in an even more depressed state. In private, the councillors feel humiliated that Kashi saved us from the flood that destroyed the city. Reciting the story of Devavrat's shame would be adding salt to a wound."

"That is no explanation. What was shameful about that episode?"

"Patience, I am getting to it. Devavrat does not shine in it for two reasons. He commits atrocities and he breaks his vow of celibacy."

"Committing an atrocity? Breaking a vow? That would make a great story. Just like Amba's story, that you implied was another mystery. I don't want you to skip any stories. Why would you skip such drama? Hastinapur the capital is history and nobody cares about its feelings. These stories are not shameful. Rather, these stories make it great. You don't have to suppress stories just because the councillors are easily embarrassed."

Vaishampaayana said, "Really? Who do you think commissioned this project?"

Bhargava's mouth was set in a crooked smile. He looked away. "Yes, yes. I know. I am not the customer."

Vaishampaayana laughed. Then he leaned forward and said softly, "The story of this *Jaya* is the story of how an empire rose out of the ashes of a crisis. An act of atrocity corrupts the imperial achievement. Even breaking his vow does not damage Devavrat's reputation as much as the story of an atrocity. It makes the city less in the eyes of people. You want me to include a sideshow of no importance."

Bhargava said, "Don't get me wrong, Vais. You know that the sideshows are why our work in writing this down will be praised. I'll support you and your apprentices for the time we spend on this sideshow."

"I am sure the city will thank you for that."

"I see. Not you? I can help you too. I'll support an additional apprentice bard for the first six years of his education. Satisfied?"

"Only one apprentice? I need..."

"Vais! I'll withdraw the offer."

"Okay, okay. One is good. Two, if you include your cook for the period of getting this written."

Bhargava looked at Chandrasekhar who nodded his head.

Bhargava said, "Yes. I can do that."

Vaishampaayana said, "Before we start, we have unfinished business to discuss. My apprentices reported on yesterday's validation sessions."

Bhargava said, "I heard. That was a most unprofessional and ridiculous performance."

"I am glad we see eye to eye. We will need to make substantial changes."

"Your apprentices need to apologise to my son and my apprentices for their behaviour."

"Huh? I am told that the offenders were your apprentices. What were you told?"

"Yesterday's validation session ended with your apprentices fighting mine over the palm leaves."

"That is not what I was told – your apprentices would not accept changes that my apprentices proposed and became angry when my students picked up the palm-leaves to point out some errors. They asked for changes to be made, but that did not happen."

"Changes, indeed! They were uncalled for. They were unnecessary. Completely not necessary. Ask Chandrasekhar here."

Vaishampaayana was not about to yield judgement to an untested third party. "Oh, no! I reviewed what my apprentices wanted – they were completely and utterly necessary."

"Give me an example."

Vaishampaayana turned to Chandrasekhar.

"Chandrasekhar, How do you write your father's name, 'Bhargava'?"

"Let's see. 'b', 'ā', 'g', 'ō', 'ā'."

"Write them down."

"OK." Chandrasekhar scribbled it down on a palm leaf. Vaishampaayana took the leaf and handed it to Bhargava.

"Now pronounce what you have, please."

"It's 'baa-go-aa'."

"Yes, good. Now do you see the problem?"

"No."

Vaishampaayana said, "He did not write it the way *I* pronounce it. I would have said 'b^hār-', 'ga', 'vā'."

Bhargava said, "Ha! You do not like the pronunciation. That's how we pronounce it in the northwest: 'baa-go-aa'. That is not a problem – dialects vary even from village to village. People understand the names even when pronounced differently. If a name is written so that it is pronounced in one way, the listener recognises the name – how the name is written hardly matters. The same is true for much else – it is only necessary to write consistently to somebody's pronunciation, anybody's pronunciation. I am sure that none of your listeners would be confused if you said 'Bagoa' instead of 'Bhargava'.

"You are insisting on your northeastern variant – that is how you pronounce my name in your accent. You mean to say my name correctly but just cannot do it. It is 'bāgoā' not 'b^{h}āṟgavā'."

Vaishampaayana felt that he was teetering at the edge of a precipice. Bhargava did not understand. That seemed unlikely – maybe he understood only too well? He chose his words carefully.

"The words that Chandrasekhar writes on the palm-leaf must be the way I, Vaishampaayana, pronounce it, for that is the traditional pronunciation used by the bards. The bards did not pronounce words the way the locals did – this was a long-standing practice of bards, predating the Kavi Sangha and going into the mists of Panchnad history. In the future, a reader should not pronounce a word differently just because a scribe chose to write the word one way that day. The next scribe might write it differently and the reader would pronounce it another way. In a few generations, the result would be documents containing a collection of inconsistent and incoherent words. This might not be a great problem with names, but it would be a problem with all other words. Our problem is not how to write so that the neighbouring village understands us – the problem is to ensure that a reader five hundred years from now understands us."

Chandrasekhar said, "I see the point you are making, sir. However, I have no choice. I have to write using the twenty-eight symbols that I have been taught to use. In addition, I can only write down what I hear. If my hearing is faulty, your apprentices can listen to a reading and correct the written words. I must express what I hear with the symbols I have. What your students should do is help me approximate the pronunciation you want."

"It is not enough to approximate the sound, Chandrasekhar. We must write the correct sound. It is important to write the exact sound."

"Sir, in my studies, our teachers made it clear to us that the writing must convey the right concept. The sound may change over time and from country to country, but as long as the right concept is written, the sound does not matter."

Vaishampaayana shook his head vigorously from side to side as he said, "No, no, no…"

Vaishampaayana's denials tapered off into silence. Nobody said anything as they contemplated what Chandrasekhar had just said. A few vighatis passed.

Then Vaishampaayana said, "I understand but do not accept what you have just said. It strikes at the very heart of a society founded on speech. I don't want to accept it. Once we start writing, we will not be able to stop and return to being the oral culture we were. This is worse than I thought – the Writ will overcome the Word."

Bhargava said, "Vais, my friend. It is all very well to contemplate the subtle consequences of our actions. However, we have to finish this. What do you suggest we do to convey the exact and correct sound?"

Vaishampaayana said, "If a new basic sound must be represented in the script, and, if your current set of symbols is not adequate, we must add a new symbol to your set of symbols. Possibly, change some of the existing symbols as well. We will need to create symbols appropriate for our language, the Kavi Sangha's language."

Chandrasekhar looked up at the sky and took a deep breath. "Uncle Vaishampaayana, you want me to invent a new script."

"We can do it together. I was not a good student when your father tried to teach me to write. I was too young, I did not understand him. Teach me your script and explain the rules of its creation. Then, let us see what we can do."

Bhargava said, "Vais, that's crazy. What makes you think we can change the script?"

Vaishampaayana said, "I have been reviewing some of the work some evenings. In the beginning, I admired the neatness and cleanliness of what you had done – the symbols lined up closely on the leaf, the rectangle created by the margins on all four sides. The variation of images across the leaf created by the symbols, set within a rigid frame of discipline, looked like music captured. It was caged poetry. It is a marvel. Is it accurate? I am sometimes considered too much of a stickler for accuracy; maybe I am, but for this project precision and accuracy is essential. The written words must be precisely the spoken word without any scope for discretion on the part of the reader; in addition the word must be accurate, not 'accurate enough'. All mistakes must be corrected."

"You are asking for the moon, my friend. Maybe you can achieve precision. But accuracy? As a caravan Master, I worry constantly that my accounting is accurate for I risk whatever profit I can make. Despite all my worrying, I must tolerate one error in every hundred numbers written in my accounting tablets. Those errors represent real profit – my partners will find every one that is in my favour and overlook the rest; my clients will do the opposite. You can surely tolerate more minor errors than I do. There is no guaranteed way to be accurate when writing."

"I do not think I am being impractical. We have a deep understanding of how to pronounce oral poetry. That should help precision. As for accuracy – we will not depend on your worrying – we will apply our techniques for accuracy in memorising. And lastly, this is not accounting – there is no profit or loss at risk here."

Chandrasekhar was shaking his head. Vaishampaayana continued, "I know from our past work that each mark stands for a sound. I gather there are rules for how sounds are put together. In essence, your script is not so different from the way we teach our bards to listen and recite. Our very first lesson consists of the recitation of the sounds that modify the sound made by another mark – the *swaras*[117] modify the *vyanjanas* to create syllables. Why, Chandrasekhar, are you disagreeing with me? You have any vowels in your script?"

Chandrasekhar said, "Five 'letters' represent vowels. Each 'letter', a scribed mark, represents a vowel and some of its variations. As you read, whenever you see that letter you make the corresponding sound."

"Only five vowels? That is surely not enough?"

"We can combine them in different ways. Sometimes, a letter will be pronounced differently based on the other letters around it. We also have letters for non-vowel sounds."

"Those are the sounds we call *vyanjanas*. How many consonants do you have?"

"Hmm... there are about twenty-three letters, that is, scribed marks, for consonants. These letters – the consonant letters – each one represents a non-vowel sound. A consonant letter and a vowel letter often represent a syllable. There are other ways of writing syllables as well – 'consonant-vowel-consonant', for instance, is also a common form of syllable. A combination of consonant letters can represent a different consonant-sound for which there is no explicit letter, just as a combination of vowel letters can represent a different vowel-sound."

117 *Swara* means "vowel"; *Vyanjana* means "consonant". After this, we will use the English word.

"What do you mean? What does a consonant letter look like and how do they combine?"

"For instance, the second letter or mark in our system is the first consonant – it is called 'bit'. You read it as the sound 'b–'. It combines with the vowel called 'alif' read as '–a' to make the first syllable of my father's name, that is, 'ba'.

"What do you mean, 'bit' is pronounced 'b'? What exactly are 'bit' and 'alif'?"

"They are names."

"A name for the consonant and the vowel? Don't the sounds name themselves?"

"Technically, it is the name for the written letter, not the sound, a subtle distinction. That is, the name is the name for the scribed mark for the sound. For instance, a word consists of some letters. You would spell a word out as I did my name a short time ago, by using the names of the letters. My father's name would be spelled, bit-alif-ra-gil-oma-alif."

Vaishampaayana said, "Chandrasekhar, you father will tell you that this is where I balked many years ago. Why do you need to spell anything? Doesn't the sound directly name the letters to use? Look, there is only one way that we break down 'Hastinapur' – it is 'Ha-sti-na-pu-ra' – the sounds are the names of the syllabic signs. What's wrong with that?"

"I don't know, sir, but this is the convention. What do you want to do?"

"Chandrasekhar, let me tell you how we train our apprentices to memorise and recite. The first lesson is to recite all the vowels, beginning with 'a'; then they learn the non-vowel sounds, that is to say the consonants, in order – first, the sounds made by opening the back of the throat – 'ka', the first consonant, the first question, and the sounds related to it – the aspirated 'kha', the voiced 'ga', the mixed aspirated and voiced 'gha', and, the nasal 'ng'; then the sounds made when the tongue caresses the teeth – 'cha' the second consonant, the first conjunction, and the sounds related to it – the aspirated 'chha', the voiced 'ja', the mixed aspirated and voiced 'jha', and, the nasal 'nj'; then the sounds made when the tongue curls back against the hard palate – 'tta', the first oath, and the sounds related to it – the aspirated 'ttha', the voiced 'dda', the mixed aspirated and voiced 'ddha', and, the nasal 'nna'; then, the sounds made by sliding the tongue past the hard palate to meet the upper teeth – 'tha', the follower, and the sounds related to it – the aspirated 'thha', the voiced 'dha', the mixed aspirated and voiced 'dhha', and, the nasal 'n'; and then, the sounds made when the lips come together and part – 'pa', the flag, and the sounds related to it – the aspirated 'pha', the voiced 'ba', the mixed aspirated and voiced 'bha', and, the nasal 'm'. This list is not complete, for we have consonants like 'ya', 'ra', 'la', 'va', and a few more, that are exceptions. Then, we have other consonants that are composed from the named sounds, for instance 'kra' is 'ka' and 'ra' joined. From these consonants and vowels we make syllables and poetry is recited with syllables – for that reason, we practise pronouncing each syllable accurately. Every syllable can be thought of as a consonant or a mixed consonant, paired with a vowel. Our poetry is measured in syllables. One hundred and eight syllables are pronounced in a *vighati* – with time for stops, that is three verses in the anustubh[118] meter of thirty-two syllables. The syllable is the unit of memorisation. Like the wheel that moves a wagon a unit distance in a revolution, the syllable drives thought in unit steps. In the Kavi Sangha we teach that the syllable is the very heartbeat of the universe – every syllable is Time itself. We train Samavedins to use the syllable as the unit of keeping time."

118 *Anustubh* is a classical Sanskrit meter for a *shloka* (verse) consisting of thirty-two syllables in two lines of sixteen syllables. Almost two-thirds of the Mahabharata is composed in this meter, the rest is in the gayatri, and a few can be considered prose.

Bhargava said, "That I know well – it's how your contract memoriser decides how much I pay when I have to register a contract."

Vaishampaayana continued, "Make up symbols appropriate for the language I am reciting. You could use the Kavi Sangha's classification of syllables."

"I understand where you are headed, sir," said Chandrasekhar. "Do you know how hard it is to construct a set of marks like these? How much effort to teach everybody to use the same symbols? To foster agreement among competing parties? As it is, there are more than two systems of scribing – I've used the one that I know, from a group called the 'People of the Sea'. Your system will stand no chance against these established writing systems."

"So? We do not break under such challenges. In any case, we are not competing with anybody. The traders have created a script for trading; we are creating one for *our* poetry. We are creating a script solely for this use."

"I understand. People have modified these scripts for private use, as ciphers – so what you are proposing is not new. My observation over all these years in caravans is that no one has proposed as radical a change as this. Most scripts are said to use between twenty and thirty symbols. The letters for many common sounds are the same or look similar. If you've learnt one script, it isn't too hard to learn another for they are all based on the same concept. However, this script, you say it will be different. What exactly do we gain?"

"What do we gain? Accuracy. Again, I insist. It doesn't matter if our script does not resemble those other scripts – we are not making it for universal use, just for our use. For that, it needs to be accurate and perfect, not universal. Call it the world's first script exclusively designed for epic poetry, our secret script. How long do you think it will take?"

850 B.C.E

Chandrasekhar looked to his father for support, but Bhargava shrugged in resignation – his friend did not seem to understand how complex the task he was proposing was. Would this slow down the project? Possibly. By how much? Bhargava didn't know. The flood had destroyed the long-distance caravan business for that year – none would be coming or going this year. He would not be working on anything until after the next harvest at the earliest. This year's harvest was meagre, destroyed in the flood. He had nothing else to do that was useful or interesting, nor, for that matter did his son. This task sounded impossible but interesting, and it would keep Chandrasekhar busy. "I don't know," he said, "I don't believe it has ever been done in this manner."

"Think about it," said Vaishampaayana. "I and my apprentices will work with Chandrasekhar and your apprentices to identify sounds for which you can create new marks. Take the rest of the day off. Work on this and let us meet tomorrow."

Bhargava said, "But, but... you said we were to continue now from the day before."

Vaishampaayana said, "Bhargava, my dear friend. I am sorry to change this schedule at the last vighati. What Chandrasekhar has to do with our apprentices is the most important task right now. If you wish, we can observe."

Bhargava said, "No... that would be a mistake. My apprentices will start showing off for me and maybe yours will too. The result will be mayhem. Let Chandrasekhar report on it. I believe it is urgent and we must restart tomorrow."

Vaishampaayana said, "Chandrasekhar, tell me now – how long this will take?"

"Sir, I don't know, but I have the glimmerings of an idea. You said to base the script on the syllables you mentioned. Every one of the base consonants, except for the ones pronounced off the soft palate, is represented in the script we are using. We can invent new symbols for the added consonants. Single letters, some old, some new, could represent the vowel sounds. Then we use the methods used by the Elamites to connect consonants to vowels. I will let you know by the mid-day meal what we can do."

Vaishampaayana said, "There's your answer, Bhargava. We will know this afternoon and we may resume tomorrow – your son knows what to do."

The Problem is Solved

Kaushambi/Hastinapur
circa 850 B.C.E.

The next day, a messenger was waiting for Vaishampaayana when he emerged from his tent that morning. The messenger delivered his message and left just as Chandrasekhar and Bhargava walked up the path to the tent.

Vaishampaayana said, "Bhargava, do you know anything about this? The city elders have asked for my presence at a meeting about my 'new project', as they call it."

Bhargava did know of it. He was responsible for it. He had been called by the city council to discuss the progress of the project. He had pulled Chandrasekhar from his scripting session and asked him to explain the status. Chandrasekhar described with great enthusiasm the new ground he was covering. The Kavi Sangha apprentices were being trained to read and write in a new script. The new script was designed to work with the language of the city and its archives. There was nothing like it in the world. Chandrasekhar had left believing he had convinced them.

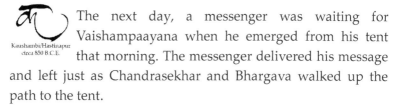

He was, of course, mistaken. When he described the new script as being 'like nothing else in the world', he had raised a danger signal, a red flag for a raging bull. Bhargava had heard from his informants that the councillors were furious – they thought the Vyaasa had hoodwinked them by defining a mammoth unfinishable project. This request to meet the Vyaasa was the result.

Vaishampaayana said, "I talked with my apprentices. Let me tell you – the Kavi Sangha seniors are critical about everything, but they had praise for you. Chandrasekhar and you have done well. Do not worry – my apprentices will learn quickly, at least how to read if not to write."

Bhargava said, "Vais, I've not seen you this enthusiastic for a long time. So, what do you think? We can be done soon?"

Vaishampaayana said, "Sooner than I imagined it. Hah! I think I can show the council the value of what I am doing."

"Will we be done in a day?"

Chandrasekhar shook his head, "I am making progress and I must thank your apprentices for their hard work and contribution. We are almost done with the set of marks to use. Next, I must practise writing to dictation."

"How much?"

"A week, perhaps. Maybe longer."

Vaishampaayana said, "Let me suggest that we continue the recital using the old script, and the errors will be fixed during the review by our apprentices. I can postpone the council meeting by a week. That should be time enough to prove this point."

The city council did not see the value of what he was doing. They were upset. The chairman, usually very deferential to the Vyaasa, grilled him. After a few welcoming remarks, he said, "Why have you held up the project we asked of you, while you train your apprentices to read and write? What is the need for this – Bhargava has all the apprentices needed to do the scribing and they already know how to read and write. Bhargava has even offered not to charge us for their services –they will not charge for their work. Why are you slowing the project down with your own innovations?

Vaishampaayana responded, "Sir, there are quality issues with using the script of the Sea-people. When the project is over, and the trader's apprentices have left, as they all will, you will need people who can read what has been written. Even the Kavi Sangha will need readers. In addition, when my apprentices know how to write, they can begin to write down important archival material that is not part of the history of the city but is about other critical matters. They will be able to teach the senior members and to help train newer apprentices. For that matter, they can even teach the councillors to read, why, even to write, if you so wish.

"In addition, the new script is so much more efficient – it will speed the project up five-fold. Let me demonstrate it."

He brought forward one of Bhargava's apprentices and one of his own. Each read from a palm leaf that they held in their hands. It was the same passage, a benediction. First, Bhargava's apprentice read it aloud from his palm-leaf. He struggled with pronouncing unfamiliar words. Many words were pronounced incorrectly – even the council could hear the difference. Some of the errors in pronunciation made them smile, for it sounded the way a child might speak. A Kavi Sangha apprentice, who read slowly, followed this but every portion sounded the way it was meant to sound. He had no difficulty determining what vowel to use.

The head of the council said, "Show me those palm leaves."

The palm-leaves were brought to him. "These are different," he said, "Are you hoodwinking us?"

Vaishampaayana hastened to explain. "They are different scripts, sir. My apprentice read from a script that we have just created. It is based on the other script, but made for our language, the language of the archives, not the language of the Mlecchas. It is easier to learn for it echoes our sounds."

"How much longer will it be before they are ready?"

"We are training all our apprentices, sir. I cannot say how long it will take – we are on completely new ground. When we teach our apprentices the oral syllabary, it takes about a week to two weeks. Very possibly, in another three weeks, they should be ready."

"Can we dispense with the trader then?"

"We will first correct all the work that has been done to date. Bhargava's apprentice will read what he wrote originally – my apprentices will determine the words that should have been written and its spelling and thus they will redo each palm-leaf. In the meantime, I will continue with Chandrasekhar and Bhargava. The trader's son is a miracle, a genius. If all goes well, we should be done with his services in a month or two. After that the Kavi Sangha will do all that is needed."

"Does this mean," said the chairman, "You have changed your mind about the utility of writing?"

"No," said Vaishampaayana, "My concerns about writing are not allayed. If anything, what I have done to fix the problem of pronunciation is more worrying. People will believe that we have solved problems with writing, that writing can be accurate and reliable, when we have only made the problem worse. For the written word cannot adjust to the living language but will become a tyrant, allowing only one way, the written way, for all time. People will come to believe that what has been written is the truth. 'It has been written,' they will say, as though that settles the truth or falsity of assertions. Our way of life will change for we will become captive to the tyranny of the written word. My original recommendation stands – we should not write this down at all but restore the Kavi Sangha to its original strength."

"That is not going to happen."

It was an astounding statement. Vaishampaayana looked at the other council members and they seemed nonchalant, seemingly unaware of the import of what had just been said.

The Kavi Sangha would not be restored! He made a snap judgement. *Better not to dignify the new policy by highlighting it, for even the chairman might not have realised the dramatic policy option he had just proposed.*

Vaishampaayana said, "Still, we must avoid the tyranny of the written word. That brings in my second recommendation, a policy to deal with the written document. Make only *one* written version of the archive. When we return to Hastinapur and re-build the temple of Nagaraja,[119] we shall keep it safely in the inner sanctum of the temple, under the control of the Vyaasa and the guardians he appoints."

"We shall see."

Vaishampaayana had come to the meeting confident and smiling. He left the meeting with a frown and a sinking heart. He had not convinced anybody, and, he might have just witnessed the birth of a new policy. *The Kavi Sangha would not be restored to its previous strength.*

His thoughts were interrupted by Bhargava's voice.

"One day you should tell me why you are so against writing. Especially considering the amazing way in which my son and your students are modifying it."

"I will," Vaishampaayana said. "The supremacy of the Kavi Sangha dies when writing becomes ubiquitous. Where else in the world do you see the poets advising the emperors? Hold on, we can discuss this later; we have work to do now."

They had reached Vaishampaayana's house. The apprentices had set up their seats. The three of them sat down.

Vaishampaayana said, "Do you recall where we left off?"

---

[119] *Nagaraja* means the "King of the Snakes". In modern times it refers to Shiva. In 850 BCE, Nagaraja was probably worshipped by the Nagas, while Shiva in the form of Pashupati literally means "Lord of Animals", would have been worshipped by the people of Kashi.

Chandrasekhar said, "Devavrat had summarised for Yudhishthira the major events after the death of Shantanu – how he and Satyavati were co-Regents for Chitrangada; how Chitrangada died soon after being crowned; how Vichitravirya died even as his wives became pregnant with his sons; and subsequently, another co-Regency as Mahendra came of age. Yudhishthira heard all of this in silence."

"Good, good. Your memory is excellent. Yudhishthira was reconciled to the Vyaasa Shukla's idea that he should not be satisfied with such a short précis of important events in the life of his grandparents and parents. A fuller story was needed.

"Then, Yudhishthira had instructed the Archivist on what he wanted the Archivist to focus on and the need to manage digressions. Following this, Yudhishthira and the Vyaasa left."

PART 5.

Bhishma, the Terrible

THE FIRST CO-REGENCY

Kaushambi/Hastinapur
circa 850 B.C.E.

Vaishampaayana continued: "Then the Regent Devavrat proceeded to tell Lomaharshana, the Archivist, the story of Chitrangada's death."

CHITRANGADA'S WAR

THE PANDAVA CAMP
CIRCA 2000 B.C.E.

Lomaharshana said, "Sir, you heard the guidelines I have been asked to establish in your narrative. Will you be able to tell me everything without halting?"

Devavrat said, "It is not easy to tell you this story. It does not deviate from your directions. What it does, though… even thinking of it creates a knot deep in my chest. As recently as three days ago, I would have claimed that this reaction has nothing to do with the history of the following years, down to this day. My encounter with Shikhandin has altered that belief – the knot is a complex one, with three strands, one of which leads unerringly to the man I just killed.

"Killing Shikhandin closed the story of my killing of Chitrangada. Yes, I will not hide it anymore. I killed Chitrangada.

Believe me, it had to be done. Killing him created that first strand of the knot that now threatens to choke me. That strand earned me my name. *Bhishma*. The Terrible. Not even *Devavrat the Terrible*. Not *Vasudeva the Terrible*. That would recognise my father's attempt to make people accept the unacceptable by calling the children he killed the incarnation of the Vasus. I was the Vasu who did not die and the sorrow and anger occasioned by that survival might have made the name acceptable. Even my given name Devavrat, *oath of the gods*, prescient in its own way for it recognises the fateful vow that made Satyavati my stepmother, was not earned. *Devavrat the Terrible* would have been fine. But just *The Terrible*? Am I *adhvaya*, sui generis, one of a kind? Is that kind the *Terrible* kind?

"Killing Chitrangada brought Amba into my life. When I lost her, the second strand was born. I had given her up for dead. Shukla says that she left me for Drupada. Drupada? No, that makes no sense. Shukla says that she has lived in hiding all these years. That does not make any sense, either. That is how her actions created the third strand that lay hidden from me until revealed by Shikhandin. These three strands, let me call them *Chitrangada-Amba-Shikhandin*, independent though they may appear to be, are knotted tightly around each other, each born of the previous one.

"Why, then, did I kill Chitrangada? The easy answer is that I saved him from a fate worse than death. When I decided to kill him, my mind was clear and without doubt; but even as I acted on that decision, my thoughts whirled and became muddled, and the purity of the initial intention was compromised. For I always wonder how it would have been different if I had been the King.

"When Chitrangada became the ruler of Hastinapur, many citizens of Hastinapur rejoiced that they were no longer subject to the rule of a Regent. The boy was just sixteen years old and under Satyavati's indulgence had become confident in his own ability to rule. I had trained him to be a warrior. He was good – he would have made an excellent commander of a battalion or even a division. That was not good enough for him – he considered himself a warrior in the tradition of Samvarana, father of the dynast Kuru. Shukla knew Chitrangada well and he would confirm how ridiculous that was. My ancestor Samvarana had become a warrior under the tutelage of the Kavi Sangha so that he could regain Hastinapur. The great Vasishtha who led the Kavi Sangha in that time took personal charge of Samvarana's education and training as a warrior. In the other cities of the west, the ones emptying out as the crisis continued, the leaders hired mercenaries. The mercenaries were the guards for trading caravans that went further west. The mercenaries guarded the leaders when they went on trips. The mercenaries maintained order; they prevented riots when the poorest felt unfairly treated. Mercenaries were the only ones who trained to fight.

"Since the time of Samvarana and Kuru, the rulers of Hastinapur have been a little different – we fight to protect ourselves from the Nagas of Panchala and to deter the Rakshasas[120] who attacked Laghu Nagapura downriver. We train for that. We protect our trade routes ourselves rather than use mercenaries. Our secrets stay with us. My father and I created even greater change by establishing an internal security force – initially a small corps to manage the influx of immigrants and the conflicts that arose between them and the Nagas. Later, we used the corps to enforce laws within our boundaries. That is how my father enforced his laws about children. He had the full support of the Kavi Sangha in this. This meant that we could no longer use the mercenaries – mercenaries only know how to make war and enforce martial law. They do not know how to

120 The Rakshasas occupied much of the Southern Peninsula, the plateau south of Laghu Nagapura, and both sides of the Ganga to the east of Laghu Nagapura.

enforce civil laws – how to take a child away from its parents without killing the parents as well.

"Having said that, I will admit that if my army had ever faced a mercenary army, our chances of victory were non-existent. You do not see mercenaries anymore – the guild of mercenaries has evaporated under the pressure of the crisis. They have no jobs because the caravans no longer head west through dangerous lands; the cities do not exist anymore and so do not need champions to fight on their behalf; and, finally, there are better opportunities for guards in the west. So the east has been abandoned.

"After my father died, it was an easy step for me to create an armed militia. I needed them to protect the dams I had built upstream from the northern boundary of Panchala. The Panchalas did not like my projects and could easily prevent me from crossing the Ganga to their side, so we chose the sites carefully. I used my militia to discourage them from coming over to our side. South and west of the Ganga, the wayward Yamuna had made the watershed unstable, and new waterworks had to be built to control the old monsoon-fed rivers. The army came in useful to coordinate the design between towns and villages and to direct the construction of dams, canals, and ponds by local workgroups. By the time Chitrangada was crowned, we had a small construction corps that could be used for projects.

"Having an army gives rulers the idea that it should be used. When Chitrangada came to power, his first wish was to use our army – my *small* army – to attack Panchala and avenge Samvarana's humiliation. *It was not enough,* he said, *that Samvarana had re-taken Hastinapur. The Panchalas had to be taught a lesson.* We, Satyavati and I, were able to dissuade him by pointing to the difficulty of launching an attack across the river. Such cooperation was rare – Satyavati and I were on opposite sides of every question that required joint action. Unfortunately, I also raised the possibility that we might not have the full support of the Nagas on our side – once this sank in, it coloured Chitrangada's attitude to the Nagas and thereafter he distrusted them. This distrust proved to be a disease difficult to extinguish even though Satyavati was a Naga – later, both Dhritarashtra and Suyodhana were infected with it.

"Chitrangada's ambitions to be recognised as a warrior had been stayed for the moment, but they never went away. The result was tragedy.

"I had continued my project of creating dams and canals wherever feasible. One of my greatest successes was restoring Varanavata, Samvarana's old abode of exile, located on the edge of Khandavaprastha at a point where the newly diverted Yamuna exited the forest. A monsoon stream ran through the shallow valley – its channel now overflowed with the waters of the Yamuna. My engineers had designed a series of crescent-shaped ponds that channelled the river, making it flow faster and deepen its median channel. The result was a river that flooded less. Canals led from the crescent ponds to Varanavata's fields much further away. As a result, the town had prospered and was slowly filling up with immigrants.

"I was visiting Varanavata when a messenger from Hastinapur delivered an urgent message. Chitrangada had received news of an incursion into Hastinapur territory at its northern extremity close to one of the branches of the Sindhu. I had not anticipated this. I had known of the incursion some weeks ago and had decided not to do anything about it. The Panchnad people claimed suzerainty over Jambudvipa but this was a formulaic suzerainty. Nobody enforces it. The incursions had become an annual event over the last twenty years. Some Naga bands had settled near there and I expected the intruders to go back as they usually did. *Who were they*, you ask. The intruders were from an uncivilised nomadic collection of tribes that called themselves 'Shaka'[121] and they came from the open plains northeast of the plateau of the Paarshavas. The mountainous and forested lands that we occupied were useless for them and they usually left after a few weeks. *Why did they come?* They came to trade. They came with lapis and agate, both polished and rough; they brought partially tanned skins of many animals, both large and small; occasionally they would have a small collection of yellow nuggets of pure gold. In the days before the disaster, Hastinapur would have viewed them as competition. *How did they come?* This was the most interesting aspect of their visit and the reason I did not try to eject them post-haste. They were in carts pulled by small horses. Not onagers[122] like we had, but horses. They did not behave like most traders – for instance, they did not bring their goods directly to the market. Instead, they would set up a camp in a secluded defensible place and they would come to the market with their goods on their backs or in small hand-drawn carts. Thus, they would never bring their horses to the trading site. Once I invited them to come with their horses for dinner – they refused. They cited cultural prohibitions that prevented them from eating with a non-Shaka. What I did not realise until much later was that they had started coming only after I built a dam across the Yamuna ravine, well within the mountains. Previously, it had been difficult to cross with carts and supplies; now, the dam provided the path. I would pay for that bit of carelessness.

121 *Shaka* refers to Scythians (as named by the Greeks) who roamed over much of the steppes of Eurasia.

122 The Indian onager is a subspecies of the Asian wild ass, of the equid family, larger than the donkey and smaller than a horse. The Indian onager is easier to tame than the other members of the family and may have been the preferred mode of transport from 3000 BCE to about 1500 BCE after which they were largely replaced by horses and oxen.

"I had sent some spies to keep track of the intruders and I would get a message every week or so. When I was not in Hastinapur, the messenger would be re-directed to me. The last messenger had gone to King Chitrangada's council-room. He tried to withdraw when he realised that I was not there, but before he could retreat the King observed him and commanded him to deliver his message. Chitrangada then expressed to his mother his dissatisfaction with my decisions, and his shock that I had put the country at risk. He decided to take our army (*my* army) and teach these intruders a lesson.

"I received a confused message from Satyavati about the matter and I returned to Hastinapur in a hurry – it still took a few days. Satyavati was in a tizzy. Sometimes she urged me to leave immediately to help Chitrangada; at other times, she fretted that I would steal from her son the credit of repelling the invaders. I kept quiet during these crying fits – what could I say? *It's my army he has taken with him, the five hundred trained fighters that I gave up to him, leaving only a small force of a hundred boys-in-training to protect the city!* Such a statement would only have made her angrier. I left as soon as I could with about fifty of my personal band – Chitrangada having left me with only a hundred men, I left half of them behind to supplement the hundred men from his army.

"There was not much we could do to go faster. Not with our onagers. The Shaka are trained horsemen – they use horses in their land for everything. It is a mystery to us how the Shaka can ride them in such a carefree manner – I have seen a horse and when angered, it is a terrifying sight. Many years ago, a trader had brought a wild horse in a cage. He showed us how it would refuse to submit to a yoke, and even if a yoke was somehow placed on its shoulders, it proved to be an uncontrollable power. Only the Shakas have mastered the secret of taming the horse. They do not part with that secret to anybody.

"We use onagers. I left as soon as I could."

2000 B.C.E

Devavrat to the Rescue

The Pandava Camp
circa 2000 B.C.E.

Devavrat continued:

"We loaded our supplies onto a dozen carts pulled by onagers. Onagers are stubborn wilful creatures but when harnessed with other onagers, they could pull carts. We needed to make speed, so we had two pulling a cart while two spare ones walked alongside. The crowd listening to a bard's stories does not always realise that it takes an army to move an army – my squad of fifty fighters needed sixty onagers and fifteen carts; forty-five of the fifty men were divided into three squads that were responsible for driving the carts.

"The day began with a meal followed by harnessing the onagers and driving for twelve ghatis. There was a break for a mid-day meal of flatbread and salted meat. In a more traditional campaign, we would have stopped to hunt for meat if the game looked promising, and we would have bartered our salted meat for hot cooked meals from local towns and villages, but we were in a hurry and we did not do that. After the meal break, we could go for another twelve ghatis or until the sun began to set. Then we would settle down for the night after a light meal, the same flatbread and salted meat.

"Our fifteen carts were loaded with three or four men each, their arms and armour, their food, as well as forage for the draft animals. Each cart selected one man to stay awake the first half of the night and a second man to keep watch during the second half. My primary worry was wild animals – the occasional tiger that was tempted by the easy prey that an onager seemed to be. In a small squad like this, the onagers of the carts on the outside might be attacked by wolf packs if they looked vulnerable. The tiger and the wolves were the most dangerous as they were not easy to dissuade.

"My second worry was the *kapi*,[123] that roamed in bands and made trouble everywhere. I've been told that these monkeys can be used as spies, and that is certainly possible but I've only found them to be nuisances. If a cart were not constantly protected, it would be ransacked. The onagers were tied to each cart on opposite sides – if they were startled at night they would panic in opposite directions, thus not moving the carts very far or going where they would not be found. Far more destruction has been caused in camps by distraught onagers than by even the fiercest enemy.

"If the destination was far away, and speed was essential, each onager would be spelled by a second onager that walked unburdened. That would double the distance we could go. Our haste added to the problems – we had to carry twice the hay and grain for feeding the onagers while cutting the number of soldiers and including one or more handlers for the additional onagers. The bottom line is that moving an army, even a small army, is not an easy task. I knew that Chitrangada had left in a hurry without enough draft animals and would have had to slow down to an achievable pace.

"Chitrangada had a lead of seven days over us but he would have moved slowly, with almost five hundred men and a couple of hundred followers who provided support. Instead of the four days we would take, he would have needed six or seven to reach the intrusion point. We have had some experience with unexpected confrontations with the Nagas of Panchala – it usually took a few days of manoeuvring and observation before it became clear who had the upper hand. Against a Panchalan force, the smaller group would configure itself in a defensive formation and send for reinforcements. The bigger group would assess its chances of total victory before those reinforcements

123 *Kapi* refers to the Indian rhesus monkey.

came and configure in an offensive formation. We inherited these forms of manoeuvring, called 'vyuhadyuta'[124] from Panchnad. It was rare for such a procedure to guarantee victory for the larger group; so, much of the time, nothing happened. A great superiority in numbers was needed before the larger group attacked. When reinforcements arrived, the forces might be equal or the relative strength might be reversed. The strategic implications of their relative strength would lead to reconfigured formations. Unless there was an overwhelming advantage for one group over the other, these manoeuvres would end in a stalemate. Both groups could withdraw and sometimes both declared victory. Sometimes, the groups might engage in battle. This could happen for various reasons – personalities of leading warriors, or an error of judgement by one side or the other, or even a momentary lapse in attention that allowed one side to get an advantage over the other.

"As I mentioned earlier, in the past I would arrange to monitor the Shaka 'visitors'. The pattern was that after a few weeks they would leave. They were not used to the never-ending forest and were a noisy bunch, especially when they rode their horses. I had a spy once who followed the Shaka back to their homeland and spent a few years with them. When he came back, he was in bad shape – a nervous wreck, his voice pitched higher than before, slurring words as though he might lose them if he slowed down, his eyes staring down and constantly moving. When he delivered the report of his two years on the road, he spoke quickly and I had to slow him down, but he was constantly speeding up as he spoke. He gave me useful information about the Shaka – unlike their peaceful behaviour when they visit us, they are extremely warlike in their own land. Every would-be warrior raises a horse – the team of horse and warrior can be terrifying when confronted on an open field.

[124] *Vyuhadyuta* means a shadow duel of opposing battle formations. See Endnotes.

"My spy described a battle he had seen when a Shaka band had attacked a caravan on their border with Parsaka – the guards protecting the caravan had formed a defensive perimeter when the Shakas were sighted. A Shaka warrior would gallop past the line just within arrow range, firing constantly. Arrows shot and spears thrown at them missed, apparently by magic. If the line wavered, the horseman might go in closer – once, an injury to a captain had distracted the soldiers near him and the horseman had managed to get in among the footmen – he had inflicted damage with a heavy sword while the guards struggled to organise. As soon as the guards regrouped the horseman had ridden out barely touched. The strategy was to make the defenders use up their arrows and lose spears thrown in haste.

"After a few days of this, the defenders became desperate and made overtures, offering tribute. The Shaka accepted the offer and came to collect – once in the camp, they rampaged through it on their horses, attacking the lightly armed guards and the defenceless traders and workers. It had been a terrifying sight – a man on a horse charging down a narrow path, slicing the walkers as they scattered to his left and to his right. They then proceeded to ransack the camp and kill most of the fighters. The few women in the caravan were taken as captives. They tortured the men for amusement, killing most of them in the process and leaving the rest maimed and injured.

"My spy had been one of the tortured ones – he shook uncontrollably as he tried to describe what had happened to him but he became increasingly incoherent when I pressed him to report clearly. I learned later that part of the torture had included castration – I retired him to a home where he was taken care of for the rest of his life. His return to me to report had been an act of perseverance and loyalty – I wish I could have done more, but the doctors shook their heads and could do little for him.

"I understood then that as long as the Shakas were far from their own land and faced with a land or people they could not conquer, they would be peaceful. If they sensed an opportunity to deploy their preferred mode of warfare, on open fields mounted on horses and dominated by the use of the bow and arrow, they would win every encounter with foot soldiers. Our Shaka traders had been peaceful because the Nagas lived in forested areas and the traders had come over mountain passes. They had come with only a few horses pulling carts. Something had changed and this time they were behaving differently.

"As I said before, we have tried using horses to pull carts with no success. In recent years we have managed to use some young female horses to pull light chariots, but it is a difficult task – these young horses are fragile, temperamental creatures that need a lot of care. Maybe Shaka horses are more docile. The hooves of our horses get tender and inflamed, they become lame, and they are easily spooked. Unlike our onagers. Onagers are placid. They will do nothing that will damage their feet, like gallop. Only the most fearsome predator will spook an onager. The only problem – it is not possible to ride an onager. I know, for I have tried.

"The Shakas use horses to make war. We have no experience with such wars. In the world of the Panchnad cities, war was rare and conducted by mercenaries as a game. Samvarana's eviction from Hastinapur and return to it was the only real war in our recent history – a smaller force was trapped by a siege and lost. I have been told of wars waged on open fields in which the horseman would be a fearsome opponent – one rider on a horse can speed by a line of infantry, dodging all arrows and spears, while shooting into the mass. One horseman can decimate a line of infantry; create a hole through which attacking troops can break a defensive wall. The onagers were useless in that role – they can pull steadily but cannot be made to go faster. An onager racing past an infantry line – the thought strayed into farce.

"Horses are not useful everywhere – a forest is no place to ride an animal like a horse. We cut paths and create trails for use by people and carts, not animals with a man sitting on top. The paths made by Nagas will not even support an onager-drawn cart. A small horse could probably make its way through the forest easily, but a slightly bigger one or one with a man on it would be blocked by branches that have to be pushed aside – a slow and noisy procession. A troop of horses, so much bigger, would have to go single file, which makes them vulnerable to attack by an enemy. That made me confident – I felt that we had nothing to fear from the Shakas. In case of conflict, we would deal with them in the forests and not on a battlefield. I had instructed my observers to avoid confronting the Shakas as much as possible and over the years they had complied. Everything had worked out well. I did not want to fight the Shakas – there is no predicting what would happen in actual battle, and the stakes were too small to risk it."

The Shaka Attack

THE PANDAVA CAMP
CIRCA 2000 B.C.E.

Devavrat continued: "Two days after we left Hastinapur, we were met by one of my observers returning with a message and a head in his cart. The head was that of one of my captains. The news stunned me. The King was missing. The Shakas had attacked us.

"My spy gave me some of the details. Chitrangada had planned to camp near the village of Seshanagaram, a Naga village that was a few yojanas from the Shaka camp. The village of Gandhanagaram was much closer, less than a yojana, and would be an observation post for his scouts. Just as they began the tedious task of setting up tents and lean-tos, a small group of women and children came streaming out of the forest.

"Gandhanagaram had been attacked. Many of the adult men had been killed. It was the season for planting seed. As was

Naga practice, the women had gone into the forest with their children to gather firewood and harvest some fruits. The able-bodied men were preparing the field for planting – this involved dragging a large wooden wedge to create a furrow. They would make the furrows of one crop at right angles to the furrows of the previous crop, so that the soil was evenly used. Because this made it harder to drag the wedge, the job required a bit more strength and only the men were considered suitable. That left a few older men and women not working at anything but relaxing in the central quadrangle of the living area.

"The Shaka horsemen had come along the trail that led to the river. It was a narrow trail and it must have been rough going, as the trail was not cut for horses. That had not deterred them. As they emerged from the trail, the horsemen had spread out along the perimeter of the field. They were quiet but it was the middle of the day and they were quite visible. There were about twenty Shakas. They did not make a sound, did not announce their intention, but they did not have to. The Nagas were not familiar with the use of a horse in warfare, but their armour and weapons were signs of what the Shakas planned. The men in the fields began to run towards the centre to get to their weapons; the women who had not gone to the forest ran into their huts; the old men and women went into the central hut. As soon as the running started, the horses started in towards the centre. They speeded up and quickly caught up with the fleeing men who were closest. The Nagas had no chance – the riders wielded bronze swords that they used expertly to kill or disable the men.

"It was fate, or perhaps ill luck, that Chitrangada had just come to this campsite south of the Naga village. The Naga women who were at the edge of the forest had seen the assault and had come to the King for help. Quick response is what I had trained my men for and within a half-ghati a squad of twenty men were ready for battle and one ghati later the Shakas watched the armoured and armed band make its way into the village clearing. Following the same tactic they had used with the Nagas, the horsemen charged the soldiers who were armed with spears and carried leather shields.

"Riding bare back, the Shaka warrior looked like a part of his horse, a second human torso with a human head. The horse came at the soldiers with terrifying speed. Chitrangada's men (*my* soldiers) were unfamiliar with such attacks. To the first soldiers to face the horses it appeared that they would be trampled. They sidestepped the horse and as the horse flashed by the horseman tried to slash at them with a sword. My men's spears protected them from that first slash but the passing of the horse unbalanced them and many of them fell to the ground. The horse stopped and turned around to run at them, but at a much slower speed. For some of my soldiers there was enough time to retrieve their spears and this time some of them succeeded in wounding the Shakas. Some of the Shakas fell off their horses and though they landed nimbly, the soldiers had some advantage over the Shakas. A few Shakas were killed – maybe five or six, and ten soldiers were killed and two were wounded. In the meantime, a second squad of soldiers had come into the opening. The Shakas realised that they were outnumbered and that they could not afford to lose so many fighters. One of the Shakas shouted and at that sound all the Shakas still on horses had wheeled them around and galloped back onto the trail they had come by. The other Shakas fought to the death. There were no captives.

"The reinforced squad of soldiers did not chase the horse-riding Shakas. This may have been a tactical error for they would have had the advantage. In hindsight, such previously unknown possibilities reveal themselves. Instead, they stopped and helped move the wounded and the dead to Chitrangada's camp. All the Naga men who had been preparing the field for planting were dead. With the departure of the Shakas, the women came in from the forest. The old men and women of the Naga village were found hiding in the innermost hut – they had been saved only because the soldiers had been so prompt in coming. A number of Naga women were missing. Discussion among the women revealed that the missing women had been foraging in the direction of the Shaka camp or along the trail to the Shaka camp.

"Chitrangada was furious. No Shaka had been captured – they had fought to the death. More of his men were dead than Shakas. There was no live captive Shaka to be grilled. Chitrangada questioned the competence of the troops I had trained. The captains tried to calm him down. Finally Chitrangada called the officers into a quickly erected tent to decide on strategy.

"That was when Chitrangada decided that more information had to be obtained about the Shakas. It was a fateful decision. The villagers knew nothing. Nobody knew how many Shakas had come, how many were warriors. *Were there any traders or was this a raid presaging more raids?* There was no answer! One of the spies said that he had seen women and children in the camp but that report never reached the King. His captains were cautious – I had trained them well. Until they knew more about the enemy, they wanted to take a defensive posture. The King was furious. *How would they get this information?* They replied: *slowly. Spies will observe from hiding*. That was what I would have done. The King had disagreed. *Just capture one, and we will wring the information out of that one.* The captains demurred politely. *We would have to send a squad and that would attract attention. Until we know more, we should avoid exposing our warriors. We only have sixty trained soldiers, the rest are fresh recruits in training.* The King was livid. *Cowards* he shouted and stormed out of the tent.

"The captains conferred among themselves and proposed a compromise to satisfy the King. A small squad would go out that night while the Shakas were still tending their wounds. They would proceed silently. The goal was to capture one of the enemy and bring him back. As far as possible they would not engage with the Shakas in any other way. It was an unwise plan made to appease the King, since nobody could oppose his wishes.

"When the captains' proposal was put to Chitrangada, he assented with a qualification – he himself would lead the squad. There was no changing his mind. The squad led by the King had left the previous night and were expected back by daybreak. They did not return when expected.

"Late that evening a second team, consisting of two Naga members of the army, was sent to determine what had happened. They were to return before nightfall. Moving quickly through the forest they arrived near the Shaka encampment with no sign of passage of the King's squad though many signs of Shakas on horses – the Shaka were not silent. They were at the point of returning and declaring failure when they came across signs of fighting in a small clearing. Some of the trees still had arrows stuck in them, other trees showed signs of damage from swords. Freshly broken branches lay around. There they had found the head of the squad's captain. It seemed obvious that there had been a fight with their squad. The spies could not spend much time looking as night was falling and the forest would be completely dark until the moon rose. They could not wait that long. It appeared that the King had lost the battle, and it was not known whether the King was dead or was a prisoner.

"The news of the King's capture or death created turmoil in the camp. The captains could not agree on a course of action. Unlike my usual practice, the King had not included them as councillors and consequently they knew very little of what he wanted to accomplish and how they were expected to back him up.

"Where was the King? Where were the soldiers who had gone with him? Another squad of spies was sent at moonrise more or less around midnight – they could not go far as the

Shakas were more active that morning and had been working on rearranging their campsite, making it more defensible. The squad returned and reported no signs of the King or the squad. The officers in charge could not agree on a course of action – they were too few to defeat the Shakas on horses, but they were needed to provide the local Naga villages with some feeling of security. They had learned this much from our past encounters with Panchala – I would guarantee the safety of Naga villages or towns that we passed through and was rewarded with help and loyalty.

"They needed reinforcements if they were to get the King back – so they sent me a messenger with the one head they had found as a way of impressing on Hastinapur the urgency of the matter. Then they deployed the troops in a defensive formation around the Naga village and waited for events to unfold. They did not know what to expect. The normal practice among the mercenaries of Panchnad was to propose exchanges of equivalent prisoners or a demand for ransom. This was usually simple except when a leading officer was captured – that would require more bargaining. The released men promised not to participate in the war. They would also exchange the bodies of the dead enemy for their own dead. That seemed obvious to my men and so they waited for a message from the Shakas. And waited. There was no overture. Nothing happened.

"With a sinking feeling in the pit of my belly, I roused my group and we set out as fast as we could. Without a leader, and missing a captain or maybe more, my five hundred would be massacred. We got to the campsite that night. At first I was pleased. A defensive perimeter had been set up. Inside it, though, was chaos. There were areas of furious activity interspersed with completely calm areas where soldiers were lounging around. There was a commotion at the eastern end of the campsite, where we usually placed a gate. People were rushing back and forth, looking for something. A few were carrying buckets of water. Nobody recognised me until I was well inside and saw one of my captains who took one look at me and shouted, 'It's the Regent! Regent Devavrat has arrived!'

"The news of my coming spread like a ripple created by a stone thrown into a pond. Very soon I had my captains and a collection of soldiers and helpers around me. The source of the commotion was a group of unfamiliar people – Nagas, mostly old men and women and children. They looked like they had been through a forest of thorns – they had blood on their clothing and clotted blood on their arms, legs, and faces. Some had hands hanging useless by their sides, barely connected to the arm. There were a few younger men, but they seemed to have suffered battle injuries – one man had his right eye covered with a cloth that looked freshly bloodied, another had been laid on the ground, his legs covered in blood.

"There were two doctors with the Hastinapur army and the Naga villages had their herbalist and physician. I could do nothing for these victims of a Shaka attack. The captains had given up hope for a parley and expected an attack in the morning. My first concern was that this camp would be targeted as it could be used to defend the other villages. My second concern was to get news of the King. Had he been killed? Why had the Shakas attacked this Naga village? There was no precedent from the many years of Shaka visits. That was meaningless – for every new behaviour, there must be a first time, and this was surely a first. I would have to ensure that this was the last.

"The Nagas from the village that the Shakas had attacked decided to make a formal appeal for my help – you know how unusual that is. Nagas help each other unasked if there is a family connection and only if there is a family connection. Any other request must be made formally. Some Nagas in frequent contact with us in Hastinapur are not such sticklers about that custom and have become more like us. There are frequent misunderstandings, situations in which a Hastinapur

Naga expected to get help from a bystander unasked, as well as situations where a bystander intervenes and is vilified by all sides in the dispute. Here, out of the ambit of Hastinapur's cultural influence, old Naga practices were still in place. The Nagas appointed a representative, one of the older men who had escaped injury by hiding in the community hut. He asked to see me and said, 'Sir, we, the Nagas of the northern hills, need your help. I am assured that my cousins in the south by the Great River are allied with you. If that is true, I invoke your help.'

"I replied 'Yes, indeed! I will help you. That would help me as well, for I come in search of my brother, the ruler of my city, who may be a captive of the Shakas. You must tell me more about these Shakas. Did you meet any of the traders?'

"This was not the first time the villagers had traded with Shakas. The Naga band that populated this village had moved here fifteen years ago. As usual, they burnt a section of the grove, cleared it of trees and shrubs, and sacrificed at the four corners to the mother Goddess. They put down the first seeds, shortly after the spring festival. They then used the trees and branches to build permanent homes – wattle-and-daub cabins with roofs made of crossed branches covered with thatch that would keep them dry during the coming rainy season. This was their age-old practice.

"The Naga band encountered the Shakas some months after the rains – they were clearly visitors for they had not been there before the spring planting season and occupied makeshift homes consisting of conical frames covered with leather. The band consisted of about ten men and women with their children. They came in covered carts pulled by horses and carried merchandise for trade. The Shakas had been peaceful – the two bands did not share a common language, but the Shakas had useful and decorative objects that they would barter for grain and vegetables. They wanted bronze but would accept copper.

"When the Nagas took the Shaka items to Hastinapur, the merchants, Kuru as well as those from Panchnad and points further west, were impressed by the size of the gemstones; they were awed by the thickness and nap of the bearskins and even the deerskin, so much larger than the native black bear and sambhar deer; and bubbled with excitement at the yellow nuggets. They wanted to know where these were from, but the Nagas kept the Shaka source a secret while the Shakas did not tell the Nagas anything. It was also made clear that the Shakas did not want the Nagas to find out. The Shakas would usually leave when the weather warmed up and the sun began its northward course back. Well before winter ended, they would be gone.

"This pattern had been in place for almost fifteen years. The ash layer created in the grove from the old burn was almost drained of its fertility and in another year or two would have to be abandoned to the forest. It was time to move on and the band had started the process of identifying a new grove to burn and settle in. In the typical case, it would take a year or two to complete such a move. The Naga band did not want to lose their exclusive access to the Shakas by moving further away, so, they moved closer to the place where the Shaka usually camped.

"Something had changed this time. The Shaka group was much larger – more than forty or fifty men had been seen, a larger number of children, many more horses and carts. They were too many for their old campsite and had instead occupied a cul-de-sac in the side of a small hill, and constructed a thorn fence with a gateway. They worked on their settlement and did not try to contact the Nagas immediately. The Nagas took the initiative and sent a small group to welcome the traders. The Shakas met them at the gate; they were formal and correct, but would not let them in.

"After a couple of weeks, the Shakas sent a small group with a cart loaded with goods for barter. This was as expected and the Nagas eagerly welcomed them to their new settlement. It did not take long for disappointment to set in. The Shakas had brought little worthy of barter. Most of the skins they brought with them would be unsaleable as they were old and worn – nothing like the large, furry, and well-cured skins from previous years. These skins showed signs of many years of use. In exchange, they asked for the same products – grains and vegetables, copper and bronze – as in previous years. The Nagas were disappointed and refused to take what was offered. The Shakas were insistent. The request to barter became demands, which the Nagas rejected. The demands became unmistakeable threats, at which point the Nagas stopped all talk and sat quietly. The Shakas were equally patient or apparently so. They sat for most of that day; we even offered them some meals; in the evening, all the Shaka got up and left silently.

"The refusal to barter was unprecedented among Nagas. It was commonly the case that every place they occupied, every time they moved, new traditions would be created and some old ones dropped – bartering with the Shaka was now a tradition here. They had been bartering with Shakas ever since the first year. Some of the older Nagas had muttered about the bad luck that breaking with tradition would bring. Others pointed out that what the Shakas had brought was itself a break with a much more ancient tradition. The Nagas did not want the Shaka skins and gold for themselves but for trade with other groups and the products offered could not be traded. Accepting the trade in the name of a tradition here would cause a break in tradition later. The Shakas were visibly upset; they spoke among themselves, glared at the Nagas, and left with their offerings.

"This attack, then, was their reply. This was not how a trader would act – even in the most difficult encounters, traders try to keep the peace. Peace had brought prosperity to the people of Panchnad. The violence of these Shakas showed that they had not come in peace to trade, but to raid or to colonise; in either case, they planned to terrorise the local population. *Were the Shakas ever traders, in the first place? Maybe we were imposing a category we understood on the behaviour of strangers.*

"'The traders who came to our tents were old men,' he said. 'They did not come riding on horses, but carried their meagre products by in a cart drawn by two of their oldest horses. They looked impoverished and appeared to be hungry.'

"'Does that mean that nobody knows anything about their camp?'

"'Sir, our chief visited them the first day to make them welcome. He wanted to assure them that we would, as always, engage in fair bartering. He knew that they would want grain, for their land did not produce any. In the meantime, if they needed grain while they were visiting they should ask, for we would not refuse. He thought this would tell them that they were welcome, even if trading was not possible. Our chief's visit is part of the tradition – it is one of the ways we assess the people we trade with.'

"This aspect of Naga tradition surprised me – it indicated a level of sophistication in managing trade with strangers that I had not been aware of.

"'I need to talk to the chief, then.'

"'He is dead, sir.'

"A dark shadow seemed to come over my heart – not a monsoon cloud promising rain, but the occasional burst that presaged a raging flood. *Was it going to be a lost cause to find my brother?* I turned away.

"'Sir! Please listen!' the Naga continued. I turned back to him.

"'The chief went with a small entourage – all men except for his oldest daughter.'

"'Where are his men?'

"'Dead, sir. They all died in the raid. His daughter is still with us.'

"The Nagas have some strange customs – at least, strange to us Kauravas who grew up with Panchnad customs. Among the Nagas, men and women played different roles in daily life – in contrast, in urban Panchnad, there was no cause for differences in roles. Of course, only women gave birth to the children, but both cultures required them to care for the infants. The Naga women foraged for fruits and nuts and edibles that grew wild and could not be cultivated. The men were the farmers and fishermen. They tilled the fields or fished – they called it giving birth to their food. In Panchnad, a guild, one of seven (not counting the mercenaries), determined the daily life and labour of its members. The only task that was reserved for men was trading – few women became traders or participated in years-long caravan trips. War was not one of the duties divided between the men and the women – both were equally unprepared to defend themselves or their village. The task of such protection was assigned to the guild of mercenaries. That guild consists mostly of men, though a few extraordinary women have been members too. In recent years, Kuru women have been sequestered out of the public eye. This had started when Samvarana sojourned in the forest with Vasishtha and rebuilt his army. Vasishtha had been insistent – no women fighters. It was a new rule previously unheard of – Vasishtha was exploiting the small strength advantage that a conditioned man has over a woman of equal training or skill. That rule continues to the present day.

"'How old is she? Is she here?'

"'She is an adult, sir. Her name is Amba. She is here in the camp.'

"I said, 'I wish to speak to her. Please ask her to come.'

The Death of Chitrangada

The Pandava Camp
Circa 2000 B.C.E.

Devavrat paused. His eyes that had been shaded by his brow opened and the shaded tent seemed to become lighter. It appeared to Lomaharshana as though the memory of Amba had blown away dark monsoon clouds covering the sun, which then shone down on the ground sparkling with rain-drops.

He continued: "That was how Amba came into my life. She was – *dare I say it* – beautiful. My mind struggled for control over my body – the face that wanted to turn to her, the lips that wanted to smile, and the feet that wanted to leap – despite the tragedy of the situation. When I first saw her, she was wearing a plain wrap that had once been white – now it was bloody and torn along the bottom edge. I learned later that she had been attending to the injured. Her dusky complexion made her smile glow. (*How many times have I felt a rush of joy at that sight and smiled back in response to her smile?*) Her face was oval with almond-shaped eyes. She wore a necklace with a single strand of beads – this revealed her age, for Naga women often wore their wealth in the form of precious necklaces and an older woman would have more to show. To say that I was smitten is to understate it. It had happened once before, when I had first met Satyavati. My heart raced and it seemed to me that everybody could hear its drumbeats. I stood still, looking at her, afraid that any movement would betray my reaction.

"'You called me, sir?' she was polite. Her eyes caught mine and I felt warmed by the smile. She looked away but not before I saw the hint of an acknowledgment. *She knows the effect she has had on me.*

"My voice died – it came out husky and low-pitched.

"'You are the chief's daughter?' I was inaudible.

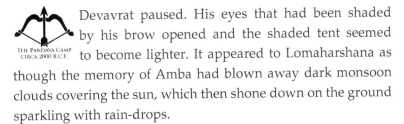

"'Excuse me, sir?' her voice was neutral but her eyes glowed.

"'You are the chief's daughter?' I said, and then berated myself for asking such an inane question. It came aloud this time and immediately the glint vanished from her eyes and her face fell and she was sombre. Her father was dead and I had reminded her of it.

"'Y-yes, sir.'

"The smile was gone from her face and like an addict to *soma*, I wanted it back. I regretted that I had reminded her. I took on a goal-driven tone. That I could handle.

"'They tell me that you went to the Shaka camp with your father.'

"'Yes, sir.'

"'What did you see?'

"'They would have come along the river bank – it is barren rocky ground that opens out into a flat, grass-covered grove. The soil there is not deep enough for planting so we do not use the grove. It was the first campsite for them. Their tents block the entrance to the grove so you can only go through the gateway they've established. The river runs white over rocks, but between the rocks it can be deeper than two of these onager-drawn carts. Inside, they have a central tent behind which are the carts in which they transported themselves. Their horses are corralled even further back so they cannot just wander away.'

"'Is it a defensible encampment?'

"'Yes. They have created a wall in the front with trees and branches. There is a small entrance, about five or six hands wide – their horses can come through. You cannot attack from the front. The river is difficult to cross and the other side is a steep hill. In the back is a rocky path uphill to a ridge that goes along the river bank.'

"'How do I get there?'

"'There is a trail from our village.'

"I grasped at a straw. Something. Anything. So that I could be with her a while longer.

"'Can you guide me and my troops?'

"'Yes.'

"'At night? Silently? Without any light?'

"'Yes, but if you make any noise they will know it.'

"'My troops will not. We will be ready a little after midnight. The half-moon should be rising.'

"She took that as dismissal and walked away. My heart was thumping. I looked around and I did not recognise the camp. The interview had been conducted in some other world.

"We gathered late that night just as the moon appeared in the east. We brought along fire arrows, with tips wrapped in cotton soaked in pine-oil, and one of my men carried the fire in a small clay bucket filled with ashes covering burning embers.

"Amba led the way. She knew the path to the village and the moon's light was just enough for us to follow. The way to the Naga village was uneventful. It took us almost five ghatis even though we kept to a normal walking pace – the running pace would have been too noisy and was not reasonable in a forest path in the dark. Amba walked carefully but without hesitation, looking at me from time to time. Her proximity was heady. I wanted to show her all that I could do, but that went beyond the exigencies of the expedition. When she talked, I was at a loss for words, my tongue felt heavy. We skirted the Naga village – Amba pointed out some landmarks in the village – the central hut in which the seniors had survived, the granary, and the communal space around which the huts were clustered, and the place in the forest that the Shaka had come through with their horses.

"We headed to that spot, for that was the beginning of the trail to the Shaka camp.

"'How long from here?' I asked.

"'About three ghatis, at the pace we are going.'

"The moon was closer to the zenith – we would have about eight ghatis before sunrise. Maybe a little less if the dawn was fogless and clear.

"'We have to move a little faster.'

"Amba looked at me. I looked back, not as a challenge but because her eyes captured mine. Maybe mine captured hers. We trapped each other in that glance.

"'We should keep to this pace to prevent accidents,' she said as we both looked away simultaneously.

"I grunted. I glanced sideways to see her smile – her teeth and eyes reflected the moonlight.

"We continued walking carefully along the path that Amba showed us. About one ghati later, we heard a rustling in the bushes. I looked at Amba. She understood my question.

"'There are no large wild animals here. A lone wolf, perhaps.'

"I took out my knife and signalled the men to stop. I wanted to investigate this myself. I moved silently towards the sound. My men knew what I wanted – they stopped and waited. Amba followed carefully.

"We came to a small clearing. There were a number of bodies scattered around. I could not make out any faces in the moonlight but some outfits were easily recognisable. These were the King's troops – he had followed my example and created uniforms for his men – not the unimpressive grey of my troops but red and gold. The gold ornaments glittered in the moonlight. Nothing was moving. Then something rustled along the opposite edge of the clearing. I went across, Amba followed.

"There was a moving body lying there. He was not dead – he responded to the sounds of our talking by getting up on his hands and knees and then tried to stand up, but his feet could not support him. I recognised the injury – he had been hamstrung, the tendons in both knees cut. From his hands and knees, he looked up towards us and Amba gasped and her hand grasped my upper arm; I don't know what I did visibly, but I was overcome by despair and sorrow for now I knew what the Shakas had done to this man. His eye sockets were empty and in the light of the moon they were dark blobs reflecting nothing. He moaned and I could not understand him. Subsequently, that sound resonated in my memories and became familiar – it was the sound made by a mouth from which the tongue has been ripped out. The man's body folded on itself and collapsed.

"I took out my knife and stepped up to him, pulled back his head and sliced the throat from one ear to the other in a single stroke. I held the thrashing body down as warm blood spurted onto my arms and flowed down onto his neck and to the ground. Slowly, the thrashing stopped. Amba made a sound. I looked up at her. She stood still and looked back at me, her eyes shining in the moonlight. I dropped my eyes – I could not bear to tie those eyes to this act. *What could I tell her?*

"Her words came to my rescue.

"'You are a kind man,' she said, 'Was he one of your men?'

"'You could say so. That was my brother.' I hugged the dead body of my brother, Satyavati's son, Chitrangada, King of Hastinapur. I let him go. He fell to the ground. I turned him so that he faced the earth. There was no reason for our men to see him thus. I got up and wiped the blade of my knife clean."

MEMORIES RELEASED BY DEATH

THE PANDAVA CAMP
CIRCA 2000 B.C.E.

After he said those words, the Regent looked at Lomaharshana –for a brief moment Lomaharshana felt like he had been thrown into the coldest Himalayan stream in the depths of winter. He could not meet the Regent's eyes – to do so would have been to leap into the vast empty gulf that is said to exist between this world of humans and the heaven of the gods. He turned his head and heard a long sigh from the Regent.

Then there was silence. Lomaharshana felt powerless to pierce that silence. *Was that even his task?* It was a silence filled with a uniform noise, a cosmic noise that, like a god, had frozen its listeners in a single moment of time. It was the primal silence that preceded the primal scream when the universe was born of the body of Brahma. Whatever it was, Lomaharshana was relieved when the Regent finally stirred.

The Regent broke his silence.

"He was my brother. When Chitrangada was born, I was twenty years older than him. My father continued to be infatuated with Satyavati – after the necessary duties of the day were done, he spent his time with Satyavati. She in turn left the rearing of her children to her maids and wet-nurses. I, too, had withdrawn from all but the most necessary of official duties. I did not see my half-brother when he was born and not for many years after.

"The monsoons had been good for a few years and for a brief period the Sarasvati flowed with water again. The refugee stream stopped as people hesitated. We always knew it was blind chance, but hope overwhelmed blind chance and the crisis seemed to abate. Some refugees even made plans to return. Those were the good years.

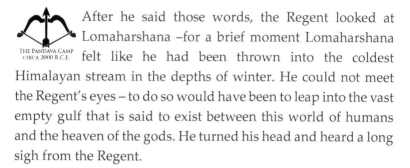

"The rains come with their own crises. A heavy rain eroded the soil under a boulder that then rolled off and damaged the levee near the womens' quarters, the place I had avoided for many years. I had to inspect the levee with my chief inspectors to assess the damage. Chitrangada was playing in the courtyard with the women. He must have been about four or five years old. I had not expected it – I thought that all the women and children had moved somewhere else. I look sufficiently like Shantanu that he must have thought it was his father – he came running up to me. Some children are unafraid of new people – that would describe Chitrangada. He paused when he realised that I was not his father, but he came up to me anyway and asked me my name. When he learned I was Devavrat, he said, 'The aunts here say that I have a brother by that name.'

"'I am that brother,' I said.

"He yelled and ran around me while I stood unsure of what to do. Then he stopped and said, 'Why are you so big? I have another brother and he is tiny. I am not allowed to play with him. Can I play with you?'

"It is hard to describe my feelings at that moment. I realised that if I had married Satyavati, this would be my son. I could not maintain my anger towards Satyavati against my half-brother. I told him that I was busy right then but that I would be certain to come and play with him later.

"I continued to avoid Satyavati – my anger and resentment against her did not go away – but I would come and play with Chitrangada. Later, when Vichitravirya was old enough, we would play as a threesome."

At this point, the Regent Devavrat stopped. Lomaharshana was listening and memorising Devavrat's words mechanically.

"He was only a child," the Regent said. The words seemed to force themselves out of his mouth. Then he stopped and closed his eyes. The silence continued. He leaned back for a moment – he had forgotten the arrow – his eyes opened as he gasped and jerked to the front; then his body relaxed in a faint. His eyes were closed and he had fallen over onto his stomach.

Lomaharshana moved forward and raised the Regent. He was surprisingly light – he had expected a greater weight. *He is old. For an old man he is holding up pretty well.*

Lomaharshana called for the nurse, who came in right away–the nurse took one look at the body in Lomaharshana's arms and moved quickly to take over from him. He asked the Archivist to move the bolster and the stuffed mat and laid the Regent down again, making sure that the arrow did not move. He picked up the Regent's wrist and with closed eyes, felt the pulse.

The nurse said, "There is a pulse. He will live, at least for now. He is a hardy man. What happened?"

"He recalled something that surprised him and he leaned back against the arrow. I think he forgot its presence."

The nurse left. The Archivist called in a passing messenger and gave him a message for the King to come after lunch if possible.

After lunch, Yudhishthira came, with Shukla, the Vyaasa, in tow. The Archivist took his place at the foot of Devavrat's bed. Devavrat was sleeping. The Vyaasa said, "He must have been exhausted."

The Archivist said, "Yes and no. He talked all morning."

"Where did he stop?"

"Just after he killed King Chitrangada. He then began explaining how he had first met Chitrangada and... I don't think he wanted to go on."

The Vyaasa stared at the Archivist. "Did he say that he killed the King himself?"

"Yes, sir. That is exactly what he said. His last words were 'That was my brother. He was only a child.'"

2000 B.C.E

"That was not the story he told Satyavati. That was not what he told anybody."

"May I get the official story as well?"

"Yes. When Devavrat came back he said that gandharva allies of the Shakas killed Chitrangada. That did not make any sense for the gandharvas have not been known to ally with anybody, even if they exist. I questioned the men who had been left behind in the camp, but they did not know how the King died. The man who found the King's body said that he had been ordered not to speak of what he had found. Did Devavrat speak of it? Did he tell everything?"

"Enough, sir."

"I can guess. The Shakas are known for their practices. When Devavrat returned, some of his troops were already calling him Bhishma. That was strange but he did not stop them. He said very little about that expedition to me or to anybody else."

The Archivist was quiet. The Vyaasa made a gesture of dismissal. "Don't worry, you can go now. Come back after you've had lunch and feel rested. You can continue if he wakes up and is ready to talk some more."

The Archivist left.

The King said, "Guru-ji, I will rely on you to keep me informed. I must leave."

The King too left. Shukla was now alone with his sleeping friend.

He sat down by Devavrat's side. These were memories from a long time ago. He had to reconstruct them as much as recall them by contemplation. Devavrat had come back with the news of Chitrangada's death, but long before he arrived with that news, a new name for the Regent had spread among the people – Bhishma. The story was that the captured Shakas, men and women and children, had been tortured in public. This had changed the people's perception of the Regent – he was no longer the young disinherited heir who had stayed loyal to the King despite being pushed aside by the ambitious new wife, but a fearsome and bloodthirsty army chief to be feared and despised. The young man who had vowed celibacy on impulse had been a friend if not a kindred spirit – the ambition that had driven the Vyaasa Shukla from the fisherman's hut to the leadership of the Kavi Sangha, an often quarrelsome and debate-prone group, was lacking in Devavrat. He had sublimated his passion in the most down-to-earth projects – building dams, ponds, and canals; addressing the issues of feeding refugees; dealing with runaway rivers; maintaining the trade route for which Hastinapur was entrepôt, expanding relations with the Nagas around Hastinapur. There were failures as well – he could not establish peace with Panchala; all his overtures to the Rakshasas east of Laghu Nagapura were ignored.

The man who had come back from the encounter with the Shakas was a silent man. The memories of his return were fogged over by the death of the King. *It was before I was the Vyaasa; I was just Shukla, the queen's brother, just another rising star in the Kavi Sangha.* The old Devavrat would have paid him a visit to describe the events of the encounter and to consider future actions – the new one barely acknowledged his old friend. Shortly thereafter, he, Shukla, had left for the great learning centre of Takshashila in the northwest, recognition of his potential to climb up the Kavi Sangha hierarchy. When he came back a year and a half later, he had expected a joyous reunion – instead, he found a man who had adapted to the new name, *Bhishma,* the Terrible. This man Bhishma had barely returned his hug and then suggested that Shukla should come and describe his experiences at Takshashila in open court. What had happened to the Devavrat who would have demanded a detailed narration, in private, of all that he had experienced? His request for a private meeting had been met with a non-committal *Yes, we should meet,* and not followed by any action.

Shukla had questioned his sister. Satyavati was still in mourning for her son Chitrangada. She had been told the official story – that gandharvas had killed Chitrangada. Devavrat's behaviour that had led to the title *Bhishma* was inexplicable. Why did he torture the Shakas? He thought it might be a lie made up by his enemies.

"Sir," a voice interrupted his reverie. The Archivist had returned. Devavrat was still asleep. The Vyaasa motioned for silence and moved outside the tent.

The Vyaasa said, "Continue with him after he has had a meal. There is more to come."

"He said he killed his brother. What greater secret could there be?"

The Archivist stopped. The Vyaasa was staring at him. "I beg your forgiveness, sir. I will arrange to make him comfortable when he wakes up. If he wishes to continue, we will. Later, I will come to you."

The Vyaasa smiled. Had he been like this as a youngster? How irritating he must have been. *I know exactly how irritating I was!* That was why he had been sent away to Takshashila to study.

"You'll do fine, Lomaharshana. Go, get this done."

Lomaharshana the Archivist watched the Vyaasa leave. He breathed a sigh – that had been close. He, Lomaharshana, at the threshold of his career in the Kavi Sangha, had talked back to the Vyaasa, the senior-most member. Yes, he was the Archivist and Archivists like him with a prodigious memory and native skill came by only once or twice a generation, but still. He was lucky that there was nobody else around – it would surely have been the end of his career. He breathed a sigh of relief.

2000 B.C.E

He went to the cook's tent and arranged for delivery of the Regent's afternoon meal. A soup made from salted roast mutton, rice, and herbs would be the most the Regent Devavrat could eat. When he returned, Devavrat's eyes were open and staring at the door. It seemed to the Archivist that Devavrat looked relieved.

"There you are," said Devavrat, "Why did you leave when I was just resting my voice?"

"You fell asleep, sir. It has been a few ghatis. Do you feel rested?"

"Rested? With this arrow in me?" Though it was a rebuke, his eyes were shining almost as though he were not in any pain.

"My apologies, sir. I must have judged incorrectly. It has been almost five ghatis and it is time for a small meal recommended by the doctor. After the meal, we can continue if you wish."

"Of course I do. I can accomplish little here. Let me satisfy your master, the Vyaasa."

The Archivist smiled – this was his assigned task and he was happiest when it made progress.

"Where did I stop? What did I tell you before my nap?"

"You were with a Naga girl, Amba, and you had just killed your brother."

Devavrat closed his eyes and took a deep breath. It was as though a monsoon cloud had moved in front of the sun. When he re-opened his eyes, they looked weary and did not shine.

"Yes. I had just met Amba. She was our guide on an expedition that night to the Shaka camp. We heard some noise and we went to investigate. Amba and I were alone when I killed Chitrangada."

"Yes," said the Archivist. "That was what you had just said."

"Must I continue? No, that was a silly question, I must continue. Let me tell you what happened after I put my brother to rest."

VENGEANCE AND LOVE

THE PANDAVA CAMP
CIRCA 2000 B.C.E.

Devavrat said, "I faced Amba. I could not read her face in the moonlight. Her eyes were wide and her right hand was placed at her throat above the heart.

"'You are a kind man,' she said, 'Was he one of the men you trained?'

"'You could say so. That was my brother.' She turned her face away from me. After I let his body drop, I stood up.

"I could not bear to see her turn away from me. Without much thought I grasped her upper arm. Her head jerked back to look at me. Her hand came up and stroked my cheek wet with the tears that were flowing unbidden. She kept her hand there for a short time and then she started to withdraw it. She was slow, for I took it in mine and held it to my face. She stood still for some time as I let the tears flow onto her fingers.

"A brief moment later, she said, 'Sir, you must continue.'

"She was right. I squeezed her hand lightly and let her take it back. We rejoined the squad.

"There is very little of surprise to report about the expedition. We reached the camp well before sunrise. The Shaka had become careless after two encounters in which they had overwhelmed our side. Otherwise, what we did would have been impossible. While the fire-throwers stayed back, the rest of us crawled slowly to the wall of branches that backed onto the first row of tents. When we were ready, we signalled with the bark of a fox. The fire-arrows hit the first row of tents. As the sleepers rushed out, we rushed over the wall and cut our way into the tents. When the Shakas realised what was going on, that they were under attack by fire from the front of their camp, they became a little more confident and came back to their tents to collect their weapons. We slaughtered them in their tents. In the meantime, the residents of the second row of tents struggled to arm themselves as their tents also caught ablaze.

"Without their horses, and with the haphazard collection of weapons, the Shaka were less formidable as enemies. Within two ghatis, we had complete control of the campsite, except for the central tent. We surrounded it and I called for surrender.

"A young boy came out, hands held out in front. 'We will surrender. Please do not kill us.'

"'Who is in there?' asked Amba.

"'My aunts and sisters, my cousins, and my grandfather and two of his friends.'

"'Tell them to come out slowly and throw their weapons to you.'

"We had sixteen prisoners – two were fighters who were supposed to protect them but had decided that it was better to live as slaves than to die there.

"That was not to be. On the way back I detoured with some of my men and picked up the King's body and the bodies of the squad he had led.

"We brought them back to the camp and the next day we went with the Naga villagers to the site of the Naga massacre. The Naga villagers gathered around us. My soldiers formed a barrier to prevent them from coming closer. I lined up the captive Shakas – women, children, and the old men. Then I brought the two fighters to the front.

"'I am looking for the King,' I said. 'Can you tell us what happened to him?'

"One man stood still. The other replied in the language of the Nagas. 'We don't know of any king.' He then whispered to his friend who nodded his head.

"I described Chitrangada – young, haughty, skin the colour of the elephant grass that grew by the banks of the Ganga, a small moustache, and the stubble of a beard.

"The quiet one nodded. He whispered to the other, who spoke.

"'Yes, we know the prisoner. He was a tough one.'

"'What happened to him?' I asked.

"They whispered some more in their own language. Then the speaker turned to me.

"'Nothing. We just kept him as a prisoner. We did not know he was the King.' He seemed to shrug as he said this. My eyes narrowed and I felt the upwelling of bile souring my mouth.

"'Nothing?'

"They conferred some more.

"'Nothing unusual.' That shrug again. My hands trembled. I struggled to control them.

"'Was he tortured?' I asked.

"More whispers. The quiet one turned his head away from me but not before he had caught my eyes and then averted his gaze. The speaker looked down as he spoke. I thought he too was avoiding my eyes.

"'No.' he said. No shrug that time. The quiet one was now looking straight at me. A sneer lurked at the corner of his lips.

"'You must tell me the truth,' I said, 'else, I will punish you.'

"The speaker looked away to my right and said, 'He was not tortured.'

"I got up and looked away and then sighed. They relaxed a bit – I had accepted their information.

"'Do you have a wife? Any children?' I asked.

"The speaker shook his head. 'No.'

"'What about your friend here? Are one of these prisoners married to him?'

"He hesitated. 'No.'

"I turned to him, my face livid. I came close and my voice fell. 'You are lying. Both of you were standing next to a woman. You had two girls by your side and he had one boy. Tell me the truth. Now.'

"The speaker backed away from me. I must have looked insane. He then pointed to one of the women. His friend looked at him and shook his head, but the speaker was not looking at him. 'That's his wife.'

"I had my soldiers bring the woman over. A boy about eleven years old grabbed her hand and pulled. My soldiers held on to the woman who held on to the crying boy.

"'Bring him instead.' I said.

"They separated the boy from the woman and brought him over. The woman now screamed and yelled. More soldiers were needed. It was hard to control the boy who yelled and shouted, calling for his mother to help him. The quiet one looked away – there was nothing he could have done. The boy was not easily controlled."

Devavrat paused. "I can't go on," he said.

The Archivist looked worried. "Why, sir? Are you tired? Hungry? Look, the soup has just come."

"No, no, I am not tired. I am… I… how can I tell this story? My gut refuses to rest. Come, Lomaharshana, pour me some soup. A few sips might soothe my heart and calm me."

The Archivist poured out two small bowls of soup. He picked one of them and brought it to Devavrat's lips. It was awkward, but he managed to keep his hands from touching the arrow. The soup was lukewarm but easy to drink. After a few sips, Devavrat waved it away.

"I cannot drink it. Why don't you have some?"

The Archivist had not intended to drink his soup, but Devavrat's eyes watched him carefully as he emptied his own bowl.

"Good," said Devavrat.

The Archivist stood attentively, waiting for the Regent to say something. The Regent lay motionless and silent, his eyes unfocused. Lomaharshana waited. Half a ghati passed and the Regent had not moved. *What should I do?* Lomaharshana thought. His voice low, Lomaharshana said, "Sir. Should I come back at a later time?" There was no response. Lomaharshana tried again, louder this time, "Sir!"

Devavrat's eyes focused on him. "Oh! Yes, you are waiting for me. I... I… was recalling what happened. Yes, let me continue from where I stopped."

Devavrat continued, "There was nobody there who could have stopped me. Instead, I was obeyed as I proceeded to do the indefensible. The boy was uncontrollable. I took out my sword and with the flat hit him on the side of his head. He collapsed in a faint and was as quiet as his father.

"How can I continue with this narration? Whatever I did that day, I did not plan it. That day I earned the name *Bhishma* (the Terrible). When I started I intended to punish only the two men – torture *them* the way they had tortured my brother. It was not hard to contemplate making them suffer. What I wanted I did not get. I wanted one thing – I wanted them to acknowledge that they had tortured the King. I wanted them to acknowledge the justice of whatever punishment I chose to inflict. That was not to be. In extenuation, I point my finger at those almost invisible shrugs – they goaded me. These are excuses for my commands that day. These are pathetic excuses – I gave the commands and maybe somebody objected. Maybe somebody objected, and I still did not listen. My men bear no blame – I hope they tried to stop me and I refused to listen. I do not know why my men followed my orders, but they did. They too had seen the King's body and perhaps the same demon that had gained ascendance over me ruled them.

"By the time I was done three children and two women lay dead on the ground, hamstrung, blind, and mute. *I have been kind.* I told the two men. *Kinder than you were to the King. They were not tortured.* I pointed to the bodies with my foot and turned one over. *See, no signs of torture. They died before they suffered much. Am I not kind? Can you acknowledge my mercy and ask for more?* The lurking smile and uncaring shrugs had come to a halt, but the stony faces and fixed eyes did not change. My captains' whispered pleas finally got through to me – my actions might turn the local Nagas against me.

"I had my men drag the two captives over to me. With careful deliberation, I did what I had to do. I did it myself, making sure that each could see what was happening to the other one. They were not dead when I was done and I left them next to their families to await death.

"The local Nagas watched unmoving from the perimeter where I had placed them. There was no sound from that group. Not then, not later. I tell myself that Amba's presence had nothing to do with my actions. She had taken part in that night's battle in the Shaka encampment. I thought that surely, that carnage should have satisfied her. Nor was she any help in moderating my anger. Her father and mother were dead – her father chopped, his head hanging from his body by a shred of muscle and bone. Her mother had run towards her husband as though at that last moment she could have helped him. They had not found her body in the field, but they found her mutilated remains in the Shaka camp. All that could be identified of her. These two would have been among her torturers. She had seen the King before he was dead. Chitrangada may have been taught a foolish arrogance by Satyavati, but he was a young man who cut an impressive figure. The Nagas must have thought that he could certainly help. People like us, raised in a city, are overwhelmed by death – she was a Naga who lived in the forest and she observed death every day, so the death I dealt did not repel her. She was angry – I wanted to show her that my anger equalled hers and that my resolution equalled hers. She had seen me cry and might think me weak and I wanted to show her that I was strong. Was she one of the local Nagas who might think that I had over-reacted when I ordered the murders of the women and children? If so, she would turn against me.

"I tell myself that I was angry and confused and did the unthinkable because I was not myself that day.

"That day, only Amba and the group that had attacked the Shaka encampment knew what I knew – that the King had been tortured the way I tortured the prisoners. The King's men, the other men from Hastinapur who had come with me, and the remaining Naga villagers saw a side of me that had never before been seen, maybe never before existed. As a result, I became *Bhishma* (the Terrible). My men took it up and over time, *Devavrat Bhishma* became just *Bhishma*.

"I look back and imagine myself not doing what I did – could that have been a different Devavrat, not the Devavrat Bhishma that I had become? Maybe I would have become somebody who could be liked and not feared. Loved and not just respected. I became Bhishma, a being to be terrified of. When does revenge edge over into insanity? I was insane that day. Later that day, we reconnoitred the route by which the Shakas had come and I discovered that they had brought their vehicles and horses over a dam that I had arranged to construct some years earlier. I did not say anything. In hindsight lies wisdom, I thought, as the sour taste of victory returned to my mouth. We followed the road and found a Shaka encampment, almost all non-fighters. We attacked and killed most of them. We left a few wounded survivors to return the way they came with the message; the uninjured we enslaved.

"We picked up the bodies of the King and the squad that had gone with him; we made them look presentable and cremated them en masse that day – the dead were already stinking and I did not see the point of taking these bodies home. Satyavati would chasten me later about my haste in cremating her son, but I did not want her to see what had happened to him. Nor did I want to tell her that the King's captains had let him leave on a spying expedition with a very small force – heads would have rolled. With their help, I invented a story of a pitched battle with an intruding army from Gandhara. This changed in the popular imagination to gandharva, magical creatures invented by a teller of tales we both know well."

The Archivist frowned. "Do you mean the current Vyaasa?"

"Yes," Devavrat said, and continued, "I saw Amba later that day – we were by ourselves and I surely was mad that day. That night I was subject to no oath – the oath that Satyavati so relied on lost its hold over me that night. I was not Devavrat, the one bound by Devavrat's oath. I told Amba to come with me that night. She too must have been insane – her father and brothers had been killed, her mother was dead; yes, she had tasted revenge, but this blood did not quench the heat of the inferno raging within her. I must have been insane to think that I could keep this secret from Satyavati. She must have found out quite soon after we returned to Hastinapur, but she kept quiet. Why did she keep quiet? Maybe by becoming *Bhishma,* I had terrified her. Maybe somebody had told her the truth behind the name. The old Devavrat had kept the vow for many years, and had proved his fealty to the part of the vow that she cared about – support her descendants as the rulers of Hastinapur. If she had made a fuss, she might have aroused the demon that was Bhishma; Devavrat, the dutiful son of his father, might have disappeared. Civil war between my supporters and hers, she knew, was unthinkable for the old Devavrat, for it would have ended his imperial plans – that day, after the death of Chitrangada, it was not something Satyavati wanted to threaten.

"That night Amba came to me willingly. I was sufficiently Devavrat that I told her of my vow. She did not understand such a vow – in her opinion it was worse than the monogamy that the Shakas required of their women. I could not explain the self-imposed restrictions I had lived with all these years. I abandoned the effort to explain, but she accepted the need for secrecy. We entered the woods silently. There was nothing gentle about what we did – my memories of my brother's dying moments intruded. She responded in kind, possibly driven by what she had seen of her dead father and mother. Our mutual rage found its outlet in sex. It was many weeks before our encounters became tender or gentle."

Devavrat paused. He was barely whispering. The Archivist moved closer to hear him. Devavrat shook his head, put out his hand and held him back. Then he winced and withdrew his hand. His voice became louder as he continued.

"The next day I faced the problem of what to do about the Naga village. The remaining Nagas – a number of women, some older men, and children of both sexes – kept a safe distance from me, the Terrible one. They were no longer a self-sustaining community. Without the men, who would till the gardens and grow the plants? Without champions who took the lead in challenging other bands, their band would lack standing in the potlatch festivals celebrated six times a year in each season. Locally related bands, clans related through sisters and mothers, vied for the right to host a festival for it was the source of prestige and respect for the band. The women formed the heart of a Naga band – the matriarch and her friends who stayed in the band and took care of the children were its heart and soul. The women managed the band. The relationship between bands could be competitive – this was displayed at the festival get-togethers.

"The men played an important role in these festivals. In most bands, the men were charged with organising the potlatch – their leader convinced the other men to help him by a mix of persuasion, charisma, and social pressure. The men who had shown themselves skilful at organising and hosting events sponsored by their band made the band an attractive one to join. The success of a potlatch did not accrue just to the men – it also accrued to the band and was useful during negotiations.

"If only a few men had died, the community could have replaced them at the next festival by pleading and persuading. The politics of these festivals was a sensitive matter – a band with men born and brought up in other bands could help garner support from their parent bands. A band with a group of men who knew how to build dams could lend these men out in exchange for other benefits. It was through the medium of festivals that each band showed off its capabilities.

"A band whose men were all dead stood alone. It would have nothing to offer and would be asking for a lot. It would command little political status and power. To compound the situation, a band that did not have enough men might become prey to wild rogue Nagas – boys and men who had never found a home band or had been expelled from their communities for some reason, usually an inability to control rage. They lived on the fringes of the Naga world, usually alone or in small groups; they did not form larger groups, for such men did not know how to cooperate with each other, either. Sometimes, rarely, an unlikely leader would emerge who coalesced a few small groups and individuals into a larger gang that could be a source of danger to the Naga bands in the neighbourhood. Such gangs were dealt with harshly when found and captured, with the leader and most of the older members being killed. Even if the women were strong enough to repel one attack by such a gang, the knowledge that a weak, poorly defended band existed attracted violent gangs.

"As a result, a band in which all or most of the men died would usually disband unless the matriarch and her women could attract good men from other bands, sometimes by bartering with the other bands.

"This was the one aspect of Naga life that I have never been able to appreciate – urban living had no place for potlatch festivals and expelled outlaws. In times of peace, it did not matter. Then, when conflict threatened, and we felt that an immediate decision was needed, the Nagas took an inordinate amount of time talking in their sessions without a decision. Every question would be debated – who would support whom, who would be in charge, why they were the best choice, what their instructions would be, and so on. You don't see much of this now because free Naga tribes are disappearing as they succumb to Panchala or come under the protection of Hastinapur.

"We stayed there for a few weeks, both to ensure that no more Shakas were coming that autumn and to help the band collect what they could from their settlement and move – nobody wanted to stay where a massacre had just taken place.. It turned out well, I thought – some of the Nagas in my army, trained by me and trusted as soldiers, saw an opportunity to return to the Naga way of life. They would have been considered wild, for many of them had left their bands at a young age, and failing to find a band, had come to me. Now they could return with the instant credibility of having worked with me. It meant that I lost a few good men, though they would prove useful later – their skill in war and organisation, and their loyalty to me, provided Hastinapur with a solid bulwark and buffer against further Shaka attacks. The Naga bands they joined are still some of Hastinapur's most faithful Northern allies despite King Suyodhana's disdain for the Nagas. *How do I know that?* Yudhishthira has sent emissaries offering an alliance – they were treated politely but sent back empty-handed. Of course, this was reported to me. All the Nagas in the Hastinapur army come from these bands, collateral descendants of Amba and her sisters.

"Amba's aunt, the matriarch of the band, was not happy with the liaison between the two of us. The Naga band was grateful for what I had done for them and they were grateful for the men who were leaving me to join them, but my actions had terrified them. Even the matriarch, cold-blooded and calculating, who had sent the first emissary asking for my help, shied away from me. The stain rubbed off on Amba – there were no secrets among the Nagas – and her people avoided her. They saw nothing wrong in Amba's sexual activity, just that it was with a monster. That exclusion is why Amba decided to come with me to Hastinapur. With the death of her mother and father, Amba's response to rejection was further withdrawal. I did not know how this was going to turn out – repeatedly, I went over the need to maintain appearances, to keep Satyavati and others from finding out, and every time I did that, the discussion led to angry words that ended with the urgency of sex.

"Amba's sisters – ten-year-old twins named Ambika and Ambalika – made a fateful decision to come to Hastinapur just for that winter. They had nothing to do with me and were under no pressure to leave. We Kauravas would have called them 'orphans' and looked for relatives who could be responsible for them, but within a Naga band, aunts and cousins took care of each other. Later, my enemies would accuse me of kidnapping the three sisters, hoping to drive a wedge between my nephews and me.

Ambika and Ambalika were excited that their sister was going to the city and wanted to go with her. Amba told everybody that she would bring back her sisters and I believe that was truly her intent.

"A sad procession returned to Hastinapur. Two months had passed. The city had been in mourning for the King and very little had been done while they waited for us. We had received daily demands for information from the Queen, along with implied accusations of treachery. I kept her well informed with the requested daily reports, but after the first few confusing days, there was nothing to report. I told her nothing of my crazed revenge, but she heard that I was now called Bhishma and that I had terrified the Nagas. She did not care to find out why I was called so, but she found it useful to broadcast my new name. A confused mélange of rumours were also reported in the town – I had kidnapped three Shaka princesses for my brother to marry; that I had been rejected by a Shaka woman and I had taken a terrible revenge. Among the people (the few people close to the ruling family) who knew of my vow, the rumour was that the unnatural celibacy had caused a mental breakdown; sometimes it was rejection by Amba that had done this; or, that I was regretting my pledge to protect Hastinapur and support Satyavati's sons in their claim to leadership. Satyavati and I agreed to suppress the story of the Shaka invasion to avoid panic – my dam-building project had made our northern border porous, and I did not want to spread panic.

"I learnt later that an extended period of drought in Shaka-desa (the land of the Shakas well to the north of the Snow Mountains) had occasioned a great migration of the Shakas into Parsaka and Mleccha-desa. My massacre proved to be politically useful in deterring further invasions – I made sure that traders going towards Parsaka and Mleccha-desa were told a lurid and bloody version of the massacre. It has been forty years since the massacre. The sleepless nights, and there have been many of those, are spent replaying the events that led to it. That I was insane with anger is no excuse – but it is possible that the story of the bloodthirsty ruler of Hastinapur kept many invaders away. When the invasion comes, as surely it must, it will not be by a small band, but a large and well-equipped army.

"I introduced Amba and her sisters as daughters of the chief of the Northern Nagas. I think the Naga residents of Hastinapur understood this exaggeration but the others did not. As the daughters of a chief, they were welcomed and treated with respect. Satyavati took them under her wing and would have made them stay with her, but Amba insisted on keeping them with herself in separate quarters. Thus began a winter of subtle gestures, meetings in dark places, sneaking out of my home and sneaking into Amba's. Ambika and Ambalika often slept through these assignations – we explained the need for secrecy and they kept our secret.

"Great happiness is followed by great sorrow – that is inevitable, and it has been so for me. Hastinapur returned to normal. That was the winter of my happiness. I did not know that come spring, Amba would disappear. With the spring thaw, the snow-fed rivers rose and, somewhere or the other, a flood threatened. I had worked to create dams on the Ganga, so Hastinapur itself was safe. We could do nothing about the Yamuna – it was a crazy river in the spring, especially the new stream going to the east of the Aravalli range. I had an idea that with the right set of structures, the Yamuna could be diverted back to its old bed to the west and the Sarasvati could become a great river again, instead of the monsoon-fed, drought-prone stream that it had become. These projects were difficult to implement for the mountain-fed rivers never dry out completely. During the winter, the cold, white snow freezes in the mountains, creating glacial ice dams at unexpected locations – melted water from higher up accumulates behind these dams. When the dam bursts, a torrent of water is released. We cannot predict when such a dam might break upstream. The breakage of a dam deeper in the mountains might release enough to break the next ice dam downstream setting off a chain of dam collapses – when that happens, the floods overwhelm our best efforts. The best times for constructing water-works are late fall, after the first ice dam forms in the mountains and holds back some water, and early spring before the ice-dams break releasing gushers. Of course, spring is also the best time for the refugees to leave their homes or temporary shelters and migrate – the weather is not too hot or too cold or too wet and animals abound in the forests. A spring migration could be followed by settling down on fallow land and creating a permanent settlement A fall migration followed a summer spent accumulating supplies to last through the winter before continuing east. Many of my water projects were smack in the middle of the migration route to Hastinapur and I thought I could use the refugees as labourers. I was wrong – the urban refugees were in no sense ready to labour on a canal project. A settled urban life changes people – they become unable to perform physical tasks with soil. These refugees were repelled by physical labour the way a child reacts to the fire that burnt it once.

"I was away for two months, almost all of it just north of the wasteland we call Khandavaprastha. I left six days before the full moon, that being the best time to travel (the moon makes the nights safe for resting), and came back two days before a full moon. When I came back, Amba was not there and nobody seemed to know where she had gone. Nobody had searched for her. Amba's house, the one I had prepared for her, was empty – it had been cleaned out after she disappeared. I could not ask Satyavati directly for that might reveal the strength of the bond between us. In any case, when it came to working with me, Satyavati could never tell me the truth. I tried to keep my relations with Amba a secret from Satyavati, so my search was low-key, the questions I asked were obtuse, and the answers I received seemed to be evasive.

"Her sisters Ambika and Ambalika were useless – they had been moved in with Satyavati – at their age they were too young to be by themselves. They also did not proffer any information. I was sure they knew something, and as I listened to their lies (*lying to my face!*) my face turned red and my hands shook. The girls began crying and their sobs attracted the attention of the servants – most of them were my agents assigned to Amba, but I had had to include a few provided by Satyavati (Amba was well-spied upon) – and as they came in, the attendants surrounded the girls and consoled them. Satyavati appeared and chided me. The appearance of these women moderated my anger – I now knew that I was capable of torture – and I was grateful for that. I stormed out and found my men standing around in two groups. Both groups had drawn their swords and were prepared for my commands, and they turned when they saw me come out by myself. That was one day that my training with the Kavi Sangha, brief as it was helped me. I sensed the tension in my men's disposition, calmed myself down, and projected calmness. Seeing me relax calmed the men, and their captains came to me. They did not say anything. I was Bhishma, my actions unpredictable. Some of my men considered me capable of torturing the girls. I do not know if I would have tortured them, if my women and men had not stopped me.

"So, I sent the girls back to their home with the northern Nagas, protected by a small armed party. The entourage came back with the girls and with disquieting news. The matriarch had died – she had been older than the other women but not that old, so her death had precipitated a crisis. Her sons had died in the Shaka attack. There was no one to inherit the role of chief. Her daughter had not partnered (that is, married) with a man who wanted to stay with this band – he would have been a viable candidate for the role. Now, she was unable to find a man who would take on the role of defence chief – a confused rumour had spread among the other Naga clans that this band was cursed. Without a credible defending force, the band's crops were at risk of being looted by wild Nagas or, sometimes, other hostile or opportunistic Naga bands. Even the Naga soldiers (*my* trained Naga soldiers) I had left behind were losing hope that the band would stay together. Ambika and Ambalika had become accustomed to living in Hastinapur and did not want to help re-create their band. Their refusal to return, even as matriarchs, was a catalyst – most of the men walked away; the women were unable to agree on a matriarch; there were not enough people left to form even one band with a good mix of older and wiser seniors and younger and more flexible youngsters. It would be a long time before such a band could provide a protective home for the girls.

"My men whom I had left behind had formed a band that offered to help Naga bands in trouble. This was how they ended up as a specialised band of Naga mercenaries. The sisters asked about Amba, but she was not there, had never come there. I questioned Ambika and Ambalika again for I could not believe that Amba would have gone anywhere without her sisters."

Devavrat paused and closed his eyes. His recital had slowed down. The Archivist did not mind – the slower Devavrat spoke, the easier it was to rehearse and memorise. Devavrat's voice, already low, had become rough, his breathing ragged.

It was late in the evening in autumn. Some trees were letting go of their leaves and were now bare. Every year when the Archivist saw a tree bare of leaves, he would worry that it would die and every spring when it came back he worried that it would be less full or less green than it had been. It was so much easier to memorise and recall, to versify and enact, he thought, than to be a farmer and worry about the rain, about floods and droughts, about planting and harvesting. His life was so much simpler than Devavrat's, without never-completed goals of peace, without subterfuge, and without plots.

2000 B.C.E

If Devavrat had simply given it all up, he could have disappeared with Amba. Lomaharshana sighed and looked at Devavrat, who had fallen asleep. How strange that he could sleep like this even though he had an arrowhead piercing his lung. *It's time to join the Vyaasa and the other Kavi Sangha members for the evening rituals.* Followed by five ghatis in the dark of rehearsing the material he had just heard, then sleep, which would inevitably consist of dreams about what he had just heard. He would then come back tomorrow with his teacher.

The Second Co-Regency

Vichitravirya

The Pandava Camp
circa 2000 B.C.E.

"Ambika and Ambalika saved me from a fate worse than death – becoming the King."

Devavrat had woken up from a dream still lurking at the edge of his consciousness – a full moon shining over the lake in Varanavata that he had built. It was his first and favourite project and it had been completed the day Vichitravirya died. He recalled gazing into that clear and cold night with a clear and simple mind – *how fortunate he was that he could not be King*. It was a serene sight and the calm carried over into his waking in which the sensation of pain in his shoulder was a tolerable anomaly. The King, the Vyaasa and the Archivist were sitting by the entrance of his tent. They moved closer to him and the Vyaasa had said, "Good! You woke up. That was a long sleep – it is almost ten ghatis after sunrise. Are you feeling unwell? Is this effort too tiring?"

Devavrat's mind was clear and but for the pain, he felt as rested as he had ever been. He said, "That is indeed late. I feel fine, though. If not for the arrow, I would jump up from bed to face the day."

"The nurse has brought you fruit mash to eat."

"I don't need it – I do not feel hungry. I cannot do anything from here, so why don't we just continue," Devavrat said. The nurse extended a small bowl of copper containing the slightly fermented mash and Devavrat slurped it. The smell of the fermented mash recalled his first meeting with the Vyaasa and made him smile. After one more slurp he said, "That's enough. I am not hungry. Tell me a story."

The Vyaasa said, "On the death of Chitrangada, Vichitravirya did not become the King right away as he was underage. You became Regent once more. Tell us about Vichitravirya's life as a King."

Devavrat eyes dropped and he pursed his lips. "That isn't a story, it is a question asking me to tell you more. Haven't I given you enough? Will you now tell me what happened to Amba?"

"I will do that, but I do not know much. I would have liked to talk to her first," said the Vyaasa.

"Amba is in custody in this camp," said Yudhishthira.

"She's here?" said Devavrat. "I assumed that she left the camp when I did not hear anything about her."

Yudhishthira said, "We detained her because she was not in her right mind. We intend to send her back to Panchala with a guard. But other events have taken precedence and she is still here."

Shukla said, "That is good! It gives me my first chance to talk to her. My friend, can you wait a little longer? Distract yourself with our questions. You were the only one here who knew Vichitravirya as a brother. Tell us about him."

2000 B.C.E

Devavrat felt under pressure to accept another postponement of his request. Would Amba talk to Shukla? She knew him from a long time ago, from a time that was less warlike even if not less tense. *She would certainly not speak to me,* he thought.

Devavrat said, "Vichitravirya? There is nothing much to say about him. Vichitravirya had been twelve when Chitrangada died, too young to be installed as King. The co-Regency of Devavrat and Satyavati was revived for another three years. He lived, he loved, and he died before he could do any damage as King."

Shukla said, "He had children. That should have been good enough. Particularly since you stayed faithful to your vow to Satyavati."

"Yes. The one thing that Vichitravirya did right was to get his wives pregnant before he died. If he hadn't done that, I would have become the King I never wanted to be. But, I wish that was enough. My old friend, I needed your advice then; but you were not there. You are right about one thing – my vow allowed me to be the ruler I wanted to be and let Satyavati's spawn be the Kings she wanted them to be. I had no desire for children."

"You could have sent for me, if you needed my advice. When I arrived, you had already become Bhishma, the unreachable."

"You do not understand."

"I understand only too well," said the Vyaasa. "I am only sorry that I did not tell you Amba's secret sooner."

Amba's secret. What was it?

"Archivist," Devavrat said. "Come here – I'll tell the rest of what I know."

"Vichitravirya was twelve when his world was changed by Chitrangada's death. He had been raised in the expectation that he would never be King, and the implied responsibilities slid off his shoulders like water off a turtle's back. He met Ambika and Ambalika at an age when he was not interested in them. They were in shock after the Shaka attack and in some awe of the city. Amba protected them, but as the months passed, they adjusted to their new situation. Amba was much older and had always been like a mother to them, so her role continued naturally. They were aware of her liaison with me, but as Nagas, they were not surprised. They were surprised that we wanted to keep it a secret, but accepted the argument that we needed to be careful – city people, after all, were different.

"If Amba was considered beautiful – I am biased and perhaps the memory is faded, but she was very beautiful – her sisters were set to be even more so. Satyavati, being a Naga herself, felt they should share a bond – she grumbled that Amba had refused her hospitality. Since Satyavati had full access to the girls, she spoiled them as though they were the daughters she never had. Amba could do nothing to stop this. Then Amba disappeared and against their preference, I attempted to send them back to the Naga band they had come from. The attempt failed and they lost any trust in me. Satyavati took them under her wing. They were always in the house when Vichitravirya visited his mother, and as the years passed, Vichitravirya grew up and began to notice them. They were beautiful creatures close to his own age and they fascinated him. Satyavati must have been happy, for she had been worried that he would find brides who might not look up to their mother-in-law. Worse, he might get a wife who aspired to power. Satyavati was confident that Ambika and Ambalika, as her protégées, would align with her and never turn on her.

"The day came that Satyavati raised the subject in open court. 'Elders of Hastinapur!' she said. 'It has been three years since my dear son, your King Chitrangada, passed away. Soon, we will crown my son, Vichitravirya, as the heir apparent. A city without a ruler cannot prosper, without a governor it will disintegrate, without a judge it will not survive. He will be all this, he will be a great king.'

"Considering that Satyavati had been an ambitious Naga girl who knew nothing of Hastinapur when she married my father, she had mastered the council language of the Kauravas. 'Yes, Mother!' I said. She frowned at my form of address. 'He is certainly of age. Let him take the charge he is born to. Let an appropriate and auspicious day be selected.'

"She smiled. The court erupted in applause and shouts of joy. My supporters could never match the ebullience of Satyavati's courtiers. Their actions always matched her moods – a deathly silence when she was angry or moody, an excess of bonhomie when she smiled. Satyavati's smile was smug. She had a surprise for me.

"'We have already suffered through the childless death of one Kaurava king,' she said.

"This was her revenge for calling her 'mother'; I was the senior Kaurava prince here and if not for my oath to my father, I would have been the Kaurava king.

"She continued, 'My son Vichitravirya is of a marriageable age. For the sake of the Kuru family, he must marry soon.'

"A chorus of agreement came from the council. I had not anticipated this proposal, and my supporters in the room stayed quiet, waiting for a signal from me. On the one hand, a crowned Vichitravirya might be an interfering monarch like his brother who wanted to display his authority and ability. In this matter, I had no options – he would be crowned when his mother considered him ready, and that was now. On the other hand, a married Vichitravirya would have interests other than public displays of authority and ability. That would let me return to executing my plans.

2000 B.C.E

"Yes, my plans. After Chitrangada's death at the hands of the Shaka, I concluded that the only way we would repel future invasions was by presenting the Shakas with a united defensive line across the foothills of the northern mountains. I needed support from the Panchnad republics on the Vipasa and Jahnavi rivers. Even if the far western republics of Moolasthan and Takshashila would not join me (and they were suffering from their own refugees), I would at least prevent the Shakas from establishing a foothold on the gateway between the west and the east. To create such a defensive line I needed to have a unified entity, an empire, if you wish. This empire would have to command the loyalty of the Nagas, the original Kuru settlers of Hastinapur, and the new Paurava refugees.

"These days the idea of an Emperor is bandied about easily – Emperor Yudhishthira and Emperor Suyodhana, as they call themselves. In those days, there was no 'Kuru Empire', even in fantasy. The refugees from the west brought along their ideas of running cities by guilds organised around critical functions, but this did not sit well with the Nagas who wanted to live in bands. It was not even acceptable to the immigrants settled in border areas who could not wait for service from a guild member with the authority and training to perform a specialised task. The Nagas had no concept of empire, though Panchala, the hostile Naga confederation across the river, was developing into a military state with imperial ambitions. To this day, we point to the Shakas and what they did to a peaceful Naga band to define and justify the empire I have created.

"The best argument for a Kuru empire came from the work I had done. As I built dams and lakes along the Ganga and tried to control the Yamuna, I realised that the local residents, whether new immigrants or older residents, had to be organised to maintain the waterworks. How were we to convince these local people – urbanites, farmers, Nagas, and even traders – of the value of long-range planning and long-term maintenance?

I could see it and acted to foster it through my waterworks projects. These hydraulic systems would survive forever if they were kept in repair. The taxes collected on the produce of the farmers and the goods shipped by traders would more than pay for the maintenance – the problem, as always, was finding qualified people to do the work.

"My focus on the long-term issues created an alliance between Hastinapur and the new immigrant-turned-farmers, who saw their interests tied to the interests of Hastinapur. If they could be trained as fighters, we could rely on them for defence. When defence was not needed they would rely on the empire to support them and their economy as needed. The Kavi Sangha supported my efforts – when Satyavati's brother Shukla came back from Takshashila he supported me and counselled his sister not to interfere with my plans. Now that he is the Vyaasa, he is too powerful and that is boring – she won't listen to him anymore and so he comes to squeeze stories out of me."

Lomaharshana glanced sideways at the Vyaasa who was sitting silently, smiling.

Shukla said, "My friend, it is good to see your spirit restored in this manner. If I had known that telling stories would cure you of your melancholy, I would have insisted on it from the first day that you came back with Amba. I would have been squeezing these stories out of you for a decade at least, instead of today in a hurry."

Devavrat said, "I like it this way, Shukla. It gives me something to do while I wait for an accident that will kill me."

"True," said the Vyaasa. "We both wait to die, you in your way and I in mine. Let us return to squeezing stories out of you. Where you find these metaphors I do not know!"

Devavrat nodded. "I must disagree – the stories of my regency would dampen any listener's spirits."

The Vyaasa and the Regent looked at each other and smiled. It seemed to Lomaharshana that the manner in which they spoke to each other surpassed language, that they were engaged in a conversation that he could hear but not comprehend. It was one of the more dubious pleasures of being a memoriser – occasionally a contract would be incomprehensible, containing encoded or cryptic references, where the word 'fish' might refer to a diamond, and 'pig' might refer to a coat of armour. Lomaharshana took the opportunity to yawn; then he rotated his upper body to stretch his abdominal muscles and the movement broke the tension.

Devavrat continued where he had left off. "When Chitrangada was alive, he was suspicious of my motives. He insisted that the cadre of armed farmers that I was training vow loyalty to him. Though the Kauravas had begun to use the words 'king', 'queen', 'prince', and 'princess' for the ruling family, they had not yet begun professing personal loyalty. That is Suyodhana's innovation – he is rigid and unswerving in his demand that all his people vow personal loyalty to him. Though I do not like to acknowledge it, that demand for personal loyalty will make the difference and ensure Suyodhana's victory over Yudhishthira. In those times, the old Kuru residents viewed us as senior chiefs and me as the leading representative of the ruling clan. There was much confusion over my oath to my father. Even my ideas about uniting for defence felt like a claim on people's loyalty and they resisted it; Chitrangada's demand for an explicit pledge of loyalty did not sit well with the people at all. With Chitrangada dead, there was no demand for a vow of loyalty, and as long as Satyavati and Vichitravirya did not ask for it, I could go back to creating a buffer region populated by armed allies who had not vowed loyalty, but worked together out of mutual interest.

"By creating an empire I would fulfil my promise to my father that I would protect the Kuru family and his descendants through Satyavati. This goal was yet to be achieved, and I would not be able to accomplish it if Vichitravirya or Satyavati interfered. All in all, the idea of Vichitravirya marrying appealed to me – both he and his mother would be distracted and not inclined to interfere with me as long as I did not interfere with them. He should marry anybody other than an ambitious princess who would question the sincerity with which I had accepted the loss of my birthright.

"I was surprised when Satyavati announced in the open court that she had found the perfect match but that she was not ready to announce it. The assembled court cajoled and pleaded with her and then she added a second surprise. She said that I was the reason she was keeping it secret – I had not yet given my permission. I let surprise reflect in my face – whatever she was doing, I would go along.

"Such surprises were the way Satyavati exercised her power in those days when she was young and certain of herself. She is too old for this kind of melodrama now; in any case, Suyodhana does not allow her to leave her quarters. She has no say in his court. He would certainly not have put up with any drama that did not come with his blessing. Seeing my surprise led her supporters to exchange knowing glances. More cajoling followed, along with an erudite discussion on the merits and demerits of marrying a local girl as opposed to one from another city. *Of course, they hoped that the great Regent Devavrat would bless the event.*

"Then Satyavati said, 'They are not local girls,' and I knew whom she meant and understood her reasons for this rigmarole. Not local girls, indeed! I had not seen Ambika and Ambalika for weeks after they had entered Satyavati's clique. My attempts to arrange a meeting or to have them visit me had been rebuffed. That was certainly Satyavati's doing.

"Satyavati continued, 'Ambika and Ambalika, the Naga princesses, have shown us their grace and elegance since they came here. My son knows them and they know him. They are well-matched.' Then she turned to me and stated the obvious, 'Ah! Devavrat, you look surprised. Sometimes the warden is the last person to learn what his wards are up to.' The court dutifully followed her in laughing at my apparent humiliation.

"'You are right,' I said. 'I am surprised. As their guardian, I should know more about their thinking. Please arrange to send them to my house.'

"There was silence in the court. A hint of a frown showed in Satyavati's perfect visage. She said, 'Of course, my son. They have been wilful girls not to visit you more often.'"

An Unsolved Mystery

The Pandava Camp
circa 2000 B.C.E.

Devavrat continued: "Satyavati was not amused, but she did not want to oppose me at that point. She sent Ambika and Ambalika, escorted by a collection of women from Satyavati's entourage. I asked to talk to them in private and they assented with ill grace – later Satyavati chastised me as though my request had been improper – as usual she overlooked my rights as guardian for the girls. I had frightened them when I sent them back to their vanishing band. They felt they could not trust me anymore. While Amba had been here, we had used my guardianship as a cover for my visits to Amba. Now I wanted to ask them about Amba's disappearance. The girls and I went to my chambers accompanied by one of Satyavati's women and another woman who was married to one of my men. Informal seats had been arranged for us. There were three large stuffed cushions arranged around a low table. In the middle was a large plate with dried fruits, rice cakes made with puffed rice and honey, and a bowl of honey with a number of dipping sticks. I indicated the cushion for them and waited for them to choose. Ambika chose the cushion furthest from the fruits. Ambalika moved towards the fruit and would have sat down next to them, but looked to Ambika who was glaring. She sat down by the other pillow leaving me closest to the fruits. Ambika looked straight ahead avoiding my eyes.

"'It has been a long time since I've seen you. Are you satisfied with my mother's hospitality? Have you made friends? Do the attendants treat you with respect?'

"Ambika replied, 'Yes, sir. We are well. You too have been well, we trust?' Ambalika looked at her sister and nodded.

"This was not good. *Why was she being formal?* I could not understand.

"'Yes, my dears. Thank you for asking. You know that I am concerned about your welfare. I promised your clan's matriarch that I would be responsible for your health and safety.'

"'Yes, sir. Thank you for your concern,' Ambika said, as Ambalika nodded again.

"'With your sister missing, I have not been able to do as I promised.'

"'Oh, you do not need to worry – we are doing fine in the care of your Matriarch, the lady Satyavati.'

"*Matriarch Satyavati? What had my stepmother been telling them?* In retrospect it was obvious what Satyavati had done, but at that time, I was befuddled.

"'I sent people to many Naga bands in search of your sister, but did not find her. Your aunt, the new matriarch, was not pleased to hear of her disappearance. She expressly asks after you and I have to reply. Would you like to return there?'

"Ambika looked away. 'Tell our band's matriarch that we are in good health. We are safe in the protection of the Hastinapur matriarch. We do not wish to return.'

"'Ambika, Ambalika,' I said. 'Please tell me – do you know what has happened to Amba?'

"'You do not know?' Ambalika said, and her sister frowned.

"'No, I do not know.'

"Ambika's eyes narrowed and she looked at me directly. I stared straight back without blinking. She looked away, and I knew that she was not going to tell me. That time, Ambalika came to my aid.

"'Why don't you know? You had asked her to come and meet you. She left in a hurry with a few of your…'

"Her sister stopped her by squeezing her upper arm.

"'My men?'

"'Yes, your men. We saw them – they were dressed in an off-white half-panchagam and brown angavastram padded with cotton. Your uniform.'

"I don't need to state the obvious. I had not called for Amba, nor had I sent an escort to bring her to me. Somebody had done this. *An enemy?* I could not think of anybody who was my enemy. Would Satyavati have the gall to do this? To what end? To kill Amba, for I was sure that if she was still alive, she would have contacted me. The men were dressed up as my troops – why make me the culprit? What was the message that convinced Amba to go with the men? *Was she dead?* What had she told the girls before she left, or what had Satyavati told them about Amba?

"Amba's disappearance was my fault. I had not protected her. Was she still alive? I could not believe that Satyavati would have had her killed. The fact that the sisters trusted Satyavati meant that they must have received some reassurance through Satyavati. Something that convinced them that she had been helping Amba. This was some devious plot by Satyavati – I did not know what she might have arranged and why the girls no longer trusted me.

"'When was this?' I asked the girls.

"'The very day you left. You sent your men for Amba. We have not seen her since.'

"'So, when I came back without Amba, why didn't you ask me?'

"They were silent.

"'Did she send you a message?'

"It looked like Ambalika might speak but then she held her tongue. Ambika spoke, 'Sir, we will not discuss Amba with you. If there is anything else you wish to ask us, please do so. Please do not ask about Amba, we cannot and will not talk.'

"I was the Regent, one of the most powerful men in the city. They were mere slips of girls. Yet, with the backing of Satyavati, they felt that they could refuse me.

"This was the story I began with. Men dressed in my troop's uniform had taken Amba away and later the girls had been told, or received a message – *from Satyavati?* – that had led them to suspect me and to seek Satyavati's protection. I stood up and gazed through the open back door at the garden that Amba had planted. Before Amba came it had been choked with weeds and grasses – it was the way to the outhouse and there was no need to decorate the path. She said that it reminded her of her Naga clear-cut fields. *Give me full rein over that piece of land,* she said. *I will set fire to it to clear the ground, and prepare it for planting.* When she said that she laughed to see the shock on the face of the old gardener who took care of the front of the house. He appealed to me, as he was terrified that she would be setting fire to all of Hastinapur, and I had to reassure him. Amba had not yet understood the obligations a master or mistress had to their employees and she treated them as though they were the almost-equal members of a Naga band.

"I could not see how to reassure the girls that I had nothing to do with Amba's disappearance.

"'I had nothing to do with Amba leaving,' I said. "Those were not my men. I know nothing of this. Can you believe that?'

"They kept quiet. I watched them to see if there was any inclination to talk. They looked away and stayed silent.

"'I need to find Amba. She was my life. I would never harm her.'

"There was a little flutter of movement when I said that Amba was my life. It did not last long, but died in the exchange of glances. Nothing I said after that had any effect. My heart began to race and I felt that I was losing control over my breathing. I needed to calm down. I changed the subject.

"I asked them about the proposal that they marry Vichitravirya. Marriage among Nagas was not taken as seriously as we did and Ambalika and Ambika acted like it was a game. They talked willingly about marriage or pairing customs among the Nagas. The Nagas only celebrated the matriarch's marriage, which occurred on the same day every year, at the full moon before the spring equinox, one moon before the spring sowing season. Other couples might decide to pair up that day as a couple and take part in the celebrations. The Hastinapur Nagas did not follow that practice, for they had moved away from many Naga traditions. I've gathered from the Nagas that Panchala follows similar customs. Ambika and Ambalika were going to be disappointed when they found that Satyavati was not going to take another spouse the same day and I did nothing to explain. They left and went back to Satyavati's care. The announcement was made and the city prepared to celebrate a coronation and a wedding."

Devavrat paused in the telling of the story. "Shukla, my friend," he said to the Vyaasa. "I've told you all that happened from the day Amba disappeared to the day my brother was crowned and wedded. Come, Shukla, tell me about Amba. Yes, yes, I know what you think, that I may be dying but still I grasp at straws."

The Vyaasa smiled, "I am not laughing at you, my friend. I smile to see that you still remember the parable of the man suspended by a straw over a snake pit. Lend me your indulgence, for if you tell us your old memories leading up to the birth of Dhritarashtra and Mahendra, the Archivist will have enough to work on in private and we can exchange these stories."

"There is little to add," said Devavrat. Vichitravirya was not cut out to be a ruler, but he represented all of Satyavati's hopes and ambitions."

Satyavati's Grandsons

THE PANDAVA CAMP
CIRCA 2000 B.C.E.

Devavrat continued, "Vichitravirya was sixteen when he was crowned King. He had not expected to become the ruler. The land had been at peace, and his brother had inherited all the martial ambitions of his ancestors. As a result, Vichitravirya's training had been mostly ignored and his education neglected. Now, he was the King. He needed to be trained in military matters, and he was supposed to have been trained in command. His education was my responsibility. I was limited in what I could do, for if I came down hard on the boy, I would get complaints from his mother Satyavati. He had to be educated in a hurry, so being soft was not an option. With Chitrangada, I had the time and opportunity to develop some rapport, but I did not have this luxury with Vichitravirya. Did this have anything to do with what happened next? Perhaps, for in hindsight, I would agree.

"I rarely saw Ambika and Ambalika. To all appearances, the girls had forgotten their clan and the events in their village and they never brought up the subject of Amba. Was Amba in touch with them? I don't know and I did not try to find out.

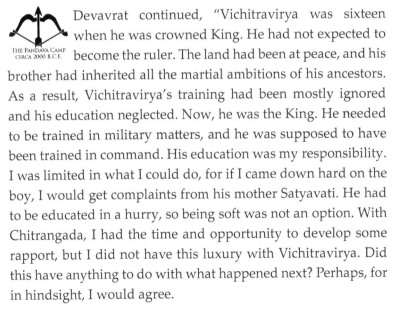

"The tedium of governance weighed heavily on Vichitravirya. He was expected to lead the council in making decisions, but the meetings bored him. All that education compressed into a tight schedule had soured any desire to rule and left only the desire to be indulged. He enjoyed the time he spent with his wives and their women and complained about the time that the official meetings took. Slowly, more and more of the administration reverted to me and the councillors turned to me for guidance and direction, while he spent time with his two wives in picnics and parties. Satyavati was not pleased, but he was still young and willing enough to practise martial arts in front of his wives.

"Seven years passed. The promise that Satyavati had extracted from Shantanu that she would mother a dynasty of rulers, would only be fulfilled if she had great-grandchildren. Satyavati was looking forward to that day – the day she could stop worrying. There was reason to worry and she voiced them to me – *why were there no children? Was there something wrong with Vichitravirya, or with Ambika and Ambalika?* Some of her women would try to assuage her worry – *he was still young. Seven years without a pregnancy between the two girls was a bit unexpected but such cases did happen.* I don't think Satyavati ever stopped worrying.

"I was out of the city inspecting a dam we had built prematurely on the Yamuna. Premature because, after keeping to one path for many years, an onrush of water down the river had broken a path upstream and now the old bed was dry and the dam was useless. We had spent much effort on planning and constructing the dam, so the settlers I had sent there were working to send the river back to its old bed. The Yamuna had not yet found a permanent path to the sea – maintenance like this was almost a routine task. However, I wanted to see the damage and talk to the engineers about the design so that we did not repeat old mistakes. That was when I received word that Vichitravirya was dead.

"I needed a day to assign power and responsibilities (that I had kept under my control) to others. Then, I left for Hastinapur, reaching it as the thirteenth day ceremonies were ending. This is one area in which I envy the Shakas' ability to ride horses, for I think on a horse I could have come in four or five days following the treeless bank of the Ganga at this point.

"The messenger had little to tell – he had been sent to fetch me as soon as the King died, so he had not had a chance to hear gossip. The news of the King's death changed everything. *The King was dead, long live the... who?* As I prepared to go to Hastinapur, the foremost thought in my mind was of the succession. I was reconciled to not being King, but it felt like Saturn, holder of destiny and arbiter of fate, demanded that I be the King, was telling me in so many ways, *You will be King,* and worked matters so I would have to assume the crown that I had surrendered so many years ago. I did not want the crown, but the thought of the rule passing out of Kuru hands was not acceptable."

The Vyaasa said, "At that point, you thought that Vichitravirya had died without children. When did you learn that Ambalika and Ambika were with child?"

"Quite soon. For seven years I had kept my expectations to myself. I left immediately, fearing the worst, but I was far from the city. As I've mentioned before, you cannot make an onager go faster than it wants to go. It took me a week. By the time I reached Hastinapur, almost two weeks had passed since his death. The city was, of course, still in mourning – white and saffron flags at every corner and the colourful gates of the city draped in white. Preparations for the ceremony of bidding farewell to the departing soul and wishing it a pleasant welcome at the home of the ancestors were in progress, the ceremony itself having been postponed. I wondered at that – these rituals should not have been held at all – my brother had died childless, but I assumed that nobody had dared to correct whatever command had come from the palace. It was a minor thing and if it helped my stepmother feel better, I was for it.

"I could only imagine what Satyavati's state of mind must have been. She had no more sons to raise to the throne, and her sons had given her no grandsons. I think she would have liked to establish a matriarchy, but she had no daughters either. When I reached Hastinapur, the city was in turmoil. The guards, some of them my agents, reported that Satyavati had been issuing commands and threats of revenge if poison were discovered. The funerary rituals usually required the body to be cremated on the third day, but at Satyavati's insistence, the body had not been cremated – it was believed that poison would prevent it from decaying – and stank. The poison tester had tasted all the food in the kitchen and any fruits, nuts and even leaves growing near the house – he was still alive. It did not satisfy Satyavati, who was not prepared to believe that Vichitravirya had died of some disease or other natural cause. She wanted results – the killer who had poisoned her son must be found, or else... Her guards had demanded access to the homes of people she thought were in the plot. No evidence had been found but that only proved that the conspiracy pervaded the entire city. They were against her because she was a Naga.

"I found out very soon that my worry was misplaced. I went straight to the palace to express my condolences to Satyavati and to the queens Ambika and Ambalika. The queens were nowhere to be found. Their attendants told me that they had gone into seclusion, almost immediately after Vichitravirya's death. Satyavati was in the council chamber. As I expected, everybody was busy with administrative trivia – there is no better task to take one's mind off distressing news.

"I left my cart with my men and went directly to the council chamber. Satyavati was there sitting on her throne. The councillors were standing. She did not see me at first for

I did not announce myself as I usually do. The caretaker of the Treasury, an old man who had fulfilled this thankless role for the city for many years, stood in front of her trembling. Satyavati was scolding him.

"'What do you mean, you can't account for twenty-five copper seals? They could have been used to pay an assassin.'

"The man was trembling and his voice came out with a slight quaver. 'Madam, this discrepancy has existed in the treasury since before your husband died.'

"He was right. Satyavati was constantly finding errors and omissions, many of which represented transactions that were not completed. Once, Shantanu had arranged to "steal" twenty-five copper seals to see if the loss was reported. The minister had reported with such an abject look of fear that Shantanu could not bear to tell him that it had been a test. Nor could he return it without making the minister suspect something. Instead Shantanu 'forgave' the minister for having committed such an error but the minister had kept the loss on the memorised accounts as a reminder. Satyavati had not known about the test. Subsequently, in the complete audit of the treasury conducted every seven years, when the treasurer completed the inventory of gold, silver, copper, and tin, he would discover the discrepancy and assume that the caretaker was trying to hide it. The error would be announced and Satyavati would berate the minister for his incompetence. At the end of it, he would be ordered to maintain the discrepancy in the archives. Satyavati was berating the minister once again, but this time the threat of punishment might be real, and everyone trembled.

"I could not bear to see this continue and I moved so that Satyavati saw me. 'Devavrat! You have come just in time. I was beginning to fear for my life. Nobody here is competent to protect the Queens as they need to be.' Then, to the minister, 'You! Go back!'

"Satyavati had never welcomed me in this fashion. I was not comfortable, for as a rule we stayed apart. I took my seat. She burst into tears – *What a miserable being I am – I get to commemorate the loss of my husband, and my children.* It was an old lament of hers, her misfortunes and her bad choices – and for a moment, I felt a knot of sympathy in my gut. Only for a moment, for this lament was usually followed by a demand for some extra consideration from the King. I tensed, waiting for the description of a problem only I could fix.

"I walked up to her seat and sat to her right – she was seated in the Queen's seat on the right of the King's seat. The seat to the right of that was for the chief councillor and I intended it as a signal to her that I preferred not to rule. She stood up and as I sat down, she said in a quiet voice, 'I have some fortunate news to announce.'

"She turned to all the other people in the room and asked them to leave for she would be discussing family matters with me. They left. Her maids stayed. She asked me to sit closer. Practices of over twenty years were being abandoned post-haste. She whispered even though only her maids (and my spies) were in the room. This was all very unusual. I felt certain that some unusual, perhaps bizarre, demand was going to follow.

"Satyavati said, 'My poor son. Fate is cruel, indeed.'

"She stopped, waiting for me to respond. I nodded. She then continued. 'For seven years, he waited anxiously for a child. The day he died, that very morning, Ambalika had missed her period, for the second time. You know how she has never missed, this time she had missed two.'

"She stopped again. I nodded again, in acknowledgement even if I did not understand why I was being told this. I had never known when any of the women were bleeding. For that matter, I did not know that Ambalika had missed any periods.

Why was she telling me this? Satyavati's words added to my confusion. Daksha, the lord of the moon, we are told fills every woman once a cycle, afflicts them with pain or tension at that time. Daksha, it seems, is not satisfied with the twenty-seven star-brides that he dallies with in that cycle. The explanation is a bit fantastic, but that is typical of doctors, seeking the cause of illness in things invisible and unknowable.

"Satyavati said, 'The doctor could only come that afternoon. She held Ambalika's hand and listened to her chest. She tasted her spit and smelled her urine and afterwards told me that Ambalika was pregnant. I had not told Ambalika or Vichitravirya – I waited for them to come in for dinner.'

"Satyavati said, 'Instead of delivering the good news to the girls, they reported bad news to me. Ambika and Ambalika were in the garden as the sun was setting. The rains were almost over, signalling the beginning of the harvest season. My son had come into their garden and Ambika and Ambalika were excited, showing him the colours limning the clouds. They said he was very happy and enjoying himself. He must have been at his poetic best, for I heard giggles and laughter. Then Vichitravirya had said, *I have a headache,* and sat down. Ambalika gave a graphic report – the shine had vanished from his eyes. She had held a hand against his temple. He turned pale even as they watched, not yet comprehending; then, he shook his head and put his finger in his ear as though he were trying to dislodge something and fell back. They rushed to pick him up but he was already unconscious. They called a few attendants who lifted him and brought him in.

"'They called the doctor back and she examined the comatose Vichitravirya. She detected a faint heartbeat and said he was not dead. At the same time, she held out no hope – without a fever or other external symptom, she could not ask him whether he was in pain or where it was located, or if some part hurt when touched or pressed and so on.'

2000 B.C.E

"Satyavati continued, 'I came in at that point. I was concerned that my son's spirit might be suffering from the uncertainty that he had no children and would suffer in the hell reserved for people whose sons do not fulfil their duty to their ancestors. Even if he was comatose, I felt he might be able to understand – so I informed Vichitravirya and his wives that they were going to have a child. I hope the news gave him some relief. Later that night he was delirious and he called on his brother to help with unseen opponents. The doctor thought that was a hopeful sign, but those were the last words he spoke.'

"Satyavati said, 'That was not the end of it. The next day we discovered that Ambika too had missed a second period and the doctor declared her pregnant too. I informed my son, comatose or not, immediately. I could not see any difference in his condition, but in my heart, I know that he felt me mourning for him. By coincidence, one of the queen's attendants, a concubine of the King, had discovered that she was pregnant two weeks earlier. It was a surfeit of babies after seven barren years that heralded the King's death.'

"Again, Satyavati waited for me to nod and I did. We were getting into deeper waters that I knew little of. I had no idea why Satyavati was so concerned about menstrual periods – I thought it might be a holdover from when the matriarch ran the family, the women were in charge of every detail, and the men were superfluous visitors. A woman's partner (a husband or sometimes just a male partner) would not be allowed to approach her for a few days every month – I think they did this so that the woman could rest, a luxury that young lovers considered superfluous. Why women laid a claim to these rest periods even after their partners had grown old, and less driven by sex, I do not know.

"Satyavati said, 'My only remaining son died that afternoon. He neither spoke nor opened his eyes, but he did become delirious moments after the doctor's assessment that he would not live long. Along with his wives, I held down his hands and legs for he thrashed them about even as we told him the news. Then, he suddenly went limp. He was dead.

"'Ambika and Ambalika were stunned – I took them to our chambers and set my women to stay with them and console them. A messenger was sent to ask you to return post-haste. Others took care of the body and plans were made for cremation as soon as possible. That is when it struck me that my son could have been poisoned. If we had chosen a date and time, and cremated him, it would have been too late to discover the cause. I decided to postpone the cremation, over-riding the objections of some traditionalists. I pointed out to them that Panchnad had an ancient practice of burying people in earthen jars, a practice that had died out in favour of cremation.'

"In this manner, I learned of the conception of my nephews. Satyavati decided that a King with an heir merited an elaborate funeral ceremony, equal to that of a Matriarch of Panchnad, a seventy-day extravaganza of solemn ritual that I was required to perform. At the ceremony, I overheard one of Satyavati's maids comment that the Queen Mother had suffered much and life was sad and unfair. I was surprised to hear Satyavati say, 'My son may have passed on, but I am blessed that both queens and even a maidservant, have become pregnant at almost the same time. We will even have at least one wet nurse we trust. A triple pregnancy is uncommon; it is an omen – my line will not die. That is why I have been able to accept the deaths of both my sons.'

"After Satyavati's explanation, I realised that the prospect of grandchildren had allowed Satyavati to be reconciled to her son's death. Of course, it wasn't that simple. She still wanted revenge against a poisoner if there was one. She felt that she would only be respected if she pursued justice and achieved it. She maintained her pressure on the city's investigators.

"Satyavati seemed to become much more relaxed after relaying all this to me. She had no choices left – after all these deaths, she could only rely on my oath; she had to rely on me. The patient hearing I gave her must have reassured her.

"It is now common knowledge that Surya, the sun, and Chandra, the moon, govern the birth of a baby. The healthy child lies in its mother's womb for at least eight moons and up to one moon beyond that. I figured that we had about thirty-two weeks to prepare for the babies' births. It was fortunate that the maidservant had become pregnant at the same time. Among the forest Nagas, the freedom of the spring ritual ensures that many women are pregnant at the same time, they all gave birth at about the same time the following winter, and so they could help one another out in taking care of and feeding a baby. A baby born at any other time was rare. The Kauravas did not follow that ritual and the city Nagas had also given it up. Children were born at all times of the year, and consequently ran the risk of not being able to find a wet nurse who could help the mother out. The Kurus of Hastinapur, like the non-matriarchal ruling families of the West, provided the wife with a trusted maid who would become a mother at the same time. Yes, my dear friend, it was controversial. How did they find the maid, how did she become pregnant, what would happen to her child – there are a hundred questions that I leave unanswered. The practice stopped because of my father's laws. Satyavati herself had given birth to Chitrangada and Vichitravirya, and I remember the tense days after each birth waiting for her milk to flow. I wondered if Satyavati had revived the practice, then decided that this was not an issue worth confronting.

"Nothing with Satyavati was simple. After poisoning had been ruled out – pieces of the King's body were fed to rats and cats that were then observed for signs of illness. I thought we were done, with the funeral. Satyavati wasn't.

"Satyavati said, 'How will these children become Kauravas?'

"What did she mean? I knew very little about conception and birth so I kept quiet.

"She continued, 'I've questioned the doctor and she said that there must be almost daily contact between a woman and her husband while she is pregnant. Then the child will inherit the features, strength, and wisdom of her husband's family. Otherwise, some stray man passing through at a vulnerable time will imprint the child. We must have a man, a Kuru, and a close relative of Shantanu stay in this house for the entire period. He does not have to do anything, just be there.'

"I was the closest relative of Shantanu. His eldest brother had died; the second had renounced his inheritance and vanished into the forest and hadn't been heard of since. For other relatives we would have to go further away into the abandoned Panchnad cities or even further up the ancestral hierarchy. The difficulty of finding such a person left only me. The proposal was out of the question and my dissent showed in my face.

"Satyavati said, 'I told the doctor that what she was proposing was impossible. I asked her for alternatives. She consulted her archives and came up with a compromise. The Kaurava relative was not required to be there for all sixty ghatis of the day. He should visit this house daily and spend the whole day-time with or near the queens.'

"The Kaurava relative, was, of course me. Spending thirty ghatis every day in this manner was out of the question too. Satyavati seemed intent on this and I could not dissuade her.

"I said, 'Wouldn't it be equally possible for the child to be influenced by a woman of Shantanu's family?'

"Even as I said this I realised that I could not shrug off this role – my father had no sisters we knew of. Satyavati replied,

'It must be you. You see why it has to be done – if we don't, the child will not be a descendant of your father. It is Shantanu who will suffer for the sin committed by his sons.'

"'Does it have to be in the same room? Does it have to be all day?' I was grasping at straws, anything that would preserve my separateness from Satyavati.

"'I don't know. I will call the doctor.'

"She gestured to a maid and asked her to fetch the doctor. We waited silently.

To my relief, the doctor was very pragmatic. She was also expert at reading my mind through my face and eyes. The next room would be fine. The night was fine too, perhaps even better than the daytime, as the aspect cast by the man would be purer. The complete investment, for it was not guaranteed, would take at least two to four months. In fact, two months would do, but that was an absolute minimum.

"I said, 'Send the Queens and their attendants over to my house before dusk. They can sleep in a room adjacent to my bedroom. In fact, they can take over a number of rooms. In the morning they can return here.'

"It was a painful four months as I had become used to a solitary life. I had to cut down on the after-dark meetings with spies and other confidential messengers. We were at peace in those days and I learned a lesson in moderation. The girls found it tedious, for I limited them to one attendant each. Shortly after the third month, they decided that they had had enough. It took a little longer before Satyavati was satisfied. In the sixth month, she declared that she was satisfied with their exposure to my Kuru aura and they were clearly showing signs of a routine pregnancy. The nightly walk to my house was getting difficult and it made sense to stop this ritual.

"In the seventh month, Satyavati announced that, in her opinion, Vichitravirya had been poisoned after all – given the time the babies were conceived, the unborn children could also have received poison. The Queens must rest so that the children would be healthy. Ambalika and Ambika were kept indoors out of sight – they did not complain. I was satisfied because it made it much easier to keep them safe. I could leave. I had expected Satyavati to relax as the months went by, the girls stayed healthy, and nothing happened. I was wrong – Satyavati was at her best contrarian self that year.

"As the weeks progressed, Satyavati became increasingly tense. Lines of worry marked her face. She was constantly demanding more and different kinds of food for the mothers-to-be. At one point I found that she had arranged to obtain live carrot plants from Takshashila where they are a medicine for blindness. The carrot, of all things! Its leaves smell and the dirty white flowers are impossible to admire. The root is eaten, a crooked purple stalk of wood with a pungent taste that the onagers love, so the cart drivers carry them when available. How do I know of Satyavati's purchase? A month before the due dates of the queens, a caravan from the west arrived carrying a hundred whole plants on the verge of flowering. A hundred plants! They had been purchased by Satyavati to be sent live from Takshashila four months earlier so that when they arrived they were just flowering. The price was staggering, bronze and copper tools for five kitchens, or equivalent gold. The order had come from Satyavati – she had told me that she wanted to order some plants. Those days I had been struggling to fit in the day's work into the time that the sun was up, so that the girls would not be disturbed at night and I had told the accountant to obey the queen without checking with me. I guess even somebody as cautious as Satyavati can lose his or her sense of purpose under stress – in this case she definitely had. I asked her in private why she had spent so much gold.

The carrots are good for pregnant mothers, she said. If they were so good, and were so expensive when imported, why hadn't she told me? I would have arranged to buy seed and grow them in my own garden. Satyavati was not troubled by the cost – she was protecting her future descendants. The worry lines did not fade from Satyavati's brow even after this rare shipment was received.

"As the seventh month ended, Ambika and Ambalika were clearly pregnant. To be frank, I learned a lot from observing this pregnancy – I received reports on their fluctuating moods, the vomiting over the first one hundred and eight days, their tiredness. When the seventh full moon passed with no sign of trouble, Satyavati withdrew with the girls from public sight. Then halfway into the eighth moon she came out with the news – Ambika and Ambalika had given birth to sons. Ambalika was first by a day. Even after nine full moons in the womb, they came out unready and unhealthy. The babies were small and sickly – Satyavati walked around moaning and cursing as though she had just given birth to them.

"The Vyaasa was to play a part in our lives once more. If it had not been for the Vyaasa, the children would have died."

"The Vyaasa Shukla?"

"No, no, that is silly. Not Shukla here but his predecessor Jaimini. Shukla, my friend, I have wished to say this to you for a long time. I am astonished by the influence that the Vyaasa Parashara has had on this family. Along with the Vyaasa Jaimini, Satyavati had daily visits from Shukla, and Krishna Dvaipaayana Paaraashara, to whom she was much attached, having cared for him as a baby.

"It is not surprising that the Vyaasa Jaimini was concerned; it is surely astonishing that the birth of my nephews was also a major concern to one future Vyaasa, Shukla, and to Krishna Dvaipaayana, a potential Vyaasa. It all begins with my father's respect for Parashara. Parashara influenced my father as the head of the Kavi Sangha, he was Shukla's teacher and Krishna Dvaipaayana's father – all three of them Parashara's children, physically or intellectually. You could almost call Parashara the root of the tree of cause and effect that has led to this war."

"My friend," Shukla said, "I wish what you say were true. Our influence has not prevented this war, despite the best efforts of the Kavi Sangha. Of Dvaipaayana, the less said, the better. For many years I despaired that he would remain in the Kavi Sangha, for he was a wayward young man. Vichitravirya's death shocked him and made him change his ways."

"Wayward young man? Unlike you, at his age? It reminds me that when he was six or so and had just started training with the Kavi Sangha, he would be teased by everybody. They would call him Shukla, to which he would respond with a vigorous *I am not like Uncle Shukla* (as he calls you), and then they called him not-Shukla. He did not like that, and one day he said, *Why don't you call my uncle the Not-Krishna,* to which people pointed out that they did – that was what 'Shukla' meant. I observed it once and was struck by the role names played in our lives. Take the name Krishna – maybe it is only a coincidence, but life is a mess of such coincidences – Shukla the Vyaasa is a not-Krishna; there is the Yadava Krishna whose support of Arjuna and the Pandavas has ensured the continuance of this war and resulted in my capture; and, there is Krishnaa Agnijyotsna, the Dark Lady, the Matriarch of Panchala whose blistering rage has not allowed this Kuru family to resolve its internal conflicts by themselves. Your nephew Krishna Dvaipaayana will find himself in good company.

"Pardon me for this digression, but I have one more observation – it is not so strange that Satyavati's family became so central to life in Hastinapur now, for Satyavati spent all her efforts and influence to ensure that her descendants would be central to Hastinapur in the future. That makes us no different than Panchala – we too have our own Dark Lady whose personal ambitions for her children have precluded compromise.

"As for your father's foster-child Krishna... ah! Krishna Dvaipaayana. What an impressive young man he became after Vichitravirya's death! You were absent, gone to the Kavi Sangha's university in Takshashila, and missed this part of his life. I think of him as a child, even though he is not much younger than us. He has become a major intellectual force in the Kavi Sangha, something I would not have predicted. As a young man people liked him, though his behaviour was irresponsible and difficult to condone. He did not like to stay in one place but would be constantly moving around – he would come and wheedle gold and silver for trading out of Satyavati and then disappear. In the beginning, I would receive reports of his activities that somehow never ended unhappily – an abandoned girl in one place would follow him but, after talking to him, go back with a wistful smile; an insulted bard would come to chide him and leave praising his kindness. The only exception seemed to be Satyavati: every visit ended with Satyavati angry and she would order him to leave. Then she would cry and with tears, she would ask him to promise to return. I think he was her sole link to your father who had raised both of them. I expect that he was rebelling against the expectations that people had for him, as the son of his birth father Parashara. As I mentioned, he changed – he visited me shortly after the birth of Vichitravirya's children. I had not seen him in many years and I was overwhelmed by his charm. He was polite, he asked after my health, and made light conversation, and left me babbling about his generosity in favouring me with a visit. I am told he has that effect on everyone.

"That was when Krishna Dvaipaayana started building a new life. Satyavati asked him to visit the babies – he obliged. He even played with them. Satyavati stopped crying after his visits. I stopped getting reports from the places he visited. Then I heard from a proud Satyavati that he had risen fast in the Kavi Sangha. He was a skilled poet and is a rising leader in the Kavi Sangha hierarchy. As I mentioned, he is even a possible Vyaasa."

Shukla said, "Archivist, that is a long digression; but do not edit it out – I'll help you clean it a bit later. Devavrat, my friend, please continue with the birth of Vichitravirya's sons!"

Devavrat said, "On the Vyaasa's advice, Satyavati placed the babies in a warm room heated by a hypocaust fired all through the day. To make sure that nothing untoward happened to the babies, her maids were in constant attendance on them. A piece of cotton would be dipped in goat's milk and squeezed into their mouths. For two months, they were fed like that. By that point they were healthier and ready for their mother's breasts, but Ambika and Ambalika were unable to lactate. It had been too long – the baby suckling at her breast is necessary for the mother to produce milk and their babies had not done that. As a coincidence, the pregnant maidservant gave birth to her own baby two weeks before Dhritarashtra and Mahendra were to be switched to mother's milk. Her baby was also a healthy boy. She was a sturdy woman – she produced enough milk for all three boys, though with three feeders she no longer had the energy to attend to the queens.

"Whoever said that nine moons of pregnancy results in healthy babies should revisit their numbers – the child of the wet-nurse, born a little late in the eleventh month was named Dharmateja – yes, the same Dharmateja who creates trouble in Hastinapur with his moralising lectures. Please understand – Dharmateja is probably the most ethical, the kindest, and the most far-sighted of Dhritarashtra's councillors (I would even include myself). His advice to settle this war peacefully enraged Suyodhana. Dharmateja was conceived a couple of weeks before the two princes but he was born well after them – a prodigy, born in eleven months! If only the two princes could have stayed in the womb for another two months – unnatural that might be, but maybe it would have resulted in healthy babies. These were not healthy babies.

"Ambalika's son was named Dhritarashtra. When he was finally ready to be shown to the public, it became clear that something was wrong with his eyes. He kept his eyes closed. If we tried to hold his eyes open by raising the lid, he would struggle violently and cry. We determined later that he could not bear to let light into his eyes. As a result, he did not look at people's faces when they looked at him or spoke to him. There was nothing wrong with his mind for he listened intently to sounds. Other than this blindness, the stay in the warm room had not hurt him at all – he was healthy and grew up to be strong. Healthy, but blind.

"Ambika's son was named Mahendra. He had been born white as milk – later he would be nicknamed *Pandu*. Even though he shared the heated room treatment along with his brother, Mahendra emerged just as pale as he had been at birth. As the years went by, his skin colour changed but unfortunately not in any uniform way. He developed large patches of pink and white skin separated by areas that were tinted brown. His eyes were pink. Like his brother he could not tolerate glare but he learned to cope with it and did not become blind. Otherwise, just like his brother, he was healthy and grew up to be physically fit. Unlike his brother, he could see."

Devavrat looked at Vyaasa, "There. I have told you of the birth of Vichitravirya's children. That is how far I will go. Now, tell me Amba's secret."

The Vyaasa smiled but only with his lips – his eyes did not and his nose flared up a bit. "Devavrat, in some ways you are so naïve. Yes, I shall tell you Amba's secret, but I did not imagine that Satyavati's secret, Ambika's secret, and Ambalika's secret were also hidden from you."

"What secrets? You smile, are you mocking me? I don't care about Satyavati's secrets – she had many. The two girls, Ambika and Ambalika were innocents who had no secrets from the world."

"No, I am not mocking you," said the Vyaasa, "I wonder... why do you want to know Amba's secret when there are so many other secrets you do not know. If you learned of a new secret, even one about Amba, what can you do with that knowledge? I fear you will not recover from your wound. You may recall the Kavi Sangha's maxim, 'that which does not lead to Action is not Knowledge'. There is no meaningful action you could take even if you knew all their secrets."

"I don't want to do anything. My father appeared in my dreams last night. I assume everybody has occasional dreams of visits by their parents, so this is not unusual. Dreams are creations of the mind. Who can say with authority that they know how dreams correspond to material things? In the last few days, a particular dream has become constant – my father appears and tells me that I have fifty-six days. Huh? Fifty-six days for what? Father said no more in the dream but vanished. The next time he appeared in a dream, he told me I had fifty-three days. When he showed up yesterday, he said that I had forty days. That is sixteen less than before. Where did my sixteen days go? I've been in bed since I was wounded. Are these sixteen days in bed the ones that are lost and that I no longer have? What will happen when there are no days left? Perhaps I will die –it would certainly be considered a miracle if I survived another forty days. What is the meaning of such a dream – I've seen scholars debate this matter for our edification, but they do not come to any agreement. Perchance in forty days, reason will have prevailed and this war will end. Maybe I will be released in forty days completely healed, and will stop having these dreams. If it is my father coming to me in a dream, he must think there is something I can do, so all that remains is for me to decide what to do.

"In any case, you promised."

"I will do as I promised. There is something only you can do in forty days," said Shukla. "Only you can bring the parties to the negotiating table."

"I've tried."

"Oh, no! You haven't. Not in the council, and not in private. In the council, Karna, Suyodhana and the rest of that gang shouted you down, but you could have stuck to your points and insisted on an honest negotiation."

"It is over. I do not wish to debate it. Even if that is the meaning of my dreams – what my father wants me to do in forty days. I call out your promise. Tell me Amba's secret. No more side-shows."

Secrets Revealed

Amba's Secret

The Pandava Camp
Circa 2000 B.C.E.

The Vyaasa dropped his eyes and took a deep breath. His shoulders slumped down. He did not move for what felt like a long time. Ten vighatis passed as Lomaharshana and Devavrat watched him. He looked up at Devavrat.

"Devavrat, why can't you see the obvious? You accuse Satyavati of all kinds of plots and dealings, but the biggest plot eludes you."

"Satyavati has plots in her blood. She had been plotting from the first day I met her."

"Satyavati has been trying to make amends ever since that first day. For much of what she did, she consulted me. She did not always do as I suggested, but I always knew what she would do. Once, only once, she plotted Amba's disappearance without asking me for advice – I was in Takshashila and could not advise her. Why didn't you, who mistrust her at every step, not think that she might have had something to do with Amba's disappearance."

"I did consider it but did not see why Satyavati would want to get rid of Amba. Even if she knew that we were lovers and that I had broken my promise, she faced a risk only if a child was born. That possibility itself gave her power over me, for she could denounce me as an oath-breaker. Civil war would be my only option and she knew that I was averse to that. Why, then, would she want Amba gone?"

"The obvious one. Consider this. Why did you and my sister plot against each other when it would have been so much easier to cooperate? After all, you agreed to split responsibilities after Shantanu died. You did that without disagreement. She handled the internal affairs of the city within Hastinapur while you made it an empire. What did you think was going to happen when you brought Amba into the arrangement?"

"I would have kept it secret. For if Satyavati found out, she could threaten to disclose it and shame me."

"Because you broke your vow?"

"Yes."

The Vyaasa touched his fingers to his forehead and took in a deep breath. Then he laughed. "My friend," he said, "You are an idiot."

The Vyaasa continued, "Vows are broken all the time. The tempest caused by that charge would have lasted half a day. Nobody would have left your side as a result. She did the next best thing – she made it appear that you were intent on getting rid of her, but were incapable of coming to a decision. That kept your potential supporters on edge. She did not expect it to be so easy. Is it possible that Amba, on the other hand, believed you would do whatever you thought needed to be done? That you would not flinch, since she knew how the name Bhishma had been earned."

Devavrat silently absorbed this news. Satyavati had kidnapped Amba and made it seem that the kidnappers were Devavrat's soldiers. *If they did not kill her, what did they do? What did this have to do with Shikhandin?* The Vyaasa watched him for some time and then said, "Satyavati told me much of this when I came back from Takshashila. Your reaction, though, surprised me."

"What surprised me was that nobody else seemed to be concerned about Amba's disappearance."

"That was to be expected. Amba had kept aloof and distant from most people. She spent time with her sisters and with Satyavati. You too, of course. She had announced that she was leaving and that took care of any worriers, like me. It was your reaction that baffled me."

"What about my reaction?"

"You seemed preoccupied and distant. All issues that came up were dealt with efficiently. You did not even talk about Amba's disappearance. You did not do anything about it."

"What I did, I did secretly. I did not want it to be publicised. She was a slice of good fortune that had come my way, and now, like all such slices, the good fortune was over."

"I assumed you knew about her pregnancy. I was puzzled that you did not seem concerned about her state of health. I was puzzled that you did not mourn the child she was carrying. Your child. I was truly puzzled by you."

Devavrat's whole body tried to turn to face the Vyaasa. He regretted it immediately, the movement pressed the arrow deeper and Devavrat stopped. He could only turn his head slightly and he looked sideways at Vyaasa.

"But it is the truth. I did not know."

The Vyaasa leaned closer, his voice a whisper. "You did not know that she was pregnant when she disappeared?"

Devavrat shook his head "No. I only found out a few days ago during the ambush. How did you know about it?"

The Vyaasa's eyes narrowed. "You never knew of the pregnancy? I... I cannot believe that."

Devavrat shook his head some more. "I've told you more than once – I just found out a few days ago when I killed Shikhandin and it was confirmed when Amba tried to kill me. How did you know?"

"The doctor told me. She thought you already knew. Amba had asked her not to tell Satyavati, but after Amba disappeared she felt she had to tell somebody responsible. I told her to keep it secret until it was needed."

Devavrat closed his eyes. "Go away," he said. "Come back later."

The Vyaasa got up slowly. He felt his bones creaking and complaining. He sighed loudly. Then he gathered the folds of the upper garment and moved towards the entrance. As he stepped through the doorway, he heard a sound from the bed – he turned around a bit too quickly and would have fallen if the Archivist had not stepped forward to hold him up. "Did you say something?" he said to Devavrat.

"Come back and finish telling me what happened to Amba."

"Yes, of course, I will," said the Vyaasa as he returned to his seat.

"Should I memorise this, sir?" said the Archivist who had been silent all along.

"Yes, yes. You have been listening haven't you?"

"Yes, sir."

"Devavrat, my friend," said the Vyaasa. "Can I begin now?"

2000 B.C.E

"Yes."

"I used to spend many months in Takshashila – even then I knew that the Kavi Sangha was going to be my life. I came back once or twice a year – the trip was tedious and took too long. The organisers of caravans seemed to show no interest in the affairs of the lands they traversed. It would be some years before I realised how much they knew that was important – they knew the border guards, they knew the officials to go to for various permissions, they knew who could provide protection and who could not, they knew who was predatory and who wasn't, and finally, they knew what could be exchanged there. I digress.

"Satyavati was in good spirits. She had taken over the care of Amba's sisters. Amba's absence did not seem to have affected anybody. Including you. Satyavati was brief when I asked about Amba – she had gone away. I could not ask you, for you had made it impossible to see you except on official business. My status as Satyavati's brother and as someone who took care of her interests allowed me much more access to her attendants. I found that Amba had employed a seamstress to help her dress in a manner appropriate to the city – the seamstress became Satyavati's eyes and ears and she talked willingly enough to me. She had realised that Amba was pregnant and she had reported it to Satyavati. I assumed that you would have known of it and that is why your behaviour puzzled me.

"I questioned Satyavati about Amba. Initially she said that Amba had announced that she was going on a trip. When I mentioned that Amba had been pregnant, she feigned shock. I then told her that I knew that she had known of the pregnancy. I reminded her that after all, she was my sister and I would protect her interests if it came to that. She swore me to secrecy. Amba had been pregnant for maybe two moons. Satyavati had always feared that such a thing would happen. She had to stop it and she could not wait for my visit to discuss it with me. She had arranged for two men, dressed in the style that you, Devavrat, had established for all your soldiers, to visit Amba with a message from you – in the message, you asked her to come to your project site, as it was significantly delayed. To Amba, this might have been interpreted as good news – it would make the public aware of their friendship. Satyavati's spy, one of Amba's maids, had reported on Amba's hope that you were preparing to acknowledge her publicly, thus ending months of secrecy. She hoped that it would include the recognition of her future child's standing in this patriarchal city. She had left the next day with the messengers. Satyavati said that Amba had asked her to take care of her sisters while she was gone. She told her sisters little – just that she was going to meet you.

"The men had been instructed to kill Amba when they were alone and make sure that her body would not be found. That was the first time my sister shocked me – I had not expected such ruthlessness. My shock showed and she began to cry and explain that she had been afraid. I berated her and she asked for my forgiveness – I told her that such forgiveness was not mine to give. Then she dropped a *vajra,* a lightning bolt. Neither the men, nor Amba had returned. Maybe Amba had managed to bribe the men or escape their custody – the men had not returned for they had failed in the mission. At any moment, Amba might come back and denounce Satyavati. To prepare for that eventuality Satyavati was kind and solicitous towards Ambika and Ambalika. When Amba did not send a message that she had arrived safely, the sisters had begun to worry. Satyavati stoked their worries about your intentions. They knew what you were capable of – they had been in the audience at the massacre. Satyavati sowed the doubts – your apparent lack of concern convinced them.

"When you returned and claimed that you had never seen Amba or sent for her, they were sure that you were lying. If you were lying, they did not want to deal with you. They avoided you. They felt powerless to denounce you; they were young, there was nothing for them to go back to; the trip that you arranged for them to their old settlement convinced them that you were trying to hide something. Satyavati was considerate and charming; she was kind and not brusque like you; they had not seen or heard of her torturing anybody the way you had treated the Shakas. For the first time, they were told of your oath of celibacy, which they knew you had broken with their sister. That only made you more of a villain. Was it possible that you had arranged to get rid of Amba – maybe not kill her but make her disappear? Over time, they became reconciled to the absence of Amba, then reconciled to life in the company of Vichitravirya and other children of that age, and finally to marriage.

"Satyavati had made no effort to determine what had happened to the men who had taken Amba away – any discovery, even if by her initiative, might result in revealing her role. She asked me to investigate in secret.

"She was my sister and I was concerned about her state of mind. The impulsive and ruthless plot bothered me – it seemed so unlike her that I investigated personally – I went out into the forest with a Naga guide skilled in the trails and pathways in the forest. We found signs of camping for the first three nights but after the third night, there was nothing. At the point where a fourth camp may have been put up, there was no evidence of habitation. We traced our way back and at one point, the guide pointed to a trail that some large animal had used that cut across the path. We followed the trail and came across bones. Pulled up behind a dense thorny bush was a skeleton. It had been scraped clean by animals and some limbs were missing. There was no flesh, nor clothing or any sign to indicate who this had been: a man, a woman, a soldier, a fisherman, a hunter, anybody … anything that would help identify the person.

"I measured the skeleton carefully – the span of the palm, the hasta – the length of the arm from elbow to the tip of the finger, the circumference of the wrist, and so on. It was not a woman.

How do I know? The Kavi Sangha has collected information on the sizes of the bones of men and women. We know.

"If it was a man's body, it could not be Amba. At best, it could be one of her guards. I was relieved. We continued to follow the trail and about a hundred hastas away, we came to the banks of the Ganga. It is a fast-flowing and wide river at this point about ten *kros*[125] south of Kampilya, the capital of Panchala. The forest vegetation continues almost up to the edge of the riverbank where it is replaced by water-loving plants. Elephant grass grew in clumps. The trail continued past the skeleton to the water's edge. The water was too far down, so this was an unlikely place for an animal's waterhole. The way the trail jutted into the water suggested a natural or artificial dock for a boat, though long abandoned. To the left a section of elephant grass had been pulled out of a four hasta-square bit of land about one hasta above the waterline. A series of footprints made by a smallish foot headed north from there along the riverbank. I stepped barefooted next to one and left a larger footprint. It seemed clear that a smaller person made the old prints. If this was Amba's route, it appeared that she had passed this way some weeks ago. North from here she would sooner or later reach a town with a ferry crossing – a quick escape to the Panchala side of the river and then the road would lead her to Kampilya, the capital city of Hastinapur's enemy. There was no point in chasing Amba this way and she would be long gone, to Panchala if she was lucky or, more likely, a victim of her own hunger or that of a tiger or a pack of wild dogs.

"Many years later, shortly before I became the Vyaasa, the Kavi Sangha started a major effort to recruit Nagas from Panchala – this was a stealthy effort to change the Panchalan opinion that the Kavi Sangha was an absolute enemy. The Kavi Sangha was identified with Hastinapur and that needed to

---

125 *Kros* is a unit of measure, about 2.25 miles. See Endnotes.

change. I was one of the interviewers – my job was to evaluate each candidate as well as debrief them for news and rumours to get any news that I could. The second year, one of the applicants, from Kampilya,[126] was a fount of gossip – as you know, the best bards are natural memorisers of whatever they hear. The rumours said that the Matriarch of Panchala was unhappy with her brother because he had brought an outside woman into his palace. Unlike other men, the brother, Drupada, sometimes also called the King[127] of the Naga band, never moved out of the band to find partners. Any permanent love relationship would require the woman to move in with him, i.e. she would leave her band. It was generally felt that there must be something wrong with such a woman if she was not in a band. However, that was not the Matriarch's reason for opposing the relationship. The lady's dialect marked her as one of the Nagas from the Hastinapur side. A year earlier, there had been news that a Naga band allied with Hastinapur had fought off invaders from across the Northern Mountains. The invasion had been stopped. There were hints of atrocities committed during the battle. Instead of enhancing the reputation of the band, the victory had lead to its collapse when it could not recruit new members. The assumption was that she was one of the women scarred by that experience. The Matriarch did not want any member of such a band in her town. It was said that she was so beautiful that Drupada had refused to obey the Matriarch's demand to verify the woman's antecedents. I learned a lot about Panchala and its rulers from that applicant – in a traditional Naga band, the matriarch would have the power to enforce her demands, but in Kampilya, the power relation

126 *Kampilya* was the capital of Panchala.

127 The title for the army chief and the brother of the Matriarch could have been "Senapati" ("Lord of the army"), but that usage mixes the two roles. He may have well been addressed as "Rajan" (meaning "resplendent one"), or "Mahanaga" ("great Naga"), or even "Nagarajan" (either "Lord of the Nagas", or "King of the Nagas"). "Nagarajan" could also be interpreted as "King according to Naga practice", i.e. the brother of the matriarch. I've translated all of these possibilities as "King".

between Matriarch and King had switched. In a deep sense, Panchala and Hastinapur were twins, twin patriarchies-to-be.

"The applicant joined the Kavi Sangha but stayed in touch with the events and gossip – I stayed in touch with him. The news that year included the lady giving birth to a son as well as the ebbing of the feud between the Matriarch and the King. The woman lived a quiet and secluded life and did not seem to care that the birth of her son was not recognised by the Matriarch. The Matriarch may have reconciled with the King, but she displayed her anger by not acknowledging the birth of the child – since the mother was not part of the Matriarch's family, the birth of the son was treated as a non-event and ignored by everybody. The King did not seem particularly distressed. As usual, this was reported and recorded in the Kavi Sangha archives.

"Even then, I suspected that the lady was Amba. I could not go to Kampilya to verify this, nor could I send another senior Kavi Sangha member. I had to rely on Naga students who went home annually. When the boy grew up, he played with the other children in the palace and city. He was sensitive about some things – he could not bear to hear gossip about his mother and he would attack the gossiper; questions about his father made him sad and he would leave the group.

"The Kavi Sangha members in Panchala, though few in number, helped me collect greater detail about the mystery woman. There is no doubt that she was Amba. I do not know how, but the brief version is that Amba found her way to the protection of the King of Panchala, Hastinapur's enemy. She raised the boy in Drupada's palace. That was Shikhandin, your son. Shikhandin. When the boy grew up he enlisted in a select group of warriors led by the Panchalan army chief Dhristadyumna, nephew of the retired, aged Drupada."[128]

---

128 *Dhrishtadyumna* will appear in later novels – he is the son of Panchala's Matriarch, brother of the Matriarch-to-be, and therefore, the King-to-be in Panchala.

"Shikhandin," said Devavrat. "He acted differently towards me. Many men feared me, but a few hated me. He was one of the few. Why did he attempt to kill me? I had to kill him in self-defence."

The Vyaasa was silent. *What can I possibly say?* He had wanted to protect his sister and so he had kept Amba's secret from Devavrat. It had seemed like a small thing whose importance soared as Devavrat increasingly became *Bhishma* – he became opaque, uncommunicative, and difficult to comprehend, and it became impossible for Shukla to tell him. Bhishma was a shell from which Devavrat only dealt with the business of empire. In the meantime, he, Shukla, had become more involved in the affairs of the Kavi Sangha and embarked on the path to becoming the Vyaasa.

Devavrat also stayed silent in his bed, staring intently at the Vyaasa.

Devavrat broke the silence. "Tell me something. Why? Why did he want his father dead? That is, if I am truly his father."

Shukla said, "It was not possible for me to meet Amba. I relied on the aspiring Kavi Sangha student – he was brother to the husband of one of Amba's maids. His wife had mentioned to him that Amba would express hate and contempt for Hastinapur. I think Amba raised Shikhandin to hate Hastinapur and to hate you. He had few friends and revealed little even to the ones closest to him, but it appears that he hated Hastinapur too. You realise that for many, many years, Devavrat, you were Hastinapur."

They both fell silent. For a long time, the Vyaasa sat and Devavrat lay still. After a ghati had passed, the Archivist, waiting for Shukla to continue, stood up quietly to stretch his limbs. Devavrat's eyes were closed.

"Sir," said the Archivist, "Sir, are we done for the day?"

2000 B.C.E

That aroused the Vyaasa out of his reverie. "Devavrat," he said. "How did you get captured?"

Devavrat did not reply and his eyes stayed closed. The Vyaasa laughed. It was indeed an opportune time to fall asleep, to avoid questions. He stood up and got ready to leave.

As he moved towards the door, Devavrat said, "Shukla, you are not done!"

"You are awake!" said the Vyaasa, "What do you mean not done? What is left to tell you?"

Devavrat said, "You promised to tell me Satyavati's secrets, Ambika and Ambalika's secret."

"It has been so many years. It isn't particularly interesting."

The Archivist said, "Don't we need to make it part of the archive?"

The Vyaasa frowned. The Archivist saw the frown and fell silent.

"Come back and finish this," said Devavrat. "It won't take long – I may know more than you think I do."

The Secret of the Three Queens

The Pandava Camp
circa 2000 B.C.E.

"Do you recall," said the Vyaasa, "What you were doing when Vichitravirya died?"

"I certainly do," said Devavrat. "How could I forget? We've gone over it all in the last few days – your Archivist has recorded it all."

"Right. I want you to think back to when his sons were born. Do you recall anything odd?"

"Odd? I think the entire situation was odd. Satyavati was as she had always been – difficult and focused on her ambition. The possible birth of my nephews allowed me to continue postponing decisions about succession and rule. If I ever became the sole candidate, I would be forced to become King and my stepmother and I would have to resolve whatever differences we had. Many years had passed since my father's death, the death of Chitrangada, my time with Amba, the death of Vichitravirya, and the many intervening years of co-Regency, but even so, I felt choked by a knot that formed in my chest, when I thought about ruling Hastinapur and fathering children to rule after me. A knot that had been tied by Satyavati the girl and pulled tight by Satyavati my stepmother."

The Vyaasa said, "This is all very good to know, my friend. Now, it seems to me that you do not want to know what you've demanded I tell you."

Devavrat replied, "I am afraid of what you will tell me. I must know it, but I would willingly put it off to the day that I die. That day is soon, maybe even today. Maybe it is now. I find that I am still afraid. Most of all I fear that which you would disclose."

"I don't know how to assure you about that. You must decide for yourself. When her son Vichitravirya died, Satyavati arranged for a surrogate father, performing the ancient rite of *niyoga* to ensure that a man who dies childless nonetheless has progeny. Your brother Vichitravirya is not the father of Dhritarashtra and Mahendra."

The Vyaasa stopped to see how Devavrat was reacting. Devavrat was silent for a long time. Then he turned to gaze at his friend. "*Niyoga?* That would have to happen after King Vichitravirya was dead, wouldn't it?"

"Yes."

"But the Queens were a few weeks pregnant when the King died. Are you telling me that it was done when the King was still alive?"

"You are right. The King was dead. The children were conceived after he died."

Devavrat's head spun. He recalled Satyavati telling him that the Queens were a few weeks pregnant. She had lied. *Why had she lied?*

"Was the father a Kuru or a Puru? Was he even sufficiently honourable to take the place of my brother? Can I still believe that I fulfilled the promise to my father?"

"Hmm... I'll let you be the judge of that. Do you recall that we were talking about Dvaipaayana visiting Satyavati with her father."

"Yes. The elusive Krishna Dvaipaayana. What about him?"

"You know that he was Guru Parashara's son."

"Yes, and your father was fostering him while Guru Parashara fulfilled his vow of silence."

"Do you know that he might well be a candidate to be the Vyaasa when I pass on."

"Yes, I have heard of his brilliant rise in the Kavi Sangha. Why should it matter to me now?"

"Do you know that his mother was Satyavati?"

Devavrat opened his mouth to say something and then stopped. Instead he started coughing as though his lungs had filled with fluid. The coughing would not stop and the nurse came over and held Devavrat so that he would not push on the arrow accidentally. Shukla waited. The coughing stopped.

Devavrat took a deep breath. Then he said, "No I did not know. Please do not tell me that everyone else knew. I cannot believe that."

"Don't fret – even your father did not know. Krishna Dvaipaayana may inherit many features of his father, but Parashara had not been seen for some years and people forget."

"So what about him, what about Parashara's son?"

"He took the place of the King and fathered children with the Queens."

Devavrat felt that time had slowed down and his thoughts strained to emerge as speech. He managed to say something.

"What?"

Shukla said, "He is the father of Dhritarashtra, Mahendra, and Dharmateja."

Devavrat said, "You mean... Krishna Dvaipaayana is the grandfather of..."His voice faltered. He continued, "...these cousins... the father of their fathers."

The Vyaasa smiled. "You are indeed a very perceptive man, my friend. You refuse to see beyond the tip of your nose. I am not implying anything I am asserting it. Satyavati asked her son to father children with the queens Ambika and Ambalika."

"I see."

Devavrat's mind whirled. *Krishna Dvaipaayana was not the one responsible. Satyavati was.* Devavrat wanted to get up and confront Satyavati who, by a single fear-induced stroke, created this world. For an eternity that lasted a few vighatis, everybody was silent.

Then Devavrat said, "Dhritarashtra and Mahendra are not Kauravas, not descended from Kuru, not my father's grand-children."

The various forms of the statement seemed to rush down a waterfall to a sea of conclusions. *They were not my nephews. Their children are not my grandnephews.*

"Yes. Those are logical inferences. They are not Kauravas."

Shukla's statement evoked more inferences. *They were Shukla's grandnephews. These children are Shukla's great grand nephews.* He felt laughter forming in his throat, a mocking laughter that threatened to suppress all thought.

Devavrat needed more time to express those thoughts. *Satyavati's actions were a long time ago. Shukla's relationship is irrelevant. What should I do now?* He made up his mind.

"I stand by my question – is their heritage worthy of Hastinapur?"

"Dhritarashtra and Mahendra are the grandchildren of Parashara."

"That is a glorious heritage, descendants of the great Vasishtha. But their mothers are Nagas of unknown descent."

"Does that matter? All you asked earlier was whether the father was noble? You have already approved the mothers."

The pieces fell in place like the fragments of a broken pot that had been re-assembled.

Shukla continued, "The Queens had become pregnant after the King's death. Both sons were born over six weeks prematurely. Only Dharmateja, born in the tenth moon after the death of the King was born at the right time. Satyavati had even arranged for the premature delivery with her shipment of carrots, the elixir of its flowers being an abortifacient. It even explained her concern over ensuring that a Kaurava should influence the babies in the womb. She had made sure that no questions would be raised, even by me, about the legitimacy of the two children!"

Devavrat struggled to focus his mind. *I never bothered to find out why Satyavati was attached to the boy. I just assumed that she was attached to him because she had taken care of him almost from birth.*

Devavrat said, "Did you know at that time?"

Shukla said, "He is my nephew. I kept quiet when I found out. He was a charming boy and I was also attached to him."

"I have no issue with his qualification to father these kings. However, I am troubled. I have failed to keep even the small promise I made to my father. Neither Mahendra nor

Dhritarashtra are Kauravas by birth. The empire I have built will pass into non-Kaurava hands."

"That's not true. You have fulfilled your promise."

"No. That's nonsense."

"You recall the oath? Of course, you must. Recite it once more."

"Yes, perfectly. I said, 'I hereby renounce all my rights to have children, and give them to my father. To you, O King, I yield my birthright. O Queen, I will not marry, I will not have children, and I will not make love to any woman. O King, my father, my right to a descendant is yours.'"

"There is more to your oath."

So, What was That Again?

The Pandava Camp
circa 2000 B.C.E.

There was another long silence. Devavrat went over the links of the story. Then he did it again. If Dhritarashtra and Mahendra were Dvaipaayana's children, then they were Satyavati's grandchildren. They were her progeny, even if they were not Shantanu's grandchildren by birth. The prediction that her descendants would rule had apparently come true. That same long-gone day he had sworn an oath – that he would not have any children and would be celibate. Yes, he had already broken the vow of celibacy, but he had been a child when he made that oath. He knew now that it had been a ridiculous vow. If Shikhandin was indeed his son, he had also broken the promise not to have children.

There was another oath. Before the wedding his father had come to him. Devavrat replayed that scene in his mind as he contemplated Shukla's words.

Shantanu had said, "My dear son. To you, I owe the happiness to which I am looking forward! I asked a lot of you, and you have given me much, much more than you had to. I hoped it was enough, but I have one more request."

Devavrat's face took on a neutral cast – his lips relaxed, the eyes blank but focused on his father who stood in front of him like a supplicant, his breathing controlled. He said, "You are my father to whom I owe my birth. You are the King, the lord of life and death in Hastinapur, to whom I owe my life. Ask and I shall give it."

Shantanu said, "I fear what will happen to Satyavati if I die prematurely. What will happen to Hastinapur, the legacy that I inherited? I need you to promise that you will take care of both."

Devavrat had closed his eyes in an effort to calm himself down. The silence had dragged on for his father. Shantanu must have construed that his son was angry with his stepmother for the oaths she had extracted from him. A few vighatis later, Shantanu said, "Please, son. At least promise that you will take care of Hastinapur and keep it strong and prosperous."

Devavrat had said, "I will make whatever oaths you wish me to make. I promise now that I will take care of your wife, my stepmother Satyavati in case you are unable to. I promise that the prophecy she talked of will come true. As long as I live, I will do all I can to keep Hastinapur safe and its rulers powerful and respected."

That was it. His father had left him alone after that. He had made this oath with the full consciousness of what it meant and with time for deliberation. The vow of celibacy had been made in the heat of the moment; this vow was made with full consciousness, but not, as fate would have it, full understanding. The first vow was made to a weak man and a fickle woman; the second was made to his father alone and to the country that he was building, the empire he was creating.

Neither Mahendra nor Dhritarashtra were Kauravas, but they were Satyavati's progeny. By crowning them, he had fulfilled his promise to his father, to fulfil the prophecy that Satyavati would be the mother of many rulers, the only vow he could bring himself to believe in. Or had he? He had taken sides – when the disagreement over policies between Mahendra and Dhritarashtra became open conflict, he had sided with Dhritarashtra, for Mahendra's proposals threatened his own vision of an imperial city. He had chosen to be neutral between Mahendra's children and Dhritarashtra's children, at least in the beginning. He had only decided to support Suyodhana's claim when Satyavati insisted that the Pandavas, as everybody called them, were adopted or otherwise not Mahendra's own sons, and not descended from her. The evidence seemed compelling – it was commonly believed that albinism was inherited and none of the Pandavas were albino, though Arjuna, Nakula, and Sahadeva were somewhat paler than the two eldest. Yudhishthira's calm demeanour was unlike any Kuru family trait. He reminded Devavrat of Parashara, but Satyavati insisted that Yudhishthira inherited nothing from her or from Shantanu. Meanwhile, Bhīma's dark skin, broad face and nose, and broad shoulders, hinted at a Rakshasa origin. If they were Satyavati's grandchildren through her son Krishna, then any Naga features could be explained, but not Rakshasa features. If he had known that neither branch of the family could claim descent from Shantanu, he might not have taken sides in their conflict. He could have refused to support Suyodhana exclusively. Or could he?

It struck him that out of fear, his father had requested the wrong oath. His father was concerned about *his* descendants through Satyavati. For that matter, if Satyavati had been asked, she would have said the same thing. They wanted him to promise to keep the kingdom safe for *Shantanu's* children *by* Satyavati. That is what he had assumed all along. On the other hand, the words of the oath only mentioned the prophecy that Shukla had quoted. In that case, he had actually lived by his oath – he had protected Hastinapur and created an empire to be ruled by Satyavati's descendants. It was not what he had thought he was doing. Was *this* the purpose of his oaths? The meaning he had assigned to his life receded further from him on every examination.

The right oath would have been far more complex, covering all the contingencies that he had faced in his life. That right oath could never have been formulated for its every condition would have screamed *treachery*. Where in the oath could he have said, your children will inherit except if none of your children live in which case my children will inherit? Where in the oath could he have said, only children by birth and not those by adoption or *niyoga*?

Such a vow had not been demanded of him either – that had been his own idea. What if he had refused to make any of these vows and, consequently, his father had not married Satyavati? Would his father have allowed him then to marry Satyavati? That was doubtful. Had his father ever known what had been sacrificed for him? That was unlikely – his father was not one to yoke his desires. *Yes, I, Devavrat, have committed a sin against my ancestors by not performing my duties to my ancestors. Nor my duties to my own spirit for I have no descendants. I will suffer for it. I expected to protect my father's children, and that would have protected him and his ancestors. The only one to suffer would be me.*[129]

Another thought struck him. If neither the Pandavas nor the Kauravas were descended from Shantanu, then he, Devavrat was the sole descendant of the king. Inadvertently, he had killed his son Shikhandin, who would have been his own sole descendant. Here in this fenced camp-city of the enemies of Hastinapur, the only two legitimate heirs to the Kuru name and fortune lay dying or had died. The descendants of Satyavati

---

[129] In Hindu belief, when a person dies without descendants, they have committed a sin against their ancestors. Some variant of this belief can be seen in many religions, major ones as well as religions only practiced in remote parts of the world. See Endnotes.

and Parashara, Naga and bard, were fighting over an empire that he, a trader and a warrior, had conceived of. He had not ruled as king, but he had constructed an edifice that, if duly maintained, would sustain a great empire. Even Indraprastha had only become possible because he had put in place dams and created lakes that controlled the Yamuna upstream. Further downstream, the Yadavas settling down on the banks of the Yamuna were profiting from his creation. Space was being created for the immigrants from the west, coming from the lands watered by the Sarasvati, all the way from the delta in the south to the northernmost point at Kaalindini where the Sutudri had twisted away from its innumerable children. With the aid of Hastinapur and the Kauravas, these refugees would inherit the triangle of land between the Ganga and the Yamuna.

The crisis was not past. Crises, he thought, more than a single crisis. When you suppress one crisis, another is born elsewhere. The Pandava-Panchala-Yadava alliance would last only as long as the rivers were good fences.

Devavrat frowned – a fog was enveloping his thoughts and he could not disperse it. This obsessive recall of his life was a foolish old man's exercise. Dying would be preferable to this unremitting torture, but every time he moved down on the arrow, the explosive needles of pain made his lungs choke and his body betrayed him by shifting back up. *Even on my deathbed,* he thought, *my ancestors refuse to accept me back.*

The Archivist said, "Sir, you've been silent for a ghati. Are you feeling well?"

Devavrat heard the urgency in his voice – it roused him from the emotionally draining morass of thought. He could take pride in the empire he had created – what matter who ruled it? Rulers were all the same, whether arrogant like Suyodhana or courteous like Yudhishthira. *A ghati? Had it really been that long?*

Devavrat said, "Where's Shukla?"

2000 B.C.E

The Archivist, who was the only other person there, said, "He'll be back, sir. He had to take a short break."

"What do you think, Lomaharshana? You've heard so much from so many different people. What do you think?"

The Archivist said, "Sir, I am merely the memoriser of people's memories. My opinions do not matter."

"Please. I will not insist, but I am at the end of my life. Indulge me."

"Sire, it is an honour to be asked for my opinion."

"Be truthful and nothing else.

"Certainly, sir. I must qualify my opinions, for what I have heard is complex. I have not arrived at a full understanding, the kind of deep familiarity that will allow me to reorganise it as a poem to be recited."

"That I know. You know that at one time I considered becoming a memoriser like you."

"You flatter me, sir. Thank you. May I ask a question?"

"Ask away. You have earned the right to ask. I will answer if I can."

"It is a question that has bothered me for some time."

"Go ahead."

Lomaharshana the Archivist said, "Sire, you were asked a question you did not answer. I think you evaded it. It is this: How did a senior commander in the Kaurava army get captured in an ambush?"

Devavrat took in a deep breath. "Overconfidence and stupidity, of course. Do you want to make it part of this story?"

"Yes, sir."

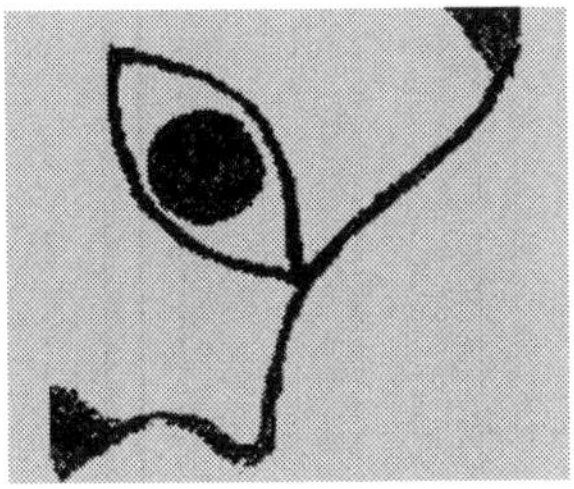

PART 6.

The Son

The Ambush

The Kaurava Council
Circa 2000 B.C.E

Devavrat said, "A man came to Hastinapur. He said he was from Panchala. He wanted to speak to the high command of the Kaurava army.

"The man was Shi... Shi... Shikhandin... Saying his name wakes up a crab in my throat. I did not know then what I know now, but I trusted him. He must have reminded me of Amba. That is why I think of her now – she was justified in trying to kill me. I wish she had succeeded.

"The man – he – Shi... Shi...khandin – he said he was a Krivi, the smallest clan in the Panchala confederation. He was authorised to make an offer that might end the war; and even if it did not, it would greatly weaken our enemy. The council held a meeting in secret – it was not in the King's main court, but in a war room in my house – it had no windows and its walls had been made thicker with more than the usual number of branches and daubed with an extra layer of mud, in order to protect against eavesdroppers. These were the rooms in which I met with spies and secret agents, with hidden entrances and secret hiding places for eavesdroppers. I arranged for a throne to be brought in – the King must look like a King, even to a traitor like this man. Such details are important. All the servants had been sent away and only two of my trusted guards were there. Kutaja, Suyodhana, Karna, Dharmateja, and Kripa[130] came. Even the blind Dhritarashtra came, accompanied by the bard Sanjaya – I seated him on the throne.

"The man was explicit. His clan did not want to go down the path of war and conquest. Four of the five clans that made up the Panchala confederation did not want this war. They would prefer to trade, not make war. He had been sent by the leaders of his clan to see if peace could be negotiated. He said, 'I can set up a meeting – one senior councillor from each of the four clans will attend. Are you interested? Can you send a senior councillor who will negotiate on your behalf?'

"Dhritarashtra smiled when he heard this. 'I have nothing but goodwill for my brother's children. Are they in agreement?'

"The man looked confused. Suyodhana rolled his eyes. 'Father,' he said, 'Perhaps you should only listen and not say a word. My cousins rely on the Somakas, the leading clan of Panchala – their wife Krishnaa Agnijyotsna is the Matriarch of Panchala – her brother Dhrishtadyumna heads the Panchalan army. This will weaken them.'

"Turning to the man he said, 'That is so, isn't it? The Somakas are the fifth clan and they are the ones who seek war.'

"The man said, 'The Somakas are the leading clan, the *first* clan. My clan, the Krivi, along with the Srinjayas, the Turvashas, and the Keshins want this war stopped.'

"Karna said, 'If that is the case, why not just stop it? Surely, the four clans are the larger part of Panchala. You do not need

130 *Kripa* is Kutaja's brother-in-law, and also skilled in martial arts. He and his sister, Kripi, were abandoned in the forest as babies, found by Shantanu, and raised in the palace.

to parlay with us if you wish to stop the war. Take your troops and go home.'

"The man gave a thin smile that did not change his face. 'It is not so simple, sir,' he said. 'The five clans have been allied for almost twenty generations. Initially an alliance of equals, it changed ten generations ago to the present one in which the Somaka are the first and the foremost. The Matriarch's family is Somaka. When she dies, the new Matriarch is not from a different clan as was agreed upon – instead the Somaka imposed a new agreement that the Matriarch's daughter be the successor. The Somaka control the army; the army controls the cities; the cities oversee the bands. It has been many years since we attempted a rebellion – the last time, our senior-most captains were arrested for treason and killed before they could make a single move.'

"'So, what is different now?'

"'Now, the Somaka king, Drishtadhyumna, brother to the Matriarch, is seeking glory in the grand alliance that will lead to the creation of a Panchalan empire. Most of our army is in the field and not in our capital city Kampilya – we can take over Kampilya and hold it for a couple of weeks until your forces come. Not much longer, for our forces are weaker than the King's, but we can hold off just long enough. We are not as naïve as we once were – our clan members in the army will escape as soon as news of the takeover is announced.'

"'Kampilya will be ours?'

"'Yes.'

"'We will control both banks of the Ganga?'

"'Yes.'

"Suyodhana's eyes had lit up and he was smiling. He slapped Karna on the back.

"Suyodhana said, 'We will still have the Pandavas and their wife serve us as slaves!'

2000 B.C.E

"Dhritarashtra spoke, 'Son, I ...'

"'Shut up, Father!'

"'Son, you...'

"'I said, shut up, didn't I? You have a soft spot for these supposed Pandava cousins. Last time, instead of sending them on their way as fraudulent pretenders, you gave them Indraprastha. See what chaos that caused.'

"Kutaja said, 'Controlling both banks of the Ganga is a desirable goal. It can only be achieved at the cost of much blood. Capturing Kampilya by subversion is much cheaper – it is worth considering.'

"Karna was infected by his friend's joyous reaction. 'Of course it is worth considering, oh great guru of strategy. We are glad that you have expressed your opinion.'

"Dharmateja, my nephew, spoke. Despite his low birth, I had brought him into the war council. He usually suggested a peaceful path when addressing a problem. He would have been an excellent trader if he had been educated. As it was, he brought the common man's sensibility to our discussions. I wish we had attended to the advice he gave that day.

"'What do we have to do to get this alliance going?'

"'Yes,' said Suyodhana, 'What exactly are you proposing?'

"The man's face lightened.

"'Four senior leaders, one from each clan, are awaiting an emissary from you. I can take him to a meeting point, about three to four days from here. It is a crossing place on the Ganga.'

"'There are a thousand crossing places on the Ganga, none of them in use since the war began.'

"'I know which one and will lead you there."

"Suyodhana said, 'We can avenge the humiliation of Samvarana.'

"Samvarana had not exacted revenge for the trouble that Panchala had caused him. Avenging Samvarana was an impossible-to-scratch itch on the Kuru psyche, one that afflicted Suyodhana the most. Kampilya had to be captured and its rulers killed, its population enslaved or driven into exile.

"Suyodhana said, 'Kampilya will be delivered to us on a platter.'

"Kutaja said, 'Whom can we send?'

"The man said, 'Anyone at your level would be senior enough to negotiate a peace.'

"Suyodhana's smile vanished. 'One of us? From this council.'

"The man said, 'Yes, sir. Any of the war leaders would be welcome.'

"'What kind of joke is this?'

"'Sir, it is no joke. Whomever you send has to be able to create a workable agreement. He should be somebody who understands the strategic issues involved in making this alliance work. He should know your own military capabilities well.'

"Kutaja said, 'We need to discuss this. Sanjaya, please escort him to the special guest room – bring him back in a ghati or so. He can wait there.'

"Sanjaya took the man to the second war room located on the other side of my house – like the first room, it was specially constructed to be secure. Back in our meeting Devavrat, Kutaja, Suyodhana, Karna, and even Dharmateja who was usually quiet, started talking at the same time. They all stopped. In Panchnad councils, there was a strict sequence in which members were expected to speak.

"Karna said, 'I like it – we get to push them back into the jungle where they came from. The cost to us? Nothing.'

"Dharmateja said, 'He made a good point about trade. This war has slowed commercial activity in all the settlements. We should never have attacked Indraprastha – instead, we should have proposed an alliance to control the entire land from the headwaters of the Ganga and Yamuna to Little Nagapura.'

"Suyodhana's upper body was shaking. If we had been standing, he might have attacked Dharmateja, but we were all seated on our assigned mats and only the King Dhritarashtra was seated on his throne, a stool set on a raised platform. His voice rose and he stared at Dharmateja as he said, 'Will you stop telling me about trade? We are not traders! You are the son of a servant; your mind is forever stuck in pettifogging details. I am not going to control the two banks by trade – my army will control the banks. We will show the Nagas our power – they will obey us. I will brook no talk of compromising with my so-called cousins. We've defeated them before; we'll defeat them again.' By the end he was shouting.

"Dharmateja's face did not change. I admire his ability to give advice calmly and show no reaction whether the advice is accepted or rejected. He merits the name *Vidura* that has been bestowed on him. Somehow, through his detachment, he developed wisdom.

"The rest of us pretended to ignore the break in protocol and looked at Kutaja.

"Kutaja said, 'We should consider this development. Any disaffection that the people of the enemy have with their leaders should be exploited. An independent Panchala will always be our enemy – a puppet ruler dependent on us is the best kind of ruler.'

"Now it was Suyodhana's turn, but he sat and glowered at us and said nothing. He had said all he wanted to say and we could go along with him, if we wanted to, but he had decided what he wanted to do.

"Dhritarashtra said, 'Can we help my brother's children out in a small way? My brother appeared in a dream last night and asked me to end this war.'

"Suyodhana rolled his eyes and muttered to himself. I could only make out 'Stupid old man.' Then he glared at his father.

"Dhritarashtra sensed his son's scorn and the throne appeared to grow around him as he cringed. He continued, 'Of course, we cannot let them hurt or exploit us in any way. Suyodhana, dear boy, you must decide that.'

"'Father, shut up!' Suyodhana said. Dhritarashtra sank into the ever-growing throne.

"Nobody said anything – I was embarrassed, I can only guess what the others thought.

"Then it was my turn and they all turned to look at me. Dharmateja's head nodded to one side – he was hinting that only I could control Suyodhana now and bring the discussion back into focus. That was when I made a mistake – I made the wrong decision. This is how it happened.

"My excuse for my error is that the last thing I expected was treachery. I can only ascribe it to Shi…Shi…Shi… the man's features that must have reminded me of Amba. In my defence, I should say that nobody expected treachery, Suyodhana included.

"'This is an opportunity to end the war victoriously, at little cost,' I said. 'We should follow up.'

"Now that first opinions had been expressed, the discussion was opened up. Kutaja picked up on my proposal. 'Who can we send? It will have to be somebody who can assess these traitors. Are they serious? Are they strong enough? Will they stay committed? Will they double-cross us, either by plan or in the heat of battle?'

"Dharmateja asked the relevant question. He said, 'What do we want from this meeting? Do we want to end this war?'

"Suyodhana did not disguise his attitude. 'It doesn't matter what we agree to. Once we have Kampilya, the Nagas will pay for their intransigence and the insult to Samvarana.'

"Dharmateja said, 'One should not negotiate in bad faith.'

"'I do not care for your moralising, old man. Just stop it.'

"Kutaja continued pressing the issue he thought was pre-eminent, 'You still need to send somebody. Who?'

"Karna spoke up. 'Let's send Dharmateja. He is expendable. And, he can prove that he is indeed Vidura, by getting us victory.'

"Suyodhana smiled. 'Yes! Dharmateja it is.'

"I objected. Dharmateja was the son of a maidservant. He was not a warrior. Dharmateja was on this council because I put him here many years ago. Suyodhana did not want to confront me directly, so he had not bothered to take Dharmateja off the council. Everybody knew that Dharmateja, however wise, would not be a credible negotiator.

"Suyodhana refused to consider anybody else. He turned to me. 'I want you to take this proposal to the man. Let him propose somebody else. You tell them that Dharmateja is your nominee.'

"Dhritarashtra said, 'That is an excellent idea. Yes, Uncle, please do as King Suyodhana says.'

"I could oppose Suyodhana, but not his father, the King even if uncrowned. Especially if that father was being browbeaten by his arrogant son, I still owed him that measure of respect.

"I went to the room where the man waited and presented the proposal to the man. He shook his head slowly when I mentioned

Dharmateja. 'Sir,' he said, 'Lord Dharmateja may be the King's brother, but he is known to be the child of a concubine. He has never been a warrior. How can you make such a suggestion – it tells me that you are not considering our offer seriously. Are we to be treated as children playing with a ball?'

"'The King's council has asked you to counter with your own proposal if you wish.'

"'It is not my place to advise your high command. The martial arts teacher Kutaja, or somebody else with his credibility, would be acceptable.'

"While I was gone, Suyodhana and Karna had revised their opinion of the offer. The successful siege of Indraprastha had emboldened Suyodhana and all his brothers. Now Karna and he thirsted for more battle and greater successes. Instead of a heroic victory over their enemies, and in particular over Panchala, this proposal would corrupt their victory.

"I returned to the council. I said, 'Dharmateja is not acceptable. My recommendation is to take his offer seriously – his clan's leaders want trade not war. The man has been sent to negotiate peace and they offer a path.'

"The rest of the council did not share Suyodhana's attitude regarding the inevitability of victory. The result was an impasse and Dhritarashtra wavered between giving in to his son and accepting the advice of the council. Dhritarashtra said, 'Uncle, you have the greatest experience of war and strategy. At the same time, my son has shown his mettle and knowledge of tactics by winning a great victory. What is the right balance between strategy and tactics? What should we do that maintains the greatest freedom of action?'

"Suyodhana groaned. He said, 'Father, you have never taken part in a war – without any experience of either tactics or strategy in war, you are spouting theory. There is no need to think about strategy – after we win, we will level Kampilya to the ground and erase all knowledge of Panchala. That is our strategy. As far as tactics are concerned – we do not need this man's help.'

"Dhritarashtra shrank even further into his seat. I felt sorry for him. I said, 'Whatever your strategy might be, you cannot ignore any tactical advantage, however small. I have met the man in private and my opinion has not changed. There is benefit in his proposal. There is risk as well.

"'Kutaja is our arms-master and war strategist. I rate him more valuable than myself. We cannot send him as an emissary. If we cannot agree on any other emissary, we should get whatever advantage we can out of his presence here. But, that is not my recommendation.'

"I continued, 'We must suggest another name.'

"Suyodhana and Karna huddled with each other, ignoring the rest of the council and me. They looked up smiling broadly and Karna said, 'The King's father has a companion: Sanjaya. He has the ear of the King's father. Who has greater authority to command the King than his father? Not only that, Sanjaya has claimed for many years that he can see activities from a distance. He will be safe from any kind of trap for he will not fall into it.'

"With each reference by Karna to Suyodhana as King, Suyodhana's smile grew wider and wider. Dhritarashtra's face had darkened and his eyes downcast. Suyodhana had taken over the role in public, but until this day, Karna and his brothers had maintained the fiction that Dhritarashtra was the King. That bastion had fallen.

"Sanjaya accompanied Dhritarashtra everywhere and was sitting behind Dhritarashtra. He looked alarmed. Then he said, 'Sir, I do not claim to see at a distance – I am not a god. I have created a *yantra*, a tool that allows me to watch from a distance. If you wish, I can show it to you and explain it as well.'

"On hearing Sanjaya's words, Suyodhana and Karna sniggered and laughed. They were being impolite and insulting to their own proposed envoy, a close friend and companion of Suyodhana's father. Sanjaya had been a member of the Kavi Sangha who had left when he failed to advance – he was not good at memorising, his diction was poor, and he was a poor wordsmith. He could not, or refused to, create the archival and historical poetry that was the Kavi Sangha's reason for being. The Kavi Sangha does not expel anyone who had been through its school – they leave of their own accord and that is what Sanjaya had done. He had become friends with Dhritarashtra and had stayed a loyal friend even as the King had aged and allowed his son to arrogate royal powers to himself. As Dhritarashtra became more and more of a figurehead, his erstwhile friends abandoned him and finally he was left with Sanjaya. Sanjaya had nothing to gain and nothing to lose; he was not a warrior; he was not a trader; he had never cared for power or wealth; he had no family – ergo, he was expendable. Nobody listened to him.

"It was not a proposal, it was an insult. Despite that, the council agreed, while Dhritarashtra did not say a word. I was directed to negotiate with the man again. I did as I was directed and took the proposal back to the man. He rejected it.

"Despite his discouragement, the man was not ready to give up. He tried once more, asking for Karna. I was in favour as was Kutaja and Dharmateja. This time, Suyodhana rejected it. 'Karna is my right arm,' he said. 'It is a ridiculous idea that we will send a warrior from the council. Tell him I refuse. Ask him to choose somebody lower down the hierarchy – even one of my brothers, perhaps.'

"I stood up. I said, 'I see no path to agreement. I will send him back.' I turned to leave the room and could hear Suyodhana and Karna still sniggering. When I was at the entrance, Suyodhana said, 'Uncle! Listen to me.' I turned to face him – he was smiling, a crooked slant to his lips, and sparkling eyes. He gave Karna a sideways glance and said, 'If you think it is such a good proposition, you go!' Karna laughed at the suggestion and slapped Suyodhana's back, saying, 'You are indeed a genius.'

"I was disheartened. I carried the refusal back to the man. In his turn, he was disappointed and depressed. His disappointment tugged at my heart. I know now why I was so accepting of this man – he had reminded me of Amba and so I was willing to trust him. I recalled past occasions when Karna, Suyodhana's closest friend, had expressed his opinion of me, 'At his age, he will be useless in battle.' Kutaja would defend me, saying, 'At his age, he is priceless in war.' The distinction was lost on Suyodhana. My counsel was not wanted and I felt that I could be most effective if I ended this war. At my age, this was the most I could hope to do. I made my decision.

"I told the man, 'I can come.' I had credibility with the council, even when they voted against me; I could converse with any and all the senior elders of the family. My strategic competence was not in question. If I came back with an agreement, it would be a good one for Hastinapur and Suyodhana would not be able to reject it.

"The man considered my proposal. I don't know what I would have done if he had rejected it. The man said, 'Sir, you are certainly the most senior member of the council. However, it is generally believed that you and Suyodhana frequently clash in the council. Will an agreement you make be acceptable to Suyodhana and his brothers?'

"Even though the man said he doubted that I could be an effective envoy, his attitude changed. His demeanour had changed from a gloomy slump to an erect stance, almost a bounce; his eyes lit up with hope.

"I said, 'I am the most senior commander of Hastinapur's forces. I have credibility.'

"'Yes, you'll do,' he said, looking at me as though I were a bird downed by an arrow, ready to be cooked for a meal. 'I'll take you to the meeting place.'

"He then laid down some rules. 'We will go by ourselves. The meeting place is on the right bank, the Hastinapur side of the Ganga; the four senior leaders of the Panchala clans will come to meet us. It will take a few days to get there.'

"I said, 'I am not young – I cannot walk at a military pace, or carry my own supplies. If we are going into the forest for more than one day, we will need a cart or carriers. Unless, you can carry all we need.'

"He frowned at me. He must have expected a much simpler expedition. He did not seem to have considered the logistics of this conclave.

"'It will be about three days. We will be on the King's Path for much of the way and you can rest in one of the many peddlers' huts.'

"'I set those up, but nobody has been maintaining them during the war. They will be run-down, if not destroyed.'

"'Good!' he said. 'We will not encounter anybody.'

"'Can you carry supplies for three days? We will need to share sentry duty at night, for there are both wolves and tigers in the forest.'

"The frown-lines around his mouth became deeper. It reminded me of something but I could not make the connection. Now I know the reason – Amba had the same lines on her face when she was disapproving something.

"'I cannot take a wedding party to the meeting site!'

"'How are your negotiators coming?'

"'All they do is cross the river at a point across from the meeting spot. Not more than one ghati to cross and another to return. They will only be exposed to watchers for a short time.'

"That did not tell me anything about the location. Between Hastinapur and Kampilya, there are thousands of crossing spots. Only some were ever put to use, mostly for trading, but even that had stopped. These days all the crossings have been abandoned.

"'We'll take a cart, an onager, and two helpers. We will avoid the King's huts, but sleep in our own tents,' he said. 'The last night we will camp half a kros from the meeting point. We will leave our helpers at our campsite and head out. We will plan to arrive a little before noon. I expect the ferry will cross at noon exactly. If all goes well, the meeting will only last one or two ghatis. We will then return and spend the night at the same campsite.'

"That is what we did. For three days, we walked in the forest along a path that the man seemed to know. At the end of the third day, the man, who had been tense all along, was relaxed. He had been concerned that we would be late, but seemingly we were not. We were a short distance from the river and that morning, all of us took the opportunity to bathe in the cool water. Then the guards replenished our water supply and fed the onager and washed it down. I waited. In the middle of the morning, the man said to me, 'It is time to go by ourselves. We are only a short distance from the meeting place.'

"My guards looked at me for guidance. We had prepared for the eventuality that I would be separated from them, so they knew what to do. I said to the men, 'You will wait here – I do not expect to be back until evening. Set up the tents so that we can spend the night here, before we return.'

"The man said, 'There is no need for that. If all goes well, we will be back by early afternoon.'

"I put on my armour and tied a scabbard for my short sword at my right hip. At the other hip I tied on a small quiver with a few arrows. Armour and swords do not make for easy travel through these forests. The man laughed and said, 'There is no reason for these precautions. See, I am unarmed. So will everybody else be who comes to this meeting.'

"I look back and think that under normal circumstances, every one of these statements from the man would have aroused my suspicions. The circumstances were not normal, and I continued to be blinded by the hint of Amba.

"The guards set to doing what they had been told to do while the man and I left for the meeting. We walked cautiously for about six ghatis. The sun had not yet reached the zenith when the man raised his hand and we stopped. We were at the edge of a clearing. From the absence of tall trees and a uniform growth of small trees, I guess it must have been left fallow for a year or two at the most. A Naga band must have lived there for there was a large thatched hut still standing. These huts deteriorate slowly, but this one appeared to be in good condition with intact roof and fresh mud daubed on the walls. It must have been maintained even after the band had left. We headed to the hut.

"The ground was very dry and as we walked, we cracked twigs lying on the path. I thought I heard a twig cracking somewhere, not below us, not by our feet. I had arranged with my guards that one of them would follow us. They were experienced trackers and would not have made a noise, but the possibility that it was my own guard allayed my suspicions. It was enough of a signal that I loosened my scabbard so that the sword would pull out easily. The man did not notice my action. There was no way to unsling my bow from my back without alerting the man, so I relied on my short sword.

"The man, who had been cautious about making noise up to this point, walked as though the need for caution was over.

I tried to stay cautious. The man glanced at me and smiled. He said, 'We are at the meeting point. We appear to be early – they will come at noon. You can relax.'

"I said, 'Maybe. Will you be careful and aware, even if you think it is safe?'

"He shrugged and said, 'As you wish.' He was still smiling. We had been together for three days and I had seen him smile, but not the smile that now appeared on his face.

"He was still smiling as he slowed down and it was a fortunate thing. Just as we entered the tent a branch shook slightly to the right of the hut, but when I turned to look I saw nothing. The hut was empty, so I turned around and backed into it.

"As a result I saw what I would not have seen otherwise. Right in front of me, across the clearing, an armed man moved from behind one tree to behind another. To the right and left of the tent I heard something that sounded like an animal moving through the brush. We were early and Shikhandin had said his negotiators would be here at noon, not for another ghati or more. This was a trap. There were no talks to be held on an impossible future peace.

"I had to deal with the man right away, not when the trap had closed. I turned around to face him, and drew my sword from its scabbard. Shikhandin – I can pronounce his name now – had entered the hut a few steps ahead of me, expecting me to follow behind him. He began to turn to the right to face me when he heard the sword being drawn. He was too slow and I did not give him any time – I lunged at his back and drove the sword through to his chest. It was a fatal blow for it went in the right side of his body and pierced his lung. Fortunately, it did not reach the heart. Now he would die a slow death. He fell towards me – when I was younger I would have sidestepped the dying body, but these days I am not fast enough and I only managed to catch him as he fell.

"I intended to use him as a shield if anybody entered through the front of thc tent. He lay gasping in my arms – I wanted to know who would be leading the ambush, but a gold chain that I had noticed a few times during the last three days around his neck was constricting his throat. I loosened the chain and found that it was attached to a pendant. I glanced at the pendant as I pulled the chain free.

"The tent seemed to glow with light – I felt that I was out in a field after the first rains of the monsoon when the earth sings with joy at the sight of the sun. Amba. Amba? Amba! Amba had chosen to re-enter my life at an inopportune moment.

"'Where did you get this?' I said. Shikhandin, I can say his name now, answered. He was dying and there were so many things he could have thought about, but he let them be and answered my question.

"'From my mother," Shikhandin said, sucking air with every breath for I had breached his lungs.

"'Where did she get it?'

"'From my father.'

Impossible! That was impossible. I had to know who his father was.

"'Who is your father? Where is he?'

"The man took another deep breath but it was not enough. He would be losing consciousness soon. *He had to answer my questions.* I had many unanswered questions. *Was Amba dead, had she been killed in the forest and her jewellery and other possessions scattered around the world, or was she alive?* There could not be another pendant like it – we had designed it together, the motif of a lotus in profile with two snakes wrapped around its stem. I put one hand over the wound to close his lungs and prevent the air from escaping. It may have helped for with his next breath he said, 'I don't know.'

"I groaned. What did that mean? That he did not know his father? Not know where he was? What did he mean?

"Then he said, 'Hastinapur.'

"That was when I noticed what I had missed all these days he had spent building my trust in him. His eyes, shaped like Amba's eyes; his lips and nose like my father's; his hands, large with shaped nails, also like my father's; the tilt of head with which Amba would express puzzlement. *Was it these familiar facets that had made me trust a supposed renegade from Panchala?*

"'Who is your mother?' I asked, though I knew the answer.

Did he say *Amba,* or did I imagine it? If he said *Amma,* wouldn't it sound like *Amba*? That was the last question he answered before he closed his eyes and lost consciousness.

"It is possible that if I had not wasted time with that question and its answer, I would have been prepared for the ambushers. Unfortunately, he had delayed me enough. I had planned to use him as a shield but I had not brought him around and I saw some movement at the periphery of my vision. There was a sword by my left hand and I reached for it. Arjuna the Pandava and Krishna the Yadava had entered the hut with bows drawn. It seemed to me that time slowed at that moment.

"In my mind, the scene is played out on a stage. I reach out with my left hand for the sword, but even before I can touch it, an arrow, moving, oh, so slowly, has cut through the seam of my front and back armour pads under my left armpit. I pick up the sword but the pain is intense and I command my mind to ignore the pain, but there is no strength in my arm as my breath leaves my body and I gasp. I stand up with the sword dragging in front of me, the first time a sword has felt like a burden. I let it drop. This scene plays itself out repeatedly, in an endless cycle.

"Arjuna and Krishna kept their bows ready but kept their distance. Some part of me could not understand – *You can come closer* I tried to say. Pain radiated from the wound. Breathing accomplished nothing. I reached around the front of my body with my right hand and could just barely reach the shaft – I wanted to pull it out but my hold was very weak and even then, when the arrow moved, the pain increased – it multiplied in leaps and bounds, and I must have fainted. The next thing I knew I was tied to the bed here, with my son Shikhandin's body at my side for me to contemplate."

The Archivist was quiet after that. Devavrat and he contemplated each other. *If I had become a memoriser, I would have been like him,* Devavrat thought.

The Archivist turned his head for he did not want Devavrat to see the tears that were clouding his vision. *A long life with so much power and he cries over a lost love.*

The door flap was pulled aside and the Vyaasa came in.

"Let us break for the day," he said. "Tomorrow we can get to the next generation."

THE LAST OF THE KAURAVAS

Kaushambi/Hastinapur
circa 850 B.C.E.

Bhargava said, "Splendid! Neither the Pandavas nor the Kauravas are Kauravas. The Hastinapur Empire, founded by a Kuru, was never ruled by a Kuru."

Vaishampaayana said, "Don't laugh. The migration from Panchnad to Bhaaratavarsha succeeded because that empire created by a Kuru supported it."

"What happened to the Nagas and the Rakshasas?"

"We will get to that. Just look all around you. They are everywhere."

"What about Mahendra and Dhritarashtra?"

"They are the next generation."

END OF BOOK 1

Appendices

APPENDIX A

ENDNOTES

A.1. Trade Routes in India

The trade route from the mouth of the Great River (Mahanadi in the modern-day state of Odisha) to Takshashila (Taxila in northern Punjab in modern-day Pakistan) was called *Uttarapatha,* the Northern Road, and much later, the Grand Trunk Road. Branches of the road split off at Kaalindini, one to the south to Panchnad, one to the north to Kashyapura. The main road continued to Takshashila. Beyond Takshashila, the trade route branched again – one route went further north into the Pamirs and joined the Silk Road near Samarkand. The other branch entered Afghanistan and crossed the Iranian desert through Malyan to Susa and points beyond. These connected Northern Jambudvipa to the cultures of the North and West.

The trade route to the south, called *Dakshinapatha,* had one terminus in the imperial capital (initially Indraprastha, then Hastinapur, later Mathura, and finally Pataliputra) where it connected with Uttarapatha. The southern route wound south along the Charmanavati (Chambal) river to Malwa and then further south through the Sahyadris and across the Vindhyas into the Deccan plateau. There was no single southern terminus, but paths spread out in all directions through hilly passes. There is some evidence that the Kolar gold mines in Karnataka were being exploited and the gold sent to Panchnad using this route as early as 2000 BCE. Branches exited via passes in the Western Ghats to ports on the Arabian (Western) Sea, from which ships would sail using the monsoon winds to Dilmun (Oman), Egypt, Ethiopia, and African ports along the eastern shores of Africa.

A.2. Standardisation

A recurring theme in the Panchnad culture was *standardisation.* This can be seen on the ground in the archaeological sites of Mohenjodaro, Harappa, Chanhudaro, Lothal, etc., where uniformity reigns to a far greater extent than other contemporary urban cultures such as Sumer. Bricks are manufactured in a standard ratio of 1:2:4, weights are found in the sequence 1, 2, 4, 8, 10, 16, and 32 (it is surely a coincidence that the "2" weight is within ten per cent of the British ounce), towns are constructed on a precise north-south axis, every town's architecture is very similar, and so on.

We have assumed that this approach applied to other areas of endeavour, such as the calendar, seasons, time, distance, arts, and even the conduct of war.

A.2.1. Annual Calendar of Panchnad & Hastinapur

Melas (fairs) are held on the two equinoxes and the two solstices. The winter solstice marks the Sun beginning its journey north, but also marks the beginning of the winter harvest period (January to March or April, depending on latitude). The spring equinox heralds the arrival of spring and is considered the start of the year. The summer solstice is the beginning of the monsoon-planting season. The autumn equinox marks the end of the monsoon harvest and the beginning of the winter planting season, ending with the winter harvest. In the parts of South Asia where three crops are possible, a summer planting and harvest season extends from March to June (spring equinox to summer solstice). Traders leave home after the winter harvest to reach their destination(s) before the monsoons begin (a leading separation motif in Sanskrit love poetry) and start on the return journey after the monsoons end to arrive home in time for the winter harvest.

A.2.2. Seasons of the Year

Season in Sanskrit	Season in English	Tamil Months	Gregorian Months
Vasanta	Spring	Chithirai, vaigāsi	Mid Apr–Mid Jun
Grishma	Summer	Āni, ādi	Mid Jun–Mid Aug
Varsha	Monsoon	Āvani, puratāci	Mid Aug–Mid Oct
Sharada	Autumn	Aippasi, kārthigai	Mid Oct–Mid Dec
Hemanta	Winter	Mārkazhi, tai	Mid Dec–Mid Feb
Sishira	Prevernal	Māsi, panguni	Mid Feb–Mid Apr

A.2.3. Measures of Time: Ghati and Vighati

G^h^aṭi and *Vig^h^aṭi,* pronounced "Gut-e" and "We-gut-e", and spelled "Ghati" and "Vighati", are the measures of time that have been used in India from ancient times. I have appropriated them for this period as we do not know what terms were used.

The day, defined from sunrise to the sunrise of the next day, was defined as approximately 60 ghatis (it is approximate because the "day" defined in this way, varies during the year). Each *ghati* in turn was divided into 60 *vighatis*. For comparison, one *vighati* is 24 seconds and one *ghati* is 24 minutes.

A.2.4. Measures of Distance: Yojana

The earth rotates once every 3600 vighatis (through 360 degrees, the modern measure of angles of a circle). In one vighati the earth will have rotated one-tenth of a degree. In that one vighati, a vertical rod that cast a small shadow pointing north at high noon (say local time in New Delhi, India) will cast a slightly bigger shadow angled slightly east by one-tenth degree with respect to north. At the same time, some distance to the west, it will be high noon (local time) and a vertical rod placed there will cast its smallest shadow pointing due north. The distance between these two rods was considered one *Yōjənə* (pronounced "Yo(re)-ju(t)-nu(t)" and spelled "Yojana") in Panchnad.

The above definition of yojana as a measure of distance is dependent on the latitude. Such a dependent definition, while useful in a culture spreading in an east-west direction (like Europe, West Asia, the Russian steppes, etc.), is not useful for a culture oriented from north to south (like South Asia, or for that matter, Egypt). A definition based on a north-south orientation would be a constant, but establishing it would depend on the exact determination of longitude (or, the circumference of the earth), which requires the use of synchronised clocking. Such a capability did not exist until late in the history of Panchnad (when the Samavedins perfected their techniques for keeping time).

A standard definition of yojana can then be obtained by selecting a well-known spot, for instance, Takshashila (the famous centre of learning and thought in historical ancient India, and in this book considered the Panchnad centre of learning, culture, and philosophy, where Kavi Sangha members went for their advanced education). The standard yojana is measured on the ground at that latitude and composed of smaller standardised units, such as the hasta (or cubit). The latitude itself can be determined easily by measuring the declination of the sun at noon on the spring or autumnal equinoxes and other spots at the same latitude can be identified, if necessary.

If measured at the equator, one-tenth of a degree would be about seven miles (11.13 km). At the latitude of Takshashila, it would be the "standard yojana" of about six miles (9.24 km), or 21,120 hastas/cubits (see below). All of Panchnad used this definition of yojana.

An average "casual" walking pace is about fifty steps per vighati or three thousand steps per ghati. The average step of the average South Asian is about two feet, so the average walking speed is approximately one mile/ghati. In six ghatis (one-tenth of a day of sixty ghatis) an average person could walk about one yojana.[131]

Allowing for meals and other breaks, and only walking in the daytime, a traveller could hike between three and four yojanas, i.e. about twenty miles/day. Walking at that pace, it would take about three months to go from Kamarupa in the east of South Asia (in Bangladesh) to Takshashila in the west of South Asia (in Pakistan), about sixteen hundred miles.

Another measure integrating time and distance is the cartwheel – a fully loaded cart with large wheels (about four feet in diameter) pulled by a single bullock or onager will make between one to five turns of the wheel every vighati – the smaller wheels two feet in diameter will make about four to eight turns in the same time. A peddler's cart pulled by either animal will move four to eight miles/hour (not an unreasonable speed), but a single bullock will work less than four hours a day at that pace. A caravan of such carts will go slower, perhaps half the speed, at eight to sixteen miles/day. The trader can make the outbound trip starting in early to mid-October (after the monsoons end) and arriving in mid-April (just before the summer heat makes it difficult).

A.2.5. Measures of Distance: Classical Sanskrit

These definitions are from Kauṭilyā's *Aṛtaśāstra* (approximate equivalents in inches are also provided):

1 angula = a finger-width, 3/4 of an inch;

4 angula = 1 dhanurgraha [bow grip], 3 inches;

---

131 The reader should be aware that this definition of the "standard yojana" is speculative and based on coincidences. At the latitude of Takshashila, the sun will "move" in one vighati a distance that a person walking east (or west) can go in six ghatis.

8 angula = 1 dhanurmushti [fist with thumb raised], 6 inches;

12 angula = 1 vitasta [span-distance of stretched out hand between the tips of a person's thumb and little finger], 9 inches;

4 vitasta = 1 aratni / 2 hasta [cubit], 18 inches;

4 aratni = 1 danda / dhanus [bow], 6 feet;

10 danda = 1 raja, 60 feet;

2 raja = 1 paridesha, 120 feet;

2000 danda / dhanus = 1 krosa / gorutta = 4000 yards or 2 1/4 miles, nearly 3.66 km;

4 krosa = 1 yojana = 9 miles, nearly 15 km.

Note that by the time of Kauṭilyā, believed to be around 300 BCE, a yojana is no longer defined using the motion of the sun but composed from smaller measures built on human dimensions.

A.2.6. Fine Arts

Centuries later, the *Natyashastra* of Bharata-muni would codify the theatrical arts and techniques, establishing *standardisation* in theatre. This began, I assume, in the cultural ideal of standardisation inherited from Panchnad before 2000 BCE. The techniques and methods of instruction used by the guild of bards became the pattern of all theatrical instruction. Speech sounds had been classified into *swara* and *vyanjana* and systematised – this made it possible to teach memorisation in a uniform manner. Every bard was capable of reciting an epic poem in exactly the same way and that skill, of learning and reciting, was attributed to the mode of instruction.

This mode of instruction was applied to all the elements of the theatre – hand movements were named *mudras* and became the basis for a semi-secret alphabet of signs and signals; exercise routines that actors practised were named *adavus* and standardised for formal instruction; emotional states were named *rasas* and there were exactly nine of these – the art of expressing the rasas on stage was named *abhinaya*.

A.2.7. Vyuhadyuta: War by Mercenaries

A *vyuha* described the deployment of an armed force intending to attack or to defend from attack. The Panchnad mercenaries' guild had developed a theory and classification of vyuhas that suited their mode of battle in which troops hired by two cities would set up challenges or duels to determine victory as efficiently as possible. Actual battles between armies only occurred if one side developed an overwhelming superiority in numbers and/or position, but this was rare. Thus, the SSC had standardised war, with the result that full-scale all-out war never happened. Until the Great War.

A.3. Panchala versus Panchnad

The names are, unfortunately, very similar.

Panchnad is the land defined by five rivers. These are the Sarasvati, the Sindhu, the Sutudri, the Yamuna, and the Drishadvati – this extends from approximately Ropar (Kaalindini) in the north to the Arabian Sea in the south, the Aravalli range in the east to Multan (Moolasthan) in the west, bounded by the rivers. An additional note: Panchnad is not the same as "Punjab" – that province, divided between India and Pakistan, overlaps with Panchnad. Punjab also means the land of five rivers, but as it turns out, only the Sutudri (renamed Sutlej) and the Sindhu (renamed Indus) are in common. Punjab also extends further northwest into the Himalayan range, but stops well short of the sea in the south, whereas Panchnad goes all the way south to the sea.

Panchala is the name of a confederation of five Naga clans (a unit much larger than band or family). It became the name of the region controlled by these five clans – on the northern side of the Ganga from Ahichhatra in the north to (possibly) as far as modern-day Kashi.

A.4. Janas and Ganas

By the eighth century BCE, a number of polities in the Gangetic plain were called "janapada" and "maha-jana-pada". Conventionally these words are translated as "republics". There are a variety of poorly-supported explanations for how these entities were governed, ranging from elections of representatives, to village "panchayats", to rule by "prominent men".

The matriarchies of Panchnad are best described as *janapadas* – citizens cast votes in an election, typically conducted in a public arena. The citizen electors are the *jana,* sometimes translated as "people", but probably refers only to those members of the city who had the right to attend assemblies and vote. The electors might select a smaller group to form a governing council – the members of such a council might be selected by election of representatives, or could be the head of a guild or other group would be termed *mahājana,* or *mahān.*

Not all residents of a city were voting citizens – servants, slaves, and other residents without property rights or without membership in a founding family may not have had such rights. These unrepresented residents were called *gana.* Sometimes a group of ganas might organise under a leader, a *ganapati.* Despite representing a disenfranchised subgroup, a ganapati would have the power to unleash chaos in a city and so would be in a position to negotiate with the city council. At the same time, a ganapati was not necessarily respected – the power of a ganapati often resided in his/her skill in controlling a mob.

A.5. Matriarchy, Matrilinearity, & Matrilocality

Before the events of this story, all the ancient peoples in South Asia were matrilocal, matriarchal, and matrilineal.

A *matrilocal* culture would see a man residing with his "wife". Very few contemporary cultures are systematically matrilocal and even they make exceptions – among the Khasis of the northeast of India, for instance, a husband stays with his wife if she is an heiress – otherwise, the wife comes to stay with the husband. Locality after marriage affects how cultures view the marriage bond – a husband who stays with his wife is unlikely to have multiple wives (unless they are his wife's sisters), and a wife who stays with her husband is unlikely to have multiple husbands (unless they are her husband's brothers). Bands in an ancient world would have been matrilocal – the need to give birth and raise the children and family make it likely (but not necessary) that a woman and her sisters would look for a place to settle down (if only for a season) to raise their children. Men, on the other hand, only settle down when they must – the permanent or semi-permanent settlements created by the women provide the men with a convenient home to which to return. Thus the man's commitment to a band is opportunistic, while the women *are* the band!

A good example of such a structure can be seen among elephants – a family group consists of a number of females headed by a matriarch and associated male elephants. The males are not necessarily bound to their band – some of the males move from band to band, while other males stay in a single band. Sometimes, a band of females will have one or two males who are permanently a part of the band, but there can be the occasional band without any permanently attached males.

Elephant bands will generally encourage young male elephants to leave on attaining puberty. Sometimes they are allowed to visit, but sometimes they are not. When a male is in heat, he will attempt to visit a band of females, and sometimes the visitor is accepted, but sometimes not. An accepted male will sometimes stay with the band after mating but may also move around to other bands of females. Male elephants, especially young ones forced to leave their band and unable to visit another (I hesitate to name "shyness" as one possible cause), will often join a group of other young males like themselves – for companionship and for protection – until they are accepted by some band of females. Occasionally, a young male might be exceptionally anti-social and does not ever get accepted by any band, male or female – such males become loners and do not survive long.

Similar family/band structures exist among other animals. Matrilocality is also common among primates, especially when the male and female are equally or almost equally strong (as with bonobos in Africa).

Matrilocality of the above type can result in gangs of unwelcome males that become a threat to other bands. Cultures develop adaptive responses to this situation – an extreme form would be killing anti-social males at an early age. The three cultures of South Asia developed different solutions – Panchnad was a trading culture and men who became traders were rarely home, thus providing a role for men who could not be controlled using purely societal means. In addition, the development of the guild of mercenaries provided an alternate way of life for anti-social men to function within the system.

The Rakshasas segregated the men into fraternities to which an adolescent had to apply for admission – these fraternities were typically associated with a number of neighbourhood bands and provided some support for their members. Admission involved initiation rites that could be deadly – the weak and/or unsocial males might suffer death or injury. Following the test, the injured male might be refused membership – a Rakshasa boy who failed to get admission would eventually die in the forest.

The Nagas had developed a uniquely cooperative culture and an unsocial male was an unusual event.[132] As a result, the

[132] Some ethnologists and ethno-geneticists have hypothesised a possibly evolutionary adaptation towards sociability among East Asian populations.

culture had no mechanism for dealing with such males – after centuries of expansion, a large (and therefore dangerous) gang of rogue Nagas formed – this resulted in the creation of an army by five large tribes that dealt with the threat. To control the army, the five tribes formed a confederation named Panchala. Panchala was ruled like a super-band, with an established settlement in the militarised city Kampilya, with a matriarch as its head, but the head of the army exercising real power.

Technically, *matriarchy* is rule by women. The women who stay in a settlement rule themselves in a variety of ways – these can be described as a primitive democracy with power deriving from seniority and experience. In the absence of resource competition with surrounding bands, such a system works reasonably well. Change threatens when competition with surrounding bands raises its head – usually over resources, but it can also happen over questions of respect, of competing alliances, or trading rights. Often, as in the potlatch competitions of the New Guinea Trobrianders, the males are the ones who create and sustain the competition over the key question *"Whose potlatch was the best?"*

The people of Panchnad had developed a form of matriarchy that was comparatively egalitarian – most real power lay in a council that advised the matriarch, and both men and women could be a part of the council.

Naga bands, as initially conceived, were also matriarchal. As described earlier, the capital Kampilya, of the confederation of Panchala, was organised like a matriarchy, but the real power, supported by an army, lay with the army chief. Battles over resources between Naga bands were rare, but when they occurred, the matriarch's brother took the lead in organising the men in each band. The matriarch's brother also organised the

---

This is a result of rice cultivation, requiring collective cooperation, as opposed to wheat cultivation that can be done by individual farmers without cooperation. It could also be the result of the cooperation required for riverine fishing – building weirs, managing fish stocks, etc..

holding of the band's potlatch and a successful festival would bring praise and respect to the band.

The Rakshasas (hunter-gatherers, unlike the slash-and-burn agriculturalist Nagas) were organised much like the Nagas with one exception – the large men's fraternities that were led by elected chiefs. These chiefs showed their skills in hunting and in organising the men when conflicts threatened – in peace time they also showed their skills by organising festivals and performances. It was in times of war that the chiefs showed that they were indispensable.

Matrilineal refers to the way inheritance works. An example of matrilinearity in the modern era was the Varma ruling family of the erstwhile state of Travancore-Cochin in South India. When the Varma king died, his eldest sister's son (i.e. the dead king's nephew) became the next king. It sounds a bit strange, but becomes comprehensible when we realise that Travancore-Cochin had been a matriarchy, but the matriarch (the eldest sister of the king) had become a figurehead without direct power. The earlier form of the inheritance rule would have been that *when the matriarch died, her daughter became the matriarch.*

A wrinkle in many matriarchal cultures is the role of the army chief. Armies and their chiefs are usually male. The army chief gains power relative to the matriarch when resource conflicts have to be repeatedly resolved by war. The army chief can come to command great military power and become a threat to the matriarch. Therefore, the army chief must be someone absolutely committed to the matriarch and the one least likely to be disloyal. In practice, this is the matriarch's brother. When a matriarch dies, her daughter becomes the matriarch. The mother's army chief would be the new matriarch's uncle, not her brother. Therefore, he might be less committed to his niece than he had been to his sister. He might be tempted to install one of his own children, if any. Therefore, when a matriarch died, her son (the brother of the new matriarch) would replace the army chief.

The existence of an army chief implies the existence of some form of warfare (conflict resolution by fighting). In Panchnad, the development of the matriarch's council suppressed the full-fledged development of the powerful army chief into a warlord. In addition, when bands became large the daughter bands would break away and this limited the power of a potential warlord – an additional inducement for bands to break up.

The army chief is a secondary locus of power in a band, technically subordinate to the matriarch, but practically independent. The system is inherently unstable and if resource pressures continue and conflicts with neighbouring bands stay unresolved, the army chief as warlord is a threat to the matriarch. The establishment of Panchala in order to deal with the menace of rogue Nagas created a super-band with a Great Matriarch and a Great Warlord with a large standing army.

In order to mitigate the threat posed by a powerful warlord, some matriarchies may have required that a warlord not have any children, however that was accomplished.[133]

All three cultures – Panchnad, Naga, and Rakshasa – were matrilineal.

A.6. Patriarchy, Patrilinearity, & Patrilocality

Hastinapur did not begin as a city, but was a traders' caravanserai sited in a frontier region. There were two reasons for this. First, going further east was difficult (and not necessary as long as the Nagas came to the site to trade). Second, creating a permanent settlement would have antagonised the local Nagas who practised slash-and-burn agriculture and moved every ten to twenty years. After Samvarana defeated Panchala, Hastinapur became the hegemon of the region surrounding it and was a *de facto* permanent settlement. However, the fiction that it was a

133 A confused conception of such a rule may have been the origin of the story of Devavrat's vow to be celibate, as well as the origin of the story of the killing of Shantanu's children. However, that would be another story.

trading caravanserai continued to be maintained (at least until Shantanu's father Pratipa declared formal independence from Panchnad).

Like all caravanserais, its male head trader led Hastinapur. If the head trader died on the road, his son or the closest trusted male relative took over – this became the pattern for inheritance in Hastinapur after Samvarana's victory. Hastinapur thus became a patrilineal and patriarchal chiefdom with the headship passing from father to son. Despite all the difficulties it caused for Hastinapur with its parental Panchnad cities, this tradition proved hard to change; instead, the divergence increased – for instance, Hastinapur's rulers began to practise patrilocality – the wife of the head trader came to live with him and her power was limited (unlike in the other Panchnad matrilocal and matrilineal cities). The women who agreed to such an arrangement had to be unusual – they were accepting a familial form that was different and joining a power system in which their power was limited. They were usually not in line to be matriarchs in their own family – the possibility of achieving some power and status, however limited, may have acted as an incentive to marry a Hastinapuri.

A.7. Dress

Both men and women dressed with two primary pieces of cloth, usually made from woven cotton – a longer piece that was wrapped around the waist to form a skirt (it would be called the *panchagam),* and a cloth wrapped about the upper body (which would be called the *angavastram).* The guild of weavers produced these to order and decorated them as required by the wearer.

A bard at a recital of a historic poem would wear a new white (undecorated) panchagam and angavastram.

Men and women tied the panchagam and angavastram differently – the male style of panchagam used a longer cloth whose first section was used to gird the loins, while the woman's style was more like a skirt hanging off a girdle. The men used the angavastram as a kind of shawl, while the women used the central section as a crosspiece to support the breasts.

An angavastram padded with cotton and wrapped securely around the chest and shoulders functioned as rudimentary armour. Cotton armour was the main protection of the "Indian"[134] infantry of the Persian Empire under Cyrus the Great as described by Herodotus – I believe that one of the earliest uses of felted cotton may have been as armour.

A.8. The Names of the Characters

The reader familiar with the Mahabharata might be puzzled by some names. I believe that during the composition of a *Jaya,* the names of the participants were modified to highlight some characteristic of, or action by the character. In addition, since the Jaya is composed by the winners, the names of the warriors of the losing side might be changed to denigrate them. Occasionally, these became the name by which they were remembered.

For instance, the martial arts teacher *Drona* may have been renamed from Kutaja, meaning "highest mountain peak". An alternate meaning of *kutaja* is "born in a jar". The word "drona" also means "jar". More specifically, the *drona* was a wooden jar that held soma during a fire sacrifice. Since soma was an intoxicating drink, the jar and the people who handled it were supposed to be drunk from its fumes and "Drona" might have been a mocking name for the teacher. Similarly, Duryodhana ("bad warrior") may have been renamed from Suyodhana ("good warrior").

The reason for such transformation by a poet is that a person can be identified by names as well as attributes. Using

134 These were from the provinces (*satrapies*) of Arachosia and Gandhara, west of the river Indus. The men were most likely mercenaries.

a descriptive name appropriate for the action being described keeps the audience interested and signals what to expect. It allows the poet to avoid repeating a name multiple times in a single verse. In addition, names can be used to signal the audience what to think of a new character that appears on stage.

A.9. Naga Culture as Imagined in this Book

The Hastinapuris gave the name "Naga" to the forest dwelling, matriarchal bands living along the Ganga. These bands occupied the forests along both banks of the Ganga, ranging from south of Hastinapur to a little east of Kashi. They translated the matriarch's title as "Nagini" ("Mother or Female Serpent"), and the title of the male chief, usually the brother of the Nagini, to "Great Serpent", i.e. "Mahanaga". This was the origin of the name "Naga" as applied to the culture – it is likely that the bands had a different name for themselves.

The Nagas practised slash-and-burn agriculture. Each band would burn a grove in the forest near a source of water for growing food plants, raising chickens, and barley. They would settle nearby, usually at the edge of the grove, for a few years, from five to twenty, depending on the fertility of the grove's layer of ash. Then they would move to a new location, not adjacent to the exhausted grove – the grove was left fallow for at least two more cycles, generally over twenty years.

The women made most decisions in the band, which was a haven for the women and the children. The matriarch's brother was the traditional head of the men's fraternity. Except for the matriarch's brother, the rest of the men joined the band on invitation. The popular men often moved from band to band, while the others acted to keep the matriarch and the women satisfied. Boys were expected to leave their bands after puberty and find other bands to join, but matriarchs and other powerful women could keep their sons in a band indefinitely. The men who were not invited by any band were considered "rogue", and lived by their wits without social support, and usually died soon after leaving their mother's band. Rogue men who survived for a long time could be dangerous, as they were often anti-social or otherwise had difficulty in social settings. If a group of rogue men formed a gang, they could be a big threat to bands; but most rogues could not cooperate with each other, and found it difficult to form a large band of rogues.

There were a number of rituals that the Nagini and the Mahanaga were expected to perform – four of these had to do with the equinoxes and the rest divided the quarters evenly. At the spring equinox, the Nagini and the Mahanaga emerged from a sacred fire, and led a bacchanalian nine days – most children were born about nine months later (around the winter solstice), and the number of children born was an indicator of the matriarch's inner strength.

A.10. Redistributive Festivals among the Nagas

Naga bands celebrated parties frequently with other Naga bands, both close and far. A group of nearby bands (typically five) would get together once a month; a larger group of twenty-five bands might meet twice a year; and festivals involving even larger groups might be held every few years. These events were organised by the men of the hosting band, sometimes in collaboration with the men of other bands. It provided an opportunity for the men to display their ability to organise, collaborate, make friends across bands, and create alliances that crossed family boundaries.

The word "potlatch" is derived from a redistributive feast held by the Trobriand Islanders of New Guinea. Similar festivals occur in other cultures as well, usually as part of a transition to settled agriculture. In the beginning, all the clans or bands would bring food and gifts for exchange; later, a clan might host the entire event by itself, and the attending clans would acknowledge the host's "big man" superiority. A feature of the Trobriand Island culture was that the men of one tribe led by a "big man" would challenge other tribes through potlatch events. Occasionally conflicts broke out and even though their conflicts rarely led to actual battles, the more successful "big men" or with bigger teams would usually win by intimidation. "Big Men" whose teams won often, grew in prestige and with time became "Big Chiefs", leaders of larger groups of men. From time to time, a prototypical "Big Chief" would host a potlatch to show off his superior organisational capabilities as well as breadth of popularity. Over time, Big Chiefs became kings and did not have to sacrifice themselves to host a potlatch – taxes would pay for redistributive feasts.

The confederation of Panchala came into existence by a military merger of five Naga clans – the men got together to handle the menace of "rogue males", who had been organised into a gang by a charismatic leader. It is an example of how the ritual of potlatch maintains a critical skill and makes possible coordinated responses to unusual events.

A.11. Language Questions

We do not know what language was spoken in 2000 BCE, or for that matter in 850 BCE. We know that after 850 BCE, many texts were written, though few samples from that early era exist. Those we know of are in Sanskrit, and after 300 BCE in Pali. I have used Gondi for personal and intimate forms of address (such as "Avva" for mother, and "Bābō" for father) used by Shantanu's children. Satyavati's brother, a Meena-Naga, uses the Dramila (or Tamil, as Tamil speakers are called in many ancient texts). For the more formal words (ghati, yojanas, etc.) spoken by the upper classes in 850 BCE, I have used Sanskritic forms, translated when it seemed necessary. I've used "Namaskar" and "Guru" as well as the honorific "-ji". This too may be an anachronism; in addition, Sanskrit does not use "-ji", so it assumes a vernacular language that was not Sanskrit. Keep in mind that over four thousand years, a language will drift along with its speakers. Some of the changes are well known – for instance, 'k' drifts to "w". There are many such changes possible and not all that is possible happens.

On the whole, I don't believe that this experiment has been wholly successful – whatever language was used as the base, including English, some result struck me as ill-fitted. So I only do this when a candidate word or concept is first used – a footnote provides the meaning. Subsequently, I use the English form.

A.12. The Myth and History of the Kauravas

A.12.1 Myth: Pururavas the Handsome

Pururavas loved Urvashi, the semi-divine *apsara,* who agreed to live with him on the condition that he would never show himself to her naked. Indra, the king of the gods, was unhappy that Urvashi no longer graced his assemblies but lived with a human. He used his *Vajra* (the thunderbolt) one night when Pururavas and Urvashi were lying together and she saw Pururavas naked and immediately left him.

A.12.2. Myth: Nahusha the Proud

Indra, the King of the gods, had committed the sin of killing a brahmin when he killed Tvastr and Vritra – as a result he could no longer appear in the courts of heaven and hid himself in shame. After many years, the gods chose Nahusha as their King. Initially a good king, he became proud and lusted after Indra's wife Sachi. Sachi prayed to the great god Shiva and was told to ask Nahusha to come to her on a palanquin hoisted by the seven Sages. The Sages were old and slow, and Nahusha was in a hurry – he kicked the shortest one, Agastya, and shouted *"Sarpa! Sarpa!"* – meaning faster. Agastya lost his patience and cursed Nahusha to become a *sarpa* (a snake). Immediately, Nahusha fell to earth as a giant python.

Later Agastya modified his curse and allowed Nahusha to be freed by his descendant Yudhishthira who would then counsel him about life and death. Centuries later, Nahusha attacked Bhima and they fought. When Yudhishthira appeared and tried to save Bhima, Nahusha was freed of the curse. This is clearly a myth as the young Yudhishthira counsels the aged Nahusha and helps him attain equilibrium.

A.12.3. Myth: Yayati the Needy

Yayati figures in two myths, the first being about his marriage to Devayani, the daughter of Shukra, the preceptor of the demons, and his cheating with Sarmishta (the daughter of the king of the demons, punished to be Devayani's maidservant). He had two sons with Devayani (Yadu and Turvasu) and three sons with Sarmishta (Druhyu, Anu, and Puru).

The second myth begins when Yayati was granted a thousand years of youth by the gods. When he reached the end of that period and began to suffer from the debilities of old age, he found that he was still unsatisfied – he wanted a few more years of youth to satisfy his desires. He had an additional gift from the gods – he could extend his youth if he could find somebody to exchange their youth for his old age. Yayati asked, but nobody would give up their youth; finally, he asked his own sons. Yadu, Druhyu, Turvasu and Anu refused, with particularly harsh words from Anu.

Puru, on the other hand, freely gave up his youth. After a few more years of extended youth, Yayati felt sorry for the son whom he had deprived of youth in this manner and gave Puru back his gift. He then made Puru his heir and sent Puru's brothers to other parts of the world. The oldest, Yadu, remained behind to go to the south of Jambudvipa and became the ancestor of the Yadavas.

A.12.4. Myth: Puru the Obedient

Puru gave up his youth to his father and in exchange became the dynast – the ruling family of Pauravas settled on the banks of the Sarasvati.

A.12.5. Pauravas: From Puru to Bharata

This is the reimagined history of the Pauravas from Ilina, a descendant of Puru to Bharata – they developed the trade routes from Panchnad in all directions, and made Panchnad a well-known trading culture,

Puru's descendant Ilina founded the city of Kaalindini (named after his mother Kaalindi, the matriarch) among the foothills of the Himalayas on the banks of the Sutudri (Sutlej). Kaalindini was on the trade route to the north into Kashyapura and points further north. Ilina developed long-distance trade to the north and to the south across the Western sea. Ilini's grandson, Bharata, began the first tentative moves towards the east, but he encountered dense forest populated by Nagas not used to long-distance trade. He pulled back and continued Ilina's work of creating a single integrated trade route from northern Gandhara and northern Vakshu to the port of Tripura in the south and across to Dilmun. Tin, lapis lazuli, and cotton textiles, became staple exports from the Sarasvati-Sindhu culture to the western world.

A.12.6. Bhaaratas: From Bharata to Kuru

This is the reimagined history of the efforts by Panchnad to trade with the Nagas to their east in the Gangetic plains.

Bharata and his descendants continued their attempts to trade with the Nagas – it was not until Hastin's reign that a trading factory was established on the banks of the Ganga at a point where the river expanded and slowed down. They sold cotton textiles and felted cotton pieces in exchange for exotic animals and fruits. Occasionally, almost pure copper ore would turn up, and once, there was great excitement when a small sample of almost twenty-five per cent pure tin ore was brought in. There was little explanation of how or where this was obtained, nor of how much was available.

This factory, managed by a head trader, was called Nagapura. It would grow to become the capital of a great empire, but it began as the outpost of a trading caravan.

The Naga polity had been changing during these years. "Rogue males" had always existed among the Nagas, but their inability to cooperate with each other meant that they lived lonely lives and died young. However, many generations before Hastin, a band of rogue males led by Takshaka had begun to threaten normal Naga life. To counteract Takshaka's band, a confederacy of the Nagas called Panchala had been formed. After much difficulty, Takshaka was defeated, his band dispersed and he was killed. In the process a settlement called Kampilya was established on the northern bank of the Ganga abut one hundred and fifty miles[135] south of Hastinapur. Kampilya functioned as a cantonment for a permanent standing army. Like the other Naga bands, Kampilya was ruled by a matriarchy, but it had a special status among the Nagas, and continued as a training centre for a permanent army. The confederacy also grew by absorbing more and more Naga bands within its protective umbrella.

Trade expanded slowly, and Nagapura grew in prosperity, and by the time of Hastin's descendant, Samvarana, it had become the single biggest settlement on the Ganga. The Nagas around Nagapura had refused to join the confederacy – that made Panchala feel threatened. Panchala attacked Nagapura

---

[135] One hundred and fifty miles is a critical span for many Bronze Age empires – a messenger walking twenty-five to thirty miles a day will take about a week to go from one end to the other (a riverboat can cut that by two or three times at most when rowing with the current and a favorable wind). This creates a two week round-trip time for administrative actions in response to events, probably a limiting factor in managing such empires. Only after the arrival of the horse did larger empires become feasible, Mesopotamia being a good example.

For what it is worth, the distance from Kaalindini to Hastinapur was approximately one hundred and fifty miles and so are the distances from Hastinapur to Kampilya, Hastinapur to Agra, Agra to Kanpur or Jhansi, Kanpur to Allahabad, and so on, all of these being ancient sites of settlement after the disappearance of the Sarasvati.

and Samvarana was driven out. Samvarana did not retire to a Panchnad city – instead he started working on regaining control of Nagapura.

Meanwhile in Panchnad, a teacher named Vasishtha had been developing new ideas of governance – this was in response to the observation that the world outside Panchnad was different. Traders returned with stories of great wars; of fortified cities under siege; of drought and famine and mass migrations. It was all a bit too much for the ordinary Panchnadis to believe.

Samvarana proved to be an excellent pupil – having suffered a loss to war, he could believe in Vasishtha. An army was organised with the help of Vasishtha's Kavi Sangha, with the help of the ex-mercenary Vishvamitra – the soldiers were all men, trained to fight and committed to the aims of the Kavi Sangha and to recovering Nagapura. After ten years in exile, Samvarana returned and found a demoralised Naga force defending Nagapura – trade had dropped to nothing, the settlement was decrepit, the surrounding Nagas no longer looked to Nagapura for luxuries obtained through trade. The Panchala army melted away and Samvarana was back in power. The Kavi Sangha and Vasishtha's reputation for wisdom soared.

After Samvarana returned to power, a steady, if small, stream of ores, mostly copper, but occasionally tin, would come by boat from the east. Tin, in particular, was extremely valuable, but there seemed to be no way to increase its supply. Samvarana's son Kuru took up the challenge to extend Nagapura's trading network to the east. Far to the east, he discovered a plateau south of the Ganga from which the river Hiranyaganga flowed – the ores came from the plateau. A small settlement called Laghu Nagapura was established. Laghu Nagapura was positioned to satisfy an increased demand for ores.

The Panchnadis encountered a new forest-dwelling culture of hunter-gatherers – Rakshasas – whom they had only heard about. The Rakshasas were hostile to trade and this hostility took many years, almost two generations, to overcome – in the meantime, Laghu Nagapura could only be used for shipping the ores out to Nagapura for smelting into bronzes.

Kuru renamed Nagapura as Hastinapur after his ancestor who founded the settlement.

A.12.7. Kauravas: From Kuru to Pratipa

This is the reimagined history of the Hastinapur trading settlement as it gained power over the local Naga inhabitants, and the city's role changed from being only a trading centre to being a hegemon.

The first few generations after Kuru were peaceful ones. Hastinapur grew in prosperity, but maintained its army – Panchala continued to be a threat. The presence of a standing army made Hastinapur the most powerful proto-state entity in its neighbourhood, the effective hegemon over the surrounding Naga bands. The surrounding Nagas had also become integrated into the trading network. The biggest issue with moving away from the slash-and-burn agricultural way of life was the difficulty of agriculture on the heavy clayey soil of the Gangetic plain.

Many local Nagas found it simpler to switch to fishing, becoming Meena-Nagas, as a way of life. There were many differences as well as similarities to the old way of life. Settlements tended to be permanent – building on stilts was expensive and so old settlements were not abandoned. In addition, the river's ability to provide fish did not degrade, as fishing continued, so frequent moving was not necessary. It was harder to spin off a new band – a new site had to be found and these had to be located along the riverbank – as there were fewer places to look at.

The new way of life was a riskier way of life. It would be put to the test by the crisis.

A.12.8. Kauravas: From Pratipa to the War

This is the period of the crisis caused by the tectonic events and the resulting changes in the flow of major rivers.

The crisis broke out very early in Pratipa's time. His son Shantanu took the lead in trying to solve the problem. However, personal issues and weaknesses dominated the family. Shantanu's first wife died, leaving a son Devavrat. The story of Devavrat from an early age is the subject of Book 1 of this series.

Spoiler Alert: What follows is a summary of this book and commentary of some aspects related to the crisis.

Wishing to marry again, Shantanu disinherited Devavrat to fulfil a promise to his second wife Satyavati. Shantanu had two sons with Satyavati. While Shantanu abandoned his duties in the pursuit of pleasure, Devavrat administered the state in consultation with the Kavi Sangha. Steps were taken to help the thousands of migrants, but the crisis grew in magnitude every year. Waterworks were constructed along the Ganga to provide water for agriculture. Land was set aside for new settlements – disputes with the Nagas over land rights increased and the Hastinapur military had to be deployed. The Nagas were not a combative culture – if two Naga bands came into conflict over land, it was usually easier for one or both to move. Therefore, the Nagas moved, and moved again; lands they would have left fallow did not stay fallow but were occupied by migrants. Though Devavrat tried to be even-handed with respect to Panchnad immigrants and Naga inhabitants, the Nagas were slowly pushed away from a growing immigrant circle centred on Hastinapur.

When Shantanu died, his son Chitrangada was crowned king but died childless. Chitrangada's brother Vichitravirya also died, leaving two sons, Dhritarashtra and Mahendra. The older son, Dhritarashtra, being blind, could not be crowned, so Mahendra became King. Mahendra was nicknamed Pandu (the Pale) and this name stuck. Mahendra's life will be the subject of a future novel in this series. Dhritarashtra had many ("a hundred") sons – they were called the Kauravas to distinguish them from the sons of Mahendra/Pandu, the five Pandavas. Suyodhana was the oldest Kaurava and Yudhishthira was the oldest Pandava. Yudhishthira should have been crowned King, but in an compromise, the Pandavas left to rule half the kingdom from Indraprastha, a settlement originally founded by Mahendra. Suyodhana, the oldest Kaurava, was declared heir to his father Dhritarashtra, but he could not be crowned while his father lived. Nevertheless, he titled himself King while Devavrat continued as Regent.

In summary, after Shantanu's death, Devavrat was Regent for about four years. After Chitrangada's death, Devavrat was Regent for about six years. After Vichitravirya's death, Devavrat was Regent for sixteen years, ending when Mahendra was crowned. After Mahendra went into exile, Devavrat acted in his stead, acting as Regent for over fifteen, possibly as long as twenty years. This regency should have ended when the Pandavas returned and Yudhishthira crowned. The compromise that sent the Pandavas to Indraprastha averted conflict but did not resolve the succession dilemma. It allowed Devavrat to continue as Regent de facto until the end of the Great War.

A.12.9. The Great War: Pandavas &Kauravas

This story is dealt with in this series of Books.

A.12.10. Pandavas: From Arjuna to Janamejaya

This is also dealt with in this series of Books.

A.12.11. The Family Tree

The Kuru family tree is shown in the inside-back cover of this book. It shows the chain of ancestors from the mythical era – Pururavas to Puru. Some of Puru's descendants, the Pauravas, are identified in the yellow box – the list only identifies the rulers whose actions are mentioned in this book and skips over many intervening rulers.

To the left is the "Vyaasa Chain" that names the sequence of Vyaasas, the head of the Kavi Sangha. The extent of a Vyaasa's role is approximately parallel to the Hastinapur ruler they were associated with – Vasishtha, for instance, is associated with Samvarana. Samvarana's ancestor Hastin founded the town of Nagapura and Samvarana's son Kuru renames the town Hastinapur.

Kuru, though a Paurava, is considered the dynast for the Kauravas, his descendants. The label "Kaurava" is used occasionally in the Mahabharata to denote all the descendants of Kuru, referring to the sons of Mahendra as well as the sons of Dhritarashtra. However, in the most common usage, "Kaurava" denotes the hundred sons of Dhritarashtra and "Pandava" denotes the five sons of Mahendra the Pale.

The crisis described in this book began towards the end of Arugvat's reign – initially a trickle that slowly grew to a population problem in Shantanu's time. Shantanu's two wives (Ganga and Satyavati) are shown along with their children, including Satyavati's child with Parashara (who also appears in the Vyaasa list).

Kunti, the Bhoja Matriarch, who comes to live in Mahendra's settlement Indraprastha, is shown with a dotted line back to her ancestor Druhyu,[136] skipping many generations. Kunti does not have daughters. Her three sons grow up in Indraprastha with the twin sons of Madri. They are, of course, the Pandavas, named after Pandu, the male head of the settlement.

---

136 *Druhyu* was one of the five sons of Yayati, and half-brother to Puru. The Bhojas, the clan that Kunti comes from, are considered to be among his descendants (though this is not certain as they also claimed descent from Yadu). The Bhojas consider themselves one of the Yadava clans that were forced to migrate from the banks of the Sarasvati.

Coloured boxes surround the warring cousins, the Pandavas and the Kauravas. The five Pandavas are joint husbands of the Panchala Matriarch Krishnaa Agnijyotsna – she and her children are not shown. Arjuna is also husband to Subhadra, the daughter of Devaki, the Matriarch of the Vrishni clan, by Vasudeva, army chief for the Bhojas and brother of Kunti. That is, Arjuna and Subhadra were first cousins. Subhadra's ancestry from Yadu is also indicated by dotted lines.

Arjuna's son by Subhadra is Abhimanyu – he died young during the war, but his son Parikshit is the only descendant of the Pandavas who survives the Great War. Following the patrilineal model of Hastinapur, Parikshit becomes the ruler of Hastinapur.

A.13. A Brief History of the Kavi Sangha

The Kavi Sangha is a completely reimagined organisation. The names of its leaders (the Vyaasas) have been chosen to correspond with sages in Hindu mythology but otherwise this is invented.

A.13.1. Vasishtha

The first Vyaasa was Vasishtha. Vasishtha was a bard – bards had always been a key part of Panchnad society for they provided the memorisation and archiving service that was used to manage the marketplace. The demand for bards was growing and the guild of bards was not able to expand fast enough. Vasishtha established a school to teach these skills to any student, and the best graduates of the school were called the Kavi Sangha. When Panchala drove Samvarana out of Nagapura, he came to Panchnad looking for help. Vasishtha took him under his wing and trained him to be a warrior; he then helped him put together an army of men prepared to fight a real war unlike the mercenaries of Panchnad. The martial arts teacher Vishvamitra was an ex-mercenary, but one with experience in the Western world, and knew about fighting such wars. Vishvamitra's unusual intellect had drawn Vasishtha to him and initially he was Vasishtha's protégé.

The Kavi Sangha's role in restoring Samvarana to Nagapura greatly enhanced its prestige and Vasishtha's reputation for wisdom. After the restoration, the Kavi Sangha and its members, especially the Vyaasa, became much sought after and every Panchnad town invited them to participate in civic affairs at the highest level. Vasishtha was the head of both the guild of bards and the school, which he managed as a single operation. He received support to train more bards and in response, he increased the range and extent of the archives maintained by the guild, now merged into the Kavi Sangha.

Many Kavi Sangha members aspired to succeed Vasishtha in the role of Vyaasa. As Vasishtha grew older, the virus of patriarchy had begun to infect him and he wanted to make his son Shakti the next Vyaasa. Shakti had been born very late in Vasishtha's life and was still a child when his father died, and another Vyaasa, Vishvamitra, was selected.

A.13.2. Vishvamitra

Vishvamitra was the obvious next candidate, but many bards objected to Vishvamitra as he was not a bard but had been a mercenary. Vishvamitra had to prove his qualifications many times, but finally succeeded in obtaining universal approval. After Vishvamitra, Bhrigu became the Vyaasa.

A.13.4. Bhrigu

Bhrigu was a systematiser – he established practices and precedents that made the Kavi Sangha a permanent institution in the life of Panchnad and Hastinapur. During this period, Hastinapur grew in power and established itself as a major trading centre. After his death, Bharadvaja became the Vyaasa.

A.13.4. Bharadvaja

Bharadvaja was the Vyaasa when Pratipa was King and the crisis began.

The Yamuna and the Sutudri changed their course, the Yamuna going east and the Sutudri further west, and both were lost to the Sarasvati. A worldwide drought that lasted almost four hundred years coincided with the riverine changes. As a result, the Sarasvati also lost its rain-fed water and it started drying up. Refugees flocked to Hastinapur. Hastinapur was overwhelmed and Pratipa asked the Vyaasa Bharadvaja for help.

Bharadvaja was a pragmatist and realist who looked for rational solutions to all problems. The flood of refugees had caused hardship. There was not enough food to go around and the Naga mode of production precluded ramping up food production rapidly. The Nagas could not be displaced easily, but their practice of leaving groves fallow for two generations made it possible to house the refugees there, even if the land was not productive. However, that was not enough and the population had to be controlled, as babies were dying from hunger. Bharadvaja suggested the "one-child-per-person" policy, that child preferably a son (a girl would contribute to later population growth while a boy could not). This law would apply to refugees who wanted to settle in Hastinapur. He wanted to encourage the Panchnad refugees to go as far east as possible, well beyond Laghu Nagapura into Rakshasa land or beyond, or to go as far west as possible, to Bahlika or even Parsaka and lands beyond. He floated a proposal to work on diverting the Yamuna back – this would be backbreaking and dangerous work, but it would restore the Sarasvati and allow the refugees to return to Panchnad. In order to encourage the refugees to participate in the diversion project, the workers would be exempted from the one-child-per-person policy. The modifications aroused anger in the older residents of Hastinapur as it was seen to favour the immigrants.

The diversion project was given up and the one-child-per-person policy applied without exemption – thus began the policy disputes that led to the Great War. Shantanu applied it to the whole population of Hastinapur in the spirit of sharing, but the policy was only enforceable because Hastinapur had become a permanently militarised state.

Bharadvaja began the use of the army to construct waterworks in areas deemed fit for settlement by immigrants. Conflicts with local Nagas were addressed quickly – since the land being expropriated was lying fallow, the Nagas frequently let the land go without a fight. Among Nagas, conflicts only occurred when two groups wanted to move to the same place at the same time – such a coincidence was rare and most often the conflict was settled by one Naga band going somewhere else. The Nagas took the same approach towards Hastinapur. Since Hastinapur-supported settlements were permanently located, the Nagas were being slowly pushed out. When conflict did become worse, the army dealt with the uncooperative Nagas harshly.

Bharadvaja died a few years after Shantanu's wife Ganga died. He was succeeded by Parashara.

A.13.5. Parashara

The Vyaasa title returned to Vasishtha's family when Parashara, son of Vasishtha's son Shakti, became the Vyaasa. Parashara was known as the "walking Vyaasa" for he walked everywhere. He had been asked by Bharadvaja to assess if the Nagas would tolerate being thrown off their land to make place for the immigrants. He concluded that the Nagas would not tolerate it. In the course of his travels, he also encouraged many Nagas to join the Kavi Sangha, with the long-term goal of extending the Kavi Sangha to the Nagas. Parashara had hidden his involvement with Satyavati from the senior members of the Kavi Sangha – the affair was not a problem, but hiding it was, and he was sentenced to a vow of silence for a few years, even though he was the Vyaasa. During this period, Satyavati married Shantanu through Shukla's machinations.

Parashara died before his punishment ran out and he was followed by Jaimini.

A.13.6. Jaimini

Jaimini became Vyaasa a year or so before Chitrangada was born. He was the opposite of Bharadvaja – where Bharadvaja had been practical and hard-nosed, Jaimini was compassionate and flexible. In particular, Jaimini objected to this use of the army to build the waterworks that helped settle immigrants and dispossess Nagas. But there seemed to be no alternative – an army was needed to keep Panchala at bay; the army had to be fed; the only way to feed it was to use it to enable increase in production or enforce laws that controlled the population. Some years after the death of Shantanu's wife, the one-child-per-person policy was lifted and that left the army only one choice – enable increase in production by replacing Nagas with settlers.

Jaimini continued the recruitment of Nagas into the Kavi Sangha. As Devavrat expected, this made the process of settling immigrants a little harder, as Naga concerns were included in each project. However, it also meant that the colonisations proceeded without too much conflict.

Jaimini died a few years after Vichitravirya's death.

A.13.7. Shukla

Jaimini's successor was Shukla, the brother of Satyavati, and the first Naga to be named Vyaasa. He was the Vyaasa through this period in which this novel (*The Last Kaurava*) is set. When he died, his nephew Krishna Dvaipaayana, son of Parashara by Satyavati, became the Vyaasa.

A.13.8. Krishna Dvaipaayana Paaraashara

Krishna Dvaipaayana as Vyaasa worked with the Archivist Lomaharshana to create order out of the archives of the war years. He composed the Jaya, a poem about the war, and performed it when asked by King Janamejaya, for a Spring Festival.

The Archivist Lomaharshana (introduced in this book) followed Krishna Dvaipaayana as Vyaasa.

A.13.9. Lomaharshana

Lomaharshana made it his mission to spread the story of the War – he made its recital an annual event coinciding with the Spring Festival.

A.14. Neologisms

Terminology invented by the author.

A.14.1. Nishkamkarnarpana

The Kavi Sangha's bards and memorisers learned early in their education to enter a trance state in which they would listen without judgement and without attachment to what was being heard. With practice and experience, the memoriser would learn to dispense with the trance state when listening, but the skill was available for use under unusual conditions. I have named this skill *niṣkāmkarṇārpaṇa* (pronounced "nish-calm-cur-narp-un-u(h)", and spelled "nishkamkarnarpana"). The word means "paying attention without attachment".

A.14.2. Nishkamsmaranadharanam

The Kavi Sangha's bards and memorisers practised a collection of mental exercises and practices used to erase unneeded memories while retaining the necessary ones. These exercises and the associated skills were called *niṣkāmsmərəṇədhārəṇəm,* pronounced Nish-calm-smu(t)-run-u(p)-th(e)-ah-run-um, and spelled nishkamsmaranadharanam, "holding on to memory without attachment".

A.15. Panchnad Geography, Politics, & History

A map of Panchnad and Northern South Asia is shown in the inside front cover of this book. It shows the geopolitical situation in 2000 BCE (the time of the events described in *The Last Kaurava*). The following conventions have been followed:

- Regions occupied by different groups and/or cultures are shown as shaded areas.
- The Laghu Nagapura and Malwa plateaus are demarcated using a dotted line.
- Cities and regions mentioned in this book (Book 1) are labelled in uppercase.
- Some modern cities have been added to help the readers orient themselves. These names are capitalised – labelled in lowercase with an initial uppercase letter. The label is placed within parentheses if an ancient town/village/city was close by.
- Rivers' names are in all lowercase and are placed alongside the river.
- A number of cities outside South Asia are also indicated.
- Some of the major passes (Khyber, Gomal, and Bolan passes in the west, the Lanak-La and the Shipki-La passes in the north, and the Nathu-La in the northeast) have been shown – they are major routes into South Asia for both trade and populations.
- Lake Mansarovar in Tibet is shown – it is generally held to be the source of the four great rivers of North India (the Sindhu (Indus), the Ganga, the Yamuna, and the Brahmaputra), and is considered

a place of pilgrimage for both Hindus and Buddhists. A number of other great rivers, of China, Burma (Myanmar), and Indochina also have their watersheds within a relatively short distance from this lake.

- At the bottom left, we show Mumbai and Daimabad. Daimabad's claim to fame is that it is the southern-most point of the sub-continent where "Bronze Age" SSC artefacts have been found.

A.15.1. Nagas and Rakshasas

The map shows a light brown region to the north and east, extending from Lake Mansarovar in the west to the eastern end of the Brahmaputra (Tsang-po) river and incorporating the delta of the Ganga/Brahmaputra. This was heavily forested and sparsely populated by the Nagas who were slash-and-burn agriculturalists. They had migrated here from the north (Tibet) and east (China and Indochina through Myanmar) many thousands of years earlier and spread over the Gangetic plain.

The reddish brown region that contains the Laghu Nagapura (now called Chota Nagpur) plateau and extends south into the South Asian peninsula was also heavily forested and sparsely populated by the hunter-gathering culture called Rakshasas (by the Nagas). The Rakshasas were descended from the earliest human migrants out of Africa (~60,000 BCE) who had left bands in settlements along the shores of the Deccan peninsula. These bands had slowly expanded into the plateau and up north into Laghu Nagapura where they may have first encountered the Nagas. The Nagas initially responded by retreating – they avoided conflict and the land seemed unlimited. As a result, the Rakshasas had come down from the Laghu Nagapura plateau, crossed the Ganga, and occupied land all the way to the Himalayas. Meanwhile the Nagas, who had discovered that the land was not limitless, began to resist, leading to the situation shown in the map.

The Rakshasas in Laghu Nagapura had developed significant mining and smelting skills in copper.

A.15.2. Panchnad

Panchnad is the brown region to the west on the map, extending from the Sarasvati in the east to the Western Himalayan foothills in the west and from the northern Himalayan foothills to the Western Sea (now called the Arabian Sea) to the south.

The city of Kaalindini (near the modern town of Ropar or Rupnagar) in northwest Panchnad is located on the banks of the Sutudri ("Hundred rivulets") as it exits the Himalayas. Before the crisis, the Sutudri drained to the south – the land being a very flat alluvial plain, the Sutudri split into a multitude of streams (hence the name). The crisis would change the Sutudri to the modern Sutlej, which turns west at Kaalindini/Ropar (and is not shown in this map). The map shows the approximate ancient course of the Sutudri as it heads south.

Before the crisis, the Sutudri merged with the Yamuna to form the Sarasvati. Tectonic events, i.e. earthquakes, changed the course of the Yamuna as shown above – it headed east at the northern ridge of the Aravalli range. As a result, the Sarasvati lost its two primary sources of water from the Himalayas. It did not dry up immediately as a third monsoon-fed river, not shown here, the Drishadvati, comes from the Aravalli range to join the Sarasvati.

A.15.3. Kururashtra

The Yamuna (as shown in its old course) formed the northwest boundary of Panchnad. The river Ganga flows parallel to the Yamuna – the town of Hastinapur (initially a trading centre called Nagapura) was founded on the western bank of the Ganga. Hastinapur controlled the land between the Yamuna and the Ganga all the way to the northern foothills. To the south, Hastinapur's control extended just past the Aravalli ridge into a scrub forest that was called Khandavaprastha. The Hastinapur-controlled area called Kururashtra is shown in pink.

A.15.4. Panchala

The eastern bank of the Ganga was under the control of Panchala, a confederation of five Naga clans that considered Hastinapur a dangerous foreign interloper. Panchala, shown in purple, was managed from the military cantonment of Kampilya. It extended along the northern foothills of the Himalayas past Hastinapur to the point where the Ganga emerged from the mountains.

A.15.5. Out of Panchnad: Pauravas &Yadavas

The map also shows the routes that the refugees leaving Panchnad followed – to the northwest, they went through the major passes towards the Afghanistan plateau. From the northern settlements on the Sarasvati, the refugees, calling themselves Pauravas, went towards Hastinapur. From the southern end of the Sarasvati, the refugees, who called themselves Yadavas, went east past the southern end of the Aravalli range and into the Malwa plateau (these areas have been left white). From the Malwa plateau, the Yadavas split into four branches – the Andhakas who stayed in Malwa; the Chedis who went east towards Kashi; the Bhojas who went along the Charmanavati River gorge and tried to settle the region between the rivers Charmanavati and the Betwah; and, lastly, the Vrishnis who headed north and tried to create settlements on the banks of the re-directed Yamuna.

The Chedis and Bhojas conflicted with the Nagas on their territory. The Chedis responded by allying with Rakshasas. The Bhojas retreated to Malwa after many failed attempts to establish settlements. The Vrishnis were lucky – the instability of the Yamuna meant that neither they nor the local Nagas had much to fight over right away. But that same instability did not help the Vrishnis' wish to create their urban centre Mathura.

The Vrishnis also followed a different model for settlement: led by their army chief Gopala Krishna (son of the matriarch Devaki by her husband the Bhoja army chief Vasudeva), they tried to create alliances with all the local powers – Hastinapur in the north, Panchala on the other side of the Ganga, and the Meena-Nagas who had migrated up the Yamuna streams – but that caused rifts with their cousins the Bhojas and Chedis.

A.15.6. Prehistory

This map does not show the other ancient migrations that led to the tripartite division of South Asia between the urban civilisation of Panchnad, the hunter-gatherer Rakshasas, and the slash-and-burn Nagas. This division had come into being well before the time of the Sarasvati disaster.

A.15.7. Jambudvipa – The Island of the "Jambul"

A.15.7.1. The Jambul

Wikipedia[137] describes two different "Jambul" fruits. One is a purple berry, tart and sweet (*Syzygium cumini*), that grows in higher elevations all over India. Alternatively, it is a pear-shaped (but smaller than a pear) fruit (*Syzygium samarangense*) with a melony pulp ranging in colour from white to red that grows all over South Asia and South East Asia. The Wikipedia reference calls both of them "Jambul", but it also calls the latter the "rose apple". It seems that the rose apple may be called "Jambul" in some parts of South East Asia as well. However, Indians asked to describe the "jambul", will describe the berry. To add to the confusion, the jambul is called "naga pazhum" in Tamil, i.e., "snake fruit", or "fruit of the Nagas".

So, is "Jambudvipa" the "Island of the Rose-Apple" or is it the "Island of the Purple Berry" or "Island of the Snake Fruit"? It is unclear to me why most Western authorities in Indian

---

137 http://en.wikipedia.org/wiki/Syzygium_cumini and http://en.wikipedia.org/wiki/Syzygium_samarangense

mythology prefer one meaning ("rose-apple") to the other. The Tamil name conjures the possibility that the name Jambudvipa connotes the original possession of the land by Nagas.

A.15.7.2. The Island

Kashmiri legend is that in the centre of Kashmir was a great lake with an island paradise in the middle. When the Earth was kidnapped by the demon Hiranyaksha and hidden in the depths of the Sea of Milk, Vishnu in the form of a boar killed Hiranyaksha and retrieved the earth by carrying it back on the tip of his tusk. The tip of the tusk punctured the edge of the great lake at a place called Varahamoola (now identified as Baramulla). The draining of the lake created the land of Kashmir.

I've "extended" the myth to create a hypothetical Panchnad myth, identifying Jambudvipa with that central island, and the draining of that lake with the emergence of the island-continent of Jambudvipa from the waters.

Jambudvipa is clearly not an island, so some people believe that it refers to all of Asia or Eurasia; some believe it refers to Asia, Europe, and Africa as a single land-mass; and, then (a deep breath is called for here), there are the people who believe that this name is a residual race memory of ancient Gondwanaland, from a time when India, Africa, Antarctica, and Australia formed one island, a mere one hundred and eighty million years ago. This is, of course, conclusively proved by its name, which translates as *Land of the Forest-Garden of the Gonds.*

A.15.8. Geography of the Western World

A.15.8.1. Egypt: Names

(From the Wikipedia entry for "Egypt")

> The English name *Egypt* is derived from the ancient Greek *Aígyptos* (Αἴγυπτος), via Middle French *Egypte* and Latin *Aegyptus*. It is reflected in early Greek Linear B tablets

as *a-ku-pi-ti-yo*. The Greek forms were borrowed from Late Egyptian (Amarna) *"Hikuptah* of Memphis", a corruption of the earlier Egyptian name *Hwt-ka-Ptah,* meaning "home of the KA (soul) of Ptah", the name of a temple to the god Ptah at Memphis.

The god Ptah was considered an ancestor of the Egyptians – one variation of the name of Ptah's temple was "Home of the Temple of the Ancestor". In Sanskrit, this would be *Pitr-vihara* ("temple of the ancestors"). Adding *"naad"* as a suffix to make *Pitr-vihara-naad* might be a culturally appropriate way to refer to Egypt.

Other names of Egypt include "The Black Land", "The Red Land", and "The Land of the Black River" – the word "black" or "red" refers to the colour of the silt that the Nile brings and deposits on the land after floods. This soil is responsible for the extraordinary fertility of the land bordering the Nile, converting a desert to one of the most productive agricultural lands in the world. The ancient Egyptians also referred to themselves as the "black" or "red" people.

The "Black River" is the Nile and it would be translated to "Krishna" in Sanskrit.

A.15.8.2. Egypt: Places, Gods, & People

Osiris (the Greek pronunciation of "Au-ser") is the great god of the ancient Egyptian religion – Indian interpreters of Egyptian religion have made much of the similarity between "Au-ser" and "Eashwar" (as the great god Shiva is known in Hinduism). There are many similarities – Au-sera could mean "the great prince/lord" and Eashwar means "lord"; Au-ser could mean "the receiver of ritual offerings", while "-eashwar" as a suffix could mean the one who has the right to a sacrifice (or ritual offerings). There is no known link between the two names, but they are ancient names in two civilisations that traded with each other.

Egyptian history mentions a people called "Punit" or "Punt" from before 1500 BCE who traded with Egypt, but came from an unknown homeland to the "east". Around 1500 BCE, the Queen-Pharaoh Hatsepshut sent an expedition to Punt with a guide – they came back with stories that could have related to eastern Somalia, but could also describe the land around Kerala in India. Later, Egyptian chronicles mention the attack of the "Sea People" said to be related to the people of Punt. The Sea People, also called Panit by the Egyptians, came to dominate trade on the Mediterranean Sea and were called Phoenicians by the Greeks. I've called them the "Western Panias", the "Pani-s" or "Bani-s" being the traders of ancient India, forerunners of the Banias in later times.

A.15.8.3. Egypt: From Matriarchy to Patriarchy

The transition from matriarchy to patriarchy took place in many ways. One example of a transitional structure is the inheritance model of the Pharaohs of Egypt, which was followed for almost four thousand years. The successor to a Pharaoh would be his son who was a *stepson* of the Great Queen (the senior-most wife of the Pharaoh) – the son had to marry the Great Queen's *daughter* (not stepdaughter) to establish his legitimacy and she would become the next Great Queen. (This is the source of the claim that Pharaohs of Egypt married their own sisters – they married one stepsister to establish their right to the throne). In practice, the system was frequently abused as some Pharaohs, once established in power, would marry other wives and declare one of them the Great Queen, and usurp the stepsister's title.

One collateral effect of this mode of inheriting power was that any other sisters of a Great Queen would be barred from marrying *anybody*. In the few cases they married, it was to men incapable of being a Pharaoh. In many cases, these sisters died of unknown causes, possibly murdered by their brother to forestall a husband from challenging the Pharaoh's fitness to rule (since *any* daughter of a Great Queen could lay claim to be her successor as the Great Queen).

A.15.8.4. Rivers

The land of the Shakas (said to be descendants of Druhyu, a son of Yayati) was called Scythia by the Greeks. North of Scythia, the Danavas (the children of Danu, one of the wives of the Sage Kashyapa) were said to occupy Siberia and Eastern Europe, through which some of the greatest rivers of the world flow but are frozen several months of the year. Many of these rivers were not known in India, though by coincidence a number of great rivers have names beginning with "D-n". Some river names from Iran to Mesopotamia are easily translated into the Sanskrit names used in this book – the Euphrates ("Well fertilised" in Greek) becomes the Su-purna ("Fulfilling well" or "Completing well"); the Tigris ("Swift" in Greek) becomes the Sindhu-of-the-west.

All the rivers to the east of India that came out of Tibet are given names that are a variant of "Ganga" – the Bo Ganga is Tsang-po/Brahmaputra/Lauhitya (Lohita's child); the Shia (Xia) Ganga is the Yang-tze, the Ho Ganga is the Huang-Ho, the Hme Ganga is the Mekong, the Naga Ganga is the Irrawady (also mother of the Great Naga Airavatha). The rivers that flow west are fast rivers, and are called Sindhu. The rivers to the northwest, the Syr Darya – called *Yaksh-arta* (the *Pure Pearl* in Persian, which is close to *Laksha-Rta* in Sanskrit, the Greek name being *Jaxartes*) and the Amu Darya (*Vakshu*, possibly meaning "good or beneficent river", also the Greek name being Oxus) were known but do not appear in this book.

A.15.8.5. Names of Countries

Afghanistan is part of the South Asian cultural landscape, but is difficult to reach, so the cultural connections were intermittent and driven by trade. Gandhara (Kandahar in modern Afghanistan) had the closest relationships. Further north, Shantanu's brother Bahlika is said to have settled in Bactria (the Greek form of Bahlika). The similarity of the names "Bahlika" and "Baluchistan" could be mere coincidence, but note that Brahui, spoken only in Baluchistan, is one of the oldest Dravidian languages known. Bactria forms part of the Vakshu (Sanskrit name for the Oxus) civilisation, also called the Bactrian-Margiana Archaeological Complex (BMAC). BMAC was an extended civilisation of fortified towns contemporary to Harappa and Mohenjodaro – the design of the settlements of BMAC could arguably be a response to the hostile conditions under which Bahlika left Panchnad.

A.15.8.6. The Khyber Pass

The name Khyber is supposed to be derived from the Semitic/ Hebrew word for "fort". There is no other name used by the West. Unfortunately, I have not been able to find a Sanskrit word for the pass itself. A plausible derivation is that the word "Khyber" is a translation of the name used by the residents. This would be "kuta" meaning fort (among other meanings). Kubera is the god of wealth in the Hindu pantheon – the Khyber was a pathway to wealth for traders going west and for raiders coming south. Hence the name "Kuberakuta", i.e. Kubera's Fort. The translation in a Semitic language to "Kubera's Khyber" is a bit strange because it sounds like "Fort's Fort", and it was simplified to "Fort", i.e. Khyber, by the Westerners.

APPENDIX B

GLOSSARY OF SANSKRIT NAMES

Name	Definition/Person/Place
Amba	Member of Naga band; goes to Hastinapura; escapes
Anashwa	Means "horseless"; son of Kuru; ancestor of Shantanu; also called Arugvat
Angavastram	Clothing: this is the upper robe that covers the torso and shoulders
Anustubh	A rhythmic form (meter) in Sanskrit poetry consisting of two lines of sixteen syllables each, each line being treated as two parts of eight syllables.
Aravalli	A mountain range in Western India stretching from Ahmedabad to Central Delhi
Arjuna	Son of Kunti and Mahendra; third Pandava
Arugvat	Means "Healthy", "Free of Disease", but also, "Red"; son of Kuru; ancestor of Shantanu; also called Anashwa
Bagoa	Northwestern pronunciation of Bhargava
Bahlika	Shantanu's brother who abdicates and migrates to Bactria or Baluchistan
Bakakula	Name ("Family of Baka") of Shantanu's driver
Bhaarata	A descendant of Bharata

Name	Definition/Person/Place
Bharadvaja	One of the Vyaasas
Bharata	Ancestor of Samvarana; in legend he is the first king to unify all of Bhaaratavarsha (but not in this novel)
Bhargava	Son of or descended from Bhrigu
Bhima	Son of Kunti; second Pandava
Bhishma	"The Terrible" – a name attached to Devavrat
Chandrasekhar	Son of Bhargava who takes over the labour of transcribing the archives of Hastinapur
Charmanavati	River; now called the Chambal
Chitrangada	Son of Satyavati and Shantanu; rumoured to have been killed in a battle with a Gandharva
Devapi	Shantanu's brother who walks off into the forest
Devavrat	Son of Ganga and Shantanu; earns the name "The Terrible" (Bhishma)
Dhrishtadyumna	Brother of Agnijyotsna ("Panchali") the Matriarch of Panchala; the army chief of Panchala during the Great War
Dhritarashtra	Son of Ambika and Vichitravirya; blind at birth; father of Suyodhana and his brothers, the Kauravas
Drona	Possibly pejorative name for Kutaja, the martial arts instructor of the cousins and others

Name	Definition/Person/Place
Druhyu	Ancestor of Bhoja clan; son of Yayati and brother to Puru (ancestor of Pauravas) and Yadu (ancestor of Yadavas)
Drupada	Army Chief of Panchala for Agnijyotsna's mother, the Matriarch of Panchala during the Third co-regency of Devavrat & Satyavati
Duhshasana	Means "Uneasily Seated"; brother of Suyodhana; possibly pejorative name of Sushasana
Duryodhana	Bad Warrior; pejorative name of Suyodhana
Dvaipaayana	Krishna Dvaipaayana is the son of Satyavati and Parashara, meaning "born on an island"
Dvapara Yuga	The third of the four Ages of mankind
Gana	The masses; the people at the bottom of the social hierarchy
Ganapathi	Lord of the Gana(s); also a god in later times; patron god of Hastinapura, who removes obstacles to trade and business
Ganesha	Another name for Ganapathi; meaning "Lord/God of the masses"
Ganga	Devavrat's mother; also, the river called the "Ganges" by the ancient Greeks and modern Englishmen
Gangaputra	Son of Ganga; also refers to Devavrat
Gayatri	A rhythmic form (meter) in Sanskrit poetry consisting of four lines of six syllables each

Name	Definition/Person/Place
Gopala	One of the smaller and less powerful Yadava clans; means "cowherd"
Hastinapur	A trading post established just beyond the frontiers of Panchnad on the banks of the Ganga, in Naga territory; also called Nagapura as it was built with Naga help
Himavat	Means "White Mountain Range" and refers to the Himalayas
Hiranyaganga	A tributary of the Ganga coming from Chota Nagpur. Now called the Sone
Ilina	Ancestor of Bharata
Indraprastha	Settlement founded by Mahendra the Pale (Pandu); short-lived capital of the Pandava kingdom
Jambudvipa	The Island of the Jambul Tree
Jaya	Means "Victory"; also a victory lay; when capitalised, as in "Jaya", it is a lay of the Great War that is the central story of this novel
Jayakumar	Friend of Vaishampaayana who dies in the flood
Kaalindini	Panchnad settlement in the Himalayan foothills closest to the point where the Sutudri emerged from the mountains; possibly, the town of Ropar/Rupnagar (though "kalindi"'s meaning "from the Yamuna" makes this dubious).
Kali Yuga	Fourth age of humanity, supposed to be in the future for Panchnad

Name	Definition/Person/Place
Kamboja	A very successful and widespread trading clan in 850 BCE; one of its Master Traders is persuaded to help write down Hastinapura's history
Kampilya	The capital of Panchala
Karna	Friend, supporter, and booster of Suyodhana
Kashi	City that saves the people of Hastinapura during the floods of 850 BCE
Kaunteya	Descendant of Kunti, i.e., the three oldest Pandavas
Kaurava	Descendent of Kuru
Kaushambi	Site occupied by the Hastinapuris escaping the floods of 850 BCE
Kavi Sangha	Means "Society of Poets"; established by Vasishtha to fulfil his plan to prevent Panchnad from possible stagnation
Khandavaprastha	Land to the southwest of Hastinapura that is suddenly inundated with the waters of the Yamuna when the crisis begins. Over the course of a century, Khandavaprastha changes from scrubland to green and fertile forest, setting the stage for conflict
Kripa	Two babies, a boy and a girl, were abandoned in the forest and found by Shantanu, who fostered them. The boy was named Kripa, and his sister was Kripi. Both became experts in the martial arts. Kripa fought in the Great War supporting Suyodhana

Name	Definition/Person/Place
Krishna Dvaipaayana	Krishna Dvaipaayana is the son of Satyavati and Parashara, Krishna means "black"
Krishna Vaasudeva	Leader of Yadavas who supports the Pandavas claim to half of Hastinapura's land.
Kuru	Dynast of family ruling Hastinapura; changes name of Nagapura to Hastinapura; establishes Laghu Nagapura; establishes riverine trade between Laghu Nagapura and Hastinapura
Kutaja	Means "mountain peak" or "jar"; may have been original name for the martial arts teacher of the cousins
Lomaharshana	Storyteller who makes hair bristle or stand on end; Kavi Sangha Archivist in the Pandava camp
Mahanadi	Called the "Great River" by Rakshasas; it goes east from Chota Nagpur plateau to the Bay of Bengal
Matsya	Panchnad name for Meena Naga clan
Mayura	Peacock; totem of Yadava clan
Meena	Naga clan
Meru	Mythical mountain, often located in the Pamirs of Tajikistan, that is the home of the gods
Moolasthan	Panchnad-Gandhara settlement near Bolan pass and Gomal pass that enter modern-day Afghanistan; one of the oldest urban settlements known in the SSC

Name	Definition/Person/Place
Naga	Forest-dwellers occupying most of the Gangetic plain except towards the east, where Rakshasas live; organised as matriarchal bands with a male war-chief; slash-and-burn agriculturalists
Nagapura	Literally, "The City of the Naga"; initial name of Hastinapura, renamed by Kuru
Nagaraja	Chief or Ruler of a Naga clan
Nishkam-karnarpana	The "focused listening" practices taught by the Kavi Sangha.
Nishkam smaranadharanam	The "memory management" practices taught by the Kavi Sangha.
Panchagam	This is the lower robe that covers the body below the waist (a similar robe used nowadays is called a "dhoti")
Panchala	Naga confederation of five clans controlling the land north of the Ganga to the foothills of the Himalayas
Panchali	Title of Matriarch of Panchala; used to refer to the Matriarch Agnijyotsna whose consorts are the five Pandavas
Panchnad	Land between Sindhu and Sarasvati rivers – centre of modern-day Pakistan. More than two thousand settlements from the Bronze Age (3000 BCE to 1500 BCE)
Pandava	Descended from Pandu

Name	Definition/Person/Place
Pandu	Named Mahendra at birth but called Pandu because he was very pale (albino); father of the Pandavas
Panini	Name of one of Vaishampaayana's apprentices
Parashara	One of the Vyaasas; father of Krishna Dvaipaayana
Pashupati	Father (lord) of animals, one of the names of Shiva
Paurava	Descendant of Puru; describes people of Northern Panchnad and settlers of Hastinapura
Pitr-vihara-naad	Land of the Temple of Ancestors; Egypt
Pratipa	Rebel, adversary; father of Shantanu
Puru	Ancestor of Kuru; Yayati's youngest son; gives up one year of his youth to his father Yayati who is unsatisfied with his thousand years; becomes the heir
Raishyava	Unicorn; one of the totems of the Sarasvati-Sindhu Culture (SSC) and portrayed on seals
Rakshasa	Hunter gatherers; Nagas gave the name "Defender" (in the Naga language) to the hunter-gathering tribes who dwelt in the forest to the east of modern-day Patna
Samavedin	A Samavedin is a Kavi Sangha bard specially trained to keep time – they were the "chronometers" of Panchnad

Name	Definition/Person/Place
Samvarana	Samvarana is driven out of Hastinapur by Panchala; his return to power is orchestrated by Vasishtha, the creator of the Kavi Sangha; establishes a standing army in Hastinapur
Sanjaya	Guru and advisor to Dhritarashtra
Sarasvati	The hidden river of Hindu myth; river bordering Panchnad on the east; dried up when it lost the snow-melt from the Yamuna (before the events of this book)
Sashidhara	Name of Shantanu's Chief Minister/ Advisor
Satyavati	Marries Shantanu and has two sons – Chitrangada and Vichitravirya, both of whom die childless; feuds with Devavrat; arranges to get Vichitravirya's widows pregnant
Savitr	One of the names for the Sun; name of one Vaishampaayana's apprentices
Shaka	Scythian
Shantanu	King of Hastinapura; husband of Ganga; father of Devavrat, Chitrangada and Vichitravirya; takes Kavi Sangha advice for addressing the refugee crisis
Shikhandin	Pandava spy who leads Devavrat into an ambush; killed by Devavrat
Shukla	Brother of Satyavati; the Vyaasa at the time of the war

Name	Definition/Person/Place
Sindhu	The ancient local name for the river Indus (which is the name given by Greeks)
Subhadra	Marries Arjuna and has a son Abhimanyu
Surya	One of the names for the Sun; name of another of Vaishampaayana's apprentices
Sutudri	Ancient name of the River Sutlej; Himalayan river that used to flow south to the Sarasvati; changed direction near the town of Kaalindini (Ropar) to flow west and is a tributary of the Sindhu (Indus);
Suyodhana	Also called Duryodhana; mortal enemy of Pandavas; son of Dhritarashtra; leader of the Kauravas
Takshashila	One of the oldest settlements in the world; centre of learning established by Vasishtha
Vaishampaayana	Vyaasa in 850 BCE charged with writing down the archives of Hastinapur
Varahamoola	The ancient name of the modern town of Baramulla in Kashmir
Varanavata	A town west of Hastinapur on the northern bank of the Yamuna river; founded by Devavrat
Vasishtha	The first Vyaasa and head of the Kavi Sangha; creates Kavi Sangha by merging the guilds of bards, poets and archivists

Name	Definition/Person/Place
Vichitravirya	Son of Shantanu by Satyavati; marries Ambika and Ambalika; dies childless, leaving behind pregnant wives
Vidura	Half-brother of Mahendra and Dhritarashtra, born of a maidservant, not a noble but a commoner; named "Dharmateja" at birth; considered both learned and street-smart, he came to be called Vidura ("The Wise")
Viduratha	Ancestor of Kuru
Vyaasa	Title of the Head of the Kavi Sangha; also means arranger/organiser/editor, recognising the many roles of the Head of the Kavi Sangha
Vyuhadyuta	A shadow duel of opposing battle formations.
Yadava	Descendant of Yadu
Yajaman	The sponsor of a ritual; one entitled to the benefits from a ritual
Yamuna	The river; changed direction, created a crisis of flooding in Khandavaprastha and a crisis of water shortage in Panchnad
Yayati	Ancestor of Kuru. Yayati enjoyed a thousand years of youth but wanted more
Yudhishthira	The oldest Pandava and the future King of Hastinapura

ABOUT THE AUTHOR

Kamesh Ramakrishna grew up in Bombay (now Mumbai) and completed his undergraduate studies at IIT-Kanpur. He went on to obtain a Ph.D. in computer science from Carnegie-Mellon University in Pittsburgh, specialising in Artificial Intelligence. He worked as a professor and a software engineer; received some patents; was software architect for some foundational products; was CTO for a startup; and in recent years, has been a consulting software architect.

For over twenty years, Kamesh has been an avid student of history, archaeology, science and philosophy and the interconnection between these disciplines. Kamesh has published the core ideas underlying this novel in two reviewed journals – *The Trumpeter* (Canada) and *The Indian Journal of Eco-criticism.*

Kamesh lives with his family in Massachusetts.

47171278R00319

Made in the USA
Lexington, KY
30 November 2015